# *The Masters of Solitude*

The thing kept coming. The sound, the hideous staccato noise composed of millions of noises, grew louder and louder and the thing came closer, across the broken stone square, pouring through the entrance, into the central chamber, over the floor, crashing like the tumid river itself against the rusted door.

In the darkness behind, Moss howled out his fear lest his brain burst. He clawed at his ears to blot out the terror of the sound like a forest of birds gone mad.

A few days before Belten, the lep flashed from the northern fringe of settlements to the masters at Karli covenstead: *Moss and Jude are back*.

Neither could tell much of what happened in Lishin. Judith was gaunt and yellow with recent fever. She begged weakly to be taken to Lorl, where she had promised to wait.

Moss was incoherent. The masters worked patiently over him; using all their skill, they linked their minds with his, but part of that mind would not respond. Not gone or destroyed, simply unreachable behind a locked door. In time, his senses returned but none of the Karli ever got a clear story out of him . . .

He had only a vague memory of carrying Judith through flood-washed streets in which bloated things turned slowly in the sluggish tide. He crossed a bridge and near the far end of it . . . yes, he was sure of that; that much he couldn't forget. Near the far end, he found the picked bones of a horse and a man.

The latter skeleton retained a tuft of black hair and a tatter of deerhide shirt. By the bones of the right hand lay a black-hilted hunter's knife.

**MARVIN KAYE** and **PARKE GODWIN**

# *The Masters of Solitude*

Futura

**An Orbit Book**



First published in Great Britain in 1979
by Magnum Books

This edition published in 1986
by Futura Pubications, a Division of
Macdonald & Co (Publishers) Ltd
London & Sydney



ISBN 0 7088 8209 9

Printed and bound in Great Britain by
Cox & Wyman Ltd, Reading

Futura Publications
A Division of
Macdonald & Co (Publishers) Ltd
Greater London House
Hampstead Road
London NW1 7QX
A BPCC plc Company

*To Sharon Jarvis, who saw that it could be born;*
*To Pat LoBrutto, who delivered it.*


## Acknowledgments

The authors are indebted for certain technical data supplied by Mark A. Roller, P.E., regional sanitary engineer with the Bureau of Water Quality Management of the Pennsylvania Department of Environmental Resources, and David G. Simpson, of the Federal Bureau of Mines.

Our gratitude to Paul Huson, the author of *Mastering Witchcraft* (Putnam, 1970), and his agent, Owen Laster of the William Morris Agency, for permission to paraphrase certain materials from that work.

Thanks must inevitably go to a number of philosophic forebears, but special mention must be made of the superb translations and exegeses of Nietzsche by Walter Kaufmann, as well as the work of Michael Novak in *The Experience of Nothingness* (Harper Colophon, 1971).

Special thanks to Ellis Grove, Frank Garner, and Richard Frank for hospitality and aid during our research trip into Karli territory.

*Contents*

*The Masters of Solitude*

Sorrow is knowledge: they who know the most
must mourn the deepest o'er the fatal truth,
the Tree of Knowledge is not that of Life.

—*Manfred,* Lord Byron

For here we have no continuing City,
but we seek one to come.

—Hebrews 13:14

*Outcast of the Covens*

In the silence of the forest, someone thought of him, and he stirred, surprised and disturbed. The bitter tang of derision burned the runes in his mind.

*Singer. Misfit.*

Better to be alone than to live among uneasy coveners casting sidelong glances at him as he passed. Sometimes the sense of separation slumbered, and he was reasonably content to be cut off from the society of those who were hardly his fellows. But tonight the ache of loneliness possessed him. He was thinking of his mother, long ago wasted and gone.

*Unfinished.*

The cave was much as he last saw it. Fox and dog lodged there over the years, hunters left the charred remains of their fires and a scattering of bones, but it was not greatly changed. He remembered where his mother lay the night she died. She was small enough for his boy's arms to carry her blanketed body to the grave gouged out of the earth with his knife.

The night air was sweet in the forest. Just before the light returned, his mind ebbed like waning tide, exposing ocean-bed memories that would soon be covered up by the neap of daylight. Pictures flared and faded: he was north, hardening his muscles at the iron forges of Wengen. He baked in the sun on coasting cotton boats, sought and did not find the fabled island of Myudah, reeled drunk in Lorl with a whore on each arm, the three revelers crying, spitting curses at the great unseen City dim in the distance.

"I've paid you well," he said, and they asked him what he wanted to do with them, but he had no hunger for love that night or at least not the kind they sold. He merely wanted them to keep him company as he violated the Self-Gate.

The women ran away, shrieking, calling Singer mad.

And he *was* half insane that night. Lurching, stumbling for nearly a mile to reach the zone, the City's electronically guarded border. Not a gate anywhere, not even a fence. Open fields stretching to the misty horizon. He plunged on past the warning marker.

The sensors scanned him, divined Singer's essence, and in the City, a metal finger flicked a seldom-used switch. When it was at last deactivated, the mercenary troops who guard the border came to collect the lifeless body, but to their amazement, they found Singer alive. They carried him, whimpering and gibbering, out of the zone and dumped him for convenience into a pigsty at Lorl. One of the crib girls nursed him in her own bed for three days while he trembled and sobbed and tried to remember who he was. At last, when he'd regained his senses, he gave her two krets for her trouble and didn't mention the two she'd stolen. It was worth it, a small price for the priceless knowledge gained.

He had finally learned something about the City.

The Self-Gate did not attack men with metal barbs or gas, did not seek vital organs to pierce or poison. Rather, it read intruders like ill-written pages, dissected their grammars, found what made each unique and measured the weak points, the flaws of personality and Self on a cold scope miles away—and calmly shredded them with unrelenting analysis.

*But I am Singer. And I am alone.*

Perhaps because of this, he was the only man ever to crawl away alive from the Self-Gate. Even so, there were horrors he dare not clearly recall of that night. He took them within, defined at last, isolated by all things he could never have nor be, an irreducible denominator. When he left the girl's bed, he began the final arc of the circle he had wandered for nearly twenty years.

He returned to the cave because there was no other place along the miles and years that was his, except for that one frail thread of knowledge, at once salvation and a burden-stone. But among men who held out no hand, in a world that opened no doors, that much at least was his: *he was Singer, and he was alone.* It had taken the better part of two decades to accept the bleak triumph of the fact. Homeless quests from one corner of the land to another. The decisive hammer blow that was the City's rejection, which yet served to bring him full-circle to the contemplation of his outcast state.

Something made him wake.

He unrolled from the blanket and knelt near the mouth of the cave in the faint tinge of gray morning light. He listened, one hand rubbing absently at the shoulder of his deerhide shirt. His ears tried to sift the silence, determine its shape.

There was no sound anywhere, and Singer realized it was the silence itself which roused him from sleep. There should be birds and squirrels, a thousand small brushings and rustlings, a wild hog lumbering through a thicket, a deer splashing in a stream, hurrying home on dainty legs from its feeding ground.

Nothing. The forest held its breath.

*North*. Something coming from the north, and the forest rejected it.

Scarcely breathing in the unnatural silence, Singer slung his quiver and slipped out of the cave. He jogged down the short slope to the trail. The hush of the forest creatures, the billion scaled, leafy things, brought back the old hunter wisdom; he was making too much noise, had to remember how to walk.

He paused, tested the set of his knife edge. In the early moted beams of the sun, he stood smaller than most forest men, but his compact frame was supple and strong. His narrow face, though deeply sunburned, showed no reddish overtones. In winter, the hue of his skin faded to a peculiar ivory, a reflection of the delicate pallor of his mother's skin.

Singer edged away from the cave, listening, seeking some trace of *lep*. Was he being stalked by the one who'd uttered his name the night before? And why was *he* in anyone's thoughts?

*Singer* . . . yes, he read his name again in the lep. The rest was a wordless feeling, a sharing, for which the Uhian dialect had no equivalent, though the meaning was clear. *Singer. Misfit.*

He hadn't intended to go by the tree. It was years, and the pain was so old and dull it was hard to remember when it had been sharp. And yet, as he stepped the brush delicately, thinking only of his feet and the need to move them with the deer's silent tread, suddenly he found himself standing before the huge trunk and his breath caught for an instant.

The deep-cut letters were stretched and distorted with the tree's growth. The grave that he had dug with nothing but a knife and eight-year-old fingers was so tramped and flattened that not even one of Garick's people could have found it, if it wasn't for the carved letters. None of them could read it, but Garick could, and that was enough. Singer wondered how often Garick walked this trail alone to read the marker scratched in the Old Language that Singer's mother taught him herself. He'd labored two days, bruising and tearing the skin of his hands, to cut the legend deep enough.

JUDITH SINGER BURYED HERE
WIFE OF GARIK
MASTER OF SHANDO
BORN IN THE CITE
DYED OF

He could neither name nor spell the cause of his mother's death. But as the miles and years fled past, he thought of that blank more than once. One day, perhaps, Garick might carve it out with his *thammay*. Singer hoped he might be there, watching as Garick reached, fumbled deep within himself to find the correct word.

*"Garick."*

*So low, he barely heard it. Then he felt her body heave feebly, close to his. His mother was crying.*

*"Garick, I wanted . . ."*

*The message was never completed. As he moved his lips to speak, Singer knew he was alone, though nearly a score of winters would pass before the full weight of the fact crushed him and provided him with a new and bitter strength.*

Eighteen years. The green forests and plains grew pale and faded, autumn after autumn, only to burst into color again upon arrival of the spring. Spendthrift nature lavished her life gift on grubs and buds, but Judith, mother of Singer, lay dead beneath the great tree. Singer grew. Many times in the ensuing years, he puzzled without success over his mother's desperate final attempt to articulate her fierce and driving purpose in a few precious syllables.

"Garick, I wanted . . ."

If there was an answer, it was buried in the silence of the years. Eighteen of them; eighteen Samman fires lit in the groves. Garick would be in his middle years now, still master of the coven, still the god. One of the richest. His wagons rolled into Mrikan trading posts from Lams till near Loomin, from harvest to the time of sun-death, bearing the vegetables and fresh apples for sida, the fermented liquor that made the Shando wealthy among forest covens.

But something important was happening this summer. Singer heard it in Lorl when the Shando rider rode in to stable his frothed horse at Korbin's trading post. Garick had written a letter in the Old Language, and Singer wondered curiously over the recipient.

The messenger had the tanned-leather face of the deepwoods

covens; he might have been anywhere between thirty and fifty. The rhythm of their lives was beaten to a different time, Singer knew. Like most of his folk, not inclined to talk among *cowan* outsiders, the man looked up in surprise when Singer's clear lep flashed into his mind: *Why did Garick write?*

The Shando threw his saddle over the fresh mount, but lepped in reply: *Plague moving east. Need help.*

*Help from where?*

"From where?" Singer repeated aloud. "Nothing stops plague." The Shando mounted and wheeled his horse out of the stable. "From where?" Singer asked again.

"City," said the messenger.

Singer couldn't believe it. Nothing short of the plague could have caused Garick to ask for assistance from the one quarter where he knew it would never come. The attempt was not mad or desperate, only futile.

The great City, silent and aloof, sealed itself off from the Shando, the Wengen, the Suffec and all the other covens of the Uhian forest. Its inhabitants were as remote and incomprehensible as the dead god of the Kriss. The City, the mysterious City, never received or sent messages.

Staring at the tree which bore his mother's unfinished epitaph, Singer thought about the plague that long ago decimated the never-large population of the Uhian forest and still returned every decade or so to take its toll. It was a dark horror story that chilled him when he was small, huddling by his father's knee, catching meanings and suppressed fears that adults vainly tried to conceal from Singer's questing mind.

*So the woods are silent. The plague is coming, and the forest knows it. But not from the west. North's the danger. Can't Garick feel it?*

His empty stomach rumbled. Singer remembered he was hungry for something more substantial than the dried rations stored in the cave. Heartier food was not too far away; he thought of the deer run he'd noted two days back. He would have to work the buck, using the old lore. Singer smiled, remembering the early time when the method still seemed genuine magic to him. Some of it, of course, was real enough, though Judith called it *patterning;* the rest was just canny hunter's sense. The deer ranged within a predictable area perhaps a mile long and a quarter as wide between his bed in the high bush and the late and early morning feeding areas. These could be traced by hoofmarks or by the long, trenched scrapings in the earth if a buck was in rut. Only past Samman in the rutting season would his range be much wider than—

*Hunt.*

The lep crashed into his wary mind like a stone shattering the placidity of a standing pond of water, incomplete, only a word, but there was a threat in it.

*Hunt.*

Singer strung his bow quickly and padded off into the forest toward the small stream that ran by his cave. Old coven habit took him now. He squatted by the stream and plunged his hands into the dark bank mud, careful not to disturb the water. Shoving aside the long, dark hair, he began methodically to streak the mud across his face and beard, fingers recalling the old patterns.

*Hunt.*

Again it came. He sent his mind out toward the direction of the lep. There were men in the forest. Shando, Garick's men. Singer listened, unmoving.

*Hunt S—*

He almost caught another word. His muddy fingers moved slowly across his thin face and he closed his eyes to concentrate. There must be more than one, he was sure. Not many, though, and not really lepping between each other. A group of men, then, perhaps three or four, each alone but bound by a common goal, each concentrating on the collective purpose. Once more the wave beat against his senses: *Hunt.* The other word was weaker, but now he could read it.

*Hunt . . . Singer . . .*

He set his mind white to guard against the leak of stray thoughts. It was probably unnecessary; they seemed nothing more than raw hunters, not masters of the inner circle. He avoided the cave that night—they'd find it for sure—and crouched with his blanket, half-dozing in the thicket bordering the deer trail.

Now there was no doubt! Three of them, leaking thoughts like water from a cracked jar. Singer read them like a scent. One was much stronger than the others. They were somewhere in a semicircle to the west, moving silently if they moved at all, not disturbing the forest like the threat of plague, but part of it. The strong sender wavered somewhat in intensity, but was always the dominant one.

It was not Garick. He would be clear as a footprint.

First light began to gray into mist, etching the deer run before him. Singer's mouth gaped in surprise: there was the buck, already there, moving slowly down the trail toward the feeding area. It was little more than a yearling, and where the rack would later come, there were protrusive nodules. Singer's fingers hooked the bowstring.

The buck stopped in the middle of the trail, dead in the open, a clear shot. Then, seeming somewhat uncertain, it took several aimless steps back and stopped again.

*Damn careless for a whitetail. They don't grow old this way.*

The bow was bending when the picture blazed into his mind. He was suddenly watching *Singer* watching the deer, seeing himself and the deer at the same time. Then the string twanged. The buck reared and bolted, sprang two galloping paces, wavered, faltered and strained as if against an invisible tether, then fell, its chest heaving. The arrow shaft protruded from the beast's shoulder.

Confused, Singer was halfway to the animal when his eye caught the regular line of trench in the growing light. A circle dug around the trail, partially covered with leaves. He cursed his stupidity. It was the magic; he'd seen it done by the masters at Karli. Once the buck was in the circle, there was no way out, not against this.

Singer froze. He was in the open now. They'd be around him. If he reached for an arrow, he'd be dead. He dropped the bow and waited, scanning the bush around him, half-expecting the impact of an arrow probably aimed at him.

"All right. I'm Singer. Who are you?" His voice, not loud, had an edge that cut the silence like a knife.

A rope coiled over him from behind, then another. He was abruptly and violently yanked off his feet. A voice, sharp as his own, came from a nearby thicket.

"Kon! Magill! He's bad as a snake. *Don't touch him!*"

Three of them, as he'd guessed. Typical Shando, well over six feet, their sun-browned faces streaked with a paste of boiled leaves that, applied skillfully to their deerskins, made them virtually invisible in the forest. They were young, the oldest barely twenty, untried and overconfident.

Singer kept his eyes on the one named Arin, the leader, long-legged, quick to laugh, with the untempered face of a callow, cocky youth on a man's body. Singer noted somewhat bitterly that Arin had Jenna's coloring, sun-freckled, his hair now reddish in deep summer, but probably a light auburn in the sunless months. And yet, for all Arin's coltish swagger, his mouth and chin hinted of a stronger cast, like Garick in the old days: the same un-self-conscious power and confidence ready to be tapped at the right time, but still an ignorant boy, the power only potential.

Kon was probably the oldest. Quiet, private, with the look of a trustworthy hound, he was never far from Arin's side. The two seemed to share an old secret. Within the already-tight circle of the three, they were almost a single unit; *a matter of similar frequencies,* Judith would have said.

The third, Magill, with his straight black hair and barely folded eyelids, sported one of the races that mixed when the Uhians were called by other, older names. A boy like the others but more aggressive, louder, quick and bluff where Kon was gentle.

Singer measured the pair, Kon and Magill. A hound and a terrier. It was easy to see how Arin led them, impossible to imagine any other arrangement.

*The Three.* He caught the phrase from Magill's mind. It was their catch name, their identification, the child-banner under which they rallied.

Taking great care not to touch Singer, they tied him with several ropes to the trunk of a tree and strung up the buck for dressing. Though Singer was the object of their hunt, they seemed more fascinated by the felled deer.

"Lookit that," Kon said with a trace of awe. "Goddam, Arin!"

The boys were jubilant; to a hunter more at home in the forest than Singer, it might have been insult. Tracking him was simple, and they barely gave him a thought that moment. The phenomenon which had them chattering and dancing about the strung buck was that Arin successfully worked staymagic on it, projecting the circle of his will around the animal's brain, a wall it could not break. No mere hunter's trick, this was master's work.

"Goddam, Arin!" Magill echoed Kon, stomping with glee. "We run deer all our lives, us three. You never did this before."

Arin was as stunned as his companions. He grinned a trifle foolishly, but said nothing.

"You wait," Magill punched Kon's arm. "He ain't gonna even *talk* to us dumb hunters now. Too good for us."

Arin started to protest, but Kon dove at him suddenly, lifted him off his feet and flipped him in the air while Magill whooped in to catch him. They piled all over Arin in joyous roughhouse, rubbing dirt and leaves into his face until he sputtered quits.

"But I *saw* it done lots," Arin explained when they let him up. "Never knew I could. Kon, I'm hungry. Dress out the buck. Let's eat and tote him home."

Kon slipped a long, black-handled knife from its sheath and slit the deer's belly with one deft stroke. Magill started a small cooking fire while Arin stared at Singer, appraising the captive with mild curiosity.

"Old Singer," Magill wondered casually, "he talk Shando?"

*"Of course I do."*

All three turned their heads, uncertain whether the smaller man had spoken to them or projected the message by lep. Singer sensed the barriers snapping in Arin's mind.

"You know me?" Arin asked, puzzled.

Singer nodded. "You're Arin. Garick's son."

Arin grinned. "Then you heard of me." He swelled a little, thinking how his reputation must have traveled among the covens. *Arin, leader of the Three.*

"I've heard of you," Singer replied with an irony lost on the youth. "What do you want with me? Why am I tied up like this?"

Arin shrugged indifferently. "Not us. Garick wants you, so that's what he gets."

"How did you find me?"

"Hell," Magill grunted. "We knew you're here. Everything on four legs run to get out of your way." He waved at the carcass. "Old white-tail not about to get caught by you. Arin put him out for bait."

Singer kept his gaze fixed curiously on Arin. The weird thing happened again, just as before, when he loosed the arrow. He was out of himself, looking *at* Singer through Arin's eyes, feeling his thoughts, still wondering, proud of the staymagic. Then it was over; Singer broke the eye contact and looked down at his tied wrists with a silent shock of realization.

They freed one of his hands and let him eat generously of the cooked meat while they sat in their own circle, ignoring him, except for the one time Magill regarded him with mingled wonder and contempt. He caught the sharing once more, though it had long since lost its power to sting.

*Misfit.*

He watched them sitting in the circle. *Habit,* Singer reflected. The circle is everything to them. In it, they rarely need spoken words to communicate. Half Shando himself, he knew the life, the magic and the way of thought that molded them. They were not masters, not of the inner circle, but still bred to the group consciousness of the coven. Without it, isolated, they might go mad or even die like certain species of bird lost from the directive identity of the flock.

The three boys talked between and through mouthfuls—half words, gestures, sometimes mere thought projected elliptically from one receptive mind to the other. They were finely tuned to each other, had been almost since their birth beds. Kon and Magill were taken in by Garick when their parents succumbed to the last onslaught of plague. Healthy children were few and cherished then. As boys, they were raised and sheltered anywhere in generous, easy-going Charzen that they chose to stay, but for the first seven years of their lives, they slept in Arin's room and ate from the same dish. He was their own, their friend, leader and pride.

*He worked staymagic, Kon!*

*Ought to be a master like his dad.*

Arin shrugged, silent as the others. *No way, not a master. I'm a hunter. We're the Three.*

Magill shook his head, lepping the image of Garick. *The god calls, you'll be a master.*

"No!" Arin said aloud, a little too strongly.

Finished with his meal, Magill wiped his hands on a wad of leaves and squinted at Singer, whistling softly. "Damn, he sure is little. What good's he to Garick?"

"Snake's little too," Kon warned. "Don't get close."

*Why not?*

*Arin says.*

*Garick says!* Arin broke in, then spoke aloud. "He's little because his mother was City. But he's supposed to be a master."

"Master!" Magill hooted in derision. "What, like Garick?"

"I heard, too," Kon said.

But Magill still scoffed, and stepped close to Singer.

"Master Singer," he sneered, "I don't believe what they say. Hear?"

"I hear," Singer said.

"So what you gonna do to us, huh? What you gonna do, master Singer?"

Singer put aside the pity he felt for the raw boy. It was a direct challenge. He knew too well that if it weren't met, Magill would bully him until the situation became intolerable.

"What you gonna do, master Singer?" Magill taunted.

Singer raised his eyes and looked into Magill's.

Later, Magill remembered, or thought he remembered the curious shape of Singer's eyes, the pupils so large that hardly any white showed.

He repeated the challenge, a little louder than necessary. "Why you waiting, *master?* What you gonna do to us, master?"

"Why do you keep saying *us,* Magill?" Singer asked quietly.

"Smart, he knows my name!" Magill laughed, but his confidence was starting to ebb; he felt odd.

"Why do you keep saying *us?"* Singer asked again. His eyes seemed to grow even larger. "What do you mean by *us?"*

"Us," the other answered, unsure of himself. "The Three."

"What three?"

"You know who. Me, Kon. Arin."

Singer shook his head solemnly. *But there's only you.*

With a shudder of fright, Magill knew suddenly that Singer didn't lie. A chill shook him. He wrenched himself around. He was alone. Alone in the forest. Only Magill.

The circle of the Three was gone, the protective oneness—Arin Kon Magill—was dissipated. No, worse, they were *never* there. Magill was alone, alone in the empty woods, lonely, and not even the fire or the buck were real. They were dreams of a life that was sheer delusion, and he was waking to the cold of a friendless world.

"ARIN!" he screamed, trying to back away. But his feet were rooted in the earth, and the probing fastenings were clenched miles below, had always been, would always be. And then he swayed and, mercifully, fell backward into the arms of his two companions.

Kon laughed raucously, but Arin swore. "Damn, I told you don't go close!"

Magill could not move. His limbs shook. Arin looked at Kon over Magill's prostrate form, nodding toward Singer. "Wrap him tight in the skins."

Arin felt the fear himself, partly caught from Magill's mind. He saw it spreading like a sinister shadow over Kon. "Hey!" he shouted, knowing he must re-establish leadership. If he were unafraid, the others wouldn't dare to be. "Come on and wrap him *up*. Then we get drunk tonight, the three of us and three *good*-lookin' women, what you say?"

Magill sat up, dazed and stupid and a little cowed. "Old Singer . . . what he do?"

"Nothing," Arin lied in a soothing voice, gently pressing Magill's shoulder. "Eye trick, that's all. Come on, we'll take him home to Garick."

They bound Singer tight in ropes and skins so that he could walk between the horses. His movements were otherwise totally restricted. He could not even turn his head.

The party set off through the woods, and as they rode, none of the Three looked directly at Singer again.

Word traveled faster than frightened birds in the Uhian forest. The Shando, the Karli, all knew almost moment to moment any happening of importance: a word caught from a speeding rider, a child playing at the edge of the woods, hooting to its mother, or the lep caught by a dozen minds and passed on from the outlying farms and cabins inward to the great stockade at Charzen, the seat of the Shando coven.

The news of the plague came that way, wordless but sure, arousing generation-old fears and spurring Garick to petition the City.

The whispers of the City's silence traveled the same route, the City decisively replying to the god of Shando by not deigning to reply.

And so sped the news of Singer's presence in the forest and his capture by young Arin. A kind of informal escort began at the furthest farms, collecting the curious as it moved. They all knew of him, of the outcast of the covens who nevertheless possessed the powers of a master—as well as one unsettling talent of his own. The older ones remembered the gifted child, eight years old and already feared. Singer, part of them and yet alone, the son of Judith with the long City name. They trouped along beside Kon and Magill, who had him tethered from two sides; they stared and were disappointed. He was absurdly small to the inbred Shando where even women ran to six feet and over, stumbling along between the horses, tightly wrapped in skins with his hands well insulated from any possible contact with bystanders. Only his head and lower legs showed. One boy aimed a stone at him, but fled with a yell when Arin, riding behind with the deer carcass, moved in swiftly to deflect him with a long-legged kick.

The noisy parade finally poured through the stockade gate at

Charzen and moved across the dusty open space in the wide U formed by the three joined log halls. A handful of chattering girls ranged beside Arin's horse, teasing him; he glanced appreciatively at their brown legs, bare and dirty under slit hide skirts, uncombed hair falling over their shoulders and faces. The girls added their high-pitched music to the cackle of hens and squealing pigs disturbed in their wallow by the procession trompling down mud and dirt as the heart of it headed for the center of the U.

"Arin!"

They slowed and halted at the sound of a voice used to authority. The crowd milled, then parted deferentially as an older, dignified woman descended the steps of the center hall and made her way toward Arin. Her hair had once been deep auburn like her son's, though darker, but it was faded to rust now, tied back in a patch of leather and held with a bone stay. She wore no jewelry except the simple iron moon-crescent of a coven goddess about her unwrinkled neck. Arin swung down to greet his mother as she held out her arms.

"Home, Jenna," he smiled.

"Smell of hunting," she said, nose wrinkled, squeezing Arin affectionately. "Must be *that*," she added, nodding toward Singer with contempt. She released Arin and moved closer to the small, dark man.

"Don't go too close, Ma," Arin cautioned.

Jenna stiffened, then said in a voice loud enough for all to hear, "I was a master before Garick. Singer can't hurt me." She stared at him, her pale eyes flint-hard. "You remember me, Singer. I'm Jenna, the goddess. Garick's woman. He doesn't do anything without me—except bring *you* here."

It was an honest statement; she deeply resented Singer's presence in Charzen. She wanted nothing to remind her of Garick's former life, least of all this face that recalled another too well—along with memories of a power that might render Shando magic practically useless. Defiantly, Jenna tried to hold Singer's eyes in a test of power but regretted it immediately. His gaze rested on her with the weight of an oppressive hand.

There was nothing to be gained by humiliating Jenna. "I remember you," Singer said. "Garick's *second* woman." He was considerate enough to drop his voice so no one heard but Jenna. Arin only saw her mouth disappear in a tight, colorless line. Then his mother turned and walked straight through the crowd and up the steps. As she strode away from Singer, the crowd sensed the pent anger in the goddess of Shando.

Arin didn't puzzle over it long. It was Jenna's business, just as Singer was Garick's. His only concern now—his and Kon's and Magill's—was to get drunk and sing under the moon and roll in a blanket tangled in long hair and smooth-hard brown legs until morning, when he would rise to laugh at his own aching head. Life was good, so damn good that Arin had to let it all out in a whoop of pure delight that carried him back into the saddle and across the dust-swirling court toward home. Kon and Magill trotted after him.

Singer, released from between the horses but still bound immobile, stared after the Three with an ironical smile on his lips, but no one sensed the longing in his heart.

They put him in a small, bare room in Garick's house, the long hall at the base of the U. After so many years away, his nose revolted at the rich-sour smells of dirt and cooking, dust, chicken dung and livestock that heavied the summer air. The Uhians were a beautiful people, but hardly the cleanest. For all their incredible magic, they had long ages ago forgotten what a germ was and how it could kill. Their medicinal remedies for infection were simple and effective, partly through the power of belief, iron constitutions and a profound knowledge of healing herbs basic in the training of masters. But major surgery and serious disease were beyond them. In the face of a viral plague or the more prevalent childbed fever, they were helpless. Since time beyond remembrance, the Uhians lived an idyll, stamping out their faith in the goddess earth to the natural rhythms of the turning year-wheel. On a healthy but narrow diet of iron and protein, they attained the tall grace of their present stature, happy, uninhibited and sexually equal, since the power that protected them, the magic, was born in women as well as men. But, isolated and inbred, they carried their own death. The thin-hipped women who rode as well as men transmitted a peculiar inelasticity of bone that made childbirth difficult and often fatal. Cross-breeding, as Judith Singer noted, could eradicate this tendency, but there was not that much intercourse between distant peoples. As many infants perished as lived past their first year. *They are,* she wrote, *like a beautiful, dying flower.*

Singer sat on the narrow cot, his hands still sheathed in skin gloves and tethered by a rope tied to a bolt on the wall, long enough to allow him complete comfort but only a small radius of movement. A chair and table in the center of the room comprised the other furniture, while a large rectangle of material like thick, bleached canvas hung from the opposite wall as decoration, painted with representative designs of the coven. The plan was in three separate panels, showing Garick outside the circle, then in the center of it, surrounded by other figures, and finally joined by Jenna in the last panel where they were represented as the god and goddess in the traditional way, Jenna crowned with candles, Garick with the antlers of a stag. Singer was still staring at it, not without bitterness, when the heavy door swung open and Garick entered alone.

The two openly measured one another.

"Well, boy."

"Well . . . master Garick."

Age had thickened Garick's tall frame very little. He was still vital, the abundant chestnut hair barely touched with gray, most of which sprayed through his mixed-color beard and mustache framing a strong, generous mouth. Like Jenna, he had put aside the functional skins for a cooler cotton robe with no ornament except an iron sunblaze hung around his strong neck. He set a jug and two wooden cups on the table and motioned Singer to it.

"The rope won't reach."

Garick put the jug and one cup on the floor, closer. "Have you eaten, boy?"

"Yes."

Garick was quiet for a moment. He poured his own cup full and seemed to study it. "It's strange to see you again," he said in the ancient tongue. To Singer's surprised look, he added, "Can you still speak Old Language?"

"Yes."

"Good." Garick sipped his drink. "It's easier for saying certain things, and I may be needing it very soon, anyway. How old are you now?"

"Twenty-six." Singer's voice seemed devoid of feeling.

"Twenty-six." Garick nodded. He allowed himself to look fully at the young man for the first time. There was a trace of uncertainty, perhaps even an odd shyness in the glance. "You're a man," Garick murmured.

A pause. Singer sipped his liquor. He might have spoken, but determined to let Garick wrestle without help with whatever was working inside him.

"How has it been?" Garick tried.

"It's been."

"Have you traveled?"

"Yes."

"Where?"

"Everywhere," said Singer. "I have my mother's curiosity. Karli, Wengen, Mrika. North where they fish, south beyond Suffec on the cotton boats. Tried to find Myudah and failed. Everywhere."

"You didn't grow very tall."

Singer looked up at him. "Neither did she."

Garick felt the sting of the words. He took a breath and another sip of sida. "How old were you when she died? Eight, nine? How much can you remember of the way it really was?"

"Enough. I buried her. For two years before that, I watched her die a day at a time while you never came because you were with Jenna. A day at a time; I'd say I knew a little about how things were."

The words sounded dull, dead things with weight to bear down the spirit more than bruise it. Garick swallowed, tried to speak, then reached a hand out to the younger man. "Singer—my son."

Singer stiffened. "You self-serving son of a bitch, you ought to choke on that word."

"You are—my—*son!*" Garick's fist crashed down on the table. "I don't know why you returned—"

"Neither do I."

"—but you did, Singer, and while you're in Charzen, you'll do as I Say."

Garick rose—not as calmly as he'd entered, Singer noted—and paced about the small room, stopping before the coven painting.

"There are things a man must do," he told Singer. "*Might* becomes *must*. How did I know then, how could I guess? I was as ignorant as Arin—drinking, plowing women, growing apples, that's all there was for me. Your mother changed things; she taught me. I saw what was ignorant and dirty here, but I saw what was good, too. The apples made my grandfather rich, my father richer, and myself an equal with the moneymen in Lorl. They know power for the money behind it. Well, I was a master—and by the time they asked me to take the crown, I knew what I could do with that money power, but not *with-*

*out* the crown. And the god must be matched with a coven master for goddess. Ever try to get something for nothing, Singer?"

There was more than dignity in his broad-backed stancc. The silent eloquence of an unassuageable pain touched Singer even as he tried to deny it.

"I loved Judith," Garick said simply. "I've gone to her grave more than once. But—things happen between people, son. They change. Your mother was City, it was deep in her. All the magic, all the love, all the power of all the circles couldn't make her think like us. Or Circle like her." He brooded over the thought. "To City, nothing matters but learning. They've got the—"

He groped for the strange word, but couldn't bring it to mind. Singer could have told him, but he remained silent.

"Anyway," Garick continued, "they pour every scrap of knowledge their impossible lifetimes can soak up into—*it*. But for what? Does anyone know? They cram that thing full of facts and guesses and theories. Nobody knows why. All around them the rest of us can rot for all they care!"

Garick sat heavily; a vein pulsed in his forehead. "Listen." He leaned across the table to his son. "The plague is moving again. You've never seen it, probably. The last time was just after—after you left. Nothing stops it, Singer. Nothing, no magic. We lost hundreds. The rest of us survived because we moved out of Charzen until it passed, and I had to fight the masters, even Jenna, to get that much. I wanted to talk to City then, but the masters wouldn't listen."

He sat back. His expression changed, hardened. "That was then; this is now. More money, more years of handling people. I've bought men and information. Anything that happens in Lorl or Filsberg is known to my coven in a matter of days. I've shared everything with them, made them the best-informed coven in Uhia. They trust me now. They nodded *yes* to the letter this time—they shook a little, but they said yes. So—I wrote. Your mother taught me a lot. There are healers in City with machines that can replace a heart or whatever you need in less time than you'd need for breakfast. I wrote, I begged for help, a meeting, an alliance, anything to save us from that suffering again. Their healers could do it. I begged, Singer. And that cold, beautiful City hasn't even bothered to answer. To them, we don't exist."

"So how is it now," Singer asked him, "to be the god?"

Garick read the irony. His lips tightened in a mirthless smile.

"How does it feel to be alone? You and I don't need to ask each other that. The Uhians are in a storm, beating on the door of a warm house while the people inside pretend not to hear. Their silence is our death."

"They've always been silent."

"Not any more."

"Always. Centuries. How can you change it?"

At first, his father appeared not to hear. He bowed his head over folded hands. He seemed older, tired. "When they wouldn't answer," he said at last, "something broke in me. Something said *now. Now or never.* The masters never change; to them, the plague comes and goes and the earth cleans herself. Well, the plague may get us this time, but not before I open up that City; not before I face them and show them what they've turned their backs on, even if I have to take their goddam City apart brick by brick."

Singer stared in disbelief. Then he began to laugh. "Destroy them? How? You should know, you of all people, there's no way."

"Not just us," Garick went on imperturbably, "all the covens: Karli, Wengen, Suffec. I'll buy, I'll borrow, I'll beg. Even the Kriss, if they'll join us."

"The Kriss?" Singer stopped laughing. "You said the Kriss?"

"I'll pay their price."

"You *are* serious."

Garick nodded.

Singer took a stiff drink. "So you bring them all together—and that's a sight I'd have to see, Kriss and covens all in a row—then what?"

"We go to the knife."

"War?" Singer said it bluntly. "You'll lose. What can you send against the City? Men and women on horses, bows and arrows. I've heard rumors in Mrika that City has weapons that can kill a dozen in the time it takes to nock an arrow, and those weapons have never been used, never been needed. You know why?"

"Yes," said Garick. "The Self-Gate."

"The Self-Gate. Do you know what that thing can do?" The energy drained out of Singer's voice; it was a haunted whisper. "What that thing can do. Coveners who've never been alone . . . suddenly there's nothing but alone. Nothing else." He looked up at his father. "Your masters would go mad; they'd cut their throats with their own thammays. That's your fight, Garick: the Gate. What have you got to push through it?"

"There's you," Garick drawled.

Singer gave him an eloquent glance coupled with a slow shaking of his head. "You think I'd help you?"

"No way." Garick grinned dryly. "But you're like Jude. She wanted to go back to City, and I think that's what Singer wants, too. You'll try that Gate someday."

The words fell like something dead at Garick's feet. "I already have."

The older man regarded him alertly. "You did what?"

"I tried it."

"The Gate?"

"That's what I said."

At length, Garick spoke: "I don't believe it."

"That's your problem, but it's true. I was drunk enough to feel immortal. I tried."

"What happened?"

"It stopped me."

"People it stops don't walk out, I hear. They're carried out dead or close to it."

"That's right. They carried me out screaming so loud they figured I'd live. I woke up in a whore's bed. She had a good heart along with an eye for profit—and a fine body, too, if I could've done anything but shake and cry." Singer gulped another drink. "I'm the only man ever to come out alive; they ought to put me in a jar somewhere. You know why, master Garick? Because most men don't know who they are. Most men never know who they are. And the Gate does."

Garick frowned, interested. "I don't understand."

"Don't try."

"You ran the Gate," Garick wondered. Abruptly, he smacked his fist into the other palm. "I was right. You *are* a match for—"

"I was beaten," Singer interrupted painfully. "Whipped."

Garick rose, an indecipherable light in his eyes. "Maybe that time. But you wanted City enough to try. When the time comes, you'll try again."

The snort of hopeless derision died when Singer looked up at Garick. Even as he would have hooted down the notion, he knew his father was not entirely wrong. There might be a time, a moment with enough courage to run that gauntlet again, but—

"No." He bowed under the bleak impossibility. "No."

"I wouldn't bet against it." Before Singer could protest further, Garick moved to the door, still lithe for all his bulk; the floorboards scarcely creaked under him. The door closed.

Singer shut his eyes and mentally followed the god of Shando into the corridor and out the front portal of the hall. There was a phrase, repeating itself again and again in Garick's mind, and Singer wanted to catch it.

He opened his eyes, startled; he hadn't heard *that* in years . . .

The phrase echoed in his mind as Garick's unguarded thoughts leaked to him. Deliberately?

*The Girdle of Solitude . . . the Girdle of Solitude.*

Singer stared through a narrow open casement and saw part of the courtyard and the stockade gate beyond. He let his mind range free, wandering over Garick's words, wondering what sort of ultimate weapon the god thought he might be able to fashion from him.

*The Girdle of Solitude.*

If that was what Garick had in mind, it still meant a second trespass beyond the safety zone surrounding the City, another exposure to the horrors of the Self-Gate. He realized he was trembling, yet even as he did, he remembered something his mother told him once.

"There is no courage without fear," she said. "The bravest is often the most frightened. And solitude is often the companion of fear."

What else did she say about loneliness? He forced himself to remember. *To be afraid is to be alone, but . . . but . . .*

"But only then does a person attain self-discovery. Pain defines and exacts the price of its wisdom."

*She was right. That's how I learned the truth.*

But even this small part of her legacy was alien in hot, dirty Charzen. Judith's philosophy, Singer realized with bleak superiority, would snap apart the psyche of a simple coven hunter like Arin, if he were forced to experience the forging pressures of lonely isolation. Coveners relied on their sense of unity, of intermingled purpose, to define and comfort one another. Theirs was not the way of the City.

A horse and rider passed across the narrow frame of his vision, a chicken ran squawking on a brainless errand. A woman trudged through the gate, a small boy trotting in order to match her long strides. Singer knew the courtyard from one dusty end to the other, from the place where the poultry ran and the hog wallow slanted to a shallow basin, dry at Lams but a deep mire in spring, to the large log hall half a mile away where Judith stood in the last days to watch Garick ride out to the ceremonial grove with young Jenna, because he was Shando after all, and Judith was City, and there was no going back.

It struck Singer that the intended siege of the City was wholly Garick's war, and it may well have been born with his mother nearly two decades earlier. Was it a direct product of the brilliant agonies of her mind, or was it a belated response of revenge on Garick's part? Singer was not sure. There were still so many fragments of the puzzle he did not possess, even after eighteen winters of growth and wondering. One thing was sure: Judith had not left the City merely to find someone like Garick, love him and bear his child. There was some beginning bedded deeply in purpose.

Once, Singer had done his best to root out scraps of her early history. They still remembered her in Lorl, the Mrikan trading town. One of the mercenary guards recalled the morning she first appeared.

"There was this wagon train, see," he told Singer; "it came through City along the Balmer passage with dried fish from the coast. Me and one of the other guards counted wagons and riders like always, and there was one more rider on the way out than went in at the east gate. Could've been a mistake in counting, but no; I heard later about her and knew that's when she left City. Didn't matter to us. We just see nobody stays inside. Don't care if there's more people in the wagon train, though it only happened that once. Our only worry is if there's less."

Singer asked more questions and learned that the wagons creaked past the checkpoint and on for a mile or so into the deep mud of Lorl's main avenue before the last cart halted briefly. A young girl jumped down. She had a backpack on her thin shoulders.

Korbin, the fat trader, remembered her best of all, and since Singer was paying for the drinks and was himself a living portrait of her, Korbin's memory grew sharper as he guzzled.

"You could tell straight she was City." He wiped the foam from his flabby mouth. "Sure, she had on wagon girl's clothes—pants, shirt, sheepskin, but all of them too big and too clean. Little? I didn't think women came that small, maybe five foot, but she carried it like twice that. I mean, when she walked in, you knew she was there. Just something about her. Young: eighteen, nineteen."

He paused to accept another drink from his host. Korbin sipped and sighed appreciatively. "Shando sida, best there is." A belch of corroboration. "Well, I thought it was strange, because *nobody* comes out of City. Couldn't personally remember it ever happening. My father was seventy-two, *he* couldn't remember anything like it. Maybe she was the only one. But there she was, laying out the goods right on this counter. Singer, you know what *oil* is? It's what I hear they use on those City machines. Syn-thet-ic pet-rol-im, she called it; rare as balls on a woman outside City.

"Well now, she lined up *fifteen* little cans of that oil right in front of me. I bought them for ten krets each and sold out two days later at eighteen apiece. A man can live good for ten days on two krets, so I give her a fair price. And she had medicine, too, all kinds, but she wouldn't sell any of *that*. She rented my shed out back, said she'd be here awhile. I asked her where she expected to end up, and you know what she says? Lishin!"

Korbin pillowed his ample belly against the counter, swirling the sida in his cup, cocking an eye at Singer.

"You know what the Uhians say about Lishin? Dead place, dead since long before the covens, thousand, maybe two thousand years. Old bridge, solid iron, leans slanty across a stinking river. Houses made out of stone and iron! Hard to believe, but that's what they say. And you won't get a Karli or a Wengen or even a Shando near it. But your mother went, I hear. She was a *drivin'* woman."

A trace of tenderness softened his voice. "I saw her when the Karli wagon brought her out of the forest the next summer. Poor little sack of bones, sick with bad-water fever, lotta other things. Couldn't tell the dirt from the sunburn on her, had to burn her deerskins before they stunk me out. She just laid up in my shed knocking down a jug, jug and a half a day. Wasn't going back to City, not going no place. Just drinking. And drinking."

The sida had mellowed the trader. He settled back in a chair, poured a round on the house, belched contentedly again. "So, Garick's your father, um? She met him right here, y'know. Now, that was a pair! Five foot of her, five miles of him. City and raw Shando, black knife, bow and all. And no fool, that Garick. Even before she came, he taught himself numbers right here at this counter, watching me tote up bills. Couldn't even write his name, but he *watched*. Smart: just because a jug's empty don't mean it can't hold water, y'know. Well, those two were for each other, anyone could see it.

She should have gone home with him then like he wanted, but she meant to see Lishin. Never found out why."

The long, slow afternoon drew out to the droning of flics. Singer looked beyond the open door into the blue-gray distance that hid City from him.

"Wonder about City people sometimes," Korbin mused. "So quiet behind that Self-Gate. Never see them. What do they *do* in there? How do they feel? Been there a good thousand years, maybe more. No one goes in, none come out—except her."

"Why?" Singer asked. "Did she ever tell you?"

"Not me." Korbin shook his head. "But there was something, had to be. I mean, she drove herself like a horse. Never saw anyone that kind of strong, man or woman. Some idea she had . . ."

In the sleepy afternoon of Charzen summer, Singer stood at the end of his tether and thought about his mother. Over the years, the shape of purpose that drove her became clearer to him, but he could still not sum her up, define the total plan that led her first to quit the City and later bring on her untimely death.

Some idea she had.

# *The Girdle of Solitude*

Judith Randall Singer had the unused, indoor look of the scholar: thin limbs, doll body with near-translucent ivory skin and large liquid brown eyes that went black when she was angry or exhausted. Young as she appeared, there was no trace of youthful uncertainty in her manner, but rather a disconcerting composure and purpose.

She spoke a little of the polyglot Mrikan, a smattering of Uhian and was well acquainted with the Old Language, though opportunities to use it were almost as infrequent outside the City as the concentrated verbal shorthand employed within its walls. No one learned much about her, but she had the knack of drawing out the usually reserved coveners to entertain her with the old song-stories they passed down from generation to generation.

She was always most eager to hear the traditional tales of the Girdle of Solitude, an ancient, fabled garment rumored to exist in dim, pre-coven times. According to legend, it bestowed the gift of invisibility on its wearer. Judith knew that *girdle* and *solitude* were among the handful of words taken directly into Uhian without change from the Old Language. She reckoned the Girdle as fact, a memory with raveled edges frayed into myth. And always, when they sang to her of the Girdle, the tantalizing refrain ran through every song—

*In Lishin, in the west*

In time, the sight of Judith became less of a novelty, and the uncurious Mrikans turned to business: the wagons were coming east.

With spring, Lorl stirred sleepily at the start of its trade year. Raw plank shelves were crammed with goods from the north and east to wait for high summer and the first wagons out of the forest covens bringing fresh and boiled fruits, vegetables, raw wool, poultry and the priceless Shando apples to be pressed into sida and sold to middlemen dealers. From late summer until first snow they came, and the merchants glowed with prosperity, trading steel ingots to the men for knives and tools and garish weaves of finished cotton and wool to the tall, wild-deer women who sometimes accompanied them. The single main street and its few tributaries roared with commerce, with coveners and middlemen alike whoring themselves cheerfully in a welter of muddy, booming profit. Then Lorl stank of dung, urine, vegetables, meat in various stages of preserve or decay, sweat, rawhide and dirt. Lorl grew dustier and seasonally richer, sandwiched as it was between the covens to the west and the silent City to the east and by the sea. The small middle class, composed of merchants and the mercenaries from the border, little cared for the fortunes of either the covens or the City except as they affected trade and provided a source of employment. Day and night the streets seethed with volatile, black-haired Wengen coveners, fish merchants, the border guards billeted in the nearby barracks, bored prostitutes in stained robes combing stiff hair in front of split-log cribs.

And through it all moved Judith, listening, listening to the rapid, slang-slurred argot, rubbing its rhythms into her mind.

In late summer the first wagons of the Karli arrived. The Karli were northern cousins to the Shando; the two covens had always been close to one another. Though Judith spent months in preparation listening to library tapes of their dialect, it was still difficult to understand them, since much of their communication was unspoken lep. The richest and poorest of the Karli looked alike; beyond the cord-belted tabard and white-hilted knife, or thammay, of the masters, they had no status symbols. Most Karli were simple sheepherders, supremely ignorant of the world beyond their covenstead, but they had a capacity for joy and shared emotions that woke in Judith curious feelings of envy. City-bred, used to a life of study and solitude, she listened hungrily when they congregated at night and the old songs were begun by a single throat to be taken up by twenty more. Hands clapped, the men and women leaped high and turned in their snaking, circular dance. Then Judith saw the soul of the Uhians. The dance might last half an hour or more until their eyes glazed and brown faces glistened with sweat as they sought through the unceasing motion for something beyond Self, touched it in one another and grew calm again.

When summer cooled and fall stole on, the Shando apple wagons came and the trading accelerated in pitch and intensity. By now Judith was used to the impossible size of the coveners crowding Korbin's store. One of the trains belonged to a grizzled monolith named Jase, who did not so much stand in the store as wear it. When he leaned over the counter toward her or Korbin, Jase was a benign mountain shadowing an insignificant valley. His apples made him rich, and his woman was a master of the inner circle. Their greatest pride—and sadness—was their son, Garick, outside by the wagon.

"Good farmer," Jase muttered over the lip of his jug, "but he couldn't raise a sneeze by magic."

Judith regarded Garick with idle curiosity. He was about nineteen, sun-burnished with a crest of thick brown hair, square mouth and laughing, intelligent eyes. She almost collided with him as he rounded a wagon corner.

"Better watch where you walk," he drawled down at her. "You so little, someone gonna step on you."

Though he was a farmer like his father, Judith began to realize there was more to Garick than that. He visited her shed often, watching hungrily as her pencil flew over the endless pages of notes.

"Where you learn that, Jude?"

"Writing? A long time ago."

"Could I learn?" He asked it lightly, but she heard the covert longing.

"Of course you can."

Garick peered down at the strange symbols with keen interest, then at Jude. The interest did not lessen. "You could learn me lots."

She stopped writing and rested her elbows on the table, suddenly aware of Garick's proximity in a new and oddly pleasant way.

"What . . . what would you like to know, Garick?"

He thought on it. "Everything."

Then Jase bellowed from the wagon. Garick stopped in the doorway, a playful grin on his face. "Jude, you got a man here in Lorl?"

It caught her completely by surprise. "What do you mean, a man?"

"You *with* a man?"

"No," she said simply, curiously. "Why should I be?"

Her answer seemed to puzzle him in turn. "Don't even go out on the hill?"

"What hill?"

Jase called again. Suddenly Garick stepped to the table, lifted Judith's small chin with his large brown fingers and kissed her.

At the contact of his hand, she stiffened. *City people don't touch!* But Garick, she realized, didn't know that. She relaxed, neither objecting nor responding, but rather experiencing the strange sensation with interested detachment, aware that this was the peculiar coven custom she'd read about.

And then, for the first time since she was a child, Judith stopped observing and cataloging data. In an alien surge of emotion, she parted her lips beneath Garick's and encircled his shoulders with her arms. After a moment, he stepped back and studied her with wonder and pleasure.

"Well, Jude," Garick said as if arriving at a decision. He turned and hurried to join his father.

Judith stood in the vacant doorway, staring. After some time, she tried to resume her work, but her pencil hovered unused over the page. She was smiling. How curious, she thought: in the quiet solitude of the City, she'd long ago charted the male-female relationship, but it was so much dry knowledge, lore well lost, words on paper like the ancient love ballads, flame entombed in the ice of time, tamed by denotation.

*The reality is different. It can't be communicated,* she realized with something of a shock. It was a small but vital chink in her City breeding.

Jase joined a large, combined wagon train to make the homeward journey. Some of the wagons would turn north for Karli at the bend of the Tomik.

As they prepared to leave, Judith decided she'd learned as much as Lorl could teach her, so she asked to go with them part of the way. Her decision—she reassured herself—was only incidentally determined by the fact that she could be with Garick a little longer. She strapped up her pack; happily, Garick hoisted her onto the wagon seat beside him. Though her motives were a puzzle, he loved her openly, admired her courage and knew her for more than a little mad.

"How long you be in Karli?" he asked.

"Until spring."

"Karli ain't half of Charzen," Garick said proudly. "Come on home with us."

"I *would* like that," she said honestly, pressing his arm. "But I have to go even further than Karli after that."

"Where?"

"To Lishin."

A sudden, pointed silence fell on the folk in the wagon. Heads turned to regard Judith in fear and astonishment. Garick's eyes widened. "Jude," he whispered, "that's *Kriss* country."

"I speak the language well enough. They're coveners like you, aren't they?"

"No, not like us," he said flatly. "They ain't Circle. Nobody goes there. Nobody wants to."

"I have to."

"Jude, you just don't know. Nobody lives in Lishin. It's *dead.*"

"Still," she persisted, "I have to go."

"Look." He tried to reason, difficult since he couldn't lep or share with Jude. "Even if you find men damfool enough to take you there —and you won't—it's clear across Blue Mountains, up and down, up and down all the way. All bush, like to kill horses, bad enough for hunters—"

She patted his hand. "Drive the wagon."

"Jude—"

Jase waved the move-out. Garick scooped up the reins and smacked them in frustration. "Lishin!" he muttered, still unable to believe it. "And I thought a *horse* was dumb!"

Coveners had few taboos, Judith learned, but they went deep; things accepted as fact though not often voiced. The Kriss was one of the strongest. Garick finally responded to her questions and spoke of them reluctantly. Kriss were outsiders, alien. They were cowan. Circle folk regarded them as unclean, and the few facts gleaned about that reclusive people did not change the view.

"They have a dead god," Garick said, the horror of otherness audible in his voice. "They love death. They sing about death like it was a woman."

As the train crawled its northwesterly arc along the Tomik River, Judith learned more about the color of the coven life, of the lush natural setting which bounded and defined them. Mornings and evenings were crimson over the forest, the air cool and delicious. Night was a new thing to her, total dark beyond the island of fire-flickered wagons, filled with sounds that frightened and woke her constantly. Garick, sleeping beside her, seemed in some way to have linked his consciousness with her own. Once, she started awake at a weird forest call. She hadn't moved, merely opened her eyes, but Garick's hand closed over hers.

"Old owl," he murmured as it sounded again. "Don't be scared."

"How do you always know when I'm awake?"

Garick turned over and lay close, his arm around her. "I'm with you." It was the only way he could explain, and Judith could not grasp his meaning.

"Why can't I do it?"

His fingers wound about her hair and temples. "You think all up here."

"Everyone does," Judith countered; the brain was the center of every act of cerebration, deliberate or instinctual. Garick sighed with the complexity of it. "City is strange," he murmured. "What they *do* all the time?"

"We think," she said. "We study. We learn."

"Then why'd *you* come out?"

It was a long time before she answered.

"I started to wonder," Judith began carefully. "And there's a thing, a—kind of weapon. In the wrong hands, it could endanger everything the City has worked for all these generations."

"You 'spect it's in Lishin?"

She nodded.

"How you know?"

"I don't. It's just an idea I have."

Garick noted the incipient weariness that crept into her face whenever she tried to speak at length, as if the effort of reducing her thoughts to the level of a covener sapped her strength. He felt a sudden rush of anger at the indefinable wall between City and himself. He struggled to express the old rage to Judith. *Why?* Why did City shut itself in? Why did they send merks, hired soldiers, to police its borders against the coveners? And why the Self-Gate, stronger than any coven magic?

"Solitude is the way of the City," Judith said a trifle sadly. "Sufficiency unto one's self. The reasons are rooted in the founding of the City. The Self-Gate, as you call it, is a method of preserving the plan of absolute independence. We keep you out because other ways of life are inimical to everything the City represents." She sighed. "But now I'm not so sure. It's clear there are many gaps in the knowledge we thought we possessed about the covens. Our theory of language, for instance—and it's an important instance—doesn't include the *lep*."

But Garick was clearly confused. Judith smiled, stroked his cheek. "There, I touch you. That alone, touching another human being, is unheard of in the City. But, Garick, I'm going to tell them. In writing, in pictures, so much that I've learned, everything I can absorb about your people. There is *so much* missing. I feel it now within me, too."

She touched him again with a subtle urgency. Her hands pulled his mouth down to hers, the way he'd done once, and in the new half-understanding between them they melted together with the beginning of wisdoms, and in the midst of the glowing new experience, Judith laughed at the tickling of Garick's beard.

When real danger came, Garick knew it long before she did.

The last night before the wagon train divided, Judith woke near dawn. With her now-chronic kidney problem, she had to leave the wagon. It was a cool, clear night that hinted of the cold to come. The moon was low, sunrise not too far away. Two guards murmured quietly by the fire, barely looking up as she passed them.

The group was camped close to the bend of the Tomik, the river at their back and open, rolling country on three sides. The morning wind rustled the trees and Judith enjoyed the last of the shimmering light on the water, pausing to watch it fade imperceptibly in the stillness. She turned back to the camp—and stopped, surprised.

Silent as the moonlight itself, the camp had come alive. The guards stood alert, listening, while men and women issued from every wagon, dressing rapidly. No word, no sound had been uttered, yet the coveners were awake and wary, responding like a flock of birds wheeling as one to avoid a swooping predator.

She found Garick slinging his quiver.

"What is it?"

"Don't know yet. Get in the wagon."

She clutched at the knife he thrust into her hand and crouched just behind the seat to watch Garick and the others. With hardly a syllable uttered, the whole group shifted to a position of defense, some lighting torches from the fires. These few, men and women alike, formed a wide-spaced perimeter around the camp, unarmed save for the torches. In the center was a larger group with bows, Garick and Jase among them. They were silent now, waiting, but still Judith could detect no danger beyond the firelight.

Later she learned from Garick that the outer defense was a ring of masters, men and women who wove their combined power into a mental wall. Somewhat the opposite of staymagic and more lethal, they called it *whitebrain.* If anything got through, it was trapped helpless in the circle, its mental functions blanketed with numbing force, and despatched by arrows. But they relied always on their magic first.

Shoulder to shoulder, arrows nocked over their bowstrings, Jase and Garick strained their senses into probes that groped to touch and shape the thing they could not see. The lep passed between them and on to the others, and all searched.

*?*

*Dogs. Wolf would howl. Packdog's too smart.*

*Cowan hunters?*

*Masters would read them. Too far east anyway.*

*Dogs.*

The same intelligence traveled swiftly through the outer rim of masters. They waited, the hush deepening. The fire played shadows over their backs. Then—

*Coming. Now.*

Judith heard a low sound, a growing snarled chorus that lifted the hair on the back of her neck. Twin points of firelight glinted, reflected in two, three, a dozen pairs of close-set eyes, weaving back and forth beyond the circle of masters. *They have no weapons. They'll be slaughtered.*

The dogs advanced in a silent rush, half a hundred of them behind the leaders, huge bounding shapes of darkness torn out of the shrouding night. The wild creatures plunged to within a few yards of the circle and faltered, skidded to a halt, sensing the invisible barrier. Torches thrust out at them, forcing them back. Slowly they retreated until they were only fire-darting eyes.

Again they came, this time hurling themselves in a mass against the mental power, wall against wall. A few of the strongest penetrated closer to the thrusting torches, wobbling dizzily as the power singed their tiny brains.

The animals neither howled nor challenged with any sound save the continuous low growl—like an idling motor, Judith remembered afterward. Garick said wolves were easy, you could always tell where they were. But wild dogs had a memory of man and man's ways. There was actually a time, it was said, when the two creatures hunted together. The dogs could think and, like men, gave no warning of an attack.

They *were* thinking out there. Their tactics changed. Without knowing what stopped them, they could nevertheless sense where the force was weakest. They concentrated their energies there. The line held, but the dogs won more ground, coming nearer. Again and again the torches jabbed out at them. One man's arm was slashed as a red-eyed shadow leaped out of nowhere to buffet the fraying edge of the power circle.

The light was graying toward dawn. Judith began to see them now, massive, nondescript mongrels, some of them three feet high at the shoulder, loping forward or retreating with malevolent, purposeful intelligence to seek another chink in the wall. The strain of concentration was telling on the masters. A young girl swayed and would have fallen, but the woman next to her caught her arm.

The dogs immediately sensed the small gap in the invisible armor. In a body, they wheeled and rushed, hurling themselves with silent purpose against the flaw point in the power, two tearing at the woman, several others breaking through in high leaps to the center before the wall of will could knit up again.

The girl keened with fear and rage, flailing at the dogs with her torch and thammay, trying to force them from the downed woman, who uttered a single wail of pain and terror. The animals staggered away from the fierce attack of the girl, pain hammering at their skulls as the masters projected redoubled power at them.

The woman lay still.

Judith's knuckles went white around the knife handle. She saw the dogs bound once more against the circle, some few breaking through the attenuated power-cast only to falter drunkenly in the wash of its force. Their snarls pitched higher into a soul-freezing shriek as their senses went white, torn asunder by the angry magic of the masters rallying with the full force of concerted fury.

Mad, half dead already, the animals charged anything that moved. Garick shot one—and then went down under snapping jaws as a huge gray beast hit his back.

*Jase!*

Drawn on another dog, Jase needed a precious instant to make the kill. He loosed the shaft and turned, but even as his muscles bunched to spring, a small figure hurtled at the dog with a cry. Judith pumped the knife up and down, slashing the dog in weak, futile strokes, not deep but enough to slow the dog's attack until Jase's blade severed its throat.

The circle was closed again. Beyond it, the pack was at last discouraged. Its sallies were weaker and more disorganized. Wisps of early morning fog laced across the open ground, and the dogs retreated further into it as arrows struck among them. Then the fog swallowed them up. They were gone. No sound rippled the morning calm except the weeping of the girl huddled over the dead woman.

Jase helped Garick to his feet. "Jude did it," he said gratefully. "Couldn't move in time."

Garick and Judith regarded the dead dog at their feet. Her hands were stained red to the wrists.

"Who . . . who's crying?" Garick stammered, panting.

"Young Jenna," said Jase. "Dogs got her ma."

Garick clutched at Judith's thin arms. "Jude, your hands. Where—?"

"Not mine." She swallowed with difficulty. "Not my blood. The dog's."

She wiped her hands mechanically on the beast's matted hair and then knotted over, gagging. Garick held her while she was sick.

The Shando buried Jenna's mother under a willow that leaned out over the river, respectfully but with little ceremony. There was more attention paid to the gangling, red-haired girl than to her dead parent. Jenna stood close to Garick—a little too close, Judith thought. The mother's thammay and coven necklace were saved for Jenna, and each was placed in her hands by one of the masters.

"She comes again," they soothed her. "So do we all."

Judith heard but did not understand. Garick tried to explain that it was no idle comfort. The world and life were all, death a brief sleep. The death-parting of friends or family was "born again in each other's sight."

Judith listened but could not believe what he was saying. It was not a case of rejecting the coven philosophy; rather she wondered how they ever could have come to accept it in the first place. She saw how reverently the hallowed objects were offered to Jenna, already a master herself with power to protect her people—the knife, the necklace, the precisely knotted cord belt—and, with a new emotion Judith didn't stop to analyze, she saw how Jenna held to Garick's arm as he led her to her father's wagon. She had been with him before Judith, Garick said—as a simple fact with no trace of boasting or to inspire jealousy. Like his people, he was so transparent as to be impenetrable.

Garick seated Jenna beside her father on the wagon and took the man's hand. "Born again," he said.

"To the Shando," the farmer murmured, then turned a canny glance at Jenna. "Good girl here, Garick. A master."

"That's true." Garick knew what was coming.

"And you been with her awhile; you two good together."

Jenna leaned over the seat to him. "Garick, come see me at the Samman fire. I'll make you happy again, the same as Sinjin." She saw where his glance shifted. "And all the other times."

Garick tried to share it with her; that was before, that was pleasure, being out on the hill together. But the other made him grow, stretched and challenged him with lessons he hungered for, deep things.

*City girl?*

*Yes.*

*Then why she leaving? Why do you want her so much?*

"Garick," she said aloud with the vehemence of it. "She going to Karli, I hear, then over Blue Mountains to Lishin. She'll die there."

Garick tried to break away. "Karli going north." He nodded with the respect due a master. "Got to see them."

Jenna persisted. *I'm now. She's maybe.*

Confused, Garick stumbled off. He saw the friend he wanted, beckoned to him, took the youth over to the wagon where Judith wrestled with her pack.

"Jude, this is Moss of the Karli." Judith saw a husky blond youth, one of those who stood in the inner defense with Garick the night before. "You'll stay with Moss and his ma in Karli. They just like Shando"—he squeezed his friend's arm—"just smell of sheep now and then."

Moss chuckled. "Kept *your* ass warm more than once, them sheep. Y'all didn't mind then." He turned to Judith and scooped up her pack in one broad hand. "Garick says be friends, we're friends. What you called?"

"Judith Randall Singer."

His eyes crinkled merrily. "*All* that?" But he glanced at Garick. *City?*

*Mine, Moss.*

*Dumb. Jenna's a good woman, a master.*

*Well, I ain't. Never be one. I pick my own woman to be with.*

*You say good-by now, boy. She going to Lishin. Won't come back.*

Garick grasped Moss' hand. "You and your ma take good care of her."

Moss sighed; Shando had good hearts but thick heads. "Do what I can for her," he promised, "long as I can." Tactfully, Moss strolled away to the far end of the wagon. Garick put his arms around Judith.

"You be in Lorl again next summer?"

She shook her head. "I'll be going home."

It hurt him. "Back to City?"

"There's so much new work for me to do now, Garick."

"But I'll be in Lorl after Lams again. Wait for me till then," he urged. "Wait for me at Korbin's."

"Garick, I can't." She tried hard to explain, but he was trying to kiss her.

"Just till after Lams, Jude. Wait for me."

"I have to study. I have to put everything into the synergizer." She was still protesting when he lifted her into his arms.

"Jude, wait for me. Wait."

Her nails dug at his back as their lips pressed together. His arms held her tight and he begged again and again. "Jude, we're not that different. I need you. Wait for me . . . please."

"Yes." Her voice was so soft, he wasn't sure he heard. "All right."

"You will? Promise."

She put her head on his chest. "I will, Garick. I guess I would have waited anyway."

There were no more words for them to say, but they remained together for a long time. At the far end of the wagon, Moss loitered patiently, studying the sky for rain signs.

By spring, Judith felt as ready as she would ever be for the hard trek to Lishin; more than that, she felt she had earned it. But it was a different woman who walked her horse beyond the last cabins of the Karli covenstead after Leddy fire. Garick might not have recognized her. The ivory skin was chapped, blistered, healed and toughened against the knife-edge wind. Her hair, always short, had grown long and stiff with dirt, gathered back in the hide strip-and-pin fashion of coven women. Her hands were hardened at work, nails broken and yellow, fingers calloused and insensitive from the pinch of frostbite while digging and sacking potatoes.

The bitter cold weather took its toll, but Judith's own stubborn courage cost her more. She bent double with cramps from trying to digest the coarse natural food. She picked lice from her body, at first horrified and then used to them during infrequent communal baths, and shivered from the pervasive cold despite her heavy clothes.

The Karli ate well most of the year, but were not very skilled at preserving vegetables. Meat lasted indefinitely, coated with ice and hung outside the door. The staple was mutton, only rarely varied with rabbit or deer since winter hunting was hard and dangerous. When not sharing the common labors, Judith treated the vitamin deficiencies of winter-hungry children, salved injuries from her own dwindling supply of medicines, poured her own vitamins down the throats of sickly infants, watched them live or die, helped bury them, helped bring new life from the wombs of their mothers, distributed her precious antibiotics to the bedded women, and saw them return to work two days later or writhe in the terminal delirium of childbed fever, defeated by the chronic bone weakness that blocked the fetus behind the unyielding pelvic arch.

Waiting, waiting for the spring and her destined journey to far Lishin, Judith sat in the light of the intricately corded Samman fire and watched new masters honored with the touching earthiness of the Five Kisses, and she studied the delicate yet exciting choreography of the coveners' sex rites. Using ancient musical notation, she codified the stuttering, interwoven vocal patterns of the dances, tapestries of five or six rhythms interlaced into a dense, accelerating fugue of cataclysmic excitement.

She filled dozens of pages with close-packed notes, sketching the parameters of a people that the City had forgotten, had never really known. She observed their language, philosophy of life and love of it, and exhaustively described the self-discipline of the masters as they protected and marshaled their formidable mental powers.

And yet, for all her study and observation, Judith could not bridge the final gap and think like a covener. She defined and dissected, but always at a distance.

For their part, the coveners understood even less of Judith. She was beyond comprehension, not worth the effort of trying, for though they liked her, she was City. Brave beyond her years and child-stature—that they rendered her, but they also knew she must be half-mad. Going over Blue Mountains to Lishin, there was no other explanation.

Garick had not underestimated the difficulty she would encounter in trying to find a guide. The Karli shunned Lishin and profoundly feared the Kriss. At first, Judith offered ten krets, but no one was interested, so she raised the fee to fifteen and then twenty krets; still, no response.

And then there was a development, an important breakthrough in her researches and she scrabbled feverishly through her old notes about the Girdle of Solitude. After Loomin, she was ready to double her price for a guide because of what she'd learned.

A young Wengen hunter was found, storm-caught and badly frozen. He revived with cheery gusto after his rescue—an ebony-haired, brown-skinned dynamo of a man who talked with his hands and poured the gossip of the northern covens, the Wengen, into everyone's ears. His name was Gannell, and he was a born storyteller. He spoke of crop and game signs, where the winter pelts ran thick, the dangers of certain places where wild dogs were most likely to range and the brief, occasional skirmishes with merks. But along with his news, he also regaled the Karli with his own people's versions of the traditional song-stories, phrasing out the lines in the characteristic glottal-stopped Wengen that scattered r's and t's like flying leaves down the whirlwind of sound his vibrant voice produced.

One night, as the snow pattered gently against the chinked log wall and the jug went round slowly, Judith listened with the others as Gannell sang of the Girdle of Solitude, and as she heard the familiar tale of the hero Callee, she caught a clue which fixed her belief that the Girdle might still exist.

Gannell sang of a time before the covens etched their sigils in iron, before the City shut its gates

*And all men had the power*
*To ride the sky, ride high on the wind*
*Like the forest path to Lorl*

and the masters fought a hopeless war against an inexhaustible Enemy. But before their inevitable defeat, the greatest of the masters built a house wherein they devised weapons of surpassing subtlety and dreadful purpose.

*And the house was in Lishin, in the west.*

Here it was, according to legend, that the origins of the Self-Gate might be traced, and the one most fearful weapon was created: the

Girdle of Solitude, with which a man might walk anywhere in broad daylight and be undetected, even with the deepest magic.

*And the Jings came near to Lishin,*
*Run, old Callee, run.*
*Put on that belt called Solitude*
*Before the day is done.*

*The masters named you top man,*
*They know you'll do what's best.*
*Ain't no sense to stop, man,*
*In Lishin, in the west.*

And the great soldier Callee did what the masters commanded and donned the Girdle of Solitude and walked out through the ranks of the Enemy, and passed over the land seeking the other lesser houses of magic, in the north, in the east, in the south.

Here Gannell rose and warmed his hands by the fire, letting the sudden pause in his tale emphasize the alteration of style. His eyes swept over the listeners, regarded Judith quizzically, passed on and focused into infinite distance. The timbre of his voice altered subtly, and the raconteur merged into the personality of his hero.

"The Jings chase me hard," whispered Callee in the guise of the covener Gannell. "I hide in a cave, but I hear them tracking me sure by my footprints. *Now,* I say. Now it's time to wear old Girdle of Solitude."

Callee-Gannell pantomimed a peculiar buckling gesture, lowered his hands to his sides, became stock-still. A hush fell over the rapt coveners; they scarcely breathed. Then, without moving his head or parting his lips, the resurrected hero murmured:

"Here they come . . . close . . . close . . . man, I do not *move.*"

Silence.

Suddenly Gannell-Callee sneezed and, with the violent sound, broke the rigid posture and instantly metamorphosed into the crouching Jing enemy.

"What's that?" the Jing asked, fearful.

"That, that, that," Gannell chanted, an echo.

"Who are you?" called the Jing.

"You, you, you," old Echo replied.

The Enemy laughed. "I see there's no one here."

"Here, here, here."

"This is our country now."

"Now, now, now."

The Enemy was cocky, triumphant. "We will rule this land a thousand years."

Silence. The Enemy caught his breath.

"We will rule this country," he repeated, somewhat shakily, "for *two* thousand years!"

"In that case," said Echo, "you won't need me!"

The assembled Karli roared at the tag line of Gannell's tale. The sound of Wengen speech was both music and shrewd sense, but the music came first. The last line of Gannell's story inflected upward in a kind of rueful half-question, a good-humored irreverency that delighted the Karli who had never heard the version. The tale of Callee was one of the oldest and generally ended with the long melancholy retreat of the hero from Lishin and the other Old Language places that would never be again. The Jings, of course, never found Callee or the Girdle of Solitude, though Callee, like all heroes, was born again to the Shando or Karli or whatever coven was singing his tale at the time. Over his jug, Gannell maintained slyly that old Callee *was* a bit on the dark side, which would make him—

"All Wengen like you," Moss grinned affectionately. "Just quieter."

"Boy," said Gannell, "you gotta know your name in this world. I mean, you gotta know who you *are*. Now, you get born smelling of apples and feeling like you gonna die rich—you're Shando. You come in smelling sheep and feeling like you *might* have two krets to leave your woman—you're Karli."

Gannell took a long drink and sighed pleasurably as the liquor warmed its way down. "But, boy, when you get born smelling shit and can't even find a hunk to sell for manure—you know your badluck ass is *Wengen!*"

Meanwhile, Judith returned to her lodging and rummaged excitedly through her notes. She'd heard the tale of Callee time and time again at Lorl, but Shando and Karli rendered the name into common Uhian, the way it was written, and it was sounded as *kah-lee*. But the Wengen dialect changed, or perhaps preserved it as *kaw-lee,* and even more important was the vestigial *muh* that Gannell tacked on the beginning of the name.

She found what she was looking for. Long ago in the City, Judith noted one of the few historical names to survive the time of the Jing conquest and subsequent reordering of the land:

*Henry MacCauley.*

The synergizer still preserved reports signed with his name on its memory banks. Always, the reports were between a military base of some sort and a trio of experimental laboratories, none of which were pin-pointed by location.

It was Judith's contention that one of the four locations could be found in Lishin.

Her price for guides soared to twenty-five krets, half in advance. It was more than young Moss could resist. The advance alone would set him up "good as Garick" when he took a woman and a household of his own. Judith needed a second guide, and the offer was snapped up by the restless, energetic Gannell. The voluble Wengen had lost his gear and pelts in the storm that almost took him.

"Hoo-*ee,* tell them Kriss we're coming"—he jammed his pack together—"gonna die rich after all."

They started north just after Leddy fire with three good horses and ample supplies.

Although the snow was gone, the way was still cold and miserably wet. They traveled thirteen days, Judith leading the horse more often than she rode it. The ancient road, no more than a scrawl of broken masonry over the mountains, pointed the way but did not pave it.

Thirteen days Judith panted over the steepening hills, coaxing, screaming at her horse while the low clouds opened with dreary regularity to drench them in chilly rain. At first, there was a warm fire at night and fresh meat from their bows, but soon Moss forbid fire except when the misery of Judith's never-dry buckskins grew more than she could bear. Gannell cursed Moss for his strictness—cheerily enough—but Moss had his reasons.

"Kriss know we coming soon enough," he stated flatly. "Why help 'em?"

Judith's throat turned into a raw passage through which she struggled for air. Her leg muscles knotted with climbing and jolting down the steep valleys, with always another hill in front of them. Sometimes, in her blankets at night, too tired to move, she saw the dim shapes of the men huddling silently together in the lep that still bound them to their own in Karli, a thread they desperately depended on.

The lep was difficult because there were only two of them, and each night it became harder, more exhausting, to touch the massed masters of Karli pulsing like a beacon from the south.

And then one night they tried in vain. Their minds blunted against something in the growing bleakness of the country. Game was scarce, and their hunter-magic was practically useless. Even Gannell grew taciturn.

"No gods come here," he muttered. "No Circle magic. Nothing."

Now Moss permitted no fires at all for any reason. They slept wet, eating meagerly of the dried pone—corn flour and dried venison—that was their staple. On the eleventh day, they skirted the remains of a small town, no more than a few brick chimneys with a large stone hulk brooding over them, choked with ivy and creeper. The sheer height of the ruin frightened Moss and Gannell. Judith would have opted to rest within its walls, but she knew the coven men well enough not to press for it. They didn't trust the place, rode well west of it, Moss scouting ahead at a wary pace.

The weather finally broke toward the end of the journey. Sun shafted thinly through the gaunt trees where Judith and Moss rested and filled water bags from a small stream. Gannell was somewhere off ahead, across the brook, along the remnant of road they still followed.

Judith stretched out with her damp-moulded blanket for a pillow. Her hooded skins and sheepskin throw-over stank of dirt, mildew and sweat. She groaned and wriggled uncomfortably in the soggy clothes. "I'd like to be dry once more before I forget what it feels like."

Moss offered her half a corn cake. He admired her strength, but never knew where it came from in someone so frail. Judith was total enigma to him; as far as he knew, she had not bedded with any man in Karli the whole winter. The waste of it shocked Gannell when he heard.

"Not even *once?*"

"Not even," Moss attested.

As Gannell stared off at Judith, his surprise evolved into a sour grin. "Well then, we ever find that old Girdle, I know a *damn* good place to hide it."

Moss smiled remembering, but there was nothing to smile at in Jude now. She looked drained and colorless. Her lips trembled.

"I hope we can rest just awhile," she said, grudging herself the admission of exhaustion.

"Didn't think you'd make it this far, Jude." The almost parental tenderness in his own voice surprised Moss, but you had to care about Jude because, goddammit, she wouldn't care about herself.

But she had to conserve now; for the last day, Judith felt a growing chill and numbness, a lightness in her head which she doggedly hid from the men. She began to answer Moss; then, suddenly, Gannell appeared out of the thick brush across the brook. A look passed between the men; Moss rose, waded the shallows and joined Gannell. They melted away into the bush.

Time passed. When they did not return, Judith got up stiffly and followed, more curious than tired. The men blended into the forest as easily as any other wild thing, but she followed the weed-grown crumbs of concrete road and a few barely visible footprints in the damp earth.

She dare not call too loud; Moss didn't allow it. She said their names softly, but got no reply. She pushed deeper into the forest.

She found them at last in a small copse where an ancient maple leaned aslant, its thick roots writhing like agonized serpents out of the ground.

"Moss, what—" Her breath caught sharply.

At the foot of the great tree, two bodies lay close together against one of the exposed roots, one cradling the other in stiffened tenderness. It was a young man and a slender girl in long, well-cut homespun robes plastered damply to their limbs. The dead boy's pale face was downed with silky first beard. The girl's yellowish hair tumbled across her delicately sculpted features. The breast of her robe was stained deep brown. Gannell pushed aside her hair to show the deep, coagulated wound in her throat.

"Bled to death," he said. "Yesterday, maybe last night."

Beautiful, sensitive faces, like some City types she knew. "Who killed them?" she asked.

The men were reluctant to answer. The thing was so abhorrent, they hardly had any words for it.

"Did it himself," Gannell managed finally. His words sounded as if they tasted bad.

"Used that." Moss pointed to the small knife by the boy's hand. "Her first, then cut his wrists. Quick for her, slow for him."

Pity and revulsion rose in Judith. "But—*why?* They're hardly grown, they're children!"

"They're Kriss," Moss cut her off. "You listen, Jude, and you take a good look at these two. You think Garick lied to you why no Circle folk come here? There's a stink to this place. Not like forest or deer or muskrat. It smells of death."

Gannell nodded gravely. "Yes."

"No magic here." Moss wrestled with something he could barely voice. "Like that place we passed, dead houses. Covens pulled 'em down long ago, planted or let the woods come back. But Kriss, they keep 'em . . . dead houses . . . don't know why."

"They're different," said Gannell. "No way to know the Kriss. Even their god is dead."

Moss took her arm. "Come on, Jude."

She held back. "We should bury them at least."

"No."

The men would not even touch the bodies. It seemed like the simplest decency to Judith, but Moss and Gannell would not be moved. Instead, they hurried her back to the camp, collected their gear and moved on, not stopping again till they were far past the spot where the suicides lay.

Soon afterward, Gannell hunted down a rattlesnake. He and Moss patiently milked the flat, ugly head into a small cup, extracting its venom. They daubed it carefully over their iron arrowheads. It was an extreme but logical measure, Moss told Judith.

"We shoot a Kriss, if he ain't dead from the arrow, he'll be too busy staying alive to give us away."

Judith swayed on her knees. She panted. Her throat was dry, her head buzzed with lightness that was partially due to the altitude of the mountain path on which they clutched their way. Objects seemed to float in front of her, insubstantial wraiths. Moss hailed her with that cautious hunter's whistle that could sound like any forest fowl he chose. She stumbled, crept along the dirt path toward them. The deep ruts of the trail ran upward and forward and then she saw where Moss and Gannell waited, dwarfed by a sheer blue panorama of sky. The brush dropped precipitously away on her right and she saw the gray valley floor far beneath.

Moss came and helped her along, putting an affectionate arm around her. The shelf where they stood was broad enough for twenty men to form a line, side by side and arms apart. It swept in a C-curve outward from the mountain wall on the left, and the broadest part of the C permitted a dizzying vista of the valley below. Moss pointed down toward the distant river and spoke into Judith's ear.

"Lishin."

She saw a dirty brown streak of river that blurred in and out of focus. A bridge spanned it, decrepit but intact, and beyond were dark oblongs of many buildings, some standing, some partially or completely demolished. East and west were larger ruins, then the rubble dwindled and merged with the lush unkempt greenery. Another clump of structures in the western distance apparently represented a different portion of the original community, but Judith could not discern them. Lishin squatted, grim and drab in contrast to the flush of early spring grassland in the valley north of the decomposing town. Small vapor ghosts clung and curled about some of the buildings closest to the riverbank. The water reached nearly level with the first deserted street.

The wind changed. A faint but distinct odor of decay crept along the shelf on which they stood.

"Told you Lishin stinks," Moss said sourly.

Judith felt hot and weak. She rubbed her eyes to clear the dizziness.

"Better rest," Gannell cautioned.

"No," she said, taking her horse's bridle. "Later, in Lishin. Come on." She hauled the lathery, spent animal after her. "Come *on.*"

The men watched her start over the ridge and down the gradual descent. They shook their heads.

*Fever.*

*Sure as frost. Saw her eyes.*

*What keeps her up?*

"Don't ask me." Moss tried to laugh; the sound rasped across his dry throat. "Don't even know why I'm here."

"Same as me, man," Gannell sighed ruefully. "Twenty-five krets and *no* brains."

The long trail down eventually stopped at a broader road in better repair than most. It dipped in the direction of Lishin, and they followed it. Late in the day, it led them past a jumble of ruined houses and up to the very foot of the old bridge.

The tottering span was brown with rust, scored with deep crevices where it had been paved. Perilous sections canted at a steep angle; one mistake in footing could throw horse and rider through the rotted railings. They crossed single file, Moss leading. Judith kept her eyes up; the entire, broad midsection of the bridge had been iron grillwork, long since rusted away to trailing brown webs. Judith could not look at the sluggish water running far below the open drop on her right; its movement accentuated her vertigo.

They were clear of it at last and back on solid ground, leading three exhausted horses along a broad, broken street that arrowed straight between crumbled piles of weed-grown masonry.

The pale daylight faded further behind new clouds. The stink of the place was unmistakable now, but that, Judith noted, was largely due to the many dead fish washed up on the filthy beachfront west of the bridge.

"Must be thousands," Moss grumbled, turning up his nose.

"It's spring," said Judith. "There might be an old, abandoned mine upstream. The early rains wash out the acid, kill the fish."

The sun dipped lower; somewhere, not far distant, a pair of cold eyes watched their progress with disapproval. The mind behind the eyes leaked no thoughts detectable by coven instinct. Its menace was still unfelt.

They made Judith rest. She was already shaking with the fever. Moss would not dare enter any building for shelter, fearing the magic it might contain, so they camped in a small hollow near the bridge but far enough away from the skeletal stone hulks to comfort the men. They wrapped Judith in blankets and gently forced her to drink horsemint tea brewed over a tiny fire. She managed to swallow it. Gannell fed her bits of pone, carefully choosing those with the most meat.

"Go on, eat," he urged gently. "How you gonna stay pretty?"

She felt better after the food. "We'll begin in the morning," she said doggedly.

Gannell felt her hot forehead dubiously. "Begin what?"

"Looking," said Judith. "Finding."

The two men shrugged and shared their exasperation.

A lep to Karli was impossible. The indefinable barrier girdling their senses left Moss and Gannell more alone than ever, and it worried at them. They slept lightly, and in the darkness, Moss noted the abhorrent smell of Lishin and the disquieting absence of normal night sounds. He heard his own pounding heart and the shallow breathing of the woman.

Still, in the morning, Judith was first into the saddle, eager to start, eyes everywhere.

"Many of these places must have been abandoned," she remarked. "That's why Lishin survives just the way it was."

They marveled at the ease with which Judith could read the numerous signs and rusted street markers, few of which remained intact. She began to sketch a rough map.

"Mark Street: probably Market." Her pencil flew. "Third Street. We'll turn up here."

The coven men followed, Moss shadowing Judith, Gannell covering the rear. The *clop* of hoofs echoed eerily around them, counterpointed by distant thunder. A few warning drops of rain spattered the ground. Suddenly, Moss' eyes narrowed. He stared at a weedy patch of sidewalk, and even as he thought it, Gannell's mind touched his. *?*

*Tracks in the dust.*

Gannell inspected them. *Fresh. This morning.*

*Two, three pair I make.*

*Kriss.*

*Yes. Stay behind for cover.*

They followed Judith, closer together now, arrows nocked to their bowstrings. Empty windows stared at them from blocks of age-darkened stone, giant mouths gaping wide to scream. They passed a high gray heap with a cupola tower, tall as thirty men. Suddenly Judith trotted her horse on to halt before a squat red pile blasted by ungentle centuries. When the men joined her, she was peering up at something on the front of the building.

"I was right!"

"About what?" Moss asked.

She slipped off the horse and brushed with both hands at crusted dirt on a greenish metal plate set in a heavy stone. The raised letters were nearly obliterated, but she traced a portion of a word with one finger, sounding it for them. "Amspor; that's all that's left, but it's enough to confirm the old maps—"

"Left of what?" Gannell wanted to know.

"The name of the town."

They both argued she was wrong. The name was Lishin, always had been.

"No!" Judith pointed at the red brick building. Much of the face was broken or eaten away. One unmarred stretch bore the letters LISHIN. *"That* says Lishin. It might have been, well, a kind of store like Korbin's in Lorl. But that's how you get the name. It's all men could see, those that could still read."

The high gray tower nearby gave her an idea. She could command an excellent view of the entire area from the upper chamber. Moss protested, but she ignored him.

"Come with me," she directed, already moving toward the entrance. "My eyes aren't so good today. I need your help."

He followed her. It was an act of cold courage that Judith never fully appreciated. His coven instincts were useless here, and the gaunt stone hulk was a dreadful unknown. He shared his fear with Gannell, received the natural sympathy in equal silence, and entered the building behind Judith, knife drawn.

Access to the tower was easy. There was a cracked but usable stairway, most of it lit by tall, narrow windows. Judith noticed nothing as they climbed, but Moss read volumes at every step.

The tower door had been opened recently. There were fresh patterns of dirt and rust on the floor. Footprints on the stairs were obvious; halfway up, a foot slipped and skidded before regaining its balance in hasty ascent. A subtle disturbance in the dust on the banister betrayed the garment sleeve that brushed across it sometime earlier. In the small stone chamber at the top, someone moved from window to window, standing some time at each, searching for . . . Moss knew the answer. His mind sought Gannell's, felt it respond.

*Don't even cover their tracks.*

*Maybe they don't care.*

*?*

*It's like they're waiting.*

It was a grisly line of thought. They dropped it. Moss looked at Judith leaning out one casement staring north. He edged carefully to the south window and waved down to Gannell.

*Jude know?*

*Not yet?*

*Don't fret her,* Gannell cautioned. *She sick enough.*

Judith's head slumped against the cool stone. Sweat shone on her forehead.

"Jude, you got the fever."

"I know, Moss."

"Didn't you put pebbles in the water?"

"You mean tablets?" She roused herself with difficulty, gazed out over the valley to the north. "They were gone three days ago."

"Jude," he said with concern and respect, "you are one goddam hardhead woman."

"Help me look." She pointed out over the vista. "I'm trying to find a place off by itself, probably with a lot of bare space around it."

Moss scanned the horizon, careful to note anything that might be movement. Then he saw something. "Big stone place north."

"No."

"Some more like it off east. Big red thing."

"Try west," Judith directed. "Wait . . . there! Southwest; I can just see it. A big, black square."

Moss looked where she pointed. He nodded. "Flat and black. Maybe two bowshot wide all around."

"Is it like a house, not tall, but something like a coven hall?"

"Looks like. What is it?"

She labored to catch her breath. She could see it now with some effort. In the middle of what once must have been an industrial park, a flat, elongated complex of building bordered by a paved square.

"That," said Judith quietly, "is the weapons house of your song-stories. The place where MacCauley—"

"Who?"

"You called him Callee. That's where he first put on the Girdle of Solitude."

As they mounted to ride, Judith held up a sheet of her notes. "What I'm looking for will probably be paper like this, many papers. It will . . . it will take—"

She swayed in the saddle, fighting the dizziness. Her body cried to rest, but Judith willed herself erect. "It will take a few days to find what I want."

The blackened ruin stood a good way from the town, out where the brown splotch of Lishin slowly faded into the surrounding green, actually not one but five buildings. The one Judith chose, after a brief inspection of the others, was a low sprawl of concrete blocks, laced with rusted steel and various synthetics, not as sturdy as the town buildings. Decay was much further advanced. Much of the roof had long ago fallen in. The face of the building stretched nearly one hundred and fifty yards across the center of the rutted asphalt.

Moss was relieved to find the entrance free of tracks. He wandered from one great, bare room to another in Judith's ferreting wake. Eventually, she discovered a cavernous chamber near one entrance; it contained nothing but a few tables and many long, straight rows of metal boxes that stood higher than the woman herself. Here at least the roof was whole.

"Must have been the file room," Judith remarked. "Moss, we'll camp and work in here."

Heavy rain began to fall just before sundown. Gannell returned from hunting, sodden and irritable, with one scrawny squirrel. He said little while Judith was awake, but after she'd swallowed some horsemint tea and a little meat, and her shivering body sank into troubled sleep, the men shared their foreboding.

*Kriss all around,* Moss lepped.

*No, gone.*

*See them?*

Gannell nodded, picking the last morsel from the squirrel bone. "Dumb *mofo* Kriss can't hide for shit. I went up the north slope, just sat quiet and watched. Road goes west along the river, and there they were, just walking their horses down the middle of it. Going where? *Dunesk.* Home, I guess."

They lapsed into silence again. The Kriss were gone; that should make them feel better, but it didn't. The underlying fear was still there with the peculiar smell that frightened their horses as well. There was something else.

*Something on the rain.*

*Yes.*

Hiding their fires was useless now, and Judith badly needed the warmth. They sheltered in the great room with the metal boxes, letting the smoke blow out of the windows, safe from the unceasing rain, but not the shapeless fear that tormented both men. Their instincts cried out to be wary, to be gone, but they could not say why. They reached out to feel and define the rain-thing, passed it back and forth between them. *Not Kriss. Not men.*

Whatever, it already terrified the white-eyed horses, straining to break from their tethering and be free of the fetid menace burdening air that should be fresh.

But they stayed to help Judith, Moss as the guardian he promised Garick, Gannell admiring the sheer stamina of the frail City woman. And no one would ever again offer them twenty-five krets in one lump. There was a degree of cold consolation: Moss, if he lived, would measure his promises with a very small spoon. Gannell, if he died now, would be the richest corpse in Uhia. It wasn't much, but it helped.

Gannell hunted the sparse game while Moss assisted Judith as she tottered grimly about the twilit chamber, dwarfed by the high rows of metal files, communicating her needs in gestures and monosyllables. The fever gained on her. She was all eyes and chalky skin and cracked, colorless lips. She labored at an old table, a blanket draped over her thin shoulders, working, working.

**A–2: Examined lab complex today. Signs of intentional internal destruction, probably while enemy advanced into valley. Couldn't be large invading force. No marks of major battle in town. Martial law, must have evacuated population. Customary. Important papers burned, some of them. Probably no time for everything. But many files filled with black ash. What I want may be gone, destroyed.**

Moss pried open the metal boxes for her as she pointed to them. He placed the meager contents in front of her—sometimes pure carbon, sometimes crumbling sheets–covered with strange symbols and words in Old Language. Her pencil described a monotonous scrawl hour after hour—

**A–5: IMPORTANT! Closet off file room . . . found several paper folders on shelf. Among them, possibly sole surviving record of Girdle. Not plans or specs, those either destroyed or taken by MacCauley. But part of file label preserved, doubtless due to small oxygen in closet. TOPSEC/GIR— Single paper within: entire name on it. Girdle of Solitude. Helps account for survival of name in Uhian: some poetic physicist who never knew what he wrought. In folder: gray sheet of paper, looks like machine copy. Travel orders for MacCauley, destination blank. There are records elsewhere here (noted A–3) of three other weapons repositories. The deduction is inevitable. The—**

Judith hesitated. She pushed the papers aside; gestured to Moss for the tattered thing she called a map.

"Only four places it could've been," she said, half to herself, "and not in Lishin—"

He didn't hear the rest, but saw the three wobbly circles drawn at various points on the map, her pencil wavering above them. Then her head dropped on one arm and she slumped across the faded colors of the ragged paper. With a huge effort, Judith pushed herself up weakly from the table.

"Moss, I need to lie down. Just a little while."

Moss stared, astonished. It was the first time she'd allowed herself to succumb to the illness raging within her. She took two faltering steps toward her blankets. Moss tried to help her, but she stopped him.

"More . . . important. Put the papers back in the box."

He laid the mouldering papers, the map and her notes in the metal box and pushed it shut.

"Moss!"

He wheeled. Judith reeled and fell against the table. Her head lolled when he lifted her.

She did not regain consciousness for two merciful days.

And then it grew dark and the rain fell. The far corners of the room were cloaked in gloom. Moss rationed dead wood to the small fire. From time to time, he bent over Judith to cool the inferno of her dry forehead with a damp rag. She twitched feebly under the blankets. Moss swore they would leave in the morning, even if he had to tie her to a horse. Otherwise, she wouldn't live a week.

They were all hungry. There was no food in Lishin, no game. It was a dead place, as the coveners always said. He wondered whether Gannell had any luck hunting cross river.

*Wengen, where are you, goddammit?*

Gannell was long overdue. It made Moss nervous. Up till the moment Judith got too sick to stay on her feet, he'd at least had her company and could lep Gannell. But now he was alone, cut off. Coven folks weren't meant to be alone. The solitude terrified him.

*Gannell!*

The hunter *had* to be cross river, hunting far up the other bank where game wasn't so scarce. But he knew enough not to stay out after dark in Lishin.

One of the horses shied outside. The other whinnied in frightened chorus. Moss went out to them, but they were impossible to calm, rearing away. The stink maddened them; it was much worse now. The whole world reeked of it.

*MOSS!*

The urgent lep stabbed his mind.

*Gannell? Where?*

*No fire! NO FIRE! Get Jude, hide!*

*Where are you?*

*No time! HIDE! It—*

And Gannell was gone. Moss was alone again, prickling with fright. He whimpered softly, animal instinct overruling reason. He hauled the terrified horses to the entrance, shooed them off; they could do better fending for themselves. He loped to the fire, scattering it. *The paper things: they were important to her.* Moss grabbed them, then heaved the child-weight of Judith into his arms and stumbled to the small closet halfway down the long room. The heavy metal door was rusted slightly ajar from the day before when Judith slipped through with a torch and found the papers.

Gannell said hide. Not run. The closet would have to do.

The opening was not large enough for him carrying Judith. While he was wrestling with the stubborn door, Moss heard the sound. *Not rain.* The alien thing he and Gannell sensed *on* the rain was coming —fast, not wary, not circling like packdogs, but straight and rapid without fear. His mind tried to encompass it but there was no recognizable shape or pattern he could define.

The thing was everywhere, like the waters of the swollen brown river lapping the streets of Lishin. A million eyes. No shape, yet countless shapes.

Moss put all his effort into the door. His muscles bunched; the thick hinges shrieked, bled rust and gave. He lifted Judith inside the tiny space and pulled the door shut. Moss squatted in darkness beside the unconscious woman. His sweating hand clutched the hilt of his knife.

The thing kept coming. The sound, the hideous staccato noise composed of millions of noises, grew louder and louder and the thing came closer, across the broken stone square, pouring through the entrance, into the central chamber, over the floor, crashing like the tumid river itself against the rusted door.

In the darkness behind, Moss howled out his fear lest his brain burst. He clawed at his ears to blot out the terror of the sound like a forest of birds gone mad.

A few days before Belten, the lep flashed from the northern fringe of settlements to the masters at Karli covenstead: *Moss and Jude are back.*

Neither could tell much of what happened in Lishin. Judith was gaunt and yellow with recent fever. She begged weakly to be taken to Lorl, where she had promised to wait.

Moss was incoherent. The masters worked patiently over him; using all their skill, they linked their minds with his, but part of that mind would not respond. Not gone or destroyed, simply unreachable behind a locked door. In time, his senses returned, but none of the Karli ever got a clear story out of him. When plied, he would regard the questioner for a moment but could not concentrate. His eyes would wander past, unfocused, staring into a darkness that never quite left him.

He had only a vague memory of carrying Judith through flood-washed streets in which bloated things turned slowly in the sluggish tide. He crossed a bridge and near the far end of it . . . yes, he was sure of that; that much he couldn't forget. Near the far end, he found the picked bones of a horse and a man.

The latter skeleton retained a tuft of black hair and a tatter of deerhide shirt. By the bones of the right hand lay a black-hilted hunter's knife.

Garick found her after Lams in Korbin's shed, coughing over a jug of liquor. She was haggard and leather-brown, but the leather was cracked, the steel will no longer malleable. When he carried her to the rumpled cot, he felt how much lighter she was.

"I came back from Lishin." She tried to smile. "I told you I'd wait."

"Jude." All his meaning crowded into the sound of her name. "Jude."

She responded feebly to his kiss.

If only she were Circle, they wouldn't need words. "It's you, Jude. Really you."

"Me." She nodded weakly. "Judith Randall Singer, Department of History, subsection on technology . . . let's have a drink."

"Jude, how long have we got?" He feared the answer. "How long before you go?"

She was very drunk but deeper than that; Judith was sick to her core. "How long? Days, weeks, years, Garick. All of futile time, my darling. I'm not going back to the City," Judith said bitterly. "I never will. They won't accept me now." She downed the sida neat. "I went to the Self-Gate and waited. They cataloged and scanned me and judged me contaminated. They were sorry, oh yes, they were very sorry. But firm. They rejected me."

The words dropped, heavy as stones. The tears came and went again and again. She wiped her streaked face with one grimy hand, always reaching for the liquor. Korbin said she'd been drunk for days.

Garick struggled to understand things totally beyond his comprehension. She said the Self-Gate had things called sensors and they read her as surely as the Uhians could lep mind to mind. The sensors fed data to the synergizer in cold symbols that weighed her fate. She spoke of viruses, antibodies, germs, and he listened and tried to understand.

"They've been without disease for hundreds of years," Judith explained. "To let me in now might kill them all." Her voice trailed off into a dry cough.

He held her, angry. "They never should've sent you to Lishin!"

"Send?" She looked up, puzzled. "They never sent me, Garick. They were horrified at my plan. The idea was an obscenity. They rejected every request I made to go. They said there was no value whatsoever in such a journey, only danger, and they warned—oh yes, I was warned—of possible exclusion should I try it alone. Well, I did. And they did. Action, reaction. Have a drink, Garick."

"Don't cry, Jude. Please don't cry. You'll come home with me. Shando life is good, Jude. I can make a place for you—"

"Me, the lepless wonder?" she asked dryly. "In a *coven?*" But he didn't heed the acid in her tone.

"Yes! You'll get better, I'll make you better if you'll listen this time. Told you not to go to Lishin, warned you myself. Damn if I know how Moss got you back alive. *Baby* going on a grown-up job."

Judith regarded him with the first trace of amusement she'd felt in days. "Garick," she said tenderly, "how old do you think I am?"

"Eighteen, nineteen," he shrugged. "Why?"

"You think of me as a baby? A little girl who took you for her first lover on this corn-shuck mattress?" She stroked his cheek with affection and a condescension that made Garick feel odd and gangling.

"Jude," he asked hoarsely, "how old *are* you?"

"Before anyone is of value to the City, they must be taught," Judith began. "The process of education takes more than one of your lifetimes, and another lifetime—eighty or ninety Belten fires, my love—is spent narrowing down to one's own chosen fragment of the puzzle, so you may begin to work." She poured and downed another formidable drink. "You told me once that the log wall around your masters' hall in Charzen is a hundred years old. The trees that fell so that those logs could be fashioned were not even seedlings when I was born."

She slid off the cot and pulled her loose robe over her head, standing bare before him. Garick saw how pitifully the small breasts had shrunk, how her ribs showed clear and the skin sagged on the once-firm hips. But Judith shook her head.

"Forget I'm a woman," she commanded him. "Look at the animal—see *our* kind of magic." She pointed to a faint red line on her side beneath the bottom rib. "Here's where they gave me three different sets of kidneys. I've had two new hearts, additional brain cells grafted on. They've cloned every organ for possible repair and replacement." She held up a glass container with a handful of pills left inside. "This bottle holds tablets that keep my metabolism at the rate it recorded when I *was* eighteen."

Garick whispered it, awed. "Then you live forever."

"No." She shook her head. "Not forever, but for a long, long time. Forever, according to an old City joke, is in the future."

Garick had been raised to accept magic as part of life, and so, impossible as it sounded, he was prepared to countenance the brand of mystery in which City was expert. Judith was smiling at him again, an acid curve of her too-delicate mouth.

"Garick, have you ever heard the word 'absurd'?"

"No."

"To be over three hundred years old, and yet a fool and not know yourself: that's absurd. I should have lived another four or five hundred of your years, perhaps more. As it is, I'll have . . . something less than that."

The hard smile softened as she bent to kiss him. "At least, I guess I'll die 'beautiful.' That's your gift to me, Garick. Till you came, 'beautiful' was only an abstract concept, a principle to be dissected by philosophers."

"Damn that City."

"But you have made me beautiful"—she knelt and slipped into his arms—"like a tyrant god pointing at a silly patchwork doll and saying 'love'—"

"Damn them." He was crying.

"—so I love you, Garick. Did you know that I was jealous of Jenna? I loved you that much; after three hundred years, that was a genuinely unique experience."

She began to cough again, and Garick guided her away from the liquor to the bed, made her lie down and stretched out beside her so she could hold on to him. The last of her strength went into that.

"I'm so tired, Garick. I want to go home."

"Listen, Jude." He pressed her close. "They said you wouldn't last the winter, but you did; said you wouldn't get over Blue Mountains, but you did; said you'd never come back alive from Lishin, and here you are! You're tougher'n I am, Jude!" He rocked her like a child in his arms, reassuring himself as well as her. "You going to have lots of years, Jude, lots of 'em. All good. You come to Shando country with me. You want to go home? From now on, *Shando's* your home. It's yours. And so am I."

It was deeply felt, but he was twenty and she was more than fifteen times older. But no, he knew better: they were both young and beautiful and they would be rich and live forever.

"Let's go home, Jude," he murmured in her ear. She nodded gratefully and, with her last ounce of strength expended in the effort, fell asleep in his arms.

---

The infant Singer first opened his eyes between Lams and Samman. His mother took the last precious anesthetic in her pack, and so was unconscious when the baby was delivered. Thus Singer was born in silence and the person closest to him did not witness his traumatic entry into life.

She wanted to name him Randall Singer after her father, but Garick wouldn't hear of such a lengthy name for a Shando boy, so they compromised and he was just Singer.

He remembered many things clearly, even as an infant: the big, new log house that smelled of raw pine and apples, the forest on three sides and the orchards rolling away to the end of creation; the laughter of his parents as they played with him on a thick sheepskin rug. In the dark winter months, he was fascinated by the huge fire curling fantastic shadows over the hearth as he strove to understand the sounds they made.

He understood his mother first, and he soon began to realize that she made one kind of sound with his father and another with himself, repeating patiently and always showing him the letters.

"Singer. Sing-er. See? S-i-n-g-e-r."

But he was six before he realized that he spoke two languages, Uhian and Old Language, as Judith called the form of speech she chose to use. He also learned that he was the only child in Charzen who could read. There were no books, but his mother printed out tales which she called history. She taught Garick at the same time, and his father roared with delight, digesting words and concepts like savory preserved fruit, spraying them out in fountains of sound like a child playing in water. Then Judith would giggle at his fooling and hurl her tiny arms around his thick shoulders, and for a while they would forget Singer, yet the child never felt alone at such times, but safer than ever.

His mother astonished him with strange tales of the City, of the streets that moved, the machines that cleaned houses, played music, flashed pictures, cooked food and thought more swiftly and deeply in a second than a hundred masters in a year. His dark, solemn little face lit up in wonder, and he loved the stories of the City best of all.

"Someday," she often said, "someday you must see it. You must go there someday."

But there were other times when his mother was remote and untouchable, as when she sat before her Mrikan mirror, lips moving silently, one finger slowly tracing the planes and lines of her face. When she rose then she saw neither child nor Garick nor house, and Singer dreaded these moments. They made him feel empty inside.

She never spoke to him of death.

Often, the big house was full of people, orchard men, Mrikan traders, legions of farmer friends. The women often came to Judith for small remedies where their own magic failed. She insisted on sanitary conditions at birthings that drove coveners to distraction, but they did what she ordered, for Shando mothers rarely died of fever when Judith delivered them.

Sometimes they died anyway. "It was that damn bone thing,

Garick. I had nothing to give her. She needed cytoxyn, massive doses."

"Your City makes it, don't they? Makes it and stores it away and probably never needs it."

"Her" City was the one sharp edge between them. She answered his bitterness with her own. "Well, the next time I go home, I must get some."

The coven masters came sometimes, as at Loomin, when they used Garick's hall for the sun-calling. They treated Judith with cool respect while Singer stared wide-eyed at their white tabards and the way they had, at the plentiful board, of eating and drinking virtually nothing. This was the price of their gift, Garick told him. To be a master needed a clear head and an iron body. Though they couldn't read or write like his mother, they were strong, clear-thinking men and women. Singer held them in awe and basked in their unforced kindness, but there was one he disliked, the young one, Jenna. When *she* caught his eyes, Singer squirmed—and yet she was soft as morning with Garick.

His father taught him as much as his mother. He learned to read the forest as easy as a page of Old Language. He began to discern the many telltale sounds of forest. Garick sang the old stories to him and tried to explain the order of things. There were always covens, he said, because men knew deep in their hearts it was an answer to life that worked for them, gave them a hold on existence. Singer thought he understood the logic of it.

And yet his father did not speak to him much of death.

"Our life is good and safe," Garick told him. And Singer believed it, playing through the long afternoons with other children at cup-and-knife games like Save the House, some attacking, some defending, pretending to raise fearsome powers like the masters:

*Master of storm, guard me east,*
*Master of lightning, guard me south,*
*Master of water, guard me west,*
*Black Bull, horn god, guard me north!*

A game, yet one deadly serious in child-longing. Singer hunched stern and silent over his defended circle and pentagram. An older boy raised his knife and plunged it unfairly into the heart of Singer's territory.

Singer's eyes seemed to turn black as the dark strength burst forth from him. His eyes caught and held the other boy's. Singer stuck out one finger and prodded his antagonist sharply, once. The other child slowly, reluctantly, put his hand on his knife and took it back, sheathing it.

Singer broke contact, and the boy ran off, crying.

"He *stole* him!" the master told Garick. "Stole little Boody, not only touched his mind but moved it, moved his hand, made him take the knife back."

"I don't believe it." Garick was stunned. "No one can do that, not even masters."

"Your son can."

"How?"

"He touched the boy," said the master, Edan. "Says he had to touch him."

After the masters left, Garick stared at Singer in mixed delight and awe. "Jude, you know what this means?"

"No."

"He could be a master."

"Of what?" Judith shot back. "Of Charzen? Of mudholes? Of pigs and stinking hunters?"

Garick was not so much angry as perplexed. "What would you save him for, Jude? City? That's dead, gone. They'll stop him at the Self-Gate like anyone else."

"But he has a mind, Garick, an excellent mind! It'd be a crime to waste that on a Samman fire."

His father was a gentle man—gentle, not weak. For the sake of his love for Judith and his son, he tried to balance her teaching against the unwritten wisdom of his own heritage. The love between his parents was a strong fabric of security over Singer, but now as he grew and his gifts developed, he sensed dangerous rents in the fabric. His mother drank more. Garick was often away from home.

Once, Singer saw his father riding with Jenna. They looked happy together.

Singer began to take instruction from the masters, much against Judith's will. He was far ahead of the other chosen children. What they labored to memorize, he could instantly write, inventing symbols where no existing ones would serve. But his fearsome power to steal the mind and shape and purpose of others began to cut him off from his peers. Nobody wanted Singer to touch him. As he grew, he learned not to use the strange power which frightened even the masters. But it grew with the rest of his gifts, and as it did, the gulf widened between his parents.

Yet, ironically, it was not his gifts but Garick's that finally split their world asunder.

Garick was riding down the orchard rows during a rainstorm, when he felt the hairs on the back of his neck prickle. Before he had time to take cover, he was prostrated by a bolt of lightning.

The orchard men reached him first, then the masters through their urgent lep, Jenna galloping in the lead. The horse had to be put out of its agony. Garick barely breathed; he was past their combined help.

When Judith and her son rode up, the crowd was already thick. Singer had an armload of blankets, and his mother plowed furiously into the throng.

"Move, damn it, *move!* Get away, let him breathe!"

She confronted Jenna over Garick's limp form.

"You can't help him," the girl challenged tersely. Judith dismissed her with a contemptuous gesture.

"And I suppose you can? He's not dying, but he could if I don't work quickly. He's in shock. Electrical shock. I suppose you know what that is, you ignorant bastards?" Her voice rising shrilly, Judith snatched the blankets from Singer and, with his fumbling help, wrapped them thickly around Garick.

Singer stared at his father, frightened. Garick's face was white, his breathing rapid and shallow. It terrified the boy, who knew so little of death.

"Get his feet up!" Judith snapped.

No one moved. Shoving, cursing, she tried to do it herself. Singer struggled to help. Then Jase moved her gently aside and tucked Garick's legs under one thick arm. Judith knelt, soaking a cloth from a water bag, wiping the pallid face.

"Rub his wrists," she muttered to her son. "Hard."

Singer obeyed, rubbing until the brown skin turned red. His own hands began to ache, but he was afraid to stop. The big hand lay limp in his. He rubbed harder.

And the limp fingers flexed; Singer felt pressure on his own fingers.

Garick's eyes blinked open. His other hand twitched on the blanket, then rose feebly to touch Judith's face.

Singer saw the look of victory his mother slashed at young Jenna.

Judith nursed him fiercely. As he recuperated, the masters of Charzen, having detected certain indicative signs, came in a delegation. They made tests after their fashion and found that Garick's ability to lep had trebled. At their request, the mystified apple farmer successfully raised a formidable cone of power.

Judith scoffed: the thing was a scientific commonplace and had been since well before the collapse of antique society. Every power the coveners called magic, she said, emanated from a specific portion of the brain for purely physiological reasons, and a mind with potential psychic ability—especially an attuned Uhian mind—could be stimulated electrically to produce conscious control of these powers.

The masters barely listened. Judith was a tolerated outsider, though she grew less tolerable with the years, a querulous, sharp-tongued woman, too quick to show contempt for their way.

Now Jase had to manage the orchards alone as Garick labored morning and night under the masters, writing things that others memorized—thanks to what he'd learned over the years from Judith. More, with her help, he was able to theorize upon the origin of powers, something that no master had ever thought out in a logical process of thought. But her aid only served to hasten the thrusting of Garick further apart from his family. He was quieter, more remote, thin with fasting. His old laughter was muted.

At Sinjin, in midsummer, Garick became a master of the inner circle.

That night, Singer hovered close to this parents, knowing something was horribly wrong. He felt for the familiar oneness, the fabric that bound them together, blanketed him in security, but it was not to be found.

His mother sat tightly on the edge of the big bed, too intent on her hands when there was nothing wrong with them. His father stood, hesitant, by the door, huge and naked except for the white tabard of his new rank. New forces, painful and wrenching tensions, passed between the two, so strong that even Judith received them in some degree, and Singer's head ached with the brutal emotions with which the air was charged.

"I'm not just a farmer now, Jude," Garick said. "I can't say no."

"I'm staying here, then. I will *not* watch."

"Jude, I love you."

"Oh?" She glared at him and shook the long gray-wisped hair from her narrow face. "And who will give you the Five Kisses? And who will straddle you?"

"Jude—"

Her face contorted with fury. "Why don't you name her?"

"Jude, I've told you—"

*"Go rut your Jenna!"*

"I've told you, that's a symbol," Garick struggled to explain in Judith's Old Language, his own inadequate to the task. "A sign of power, of life." He sat down beside her. "Nothing happens in the circle."

She raised her head, weary and haggard. "But how much out of it? She's already pregnant and making no secret of it. She might have waited just a little while. It won't be long."

Singer was afraid to understand what she meant, but a new kind of anguish welled up in his breast.

"No, I won't lie. I've been lonely," Garick said. "You make me lonely. If you didn't drink so damn much—"

"The sight of you with Jenna goes easier with a drink!"

"Jenna is . . . only Jenna," he grated. "I love *you.*"

"Then, if you love me, tell them *no.*"

"I can't!" Garick uncoiled his great mass from the bed, paced to the door. "This ain't—this *isn't* pride, not for me, not for Jenna. Jude, I've given in to you everywhere I can, but this is *my* way, and these are my people—and I'll tell you, if a new world ever comes, we coveners are the ones who'll bring it to birth, not that almighty damn City. Not those fat Mrikans counting their money. *Us.* Once, just once, you have to understand *me,* because what I was born with—and what you've taught me—"

But Singer never heard the end of the thought, for just then the house grew rosy with the flickering illumination of a ring of torches. The masters had come for his father.

Garick hesitated at the door. "Judith, I do love you. I owe you so much."

"Yes, you do." She forced a calm smile, though her son sensed the stifled longing behind it. "You owe me your life and most of your mind, and all of your learning. And your son. That's quite a debt. *Think you can pay it back?"*

As always, Garick felt inadequate before her. He slipped through the door and padded soundlessly away to meet his future.

The child Singer plucked at his mother's knee, tried to climb into her lap. She rose, ignoring him, and walked stiffly out of the room to pour herself a drink.

Singer stood alone for a long time, choking back sobs.

He had been told not to go near the circle grove, but something impelled him to disobey this once. He ran desperately as if he could stop the thing he didn't understand, halt the rush of time and bring his father back. He willed his short legs to pump as swiftly as a deer's. Noiseless as his father, he drew near the fire-lit grove, small creatures scuttling out of his headlong path. Panting to a halt just beyond the firelight, he watched with heaving chest and an aching heart. His father was already in the circle, past the first course sunways when challenge after challenge was met with ritual response. Now he lay naked with the other men near the rim of the trenched circle. The music rose from the thronged ring of watchers; one rhythm, then another and another intermingled as the female masters moved sinuously outward from the center, flames licking tongues of light along the shining supple contours of their bodies.

Jenna stood naked over Garick and raised her hands to unpin the red mass of hair, letting it cascade over her shoulders. Other women mirrored her movements, each poised above a supine male. Even far away, Singer could see the new hard rotundity of Jenna's belly. She knelt and straddled Garick.

*No! Don't!*

Singer started toward them, a cry building in his throat, but stopped. To reach them would be to cross and break the circle, dare the power built up in it. Impossible at his age! He clubbed impotently with small fists.

It would be years before Singer found a name for the thing that died that night, but even as he watched, he knew something very special and private was gone forever.

He dragged away from the grove, a new, forlorn heaviness in his steps. Joy was dead, but the noises of *their* joy mocked him everywhere. He slammed the door in a vain attempt to shut out the music and laughter of a festival to which he was not, never would be invited.

"Garick?"

His mother swayed uncertainly in front of her mirror. The tension in the muscles of her neck and back showed him that she was in pain. It came often now.

Judith looked down at her small son. She put aside the jug and reached out to ruffle his hair, but a new spasm of pain tore at her.

"Mama?"

"It's all right."

Desperately, Singer flung his arms around her and tried, between sobs, to tell her she was so much more beautiful than Red Jenna and always would be. She cradled his head for a long time, rocking him gently. Then she sat him down and held his gaze with grave, shadow-circled eyes.

"I want you to listen to me," she said, not sadly now but with a sense of quiet, final purpose. "I have something very important to tell you. Will you pay attention?"

He thought it might be something about his father, but when she spoke, it was just about old Callee. He was hurt that she would treat him like a baby when he knew too well what was happening.

"Don't want to be told stories." He pulled away from her sullenly. "Callee's not true."

His mother spun him around; the fierce new light in her eyes riveted him where he stood.

"Now listen and *remember,"* she commanded. "The story of Callee is true! I proved it before you were born. You're going to learn it better than anyone ever has."

"Why?" he protested. "What good is it? Dad—"

"It'll be hard enough to teach you all of it, but I'll do it somehow. Someday you may be able to finish the work I failed to complete. And then, even more important . . ."

The pain took her again. Her nails left marks on his wrist. When the spasm passed, she continued weakly. "No time. You'll learn what I tell you. *Hear me?"*

His voice was thin with fear. "Yes."

"Good," said Judith. "Now, there once was a man named Callee, for that's how you know him. But time rounds the edges of words and names. He was really MacCauley, Henry MacCauley, and in the last of the old days in the place called Lishin . . ."

Arin was born at Loomin with considerable rejoicing in Charzen. Singer understood that the infant was a brother of some kind.

Garick stayed away most of the time now. His first son tried to balance between the two riven worlds and paid the price. The masters began to despair of him; for all his early promise, he had become an insolent, unteachable rebel, clearly spoiled by his mother. Perhaps he was not meant for Circle after all.

When Garick tried to talk to his son, he encountered a wall. Instead of arguing, the older man forbore to harass either Singer or Judith. His own life was changing too rapidly.

The elderly master who wore the antler crown of the god died in the spring. Garick's mother, Tuli, having shared the title, proposed to step down in favor of Jenna, provided Garick be named god.

Judith watched it all with a sharp eye, but the sardonic smile on her lips masked the now-constant pain that assailed both heart and body. She knew the assumption of Garick was inevitable. The Shando were beginning to see the wisdom of more political considerations in their choice of a god. For fifty years, the apples drew Mrikan traders to Charzen, forging the money links that stretched beyond Circle. To crown Garick would concentrate wealth in the antler crown, as well as a name known in trading from Wengen to Suffec, a name that could extend the long arm of influence to the very edge of City itself.

And so, in his twenty-seventh year, Garick became god of the Shando. Next to him, the gleam from her candle coronet less bright than the triumph in her eye, sat Jenna, the new goddess.

There was a certain historical coincidence not noted at the time. Garick was the youngest Circle god ever crowned. A few months earlier, the Kriss chose their youngest chief elder, an energetic, forceful man called Uriah. Like Garick, he was not afraid to use a new idea for an old purpose.

Now the house by the orchards was nearly empty. Few came except the women sent by Garick to help Judith with chores beyond her strength, which was failing more swiftly than any but Singer realized. She made a joke of it with him. If he caught her wincing, she would groan comically.

"I'm falling apart like bad plumbing."

It was agony to the boy, and yet, sheltered so long from the stark arithmetic of death, he clung to her, perversely fascinated by the process of dissolution. As her body failed, at last the sharp mind started to grow blunt. But as she felt it falter, she drove herself more cruelly than at Lishin, tormenting herself to express thoughts that eluded her. The words were maddeningly cumbersome things, expressing too few concepts too slowly. She longed for the concise verbal shorthand of the City, but lacking that, she pummeled Singer with facts and concepts, cramming his brain with an encyclopedia of data that he could not hope to assimilate. The hours and days were too brief to tell him everything about her view of life and the purpose of Man as postulated in the long centuries of her work within the City.

And still she coughed and forced her dry throat to talk and talk at him, insisting that he remember. Sometimes, of course, he could not follow her at all in the desperate turnings of her logic, for she would go off at tangents as the City philosophy beckoned her down abstruse corridors of speculation endless as the miles of books and machines she described.

One thing she said stuck in his mind because of the oddity of the picture, though he had no idea what it meant. "The City and the covens will break each other, as on a wheel. But the wheel won't turn until—" A fit of coughing interrupted Judith, and she never finished the thought.

All his life, Singer had been half City, half Shando, but now Judith buried most of what was coven beneath the mountain of treasures she heaped upon her son. Divorced from his father's customs and way of life, Singer began to long for the City. But there was no time to talk of it, for still his mother reeled off facts and speculated on the shape of the sundered society in which they dwelt, but before he could perceive where her investigations must lead, she returned to her search at Lishin and told, over and over, the moment when she learned that the hero Callee was Henry MacCauley. More and more frequently, Judith rambled and repeated herself.

The summer after Arin was born, Singer came home one day from playing alone in the forest. There were two horses at the front door; they were saddled with packs attached. He thought perhaps his father had come on one of his rare visits, but the house was silent.

His mother was not at the long table with a jug, nor by the kitchen hearth or in the neglected garden. She lay in the big bed, and the sight of her stopped him in the doorway.

Death was on her, clear as a command. She was pasty white and stiff with suppressed pain. Only her eyes were fiercely, yearningly alive. And yet, she had bathed and combed out her hair, tying it back with a bit of scarlet cloth. She wore a soft white cotton robe that hung loose about her emaciated body.

She stretched out her hands to him. Her appearance frightened Singer all the more for her loveliness.

"You—you look—"

"Beautiful?" She laughed with gentle irony. "Your father always thought so, and I think he had good taste. Come here, I want to hug you. When was the last time I told you how much I love you?" She coughed, and the violent spasm left her even weaker. She took his hand. "Oh, you're dirty! Have you been playing in the mud again, my baby?"

There was a time when the word would have rankled, when he would have thought his stature demeaned, but now the boy compressed his lips and blinked to fight back the tears. He explained how he had found a fox and tried to work staymagic on it, but old fox just laughed at him.

"Never mind," said Judith. "There are new skins in your room. Go wash and put them on. It's time to go."

"Where?"

"East," Judith replied. "It's time to show you the City. One last gift."

His heart leaped at the word. Above all his dreams of magic, adventure and other boyish enthusiasms there hovered, remote and irresistible, the City . . .

"Hurry," his mother urged. "The horses are ready."

They could not travel fast. Most of the time, Singer had to walk his horse to stay with his mother. By the middle of the next day, they had made barely twenty miles into the forest. Wary for packdogs or cowan hunters, the youth rode as he had been taught in strange country, arrow ready and smeared with pokeberry.

He glanced back to see Judith. She was bent double over the horse's neck, and as he turned, she tried to halt the animal. He trotted back to her.

"Get me down," she panted.

She could not ride further without rest. Not far back, Singer had noted a small cave of the sort that hunters used on brief trips. They made their way to it, and he saw it would do them very well. He made a bed of pine boughs and spread their blankets over them for her, fetching fresh water to bathe the sweat from her face. He tried to make her eat a little of the food they packed, but Judith listlessly waved it away. He built a fire at the cave mouth to keep her warm without the smoke bothering her.

Time passed. Now and then Singer tried to make conversation to dispel the loneliness, but Judith lay just the way he had settled her and did not utter a sound. His hands knotted into fists to push back the inarticulate tears that burned behind his eyelids. The Shando in him knew what was coming, but even though his knife was no thammay, he dug desperately in the earth around her, drawing the circle, filling it with every remembered rune of protection, and then he crouched by her with the knife. Death might take her, but he was determined it would not be this night, not in his circle.

The darkness was measured in owl cries and the susurration of crickets. A fox padded by the cave, sniffed curiously and went away. Singer lay close to her, cushioning his mother's head with one stiff arm.

Just before morning, he woke suddenly as if someone had kicked him; he listened. His mother still breathed very slowly, but she was awake; he knew without looking. In the silence, her voice was very weak, but composed and clear. She spoke in the Old Language, whose music he had come to love.

"It's time we said good-by, baby."

He raised on one elbow, stiff from the awkward position he'd held all night. "Does it hurt?"

"No," she whispered. "I'm like an old clock running down to stillness. But you never saw a clock, did you?"

He shook his head, the tears welling up in his eyes. He fought them back.

"There are clocks there," she said.

"In the City?"

"Yes. Oh, my baby, I so much wanted to show it to you. Go there after I'm gone. Promise me you'll see the City. So much of me is still there, and you must bring the rest back . . ."

"The rest?"

"All I taught you." But there was no strength left. She had to lie still and just breathe for a while. Then: "Go there; perhaps not now, but when you're older. They'll need you there, my baby."

Her fingers closed over his, cold.

"Perhaps," she whispered, "perhaps I'll tell you more in the morning. I'll be stronger then. I'll tell you about the City when it's light."

She closed her eyes. Singer shifted his position and lay on his stomach. He was very tired. In a little while, he felt one of the blankets spread gently over his shoulders, and realized what such a simple effort must have cost her, but he couldn't speak. He was balancing already on the soft edge of sleep. Time passed. He breathed more deeply. Then, abruptly, he woke.

*"Garick."*

So low he barely heard it. Then he felt her body heave feebly close to his. His mother was crying.

"Garick, I wanted . . ."

The message was never completed. The morning wind blew fresh through the cave mouth and across his frail circle, and it was cold. As he moved his lips to speak, Singer knew he was alone, though nearly a score of winters would pass before the full enormity of the fact provided him with a new and bitter strength.

They found Singer wandering near the cave. The god and goddess met the returning hunters as they rode into the stockade yard with the small boy whose feet dangled ludicrously short of the stirrups. A curious crowd gathered around them.

"Found him a day east," the hunters reported. "Other horse, too."

They eased their mounts aside as Garick shouldered his way through to his son.

"And Judith?"

No one spoke. A horse snuffled in the silence.

"Then she's dead." Garick's voice seemed devoid of emotion or strength. "Where?"

"I buried her," Singer said tightly. "The grave's marked. You can read it."

Father and son faced each other. *If he touches me,* Singer thought, *I'll cut him with the knife that dug her grave.*

Garick seemed to read that thought and more. He didn't reach for Singer: instead, he looked blindly at Jenna, who waited impassively with the baby Arin in her arms, mumbled his thanks to the hunters, and turned slowly back up the steps toward the god's hall. Singer stiffened; it was not enough. He would not let him go without taking all his tangled love and hatred for the man who was his father and hurling it at his back in one agonized cry that rang down the years for both of them.

*"You can read it."*

Singer kicked the horse's flank; it reared and plunged through the open gate.

The hunters wondered if they should follow again, but the god of Shando was turned away, frozen on the steps, his broad back a slumped curve of misery. They looked to Jenna for instruction. "Go after him?"

She shifted Arin to her other arm, waiting. *Garick?*

His mind was closed off—as always. She had not won anything. *Always her,* Jenna thought. *Even dead, it's always her.*

"Go after him," she ordered the hunters. Then, lower: "But don't find him."

She watched the small rider on the horse as the animal cleared a rail fence in a clean bound. The hunters began their barren pursuit, but Singer galloped straight as an arrow across the meadow and toward the forest and down the years.

# *The Broken Circle*

Whenever Magill got drunk, he fought Kon. If Kon drank, too, disputes were settled by Arin's easygoing sense. But when all three drank, they all fought and Arin always won, and then they hooted off for a night on the hill with blankets and sida and girls, and things stayed in balance. It had always been this way, always would be.

The balance that night was gloriously assured. Elin opened her eyes as the sun inched over the grassy slope. Her long arms and legs snaked out from under the blankets, stretching luxuriously. She yawned and sat up, knuckling the sleep from languid gray eyes that never quite lost their expression of sleepy ease. Next to her, Arin slept on his stomach. With what he drank and loving till the moon went down, he would sleep till high sun.

The brown legs jackknifed under her; Elin rose, bathing her bare brown, sun-freckled skin in the first of the sun. She stretched again, tasting the air, scratching vigorously at her scalp, digging her fingers under the long red hair, lashing it in thick tumbles about her face and down her back.

She was what Judith Singer once noted as the classic Uhian female type, six-foot-one—"six'n a bit" Elin reckoned it—and most of it legs. No special stamp of feature made her beautiful; rather a fluid ease and enjoyment of her body, all the more graceful for its complete unconsciousness.

She swept the hair out of her face with a feline gesture, squinting at the distant rider bobbing across the meadow toward their hill, then curled down again next to Arin.

"Hey," she murmured to the shrouded head.

There was no response. He might have been dead.

Elin dragged the blanket from his naked rump, running her lips over his back, letting her hair brush over his thighs in the way she knew he loved. Then she shook him.

"Arin, it's light. Ma'll want me."

One hand groped for the blanket. He hauled it over his tousled head, trying to shut out the loud, too-bright world. "Gzz . . ." said Arin.

She smacked him on the butt. "Arin, you still drunk?"

A weak groan issued from the depths of the blanket. "Lemme 'lone. Feel so bad, gonna die soon, anyway."

Elin snuggled closer and kissed him. "You still taste like sida."

He stirred, mumbling. "How're you?"

"Just fine, Arin."

" 'Sgood," he grunted, eyes still closed. "Now, *who* are you?"

"You son of a bitch!" she giggled. "Still drunk, bare-ass and a rider coming up the hill."

"Gimme my skins."

"Hell with that. Gimme a kiss."

Arin sat up, holding his head as if it were an overripe fruit. Down the hill, Magill roared his good spirits to the morning and a girl next to him squealed. Then a whisper of grass, barely disturbed by Kon's foot, and the oldest, most private of the Three knelt by his friend.

"Rider, Arin."

Elin cocooned herself in the blanket and stood up. "Oh, it's Jay." She frowned.

"Thought so," Kon mused. "Don't ride like Shando. Where's he from?"

"Came last year," the girl said. "Western coven, he told me."

Most of Arin's brain was still dozing in the blanket. The small remainder working in his behalf remembered that Jay was the odd one always after Elin to live with him. Arin wondered absently why she didn't. Jay worked hard, his fields were as good as any, and there wasn't a finer-looking man in Charzen. Still, he was odd. Arin never saw him smile at anything.

Down the hill, bare and brown, Magill cupped his hand around his mouth. "HEY, ARIN!"

Arin winced.

"OLD JAY COMIN'!"

"Kon," Arin pleaded huskily, "tell'im I know."

They waited as Jay rode up. He was delicate, almost clean-cut in comparison to Kon or Arin. He would have been handsome, but the stern intensity of his manner interfered. He reminded Arin a little of Singer.

"Elin." Jay gave her a dark look. "What are you doing here?"

She switched the blanket around her—with a hint of pique, Kon noted. "Getting up. Just felt like a night on the hill, and I 'spect I'll be ninety before *you* get around to asking me."

The answer clearly hurt him, but there was contempt, too, in his expression. His eyes sought Arin. Garick's son was too sick to read anything, but the hate did not escape the watchful Kon.

"Arin, I came for you. You're wanted."

"Who by? Garick?"

"And your mother."

"Be along soon, tell'em. Don't feel so good now."

"Tell them yourself," Jay snapped, staring once more at Elin. "They're wearing the crowns today, and the masters are there. They said *now.*"

"Jay," Elin came close to his stirrup, looking up at him. "I waited for you last night."

For an instant, something stood out behind the frowning disapproval, then Jay wheeled the horse about. "Your mother will want you. You should be working."

"Oh, Jay," she laughed, "don't you ever smile? Look so nice when you do."

He flicked the reins and trotted away.

The Three wove toward the stockade like weary dogs on a hot day, Arin still dripping from his immersion in a cold brook. Kon and Magill supported him between them, speculating on the contrariness of Jay.

*Think he'd quit,* Kon allowed. *Could have any girl in Charzen except her.*

*No 'cept,* Magill corrected. *He could have her. She said yes, Jay said no.*

"G'wan, who said that?"

"Elin said. Old Jay like a skunk going in a hole too small. Hard to get something in his head. But once it's there, god*dam* hard to get it out."

They agreed it was insanity. Jay wanted Elin and only Elin, and there was no reading the man. If he wanted her, why not take her when she offered? They appealed to Arin, now, since he was the smartest. Did he ever know any woman so good he'd give up all the others. *All?*

*No,* Arin lied.

He didn't feel like talking or sharing at all, but beyond that, and even though they were the Three, there was one thing Arin could not share with Kon or Gill. Her name was Shalane.

They met three summers earlier when he was buying spun wool in Karli for Jenna, and nothing would do the hospitable Moss and Maysa except Arin stayed with them. Arin found his father's old friend a strong, kindly man with sudden, unaccountable silences. Not solitary like Garick, Moss' habits were all the stranger for the warmth of the man. At times he would shut his mind off from everyone, and there was one rainy day, Arin remembered, when Moss would not speak or lep or even leave his bedroom.

But Maysa talked Arin blue about their youngest girl, only sixteen and pledged to the inner circle.

And such a girl! No slow-easy lazing along like Elin. Shalane ran, bounded, quivered with life, too much of it, too vulnerable, too easily hurt. Nothing in her was hidden; happiness or hurt darkened or lighted her face in the instant, and she had a way of saying *Hey, Arin* that shared worlds more than it said. They had little time together, though. By rigid custom, she couldn't be with men during her fasting, purification and study.

She drove Arin wild with the quandary of it. Sometimes it seemed Shalane went out of her way to see him; other times he was sure she avoided him. He wouldn't have cared with any other girl, but the *woman* of Shalane made him feel like a sharp knife. No, more than that, there was a deep, tender thing that left him staring sleepless at the moon nights on end. Because they couldn't touch, the simplest contact, the accidental brushing of fingers across a table became as exciting as going into her. He would hold it in his memory and imagine her hand stroking down his cheek, his shoulders, across his chest, and tighten in the throat with it.

Arin began to think he was downright sick. Any other girl he'd enjoyed, he could imagine—even watch—out on the hill with other men, and feel nothing deeper than physical excitement or—depending on the girl—perhaps a yawn. And this was not strange. The coven way was easy and untrammeled. Women were as free as men, always had been, the only way people could live, and Arin knew it.

And yet . . . Shalane. He wanted her for himself alone, as if he were thirty already and tired of the hill and ready to sit home with just one woman.

The week he left for Charzen, Shalane was closeted with the

masters and never home. He delayed his going, hoping she'd come, but finally had to cinch up, hug Moss and Maysa and ride. Still, he went the long way around past the masters' hall and held up there, pretending his horse had a stone in its hoof, but dammit, even that couldn't hold him here in the stockade yard much longer—

"Hey, Arin."

And there she was on the steps of the hall, barefoot in a fresh white robe, her yellow hair pinned back, smiling at him. She had big front teeth; they looked bigger now with her face thin from fasting. He wanted to run to her and tell her how beautiful she was, but it wouldn't do now. Any other time out of all their lives . . .

"Hey," he managed.

"You going?" *Don't.*

*Have to.*

"I'll be a master at Lams," she said. "I wanted you to be there."

*Yes.*

"Arin, why's Garick call you dumb?"

"Garick's the smart one."

She smiled then. "You know what, Arin. I think he's some kind of wrong." Shalane raised her hand in a gesture of farewell already stamped with its own singular grace. She was indeed nearly a master. "See you."

"I'd like that." He swung into the saddle. "When?"

"Sometime on the hill," said Shalane. She opened the door and vanished into the hall.

Three years. He always meant to go back, but there was invariably something to postpone it: wagons to Lorl, the orchards, running deer with Kon and Gill, the easy, convenient loving with Elin, like a good meal and a jug after a hard day. Sometimes he knew Garick was right: he was lazy and useless, but he only returned the warm smile old goddess earth gave him, and *she* never hurried about anything.

He had a good lep. Sometimes he tried to touch Shalane with it and thought he could feel her mind fold into his, not words, just sharing, closer even than Kon.

Three years. He'd *meant* to go back . . .

Since his own actions made little sense, he had to allow for Jay, strange as the man was. If Jay cared that much for Elin, it might explain the sour, sunless way he lived his life.

Arin's head still felt wretched and he desperately, passionately, wanted to lie down, even if he had to wrench it off his neck to do so. He did not want, of all things, to have to stand formally before the god and goddess, parents or no—and sure as frost, he did *not* want to deal with the taut-bowstring threat of Jay, standing flat-footed by his horse, blocking his passage in the middle of the stockade yard.

"Arin!"

Always ready to battle for Arin, Magill appraised the situation. *Wants a fight, Arin.*

Kon agreed silently, but Arin gave them both a gentle push. *Who'd hit a man sick as me?* "Go ahead, walk on."

They shrugged and drifted away. Arin walked unsteadily toward Jay. His head ached viciously, but it still felt better than his stomach.

"What you want, Jay?"

The other's mouth worked. "I—I wanted Elin."

"Tell her. She ain't with me."

He saw Jay's hand tremble with the anger building in him, like some subterranean fire.

"Not now!" he spat. "You dirtied her."

Arin blinked, uncomprehending. "Huh?"

"You know what that makes her?" Jay seethed. "You know what it does to her soul?"

Arin was genuinely bewildered. "No, what?"

Dulled with sickness, he never saw the fist coming. Even as he crashed on his butt, he wondered what hit him. The blood trickled from his split lip. Jay hovered over him.

"Get up, Arin. I'm gonna hurt you bad."

Arin sat still, looking up at him. Anger rose, boiled, simmered and then cooled. Neither Jay nor Elin were worth the effort.

"I don't fight over her, Jay. Go 'way."

"You won't fight?"

"She'll be with you the same as me. You don't want her, don't fret me about it." Arin wiped more blood from his lip. "Go away."

"Filth!" Jay screamed, swinging himself into the saddle. "You! Kon, Magill! All of you! Drinking and rutting, dirtying the world—animals! How can you stand to live?"

Jay heeled the horse sharply. The beast leaped into a startled gallop out through the open stockade gate.

Most of what he'd said was lost on Arin, sitting miserably in the dust, his head swimming, stomach heaving. He didn't much care about it except to agree with Magill. There was no reading old strange Jay.

Arin paused long enough to wash off and change into a clean cotton robe. Then he opened the doors to the center hall and entered.

They were waiting, his parents and half a dozen of the older masters, the core power of Shando: Tuli, his grandmother, once the goddess, and old Edan, master of masters, who had in his care the teaching of initiates, most powerful after the god and goddess.

Arin approached his parents with precarious dignity and knelt before the two crowns. Garick noted the bruised lip and the other slight lump, a gift from Magill the night before. His son looked like a sick chicken in need of a place to die.

"We heard," Garick began, "how you worked staymagic on the deer to bait Singer."

Arin nodded wanly; his stomach convulsed in warning.

"Edan will test you," Jenna said. "If he finds you can raise power—"

"And can stand the trials of the masters' way," Garick interjected, and Arin saw the bleak doubt in his father's face, "then, Arin, you may be called."

Jenna beamed proudly at her son. She noted his pallid color and attributed it to stunned surprise. Garick held no such illusion.

Now old Edan hobbled forward and spoke to Arin. Frail though he was, his voice echoed powerfully in the great room.

"The masters are the bone in Shando flesh, Arin. Our magic leads, our power protects. All coveners have some gift; it makes us what we are, but only a few can be heated and shaped like iron for Circle. To be a master will ask from you everything you are. No word, no law will deny you the things that are good to men and women—the food to the stomach, the love that's good for the heart—but the iron of the master's way, once it blends with your strength, will be stronger than any other law. Your body will be like a dog kept half-hungry to do what your power wills, without question or argument or failure. Who knows if you're strong enough, but will you try it?"

For a brief moment, Edan mistook the rapt preoccupation in Arin's face for devout inspiration. Arin swallowed with difficulty—twice—then, with a pathetic sound, doubled over and was violently sick on the floor. When it passed, he sensed that he was the center of a stunned silence.

"Aw, ma," he choked, "*damn,* I'm sorry."

She did not reply. Jenna was rigid with shame. She turned to Garick, who sat with his head lowered. His tightly compressed lips might be locked over anger or something else. Garick laughed at strange things. Whatever, he mastered it and spoke in a low voice to her: "Take the masters outside, Jenna."

"But—"

"Take them outside—and wait."

Garick did not move until the door closed behind the last of them. Arin was wilted on a bench, head in his hands. Garick reached him in three strides, hooked a pitcher of water in long fingers and emptied it over Arin's head.

"Sit up, boy!" There was an edge to his voice. "Some have cried when called into the circle, others have been afraid—but you, Arin, you're the first who ever puked!"

Arin felt small as a toad. "I shamed you."

"You?" Garick measured him sadly. "I never expected better from you. If I could trust him, I'd be glad to send Singer in your place."

*Singer?*

"Why not?" Garick challenged, hands on narrow hips. "Singer could have been a master. He could bend minds with his will when he was seven. No master can do what he can, not even Edan. But Jenna thinks you're fit for the circle. Perhaps she wants to prove Singer isn't the only—"

He broke off in dry bitterness, but it touched something in Arin never spoken before.

"He's yours, isn't he? Not Jenna's. Yours."

Garick nodded. "Yes."

"Someone said once. I didn't believe. Only if I could hear it from you."

"So now," said Garick, "you've heard."

"We're part brothers, then? Me and *that?*"

"You could do worse, boy." Garick laid the antler crown on the bench beside Arin. There was an awkward silence. Arin knew no words for the things that had to be said, but the time had arrived when they must somehow be voiced. It was painful; he loved his father but knew he would never be half the man.

"You don't count me much, Garick."

"No," the older man admitted sadly. "Not much. Not bad, not good. I've watched you drink and rut and loaf your way to being a man, the easiest life in Charzen. A little work in the orchards, a train to Lorl now and then and the rest of the time it's you and Kon and Magill—*the Three.*" Garick's lips twisted in derision. "Three *what,* Arin?"

"You didn't want me to be a hunter?"

Garick sighed. "I let you be one. You were always . . . an afterthought. I didn't need you then. Now I do."

Arin clasped his hands between his long, sprawling legs. A strange feeling was birthing inside him and it ached. He felt himself beginning to lose a comfortable thing too long taken for granted.

"So," he said, "you'd rather use Singer."

"Forget what I said," Garick replied, sensing the unfamiliar pangs growing in his son, "I'm sending you."

"Where?"

"A long way," said his father. "To the Karli. To the Wengen and the Kriss. Others go south to Suffec."

Arin looked up. "Kriss are cowan."

"They're still Uhians. I want every man who'll fight with us."

"Fight?" Arin's head rejected the concept. Circle never fought. An enemy large enough to need such numbers as Garick suggested was beyond him. "Fight who?"

"The City."

Arin nearly fell off the bench. "Dad—you been drinking, too?"

"I know what you're thinking and I don't want to hear it," Garick stated wearily. "We'll die, I know. We'll die anyway. There's a plague in the forest, moving this way. They say the plague comes and goes, and no one knows where it starts, but last time it took half of Charzen. I'm not about to sit back and watch it happen again. Arin, that's been our way too long—sitting back and hoping this will pass and that won't happen, and all the time, time itself will pass and we'll be well." Garick paced from one end of the hall to the other, restless with energy and purpose. "I've often wondered what we'd do if City ever sent their merks to finish us. Probably the only reason why they haven't is because we're not that important to them. But even without that, and even without the plague, we're dying, Arin, because we don't change, don't build, don't *grow.*"

His father was talking gibberish now. "Circle can't change! How could it?"

"All life changes," Garick contradicted, "or it dies."

"Who says?"

"Someone who taught me more than just that." Garick continued his pacing, beating out the thoughts in rhythm, step by step. "Perhaps she taught me too much then. Now I see, and Singer must, too." Garick observed his son and realized he was totally unable to comprehend the words. "Look, Arin," he emphasized, "it's not to end Circle but to keep it alive that we have to grow and learn and fight."

"But fight to do *what?*"

"To open up that City at last *and make them talk to us!*"

Arin stared at his father, convinced that Garick had gone mad. Garick, picking up the thought, halted before the god's chair, then ascended the dais and sat, his tone brusquely altered.

"Now hear me, Arin. We've lepped to Karli. They've passed it on. They know my wish. I don't know yet whether they'll join us. It will take more than a lep to convince them to cooperate, it will need strong, smart talk. But Hoban and the Karli masters won't listen to anyone but another master. If he happens to be Garick's son, they'll listen very carefully. You'll have money, a lot of it. I'm going to buy them. If City can buy soldiers, so can I."

"Karli don't care about money," Arin argued.

"They just never had enough to care about."

"Not Karli," the boy answered, surprised at his own thinking, but sure it was true. Shando had ties to Mrika through Garick, but Karli was pure, old-fashioned Circle. You couldn't budge them out of their ways, not old Hoban the god, not even Shalane, young as she was. But the hard thinking cleared his head. "So this is what you wanted me for?"

His father nodded. "Say yes, and we'll see how much you can carry without breaking. Say yes, and you'll start tomorrow with Edan. You'll purify yourself as I did. You'll eat when and what he says, you'll fast when he tells you. You'll learn twice as fast as I did, because you don't have time for more. You won't drink at all. If I find you in the same *room* with an open jug, I'll boot your ass so high, you'll wear it for a hat. You'll clear that brain your mother claims you own, and you'll remember every single thing that Edan teaches you. And when Edan's done for the day—*every* day—you'll come to me to learn Old Language."

"But no masters learn that," Arin protested. "Why should they?"

*"I* did"—Garick was intractable—"and you will, too, so you can *think,* Arin, think about something a little higher than your belly and

your balls. You'll learn it so you can find words to bring the Uhians to my side. And for another reason, even harder, but we won't speak of that now. Say yes to Edan and, when you're ready, you'll ride with twelve men so you'll have a strong lep to keep me close to what you're doing." His bleak expression betrayed the ghost of something warmer. "I don't know how far you'll have to ride, or how long. You may not come back at all, but if you do—son—you'll be more than a hunter in a hide shirt."

It was a huge thing to consider, more than Arin could encompass now or even in after-hours when he walked alone in the orchards, frightened and confused. The youth wiped the bleariness from his eyes, brushing a strand of auburn hair aside. One thought passed fleetingly through his mind. Shalane was in Karli . . .

For the first time, Arin looked directly at his father. There was a lot more than just a man to Garick, deep things. Arin's mind never before dealt with complexities. The things he must say were not easy, but his father knew words better than anyone. Arin did what he could to drag out the best of his own tiny store.

"You never said that before," he struggled, "I mean, you never said about—needing me. Never talked to me, maybe hey, good-by, that's all. You don't even talk to Jenna."

"No." A memory rustled like dead leaves around Garick's heart. He didn't talk to Jenna. There was nothing to say. He got what he paid for.

"I never talk much," Arin went on. "Maybe once with Shalane. Kon and Magill, we share, don't need much words. I don't know." He strained after clear meaning. "Maybe I *am* a dumb sumbitch. I mean—what's there to think about? Horses, deer . . . but maybe . . ."

He rose from the bench, hands outstretched in frustrated inability to explain, a supplicatory gesture. Then he picked up the antler crown and carried it to Garick, holding it out with dignity and respect.

*He's like I was,* thought Garick, *just as dumb, probably as good. And in his own way, just as proud.*

He took the crown. His son bowed to the symbol and stood straight before him.

"Give me Kon and Magill as two of my twelve. I'll try to learn from Edan. When you tell me, I ride."

The dead leaves rustled again; something in Garick stirred deeply.

His eyes burned. The emotion surprised him. He gripped his son's hand.

"Yes, Arin."

*Perhaps yes. Arin is forest, and they'll follow him. And then, Jude, I'll ram Singer into that City like an arrow in the gut!*

The god raised his voice, vital with hope, to carry beyond the closed doors.

"Jenna! Bring in the masters!"

He glanced down at the floor, then grinned dryly at Arin. "And *you* get a cloth, quick. Clean up your offering before they slip and break their necks."

Kon and Magill lolled on the steps waiting for Arin. They had a fresh jug, and Jay was gone from Charzen for good, they heard, saddle, blanket and gear, and what was wrong with Arin that he wouldn't drink with them?

"Let's walk," Arin said, arms around both of them, trying to share what he understood of this new thing.

*We ride.*

*The Three?*

*And ten more. A long way, maybe a year.*

*Where?*

*All the north covens.*

*Old Garick said?*

"The god said it, Gill."

Magill nodded. They both accepted it without further question, as with anything Arin told them.

He reserved telling them about the Kriss, although he knew they would, of course, accept that, too.

*Or would they?*

*Would we what?*

Arin looked at Kon. "Nothing." It was the first time he'd ever excluded Kon from his thoughts.

Arin suddenly realized he was weighing both his friends like tools that must be shaped to a purpose, perhaps broken. It brought him a sorrow. The love he had for them was like a wound in his chest, and how could he detach himself from the Three, shutting his mind, withholding information, judging them like a superior when he was just a dumb hide-shirt hunter, too—like Garick said.

Arin, once the core and center of the Three, began to sense the weight and burden of a new loneliness, and as he did, his thoughts turned—as they would many times again—to Singer, who knew the silence of the forest and the spirit better than anyone in the Uhian world. Singer, the outcast. His half brother.

They put Singer in the room where he'd slept as a boy. Ever since Judith's death, her log hall had been used as a council house and also as Edan's school for new masters. Every day, Singer heard Arin come and go out of other parts of the building.

It was barely imprisonment. He was lightly shackled by a long rope that allowed him the whole, spacious room and part of the overgrown garden beyond his door. The food came promptly and hot from Garick's own table, and Judith's few remaining books were placed at his disposal. For the time being, Singer accepted his fate. He talked easily with Garick when he came, which was fairly often, and showed no further hostility to his father, though he did nothing to give him the impression that he would play any part in Garick's war against the City. When he was alone, Singer reread his mother's books, the pages black-scrawled with Garick's notes.

The long summer days stretched out toward Lams, but not without rhythm or measure. He followed the progress of his half brother as he was pledged for a master. He heard Arin practice the tedious song-patterns every day, sound exercises to free the breathing and relax the disciplined body ever deeper into the concentration necessary for magic.

In the fragrant air at dusk, Singer sat one twilight in the doorway to his garden. The lep was unusually strong, and it concerned the new master. He shut his eyes and read it. Arin was going somewhere.

*Arin needs—*

The young man was thinner now and quietly composed, the fasting and denial imposed on him by Edan already stamping their mark on his carefree manner, altering his gait to a more deliberate tread. Arin talked with certain other coveners in front of the log hall. Singer concentrated on their lep.

*Arin needs riders—*

And some listened to Arin, while others walked away. The people talked late over the fire, discussing the quest the god imposed on the young hunter, leaking thoughts that Singer read as easily as a primer.

*New thing, Garick's making.*

*Not Circle ways.*

The coveners felt carefully at the new thing, but even though they were suspicious, Singer noted one constant—the ancient fear and distrust of the City. But still, some said, Garick was mad. He'd beggar himself before he was through, buying Circle folk, turning them into merks.

*Not our way. Circle's earth . . .*

*And sun.*

*And seed growing. Not going to the knife.*

Yet a few coveners did respond to Arin's call. Kon and Magill naturally. And still, the trinity was not quite the same. As the impressions filtered through Singer's mind, the Three would not exist much longer. It was going to be leader and followers.

*Arin needs riders. North—*

Lams passed, the days cooled and the first tinge of yellow splotched the verdant world. Arin continued to come and go at the hall. Once he paused at the corner of the house as if he thought to enter Singer's door, but he went away. Singer followed him as he mingled with the young men Kon brought to see him, and the message was repeated once more.

*—needs riders north to Karli. And to the Wengen—*

At Milemas, midpoint in the year-wheel between Lams and Samman, Arin joined the masters. Singer stood in the doorway, hearing the staccato music from the grove. It brought the return of phantom pain, that night he'd run with deer-magic in his legs to stop what couldn't be halted. He shut the door against it. And still the thoughts entered his mind, the same burthen, so familiar to him now, but not yet done with in the coven.

*North to Karli. And to the Wengen. And even—*

Singer lay unmoving for hours as the power pulsed around him. Arin's signal was trebled now. He was making choices, feeling at men and women like pools of power, measuring their use and depth.

*And even to the Kriss—*

The traditional concept of thirteen had dwindled. Volunteers were few, and less than half of them were suitable. Singer was amused in a sour sort of way. Arin's chosen had their work cut out.

*To go beyond Circle, to ride no matter how long or far, to make change where no change has ever been—*

Gradually the shape of Arin's band—its temper and tang—emerged in Singer's mind, not as images but instinct and essence.

Arin was the leader. Close to him was the rock, the strength barely apart from Arin's own spirit, long rounded to his use like river-bed stone. Kon. Next to him, the other, lesser strength, puzzled by change, wishing to hurt it for the hurt it caused, the new distance between the Three. Yet loyal and struggling to accept if he could. Magill.

*Three,* Singer tallied in his mind.

Then someone young, rebellious, unstable. Powerful but diffused, self unmastered. A reject of Edan's, not quite acceptable as a potential master. Holder.

*Four.*

Someone else now, slower, more stolid, measured thought over feeling. Slow to act. Slower to anger. Nothing done in haste. Someone older and surer, but deep-shaded with regret. Old bitterness tamed. Hara, the hunter.

*Five.*

Young again, very young, sharp, quick, a lep strong as Arin's incredible power. Courage and a natural fear inspiring it. Clay, kinsman of Jenna.

*Six.*

Two together now, two joined as one and impossible to separate. Twins, brother and sister, young. A stillness like daybreak in a forest glade, the hush of deer couched in green bush, the whisper of rustling leaves. Power running soundless and deep as ocean current, a call and response joined in one wordless fluted sound. Sand. Teela, his sister. Twins from down Suffec.

*Not eight. Seven.*

No more came for a long time. Singer felt his brother's decision, the choice to mold his circle from the seven: Arin. Kon. Magill. Holder. Hara. Clay. Sand-Teela.

Dressed in brown-streaked skins, Arin's people knelt or squatted around him as he drew precise lines in the dirt to illustrate his orders. He spoke easily and without hesitation. Edan's discipline had cut the fat from his idle mind, leaving it clear and placid so he could instruct his seven without the fumbling that might lessen their confidence in him.

Lep was better suited to feeling and action than the many-leveled thoughts he needed to instruct them. He employed the structuring of Old Language, Garick's gift to him. It was a tongue that had more words than Arin thought could exist, tediously pronounced but much like Uhian once he saw the logic of it. *Logic* was the keynote, making sense with words rather than life-things. The concept of *concept* had nearly ruptured his mind, a thing-of-things you couldn't see, an *idea* that could be added to other ideas and put into action.

Translating to speech was hard. Time after time he glanced up to see if the others were following him. Clay did; he was a quick one. Kon maybe, too, though time on time, Arin caught himself slipping into the lifetime habit of lep with his friend. Lep they understood better, but they all had to think on their own now. The journey and its needs and purposes were new, outside Circle. They had to understand words.

They were a broken circle in more ways than one.

Arin stopped speaking and looked at them. The twins seemed attentive. Blond and brown-skinned with colorless, feral eyes, they were within a finger's width of the same height, the girl's wheat-toned hair chopped short as her brother's. But for the slight widening of Teela's hips, they were indistinguishable, voices low and whisper-shy, unused to the need for speech. That was partly the way of the Suffec, the most silent, most sharing of the covens. It was partly, too, their own especial way: never separated, without parents for most of their sixteen years, they'd ridden north when game ran scarce in the fringe lands between Shando and Suffec. Circle was deep in them, but Arin was the first real master they'd ever known.

Clay and Hara were easier to reach since both had spent time among different peoples. At sixteen, Clay rode a short time with the merks in Lorl who—among other duties—acted as border patrol for the City. But Circle was too strong in Clay, and he left rather than fight against his own kind, as sometimes the merks were required to do, especially when the Wengen raided outpost towns like Filsberg for forage spoils in a hard winter.

Hara had trapped north of Karli and knew something of the Blue Mountains. He was nearly as tall as Kon and just about as quiet.

Only Holder bothered Arin. Chosen for his lep power, there was, though, an incompleteness about the sandy-haired youth, a corrosive jealousy that Arin could not quite trust. Holder barely listened to instructions. He gave the impression he could devise a better plan himself with half a chance, and thus gave Arin the most minimal respect due a master.

"Got to be in Karli by Samman," Arin said, "so I can join the masters at the fire and speak to them later. We leave in two days. Each carries twenty arrows and three pounds of corn meal, knife, extra clothes. Sand, you pick up the meat and dried apples, then come to the god's hall tonight and help Teela bake as much pone as we can carry."

Holder nudged Sand. "And eight jugs of sida."

"One," Arin corrected.

"What!"

"One for the cold at night. Don't waste talk, boy." With his pointer stick, he drew the long Cumlan Valley running north from Charzen and let Hara sketch in the open, unforested ground as he remembered it, places where they were most vulnerable to cowans or merk patrols. Looking over Hara's shoulder, Clay verified the map, absently massaging the dark stubble just beginning to shadow his sharp chin. "It's a way west for merks," he judged, "but they been seen there."

The merks never used to be a problem, not much of one anyway, but things started to change gradually over the years, and now they were a far greater danger than the roving nomad cowans.

Clay took the stick from Hara and etched the serpentine arc of the Tasco River. "East of the headwater," he explained, "lot of open ground." *No trouble for horses*. He caught his lapse, grinned apologetically at Arin and repeated it aloud. "We should stay west and walk careful."

"What happens," asked Holder, "if one of us wants to come back?"

There was a palpable shift; one by one, the group regarded Arin, wondering how he'd handle the subtle challenge in Holder's question. Arin didn't move. Only his eyes lifted to fix Holder's for a long moment.

"You come alone," the master replied. "If you can make it."

Holder felt uncomfortable under their eyes, but flashed an insolent smirk. "*I* could make it."

"That's good," said Arin. "Because, if you're wrong, you'll be wrong all alone."

Hara toyed with his knife. "Gives you a warm feeling, don't it, Holder-boy?"

There were no further questions.

When the instructions were complete and understood, Arin dismissed the group and rested under the tree with Kon and Magill.

The latter shifted about awkwardly. Gradually, through the summer and Arin's withdrawal into his own preparations, Magill sensed and resented the new distance between them.

He got up, slung his bow and prepared to use the rest of the day to hunt coon. He had a taste for the rich meat fried in its own fat and sided with greens and cornbread that might not be satisfied again before Karli. Kon and Arin watched him saunter off toward the forest.

*Magill feels away from me,* Arin shared, an action that was almost a luxury now.

*No,* Kon disagreed. *You're away from us. No more Three.*

*Why?*

*Don't know. Just feels different.*

"Kon, all the others had questions. You just listen and go along and don't say a thing."

"You said ride." Kon settled against the tree trunk. "So we ride."

*Stay close, Kon. Be the chain that holds them to me.*

His friend shut himself off for a space from Arin. Then the clouds in his mind dissipated.

*Long as I can,* he lepped.

And then one more joined the broken circle.

Singer caught it first, before she even came to Arin. Young. Deep rhythms, powerful but with a different strength from the others. Reason still unclear, but driven by some kind of need.

THERFOR

Arin rubbed his tired eyes and moved the candles closer to the page printed in Garick's bold script. He dipped his pen in pokeberry ink and lettered the new word again.

THEREFORE—IS LIKE—

Is like what? Means what? His pen hovered, then jabbed swiftly at the paper.

IS LIKE—SINCE THAT IS SO, THIS IS SO.

The lessons with Garick were mostly by lep, which tapped Arin directly into his father's superior knowledge and cut the learning process to a fraction of its normal time. It was this fact, rather than innate genius, that bred so many scholars among Circle folk in later centuries. With lep specialized to a learning process, knowledge could be absorbed almost as fast as a recording mechanism.

He laid the pen aside. The cool dusk beyond his open window was alive with wakening night sounds. Arin breathed deeply, relaxing as Edan had taught him to conserve and refresh energy. In the gloom beyond the island of candlelight, the door opened and two figures loomed into view.

Arin rose respectfully at his mother's presence. She was dressed simply, her sole ornamentation the iron moon-crescent that hung from her neck. Her auburn hair was tied back. Jenna strode to his table. The other, the tall young woman, hung back behind her.

"Girl wants to see you, Arin. Told her you've got no time, leaving day after tomorrow. You tell her to come?"

"All right." Kon had mentioned something about Elin that afternoon. "I told her, yes."

Elin stepped into the light. It was practically the first time they'd seen each other since the morning old Jay banged him while he was too sick to see it coming.

"Hey, Arin," Elin said shyly.

Jenna snorted and turned away. "Hell, kiss 'em all good-by, then." She leveled an authoritarian finger. "But get some sleep, Arin. These fool books got your eyes squinty as old Edan's."

The door slammed, punctuating her disapproval.

"Hey, Elin." He gave her a light, affectionate hug, realizing with a stab of sensual memory how much more beautiful than Shalane she was.

Elin's unbound hair tumbled about the shoulders of the fox cloak thrown over her robe, almost the same red-brown hue. No matter what she wore, Elin had a way of looking almost naked in her clothes. Her smoky, sleepy gray eyes appraised him now much as they had by moonlight or dawn on the hill. She pulled a chair close to his table.

"Well, don't you look fine, master Arin. Ain't said hey since—when was it?"

He felt awkward and kind. "When Jay left."

"Jay. Yes." Elin looked away. "Since last time on the hill. Been back there sometimes with Gill. It . . . I don't know."

He had to say it. "We're not together any more, Elin."

"Oh, hell, it ain't that." She smiled and waved the notion away so easily his vanity twinged. "Just–don't want to stay home any more." Reflective, a little sad. Then her sultry eyes lifted to him. "I can hunt and fight. You're short for lep."

? Though he knew what she was going to ask.

*Want to go, Arin.*

He read the flavor of her thought: strong, almost desperate need. Not for him, maybe not for anything Elin could name herself. She tossed the heavy hair over her shoulder.

"Nothing for me here. I'm nineteen since Leddy, and where I been outside Charzen? You got one woman, anyway. Teela." Elin made a face at Arin. "What log you find *her* under? Look like she never been inside a house."

"That's why she's going," he said. "You're more farm than forest."

"Hell, I can ride in my sleep."

"We all can."

*I'm a good lep.*

"Come on." He rose and went around the table to take her hands. "I'm glad you came. I don't have all the lep we need, but not you, Elin. You know Kon and Gill; rest are the same, half wild like deer. You're a home girl."

Elin tilted her head back to look at him. "All those times out on the hill and you never knew me at all." She was still smiling lazily up at him when the power slammed so hard into his mind that Arin blinked.

*Need to go!*

*Why?*

*Take me!*

Arin sat down again, considering. Her power wasn't a master's but much more than he would have guessed from Elin. He opened his senses and felt for the mind of the long-bodied girl lounging carelessly in her chair. The ease of manner was a mask. She'd always seemed close to the surface, easy to read. But now all was drawn back into shadow. Something—he couldn't shape it—was carving a different woman from the raw girl. Garick, who was more than tolerably wise, said once that you could always learn from women. And his band *was* short of lep . . .

"Come here, Elin."

They shared a memory of warmth without desire. He ran her luxuriant hair through his fingers.

"Didn't come for that, Arin."

"No, just you'll have to cut all this short like Teela."

Her sudden grin was like sunrise. "I can go? Real? I'll ride good, Arin!" She laughed and shook out the river of hair. "I'll cut it, but not like her. Look like she chops it with a knife."

Arin laughed with her. "She does. Teela's out in the kitchen now, with Sand. Go help them bake the pone."

Elin unclasped her fox cloak and slung it over one arm. "Help? I'll be showing her how."

"Don't talk at her too much, Elin. She's not used to it."

*Eight.*

Singer counted the last. Elin. Discounting the Sand-Teela unity, nine bodies in all, young, strong, the best of Shando.

He wondered how many of them would come back.

He walked to the table where his mother's notebook lay open. Not the one she'd left in Lishin, but a sort of diary of her thoughts and perceptions. Garick had kept it and read it more than once over the eighteen years since she'd died.

It was so long ago that she'd tried to hammer all of her wisdom and intent into Singer. Brilliant though he was, he was still too young to assimilate much of it, and at last, the complexity of her purpose grew dim in his mind along with the image of her. But the diary started to bring some of it back to the surface.

He shut his eyes and opened the floodgates of deep-buried memory. He tried to see Judith as she was before the sickness took her: the huge eyes in the narrow face, a storehouse of fun and indomitable energy, alert, quick, always a little absurd in homespun and skins.

His eyes skimmed the writing on the page.

*There is not one world, but millions. Every man is alone, a lonely planet in the Void. We are each a distinct cosmos, apart, an island of waking action between nightmare and dream. Yet each of us is subject to change from without and within, especially from within,* if we will it. *And what is change in one—*

"Yes!" Singer said aloud, excited. *"Yes!"*

*And what is change in one—*

The rest of the sentence was on the page, but suddenly it was spoken behind him in the sharp intonations that he had not heard for eighteen years.

". . . becomes history for the mass."

He whirled with a startled cry, vulnerable and unprepared. Sudden tears stung his eyes.

Judith stood in the doorway.

His throat contracted. He swallowed.

*"Mama?"*

Singer lurched a step toward her before the merest wavering of her image tripped his instinct, slamming a white barrier down on his mind. He glared at the open doorway.

Arin filled it.

"Little brother's grown some, Singer."

No more the gangling boy-man of midsummer, the rough-hewn substance of Arin had been carved by Edan and Garick into clear purpose, serene, poised and resourceful.

For whatever motive, Arin had skillfully tapped Singer's image of Judith and the words as he read them and woven them into a cruel, complicated eye trick. Even now Singer felt the tongues of power lick about the edges of his clamped will. The deceptive ease of Arin's lounging stance did not diminish the alertness in every line of his body.

Singer's throat was still tight. "You bastard. Why'd you do that?"

"Wanted to try myself against the best. Sit down; I can read that you want to."

"Stop trying to impress me." Singer dropped onto a stool. "What do you want?"

Casually, as Arin's will still probed for any weakness, testing the limits of Singer's strength: "So you're my brother."

"Garick's mistake, not mine." Singer eased into lep to keep the other's darting will occupied. *What?*

*Need what you know, Singer. Different places and men. Other ways. Tell me.*

*Why?*

Arin grinned. *Why not?*

Singer gradually relaxed. His brother was sincere, he wanted to be taught. "Why not?" he repeated, regarding Arin with a curious look, oddly shy.

In words and lep, he spoke of things he'd never told any other, of the places where the restless current of years had drifted him; of the iron-makers near the City and the north beyond where the masters talked through their noses and smelled of fish; how each people brought their own distinctive color or tang to shade Circle this way or that. As he talked, Singer grew more animated, enjoying the sensation of speaking, for once, with someone who was eager for what he had to offer, who didn't push him away, mentally or physically, or label him "misfit."

"How about Wengen?" Arin pressed.

"North or south? North, they're light as you. The further south you go, the darker they get. They talk more, brag a little, curse like a storm. Old Language had a good deal of color; their dialect's kept a lot of it."

"What about the merks?"

"What about them? For safety, you'd better stay in the deep woods. Shando are fish-in-water there. Ride clear of the merks. On open ground, you're no match for them."

*And the Kriss?*

Singer caught a word from Arin's mind and he guarded against an involuntary telltale stiffening of his spine. *Lishin.* He wondered how much Garick knew of Lishin, how much he'd told Arin. Most of it was lost. His mother hadn't remembered too many details, other than the proving of the truth of the Callee legends. Moss never spoke of it, Singer heard, though he hadn't met the Karli man in his wanderings.

*And the Kriss?* Arin repeated.

"Didn't see 'em. Never wanted to."

"Garick's going to pay them to join us."

Singer shrugged. "My mother went into their territory. She never saw them, either. But she barely got out alive."

"I'll see them," Arin said calmly.

"Sure, you'll dazzle the world." Singer was silent for a moment, then looked at Arin. "When you get to Karli, talk to Moss. He was with my mother."

"Moss?" Arin brightened. "I know his girl, Shalane."

"Well, talk to him. All I ever heard of Kriss is bad, not just superstition. Keep your men away from their women, I'd guess. And your two women—"

Arin stiffened. "You know who's in my circle?"

"Your broken circle," Singer corrected. "Yes. I know a lot of things. You've got plenty of worries already, and you're scared to death."

"Why do you say that?" Arin asked frostily.

Singer sighed negligently—bored. "Because it's all in your mind, along with the worry. You're as easy to get into as a crib girl's pants. And you're still *little* brother."

A flush reddened Arin's brown face. Singer *had* read more than he wished to share. He had come to learn, yes, and he'd enjoyed listening to the other, but partly, Arin had come to show him.

"You were always the best," he said bitterly, "you and that City mother of yours, always pushing me and Jenna back, so damn special. That's all I heard from Garick. He even told me he'd rather send *you*, not me—"

"I know," said Singer with languid superiority.

Arin got up and began to pace in agitation, taking care not to get too close to Singer. "Because I was nothing, that's what he told me, a dumb hide-shirt hunter. But I showed him. I almost starved the first week, thought I'd break with what Edan put me through. Thought my head'd split learning Old Language from Garick. *Thought*. But I didn't break, and my head stayed in one piece, and Garick don't . . . *doesn't* look down at me any more. I showed him." He stopped pacing. "Now I'm going to show you."

Singer yawned, his gaze remote. "Why?"

"Kon and the others, they're my people. I've got to be the best for them."

"How noble, little brother."

"Stand up!"

"All right, Arin." Singer uncoiled, rose from the stool, and as he did, Arin realized he was facing a master, alert yet relaxed, with no hint of imbalance. Garick had not lied about Singer's potential power.

They faced one another. Arin's will probed the suddenly charged air for the extent of the other's strength.

Even braced for it, he recoiled from the shock when it came. The flexible steel of Singer's will struck and coiled about him.

Arin tried to meet each twisting salient with an arm of his own, but there were too many. It was incredible; he gasped; the room blurred from his sight.

Arin was alone on a barren, featureless plain, alone at night, a dull moon shining friendlessly down. Alone. Not apart temporarily from Circle. *Alone*. The hideous vacuum of total isolation, of no connection with anyone, any other consciousness, smashed against him so hard he thought his mind would shatter. No Circle. No Shando. They did not exist. They *never* existed. He was so small, separate and stupid, drunk with the mere illusion of personal significance and—

*No!*

He was *not* alone. There was Singer, and he was battling him. This was Singer's isolation, the painful lost wandering, eighteen years drawn away, shred by shred, from any hope of home, of belonging.

And if it was Singer's loneliness, then Singer existed, and . . . and . . .

And Arin wrenched clear of it. The room returned. He redoubled his efforts in a frantic burst of power. At last he caught the faintest telltale, merely a quiver of Singer's hand, but recognized it as the first indication that his brother was now approaching maximum strength, nearly spent. Arin, who'd only allowed himself a passive role, gauging the measure of his opponent, still had his power husbanded; it flooded back and stored, mounted.

Now he pressed. Hard. Ruthless. One by one, the hydra-arms of power loosened, fell away. At last, Singer began to crumple in his turn, wilting, writhing sideways in empathy with his dwindling power store, even as Arin's continued to build and build. He did it with a cold absence of passion. It was necessary—for Kon and his folk. His magic was their lifeline, it had to hold.

"All right. Enough!" Singer gasped, tottering, slumping to the floor, rolling weakly on his back. "All right. You're . . . you're good, Arin."

Done without fear, anger or ambition, Arin asserted to himself. For a larger purpose.

He was ready.

The cool morning was red and yellow with early fall tints when Arin led his people into line before the god's hall.

Garick, Jenna, Edan, Tuli and the other masters ranged on the massive, worn wooden steps. Some of the Shando were gathered to see them off; not a large crowd. There was harvesting still to be done, so not many attended, though there were a muster of pigs snuffling and rooting about with no sense of occasion.

Garick surveyed them with an ache of pride. Their youth was like a sudden, soft hand laid on his heart. The radiant luxury of Elin's hair was clipped short but, refusing to lie close to her scalp, sprang out in a sunburst about her face. Teela looked skittish as her horse, still unused to crowds. She stood next to Sand, and they held one another's hands.

They all bowed to the antler crowns as the god and goddess came among them, while Edan and Tuli began the song that was taken up by the watchers, rhythmic and wordless, a wistful song of parting. Jenna presented the gifts: new green robes of finespun wool for the Samman fire at Karli. Tuli had sewn the customary Circle patterns into the hems in yellow, and each bore in red on the left shoulder a new insignia of Garick's device.

It was a broken circle, the sundered edges reaching out as if to encompass more than its allotted radius.

Then Jenna's wiry arms were around Arin. She whispered against his cheek. The flinty look he knew so well softened now.

Tuli cupped his face in her calloused brown hands, spoke her blessing and then Arin faced Garick.

"You know what to say to Hoban?"

"Yes, but . . ."

His father's hand rested on his shoulder. "Yes, son?"

"If I don't get back—"

Garick rode over the thought. "Then born again, Arin."

"To the Shando." He was glad for something to say to cover what he felt. Both men paused shyly, aware of their closeness. Garick embraced Arin.

"Go now," he said. "While they're singing for you."

Arin bowed again to the crown, then turned to his people. "Let's ride."

They filed out through the stockade gate. Elin, the last rider, turned to search the singing people's faces till she saw her mother. She raised an arm to wave. She would have ridden on after the others, but there was pleasure in the music and she paused to hear the end of it. Magill rode up beside her.

"Hey, slow'n-lazy," he said, "you comin'?"

"The song." Elin smiled. "Never heard it so pretty before." She wheeled and trotted through the gate. Magill swung his arm in a sweeping arc to Garick, whooped his lusty farewell and cantered after her.

They came down the high-spined ridges into the valley, increasingly alert as the last Shando settlements were left behind. The group fell into a natural fit from the beginning. Sand and Teela were Arin's advance eyes, slipping through the forest before the rest of them like the prow of a boat. The twins slept together, went forward before the others woke and were not seen again until Arin gathered them in for the evening lep to Charzen.

They all worked well together, except Holder, who tried Arin's patience, taking his sweet time when summoned, always with an airy excuse, always sure a better route lay higher up or further down. He would wander off on his own when he should be riding in tight on their flank with his eyes open. And he came close to a fight with the twins. Teela slept with her brother and no other man. In the tolerant coven way it was their own affair, like the hunters who sometimes preferred each other to women. Magill, refused by Teela, went off to curl up with Elin and forget it, but Holder pushed, and the twins would have slit him open if Arin hadn't stepped in.

"He's a boy," Arin despaired. "Wish he had half Clay's sense."

Kon summed it up. "You're a master, he's not. He can't take that."

Clay and Hara took discipline well, riding Arin's flank like slant shadows. Elin trailed behind with Magill and Kon shuttled back and forth as needed, taking as much responsibility from Arin's shoulders as he could. On his own shrewd initiative, he switched Holder so he rode under Hara's cool, no-nonsense supervision, and let Clay ride alone. It worked better then. Arin had enough on his mind without Holder always nibbling at his nerves.

Cook fires were rare and forbidden at night. When they did stop to eat, Elin fetched the wood and mixed the corn meal when their baked pone was gone, always managing a trove of horsemint or goldenrod for tea when they ran low. She fussed at how little Arin ate even if he *was* a master, and joked with the other men, giving them a little bit of home, a softness to temper the hard ride. Arin thought at first she might come to him at night out of habit, and was relieved to find that was dead for her, too. Magill slept with her now and then, and she was warm and comforting but not like the old, wild Elin. Her heart wasn't in it any more.

Three days . . . four . . . five. Sometimes the forest was a riot of red and orange, sometimes their horses' hooves whispered through miles of dull green jackpine over a deep carpet of brown needles with the high sun warm on their backs. Clay reported no sign of merks. It was an easy journey, but game was unusually scarce. Still, they weren't short for food, but the lack of fresh animal signs struck them as odd.

"Scared off." Hara raked reflective fingers through the loam near his foot. "It's rut time, should be scrapes all over. Saw one."

"What scared off a whole forest?" Magill wondered.

Arin sat cross-legged opposite them and let Hara and Magill measure their own thoughts. Hara was the oldest, nearly thirty, spoke little and only when he was sure of himself. There had been a farm, but Hara wasn't good at growing. The fields grudged a scrawny living, and then his woman died of a fever and the babies, too, because the masters could do nothing for them except to ease the passage to death, and the Jude woman wasn't there any more with her own magic against sickness as in Hara's youth. Their loss went deep into him. They were all that kept him on the land. After that, he'd drifted north and trapped with the Karli and Wengen, and at last the silence of the forest touched him and Hara accepted its solitude.

"Raised a buck and doe," he considered. "This time of year, old buck should fight anything that moves. Ran scared, but not from me. Something up ahead."

Arin looked up to see the wedge of geese honking south against the red underlining of a cloud. *Sand.*

The response was instantaneous: *?*

*Game signs?*

The boy's power murmured softly in his mind like a quiet brook. *Nothing. Still.*

He read no more from the twins all afternoon. At the gather-in, they squatted together munching pone. Arin had to ask, since they never spoke first. Sand licked the crumbs from his mouth like a contented dog. *No signs.*

Arin turned to Teela. Her pale eyes always seemed strange in contrast to the deep tan of her skin. He spoke gently; like an animal, she divined more of sound than spoken words.

*All run away.* She glanced at the others as if seeking their permission to speak, and said, "Something coming," then, ducking her cropped head in embarrassment, shared the wordless knowledge with Arin alone.

After the lep, Arin went apart from the others on the pretext of inspecting his saddle. He needed to think. They were getting close to Karli. There might be a hunting party out, of course—but what Teela imparted had no man-shape, no—

Arin's hand paused on the cinch strap. The truth suddenly weighed down on him. There was no room for doubt. He *knew* what confronted them, and was chilled by the knowledge. His instincts clamored for him to run, but his mind hushed them.

He could not tell the others, no matter how much he needed to share his fears. The dreaded thing was still no place he could point to. Any change in their route might still run them square into it. Best keep it to himself until the sense of it told him where.

If it had no shape, it had a name. Plague.

The next day was the beginning of the long nightmare.

Its icy breath blew on Arin in his sleep. He dreamed he was alone beneath a midnight sky pierced with the empty sockets of burned-out stars. Close by him, a cadaverous stag of enormous proportions stood; its skin clung to ribs that seemed bare bone in the feeble light of the waning moon. The animal's breath rasped unnaturally loud. After a time, the sound began to fade, and with it, the animal itself grew misty, dim, and was gone, leaving behind, suspended in the air, its enormous rack, the points too plentiful to count. But as Arin watched, the many branchings of the antlers crumbled, one by one, and also disappeared, leaving him alone with a profound sense of wretchedness within.

And then he hovered high in the morning air in a place old beyond counted years, but though it glowed with early light, it hid from him more than it revealed. It was *alive* with an unseen evil so immense that his senses tottered beneath the undefined impact. Far below, a murmuring of sludgy water, a river brown with acid, dung and death, stinking of all three. A rotting bridge. And somewhere else, approaching, a thing so hideous Arin's teeth began to chatter in fright. What it was he could not tell, but it was unwholesome, filthy and totally malignant.

Before the panic drove his reason beyond the point of endurance, Arin woke, cold despite the blankets and furs. Nearby, Kon snored peacefully, Elin a little further off. The familiar stars shone clear in the autumn sky, no longer the old friendly guardians of his sleep, but a million impersonal eyes that saw but did not see, looking down with crushing indifference on the insignificant thing that called itself Arin.

He raised his head, trying to catch at the companionship all Shando hunters feel with the unseen creatures of the forest, but that oneness, too, was gone. No spirit shared from tree to tree; there was no Uhia, only trees beyond trees choked in brush and thornbrake. The little things were still there, the tiny animals, but suddenly Arin could not understand why they spawned without pattern, living, eating, killing, dying not as a whole, but fragmented, divorced from purpose, thoroughly meaningless. A cold breeze that hinted of the nearness of morning whispered the forest leaves into syllables. He was a thing, Arin, alone, encased in a frail skin. Nearby, far away, another man slept in his own thin protection, and beyond a woman somehow not quite as frail, but still utterly alone, without a reason for being there except she wasn't somewhere else.

Lonely places—what did Old Language call those things?—islands. Islands lost in a sea of indifference. Or hostility.

That morning he rode alone, gloomy, unable to touch the others or share with them. When Holder replied to some minor question with his usual flippant impertinence, Arin dressed him down stingingly so all could hear, then sent him off on forward point where he'd be too busy probing the forest to mouth off.

"That smart?" Kon questioned. "Putting Holder on point?"

Arin replied a little too sharply. "Wants me to treat him like a man, let him take a man's worry. It won't kill him."

At least they were getting close to Karli, would be there next day or day after at the latest. He thought he might try a lep to them that evening at the gather-in.

*Hold up!* Sand and Teela together, urgent.

*Teela coming back.*

Responses from his other folk crowded into his mind. Arin lepped a gather-in, then moved forward to meet Teela. The broken circle clustered about her, all except for Sand and Holder still forward.

*Cowans,* she shared.

They strung their bows without a word.

*How many?*

*Three men. Sick.*

All eyes turned to Arin. He paused only a moment. They had to know. He had to tell them now.

"It's plague," he said flatly. *Sand, Holder. Come back.*

Cowan hunters—wandering groups of men—were one of the cardinal dangers of the Uhian forest. They were not Circle and lived by no law but their own. Without lep, never numerous, they weren't dangerous to a settlement like Charzen, but a small party could be outnumbered and killed for their superior weapons and clothing. Coveners avoided them, killed with reluctance when necessary. Circle was a celebration of life; killing ended it and was not lightly done. Every one of Arin's people knew this as they waited his orders.

It would be wrong to avoid the cowans. They'd die for sure, they all knew, but before then, they might pass on the sickness. *Maybe Karli has it already,* Magill thought.

There was the barest rustle, almost inaudible. Sand's horse stepped softly through the underbrush, and the boy reined up by Arin.

*Where's Holder?*

*Talking.*

"Who to?"

*Cowans.*

Arin's breath was an indrawn hiss. He vaulted back into the saddle. "All of you, stonethrow behind me. Come on!"

He urged the mare forward, fear like a cold lump in his stomach. He shouldn't have sent Holder on point. He did it in a moment of impatience, but he didn't think the plague was that close.

He sealed his mind from the others as the cold necessity stabbed at him, again and again. *The cowans have to die.* The horse stumbled, righted her footing, paced ahead swiftly.

*What about Holder?* No question; if he'd been close to them, touched them. *My fault!* Arin felt sick; he was glad there was nothing in his stomach. *My fault.* The sense of nightmare revived, he remembered the skeletal stag, the gaping sockets that once were stars, and wondered, briefly, coldly, why he should worry about a thing like fault. It was meaningless.

*Here.*

He caught Holder's lep as he broke out of the brush into an open glade carpeted thick with dry leaves that crackled loud under Soogees' delicate hooves. Tongue cleaving thickly to the roof of his mouth, Arin slowed the mare to a deliberate walk.

Three of them, like Teela said. They lay at the far end of the glade, filthy and tattered. His nostrils dilated in revolt at their foreign smell.

One slumped against a tree, but the others looked dead already, their faces far too dark for sun or dirt. Even at a distance, Arin could read the signs of pox on one face—the man Holder was supporting, arm around the slumped back as the dying man gulped from Holder's water bag. As the head tilted up, Arin saw the large, ugly boil on the throat.

Arin waited, not daring to let himself think or feel. The others eased up behind him, ranging out to either side, but though he could see them, Arin knew he could no longer touch any of them. Not then. Maybe not again.

His voice was lifeless. "Get ready."

Arrows rattled from their quivers.

Holder seemed oblivious to everything. The plague, to him, was an old man's dull story told by the fire.

*I found the cowans,* he lepped, but the look on his face told Arin more. I *did*.

Arin knew how Holder thought. He'd been ridden hard by the master ever since leaving home, now he had information important to the group, picked up from the dying cowan, and only Holder could tell Arin, show him up at the same time to the rest of the group. Who's important now? Arin or Holder?

Arin shivered, bleak and cold in the saddle. *Tell.*

A grin flickered on Holder's lips. "Was ten of them. Got sick north of Karli."

"Not *west?*"

"North. All dead but these. Too weak to hunt, got chased away from Karli." He patted the cowan's shoulder. "Don't worry about 'em, Arin, no trouble. Just wanted a little water and—"

"Holder," Magill murmured in a choked voice. "You goddam fool!"

"Huh?" Holder still had the quizzical look on his face when the arrow tore the man's body away from him. The cowan's body twitched once as it slid sideways out of Holder's arms. Before he could speak again, two more arrows struck the other two cowans. Holder gawked at his companions, the water bag dangling from one hand. "What . . . ?"

Arin pointed at the dead man near the boy's feet. "That's plague. You can't come back."

"Huh?" Holder stared at him blankly. "What you talking about? Barely touched him." He bridled at the look in Arin's eyes; worse, he misunderstood it. *You never liked me, Arin.* But then, with a sick comprehension, he read the solid wall of adamant minds. He was apart. Alone. He couldn't come back, not even the few feet that separated them now. Bitterly, he turned on Arin.

"All right, you finally shucked me. That's what you wanted. I'll go home."

Kon eased his horse forward a pace or two. "Can't go home, Holder. Can't go to Karli."

The boy's eyes fixed him with a wild look. "Where then? What—?"

"Got to be alone till you know you're clean of it," Kon said. "Ride out, boy."

"No." Arin's single word lashed across their minds like a whip. Kon understood it first, the full horror of the thing, felt for Arin's mind but it was shut off from him. Arin was as alone as Holder.

The others understood now. Magill's lips moved wordlessly. Clay shook his head, stunned. The twins looked like animals crouched to flee. The thing was unthinkable.

"I'm sorry." Arin snapped erect, bow bent.

Holder screamed.

The *thum* was loud in the clearing, even louder than Holder's scream. The arrow slammed him back against the tree, and even as it flew, Magill and Hara surged forward in a futile attempt to stop it.

*Back!* It was both Arin and Kon. Arin wheeled his mare against Magill's so that the two animals collided neck to neck. Kon nudged his horse smoothly into Hara's path.

The others sat transfixed with horror, Elin's eyes shut tight against the reality of it, the twins huddled together as Holder's legs gave way. Head and arms hanging limp, his body slid down the tree to an awkward sitting position.

Arin had killed within Circle, a thing so utterly inconceivable, there was no name for it. He faced his people.

"He would have killed us all. And more than us. We might've taken the plague into Karli."

Nobody moved.

"We won't bury him. We won't touch him. Let the forest clean itself."

He felt the blank wall of disbelief. Then the sharing wavered; Clay stirred, Magill unstrung his bow. They couldn't accept it all yet, Arin knew. He wondered if they'd obey him now.

"Sand, Teela. Out ahead like before," he ordered. "Clay on my left."

Glad for something physical to do, the three swung their horses about and moved swiftly away. None of them looked at Holder again.

"Hara out right. Magill, Elin behind."

The reins hung slack in Magill's fingers. He made no effort to move. Kon eased up beside him, gentle but firm. "Go on, Gill."

Magill sat with his head lowered. "Born again, Holder."

"To the Shando," Elin murmured.

"That's right," Kon affirmed in the same tone. "Go on, now."

Magill flipped the reins and moved off, followed by Elin.

Only Kon remained. Arin searched the homely, loved face, felt for Kon to share the agony, but his friend was closed off from him now.

"Where you want me, Arin?"

*Stay close.*

*Leave me alone.* Kon turned his horse and rode well ahead of Arin so they couldn't talk.

With Karli so close, danger was minimal. Because they badly needed something of warmth and cheer, Arin allowed a sturdy cook fire and worked staymagic on two possums for Elin to fry. They gathered after the meal for a lep home to Charzen. Arin sensed a certain gratitude in the others, especially Clay, to make contact with the full circle of masters. Magill sat a little apart, brooding, waiting to lep the news of Holder's death.

And the story pulsed forth from their gathering to the masters at Charzen: the cowans, Holder's blunder, Arin's sentence and his refusal to permit burial.

They waited for the masters to reply.

They didn't have to wait long. When it came, Arin knew immediately that it was not Tuli or Jenna or even Edan who generated such unwavering strength.

*Arin is the master,* Garick lepped. *Tend your folk.*

After the god had spoken, they remained by the fire listening to the chill, rising wind. They stared into the blaze, pressed close together like frightened hounds.

Chin on his knees, Arin searched for what they refused him now. Only in Elin did he feel a willingness to reach out, a pity.

She offered him the single jug of sida which all but Arin had shared since home. Magill watched as he accepted it.

*Would've been more if he listened to Holder.*

"Go ahead," Elin urged, "take a little more. You don't eat enough. It'll keep out the cold." Arin barely wet his lips. "More," she said. He took a good swallow and let it burn down inside. He wasn't used to it any more. Elin's hand found his. *Talk to them, Arin. Share.*

They looked at Arin when he spoke, his face so thin the firelight danced shadows and planes of light over the angles of his nose, cheeks and chin.

"Some things are hard to understand," he began. "This is a changing, a new thing. The god said to me, 'Tell the Karli, where we have been masters, we must now be kings. Where life was all, now we spend it for something more.' "

They looked as lost as ever. None of them knew what a king was, and what could be more than life?

"King's like a master," Arin explained. *And as lonely,* he thought, but he didn't share that with them. Another thought rose unbidden, but he kept that from them, too. *Only give them what they can understand. Don't drown them in fear.*

"We'll lep to Karli now, tell them we're here."

Willingly, they submerged their private doubts and worries into the oneness of Circle, massing their power behind Arin in the repeated call until the answering challenge came: *Who?*

*Shando. Garick's folk. Watch for us tomorrow.*

The answer reassured them; they were expected. Then: *What master?*

Arin paused. Something so new, something none of them understood, and led by one as confused as the rest, but already a little apart . . .

*What master?*

Then, surging above the confused emotions churning inside him, his power leaped into life, redoubling itself, channeling his doubt to will, power beyond the need, beyond anything Arin ever before had summoned.

*The master Arin—Garick's son.*

The great surge of strength startled his folk. Their heads lifted simultaneously and they looked at Arin as he stood over them and the farewell from Karli faded voice by voice until it was a single, exultant note.

*Arin! Arin!*

The fading voice still sang his name.

His throat tight, his heart pounding, Arin moved quickly away from the others into the darkness, leaning his head against the cool bark of a sapling.

*Arin!* Fading, but still joyful.

Shalane's voice.

Three years, but she hadn't forgotten. He wanted to cry with relief and happiness, but something prevented him.

He could still see Holder falling, falling, and the dying sound of

Shalane's welcome mingled with Holder's cry as the arrow slammed the boy and slammed him, again and again, against the tree.

Arin's breath rasped in his lungs like a sob. He realized he'd heard the sound before, in his dream.

Once, at his lessons, Singer asked his mother the difference between Shando and Karli.

"Garick's money," she said.

Perhaps for their peace of mind, the Karli were blessed in having no large money crop. They sold wool and some produce to Lorl and Towzen, but only their surplus. They lived unhurried, insular lives, rarely visiting, but farming, hunting and holding to the pure Circle way.

**Sometimes in a hard winter,** Judith wrote of them in her early days away from the City, **there is not enough to eat, sometimes the Karli sicken and die. But the recurring bitter experience never turns them sour. Life is their religion, so all-pervading there is no word for it except "Circle," and it includes hardship, suffering and death, and yet they have a sense of joy and oneness too deep to speak. One hears it in their song, sees it in the ceremonies of their fire-days when the general love-making—as much worship as pleasure—is so rigorous that Karli women would be continually pregnant if they were not tuned with uncanny precision to the cycle of their own bodies. And since even the rare miscalculations grow tall and healthy as the rest, it only serves to reassure them how beautiful life is. So sad, so perversely impressive. If they seem to us dirty, diseased and ignorant, we are, of course, right, but I notice that, like certain fashionable ancient paradoxical philosophies, it is possible to be a bit in error even when all conclusions check and verify and are thoroughly correct.**

The grizzled shepherd counted the horses picking their way down the last rocky slope beyond his meadow. Shading his eyes, he admired the animals—small head, long-limbed, built more for speed than endurance. An old tale said Shando horses came of stock bred for racing, as if a horse had no other work to do.

"Hee—ee-*ah!*" He barged through the milling sheep, waving the riders on. "Y'all hungry?"

"Damn if *that* ain't nice," sighed the saddle-weary Magill. Elin was too worn to look up.

"What? Food?"

"No. Someone smiling for a change."

All along their route, the Karli and their children met them with gifts of fruit, sida, chunks of cooked meat still sizzling, carried out of a cabin on sticks by a grinning girl. Now rhythms drifted to them, beaten out by many hands, intoned by as many voices. Still wary of strangers, Teela shied close to her brother, but Magill lazed along, one foot tucked up around the saddle horn, stickily sharing a jar of pears with Elin. In his quieter way, Kon was glad, too. The laughter and shouted welcome, the song swelling louder with each step, brought a little certainty back into his cosmos. Arin had shocked and confused him for a time, but Arin was the pole of his world. Kon could no more veer from that pole than old north star could up and fly south. Arin felt the rift close gently as they rode together in silence.

And Hara yelled to the trappers he knew, and Clay saw how the girls turned out in their Lorlcloth best, riots of garish, clashing color swirling about them. He noted which were the prettiest and most friendly, eager to be chosen for Samman night.

Teela marveled at the bright clothes. Clay said her new green robe wasn't a skin but hair from a sheep, but since she had never seen a sheep until today, it seemed nonsense. To learn still later that the stuff called cotton wasn't even hair but grew out of the ground, well . . .

" 'Strue," Sand verified. "It grows."

*Skin!*

*Grows! Arin said.*

*Goddam Shando.* Teela was darkly unconvinced. *Lie your ass blue, you let them.*

*Shando coming! Shando!*

The little girl clutched at her mother's skirt. "Ma, they got no faces!"

"No, no, they paint like the woods, same as dad when he hunts. Washes off."

Two riders, a man and woman, lanced over the last hill before the stockade, dashing toward the Shando. Arin's heart skipped a beat. The blond girl wore a white tabard over her hide trousers and bright red shirt.

"Arin!"

"Stay here, Kon." The grateful cry burst silently in Arin as he pushed the horse into a ground-eating gallop to meet her halfway up the rise, and still she was calling his name.

"Arin—Arin—"

Her long leg swung over the pommel as the other foot expertly cleared the stirrup. She was afoot and running to him before her horse slid to a stiff-legged halt. Arin swung down and met her open arms, and then he was holding Shalane tight, and they tried to talk but words were useless and the lep was so interwound, it was impossible to tell one from the other. Oh, he'd grown so tall, and her hair was thick now like Elin's—*Who's Elin? Never mind.* And she hadn't and couldn't forget him even though they met at the worst time in the world when she was new-pledged to Circle and . . . and everything, and her eyes weren't really blue at all but a sort of green, and he still remembered the whitish scar on her hand where old fox bit her when she tried to tame him, and how long would he stay? *That long?* There'd be days and days and days and nights, and she was so proud of his mastership, and he'd be staying with her and—

"Moss!" Shalane whirled, glowing, one arm around Arin as her father trotted up. *He's here.*

Moss leaned out of the saddle, hand open. "Hey, Arin. Old Garick still mean as ever?"

"And *then* some!" Arin grasped the offered hand.

While the others rode up, he waited with Shalane. In their excitement, the dignity of masters was haphazard and a little dizzy. The broken circle was presented to Shalane. She tried to remember names, seeing only their strain and weariness. Shalane spread her arms wide to embrace them all. "There's a place for all of you. But you're only eight. The Charzen lep said—"

The pain she caught from Arin choked the word in her throat. "Oh."

"Masters waiting at the hall," Moss drawled. "Think you can spare the time to say hey?"

"Oh-h, I forgot, Arin!" With a shout of laughter she was in the saddle again. "They sent me after you."

"Listen to her," Moss guffawed. "Hoban says send a master to meet them, and this one's on a horse so fast, old shadow got left behind."

All the way to the stockade, shouting *hey, hey* to women and dirty, excited children who made a lengthening tail to their party, Shalane rode at his knee until they ranged into line before aged Hoban and Tilda, the god and goddess, and the grouped masters of Karli. Arin bowed to the antler crowns and waited while the old man and woman looked through him and weighed everything he was.

"Have you brought us the knife, Arin?" Hoban asked.

"More than that." Arin spoke loud enough for the masters to hear. He swept his arm out to his Shando. Long after what he said was forgotten, the picture stayed with him: the last of the sun splashing the stockade court with fire, touching Elin's hair, ruddying Clay's face. "These are my folk. Garick's broken circle. Shando's best."

And he remembered another thing, a thought: *what if, like Holder, I have to kill them all? What sharing then, master Arin?*

Shalane entered the inner circle at sixteen, perhaps too early, it was thought, for a girl who bubbled with life like a kettle on a hot stove. Power was there to spare, and Shalane wore it like her tabard, always a little askew and tucked up into her cord belt to give her long legs their striding freedom. She had a talent for horses along with her other gifts and had broken much of the new Karli stock. In the saddle or without one, she grew out of a horse's back. Rearing or bucking, hugging the plunging neck or near flat along the rump, she could not be dislodged, and the vicious brute that tried to roll on her would find her gone and back again as soon as it regained its footing.

The youngest of four children, the others long since moved out with families of their own, she had her mother Maysa's round face and full mouth half-parted over prominent front teeth, but her coloring was Moss, light blonde, her skin darker than her hair most of the year.

Shalane had no shadows about her; she stood clear in the high noon sun, glowing with life, and the man who couldn't love her, Arin knew, was either dead or declining fast. When he returned to Charzen, she had to be with him.

He housed his people quickly—there was no lack of offers—and followed Moss and Shalane for a mile or so over the rolling, sheep-nibbled meadows, past Moss' well-kept fields where the corn stood shocked against winter, to the long, low house where Maysa waited at the door to welcome them.

It was not the cavernous hall at Charzen but warmer somehow. It was furnished with a surprising amount of Mrikan luxuries—glazed pottery dishes, metal lamps, fine but faded cloth tapestries and a large iron stove in the kitchen. Maysa was more grateful than proud for the stove, which Moss, in a flash of generous insight, had bought in Towzen. It cooked with an even temperature and saved her hours of work. Most of the things were bought in the beginning when Moss left off hunting, cleared the land and built the house.

"We were rich." Maysa fondled the memory. "We had twenty-five krets. More money than Karli folk ever see at one time. Moss made it all one spring."

Moss said nothing.

"In Lishin?" Arin prompted.

"Yes. He was sick after that. He was . . . away from us." A look from Moss; she shrugged off the distasteful subject. "We don't talk about it."

They sat down to eat in the wide kitchen, warmed by the great stove. Shalane and Arin took only the smallest portions and drank water though polite custom served an abundance and let the masters exercise their own self-discipline in meager choices. The talk was warm as the food.

"Two of you made us laugh, first time you met." Maysa shoveled more greens onto Moss' plate. "Lane stuck up there in the masters' hall and you ready to pop."

"Near had to tie them down," Moss chuckled. He looked at the young man with that elusive nuance in his expression that reminded Arin, for no apparent reason, of Singer. "Time is a good thing."

"Well now, what's that mean?" Maysa wondered.

"Oh, just they're older now, and Arin—remember how he was? Too damn lazy to wipe his mouth."

Shalane laced her fingers in Arin's. "He's tired, too."

The food, the sharing, the loving house-feel worked treacherously on Arin's fatigue. His eyes drooped already.

"I am tired, Moss. But sometime soon I need to talk to you."

"Any time. Morning's best. Like to watch the sun come up."

Maysa plunked the refilled bowl on the table and hugged Moss from behind. "Sure. Come sunup, there's old Moss out with the birds." She smiled over his shoulder at the young people and sighed with the pure fun of being. "Moss, I'm gonna get you half drunk tonight. Half, I said—"

He nuzzled her hair. "And?"

She bit his ear. "Then I'm gonna tear you up. Lane, take Arin in 'fore he falls asleep in his plate."

He remembered Shalane's room as being more amply furnished before her mastership. It was almost bare now with the usual circle marked out on the floor, open at the north end, to be sealed with chalk when she entered to work alone or generate power. Arin wondered what she would think of his own chamber at home, the traditional instruments of art buried under inkpots, lists of hard-learned words and the manuscripts Garick wrote out for him. A plain table held her cup and thammay and consecrated bowl together with several jars of herbs.

And her bed was no way big enough for both of them.

"Sure is." Shalane hugged him. "I sleep close."

Arin slumped down on the bed to remove his shoes. The fir-needle mattress scrunched invitingly under him as he watched Shalane. The candle flames shuddered in the breath of her eager movements as the tabard was flung over her head, followed by the shirt and hide trousers. Shalane stood proud and bare before him like a favored colt waiting for a caress. Living near-naked from Sinjin to Milemas darkened her fair skin to dull gold except for the meager pale strip about her slim hips. She helped pull off the rest of his clothes, then tumbled over onto the bed, arms and legs twining with his.

*Look at us, Arin. We're like morning.*

"You're really here." Her hand brushed down his stomach to rest between his legs, not hungrily, but savoring the journey inch by inch. But the weights were too heavy on him; he couldn't respond beyond a flicker. The beautiful, soft bed sucked him down, away from her mouth and thighs toward delicious sleep, the warmth of her like another blanket over him. Arin drifted, his muscles still responding to the phantom movement of the saddle, and Hara should be out on his right, the twins up front, and Holder—

The arrow smashed Holder back against the tree.

Arin jerked. His eyes shot open as he came back to time and Shalane. She laughed, a warm, contented sound deep in her throat.

"Wha'zzat?" he murmured.

"You," she whispered, "trying to stay awake just for me." She snuggled down beside him, mouth against his throat. Her chuckle vibrated softly through him. "You couldn't go in me now with thirteen masters helping you get it up. Sleep now . . . sleep."

He was the same Arin she remembered, but shadowed with a new element she couldn't define. Perhaps it was the forced speed of his pledging. Shalane didn't ponder on it. Being nineteen, healthy and untroubled as spring, she slept.

"Master Shalane!"

The young farmer paused with his arms on the well rope and waved to Shalane and Arin swinging hand in hand down the path in front of his cabin. "Y'all stop and sit," he invited.

"Can't, Jon," Shalane yelled back. "Got to get the boys and cut Samman logs."

Jon gave the rope another lusty jerk. "Morning, master Arin."

"Never saw prettier," Arin nodded. They waved again and disappeared into the trees.

Jon filled the bucket and replenished the iron pot into which Elin and his woman, Cat, were paring potatoes. Cat tried to ease herself on the specially cushioned chair, big with the imminent child. "Elin, give me some more. Got to get these done *some*time today. They always send Shalane," she grinned, her knife sending the skin curling away from the white meat, "because she sings stories to the boys while they cut and, hell, she ain't no older'n them herself."

Because of the child, Cat couldn't dance this Samman night as she used to, so she and Jon would stand and watch until her back got tired, then come home for a quiet meal. They wouldn't mind missing it because this turning of the year-wheel would bring the child-gift.

"Bet Elin will dance all night," Cat said, pretending she was telling true, but knowing it wouldn't be. The Shando girl helped her prepare for Samman willingly enough but with none of the normal anticipation. *Like me,* Cat thought, flicking a paring from her knife. *So many dances, so many nights on the hill. They're good, they have their time. But sooner or later, there has to be more than that. For some it's late. Some early. For her, it's now.*

"Girl—" Cat was barely older than Elin, but the house and Jon and the coming child entitled her to the difference. "You don't want to stay at the fire tonight, y'all come home with us."

Elin went on peeling. "Maybe I will."

Jon rested his head lightly against the swell of Cat's stomach. "Now, who was that you asked about?"

Elin plopped the nude potato in the pot. "Oh, I 'spect he might've rode through Karli after Sinjin. Sort of quiet, didn't smile much."

Jon considered. "There was a Wengen trapper. Real dark, kinky hair."

*No. White skin, real white. Smooth.*

*Wait.* Jon remembered. "Not too big? No beard, didn't sit a horse too good?"

"Yes." Elin's eyes for a moment lost their withdrawn, secretive expression. "Jay. His name's Jay."

Long before the sun touched the hills to the west, coveners drifted in couples and groups toward the ceremonial grove, a wide perimeter hewn out of the forest where oak, beech and walnut grew thickest. The people ranged themselves around the trench worn into the earth with centuries of Circle. Standing with Shalane, Arin saw how the green robes of his broken circle stood out in the sea of dun hide and homespun. Garick's subtle display of Shando wealth.

At the east of the perimeter, old Hoban and Tilda, the god and goddess, watched the sun's descent with their arms crossed. When the lower curve of the orb sat on the horizon, Hoban raised his arms.

"The year is done. The wheel turns again."

Once more the way between earth and the spirits that moved it was open for the reaffirmation of faith. Now the sun left his earthly house to wander as he must. Now came the shadowed time, the death from which, at Loomin, its darkest point, the sun must be wooed back to warm the earth. No one seriously doubted the summer would come again, but it served to refresh their connection with life—and perhaps old sun got lonely. Now the god Hoban became death, to be reached and touched like the sun at its furthest point before the return of the goddess with life and plenty. The dances, the symbolic joining of sky and earth by the male and female masters, all shaped to this need and truth.

Tilda pointed into the center of the grove. "Set my fire so I can come home."

Two masters stepped out, unwinding the long, knotted cords that belted their tabards. East and west from the grove's center they measured the circle to be cast, until they marked out a radius of thirty-six feet. In the center, the logs of the Samman fire were laid in nine tiers of nine sacred woods shining with the grease that would ignite them quickly.

The masters' thammays dug into the age-worn trench, tracing it sunways from north to north again with two parallel outer cuts until three clear new lines six inches apart encircled the waiting pyre. Salt and water were sprinkled into the trench and torches set at the four cardinal points. So with the four elements of earth, water, fire and air was the circle purified and ready to raise power.

They must go naked into the circle. Even as Arin thought it, Kon was at his elbow: "Keep your things for you, Arin."

"And mine." Shalane stripped off the tabard, clasping Arin's hand. "Let's go in together."

First thru the north gate, Hoban and Tilda took their positions in the east. The others formed from them around the inner perimeter until they made thirteen. One master remained outside as a courtesy to Arin that he might complete the circle.

Tilda raised her hoarse voice: "Sky fire, come to earth!"

The torch was thrust into the waiting pyre; the greased logs sputted and hissed. Little tongues of flame licked out from the bottom tier. As the crackling deepened to a lusty roar, the massed voices resonated on a single deep note rhythmed by soft clapping.

Shalane moved close to Arin. As she whispered to him, her small, oil-rubbed breasts pressed against his arm. "It's Young Girl. It's my turn this year." She squeezed his hand and stepped out to make one stiff-walking circuit of the fire. At the cardinal points, Shalane dropped to her knees, striking the ground with her open hand.

"Mother! Be big with life! Mother, be full of food."

The oil articulated the muscles of her supple body, the saddle-hardened inner thighs flexing as she moved, but her brown cheeks shone with more than the oil. Arin saw the flush of secret pride that he was watching. Again she bent to earth.

"Mother, let them find each other,
The buck and doe,
The bull and cow,
the rain and seed . . ."

The voice note shifted up, the clapping increased. Shalane let the cadence take her graceful movements. Again she wilted, supple as a reed, to earth, striking her hand in the dirt.

"Mother, give us back the seed."

Arin felt his mind flowing into the massed power of the circle, yet, as never before, a part of him watched from a distance, a kind of worm in his mind, a whisperer from the blind stars voiced what could never be shared with Kon or even Shalane. *When we've gone where we must, done what we have to—*

"Give us back the life."

*How much of this will be left?*

"Be full of food for Circle's need."

*Though this may be good, this may be truth and that girl herself a pang of beauty, the fire that will burn clean may be another fire.*

Arin willed the worm to silence. Now the deep monotone of the voices outside the circle became a song, more rapidly cadenced than before; against the long arc of the melody carried by the men, the woman-sound wove its counterpoint for the meeting dance, the touching of death before the return of the goddess. Shalane returned to his side, calm as if touched by a god, brushing across him as she took her place. Where their skin touched, it seemed to tingle, and by her new, undulant movements, she invited him into the dance with her. The music took Arin. He ceased to think, body swaying in exact unison with Shalane's, three times right and left they wove to the syncopated hands.

The masters began a spiraling, intricate passage toward Hoban, rigid and still in the east, a turning wheel snaking southward and leftways, weaving around and ever closer to the god until the first touched him and, turning, danced back sunways through the approaching masters—wheels turning on wheels within the wheel of life, their minds free of Self, reaching for and clasping the others as the music swiftened again.

A surge of hot joy shot through Arin as Shalane's mind folded into his. He spun, ecstatic. They were one, then three, five linked beings, and a swell of admiration buzzed among the watchers as Arin, Shalane and the three next masters moved for an extended space as one body, five mirror images, until each returned to his original point.

The music pitched higher still, now sharp and agitated. The power was a living entity in the circle, no minds but Mind, no many but One, woven with the music that surged to an impossible tempo and suspended suddenly, unfinished, crying for completion. In answer, the high-pitched resolution began among the women, sweet with promise, painful in its need, fading to silence as Tilda stepped out from the east of the circle to stand silhouetted against the fire.

This utterly silent dance was performed only twice during the year, at Belten and Samman. The coveners waited in hushed awe. Now and at no other time the masters displayed their powers: the dance of seasons, life—the goddess—generous, ready to be wooed and as ready to elude, cast aside and deny the men unskilled in her truths. Tilda dropped on her thick haunches. Her lep struck sharply through the coven's single mind.

*So I go now as Sinjin rabbit.*
*Catch me, catch me if you can.*

Her body flowed forward in a curiously nonhuman movement. The woman-figure shrank, blurred, distorted and was not. The rabbit's nose twitched impertinently at the masters. As one body, eleven masters crouched, stretched forward, bodies curved and elongated. Only Hoban remained unmoving at the circle's east.

*And we go now as weasel at Sinjin*
*To catch and bring you home again.*

The rabbit bounded one complete round of the fire, the line of weasels undulating after, when the goddess lep spoke again.

*So I go now as a deer at Lams.*
*Catch me, catch me if you can.*

The great, sleek doe lifted her delicate head to face her pursuers. Where eleven weasels had slunk across the flickering ground, eleven huge pack dogs waited. The hushed circle vibrated with their low snarling. Contemptuous, the doe wheeled and paced away, the air heavy with the musk from her hock glands.

Teela blinked; Sand's nose delivered its verdict. This was the truth of *dog*. Circle ceremonies were few and crude in wild Suffec, but *dog* was a dark reality. His sister would have run away but he caught her and shared her fear before it burst and poisoned them separately. They shrank close together, hands on knives, ready in a moment to run away. But then, firm hands were laid on their shoulders.

*Only the masters,* Kon soothed. *Look again.*

The primal howl lifted from the circle. The doe was gone. Limned against the fire the old wolf, heavy-haunched and gray-muzzled, sang its winter hunger and loneliness.

*So I go now as Loomin wolf.*
*Old wolf cries in the Loomin dark.*
*Catch me, catch me if you can.*

"See," said Kon to trembling Teela. The masters stood as before, eleven of them ringing the huge animal.

*And we go now as Circle men*
*To bring the goddess home again.*

Eleven masters moved in on the trapped wolf, eleven arms raised and swooped down to clutch the rough hair. Then Tilda herself was raised up, her bronzed arms lifted over them all.

*And I will come home again.*

"Dogs," Sand hissed. "You didn't see?"

Kon patted his shoulder. "I saw."

Teela glowered. *Dogs took our folks. Scared.*

Kon held them close to him, raw and incongruous in their rich green robes, like foxes tangled for a moment in a sack before they tore themselves loose.

"Me, too," he told them. It was a lie, but they loved him a little for it.

*Listen.*

The sun was gone, leaving only a thin red line over the western hills. To the east, first stars winked clearly as the poignant, yearning chord lifted again among the women, and the female masters formed an inner circle about the fire. At the first rap of the hand rhythms, they wove forward toward the now supine men for the marriage of sky and earth.

Arin saw first the unbound hair hanging about Shalane's face and shoulders like the mane of an untamed mare. Her body was cut sharply out of darkness against the firelight, but where the light licked about her sides, the sweat of her exertions mixed with oil sheen. They had moved side by side in the dances, touching again and again, an arm or leg, each contact stinging with their need, till it was a secret, aching awareness between them. Though this was symbol only, he couldn't avoid being ready for her. He lay staring at the deep blue canopy of sky and stars, while his every fiber strained toward Shalane.

The music altered subtly, rising a half-step, begging for completion. Shalane crouched over him. Her face, dim in silhouette, still shone with oil and sweat. Her hand felt hot on his loins as she found him. When the throated chord rose to a resolution, Shalane put him in her.

Arin gasped; she answered with a tiny smile barely visible in the shadow of her hair. Usually there was no entry at all but a mere touching of loins, but in entering her, Arin found her as ready as himself and felt the small, bee-sting urgency begin of itself. Needing no movement, the convulsion grew, lashed upward by the stimulation of her deep muscles, which clasped and unclasped him in secret. He groaned deeply and his nails raked the earth. The pulsing grew to a delicious agony, burst and trembled away in helpless release under the gentle, inexorable milking of her still body. Shalane bent low over him; for a moment her hair made a fragrant private place for the two of them.

"Sky and earth," she murmured.

But the doubting worm in his mind whispered, *This may be the last. This may never come again.*

*No!*

Too late he tried to lock it away from her. Shalane caught the essence of it. Confused, she pulled away from him slightly. "Arin?"

He caught at her hands. "Not you. Not you, Shalane."

But for a short, cold breath of time, she had been joined to a stranger.

With the marriage of sky and earth, the circle dissolved in a rush of shouting, laughing coveners. New logs were stacked on the flagging fire. A savor compounded of delicious aromas floated from the long tables at one end of the grove. Meats aged and hung for a week in a special shed by a shaded, cool brook were sliced in inexhaustible portions onto wooden platters—venison, pork, chicken, coon, dark possum sizzling in its own fat, gamey squirrel on spits, yellow corn ears stacked in gold pyramids and basted with meat drippings.

At cold, dark Grannog when the lean belly digested dried peas, let it remember this night's feast and the goddess earth's never-broken promise of more. This was a night for the enduring truths of life—worship of the earth, love and abundance. For tonight, it was the succulent meats and the strange bread baked of rye, wagon-jolted all the way from Lorl along with fine white flour dearly bought at Korbin's and mixed with eggs, butter, milk and the almost mythical stuff called *sugar*—and baked into cake beside which the freshest bread paled in taste to sawdust, and scarce as it was, given with a hug and a kiss to the children. And so the Karli celebrated Samman.

The firelit grove was awash with raucous joy, the clatter of knives on plates, the *poonk* of unstoppered jugs. Magill blurred on past Arin, hooting, a girl under each arm; Hara had found a jug and a stocky sheepherder woman more than half Wengen by the black hair and olive skin. She knew her father only by name and tales, a trapper who wintered once in Karli before the forest took him at last. Gannell he was called.

Arin and Shalane shouldered through the crowds to a table. Laden plates were offered, but Shalane took only two cups of water and two small pieces of pork as their part of the feast. She grinned up at Arin.

"I'm all sweat, Arin. Wipe my face."

He took a clean cloth from the table and, as he smoothed it tenderly over her cheeks, Shalane cupped his hands against her, pulling him close. "I can still feel you in me."

The music began again, a few ragged voices at first, but quickly grew to the accompanying hand rhythms. Shalane started to lead Arin out, but he pulled her back. "You don't want to dance now."

She read the need, open and happy as a child. "No. No." She was already pulling him away. "Let's go home. I made juice for when we get back. Apples and pears and things."

Beyond the island of light, she broke away from him and ran laughing, her long strides noiseless in the dry grass, no sound but the rustle of her tabard. Arin followed, not as sure of the ground. Once he fell jogging pell-mell down a hill following the faint wraith of her white tabard bobbing toward the small wood and home. They bounded up the steps, through the door, and then clung together, panting and a little silly before Shalane lighted a candle.

Moss and Maysa were still at the grove; the house was quiet. Shalane filled two cups from a jug and brought one to Arin.

They lay down on the narrow bed, sipping the drink. Senses sharpened by habitual fasting, Arin fancied the trace of some taste beside fruit; violet petals or perhaps cowslip—he wondered if she'd put love herbs in the jug.

Shalane traced a finger along his cheek. "I don't need magic to hold you."

*You read that?*

*Sometimes I can. I'm so close to you.*

They undressed without parting, careless of where the clothes dropped, and wound together beneath the blankets. A warmth not quite like drowsiness stole over Arin. The periphery of his vision narrowed. The room and the candle were there, but dim and chimerical. Only Shalane was vivid, with the shadows that flitted across her parted mouth and the urgency that drew him on even as she held him back. Lashed by his own need, he was surprised to be held off like this. With Elin or others, it had always been a simple, animal thing. Shalane would give herself, but it was like Garick's gift of a manuscript that must be read from the first page slowly, with mounting clarity and excitement until the clear, joyous realization of its entire meaning.

"Give me your hand." She guided it. *There. Like that.* "Don't hurry." *Please don't hurry.*

There were gates to be unlocked, places to be explored—and the keys, she taught him, were his own hands and lips.

*Yes. Like that.* Her hand stroking his hair closed on it in a cruel grip. "Kiss me." *There. Yes.* "Yes . . ."

She taught him the pleasure of pleasure given without taking, not teaching him women but the one and many truths of herself before it blended into his being for good, and Shalane thrashed twice in her own deep convulsions before her trembling body clasped him with strong legs and fingers that trailed red welts down his back as he entered her deeply.

She drew more than his body into hers, she called forth his spirit, and with the need for her and the mercurial lep that bound them closer than flesh, he shared his pain. In the middle of love, they talked or shared; in the middle of talk, there was love to be made. Into the open, welcoming vessel that was Shalane, Arin poured the agony of his doubts, the loneliness yoked on him by Garick's mission, the recurrent horror of Holder falling back against the tree, forever dying and never dead. Joys, terrors, small wisdoms never shared even with Kon were passed to her and from her into him until, in the way of their kind, each was totally permeated with the other, filled, fulfilled. They drifted across the night in small wonders. Again and again, when they thought there could be nothing higher, they soared beyond it with no descent between ecstasies, weightless birds resting on mere clouds as they hungered higher for the sun.

The moon went down and still there was no sleep. Moss and Maysa came home from the grove, riotous and musical, mellowly boisterous with sida and thunderously in love. Arin and Shalane giggled like children under the blankets, happy that happiness extended beyond themselves, encompassing those they loved, too. And *yes*—as they drooped at last toward sleep—*yes,* she would come to Charzen, when Arin's mission was done. She'd be with him; she *was* with him.

*There's nowhere else*. She kissed his fingers.

But the worm in his mind murmured, *There's Lishin.*

He pushed the thought away, angry that the heavy burden his father put on him would never entirely cease to weigh him down. For once, though, Shalane was too flushed with her own happiness to pick up the transitory shadow within Arin. She stretched on her knees and elbows like a cat, sniffing with delight at her hands and arms.

"I smell like you all over. I don't want to wash you off me."

She settled down at length, one arm over him and one leg between his, pulling the blankets over them. The candle was long burned out, and the morning crept in at the window as Arin sank into the first real rest he'd had for long months. At last, there were no doubts, not here in Shalane's arms, no Holder, and the worm was stilled.

But on the brink of sleep, the last light of impassive stars looked down on him, cold and foreign and small.

The days with Shalane were happiness itself, but Arin watched the sky. Trappers took pelts thicker than in a run of years, the harvest corn was heavily husked, squirrel nests burst with hoarded nuts—all the signs of a hard winter warned him to be north with the Wengen before snow closed him in.

"We ride soon or not at all," he fretted to Shalane. "Dammit, your masters saw the cowans; they know there's plague, and what I do? I sit and wait while Hoban thinks."

Shalane yearned to help him. She didn't understand all of Arin. She accepted that; sometimes an enticement, but now a pain. And she could tell him nothing. The lamps burned late in the masters' hall, but she and the two other young masters were not included. She listened to Arin's arguments, the undeniable need for an alliance against City, to get in, to get help. As he had tapped Garick's knowledge, so she imperfectly absorbed his.

*If I said fight, Lane, would you come?*

*Yes, Arin.*

"Would you call the Karli to follow you?"

She hesitated, serious. "We're life. You want us to put our hands in death clean up to the elbow."

*Would you?*

"Yes. If it went to the knife, I would." *But wait for now. Be with me.*

He waited with Shalane. Every day their spirits laced tighter and deeper, and every day the sun rode a little lower at its zenith. The red leaves dulled and fell, crackling dryly underfoot. Magill grumbled. Cat's baby was born. Clay rode off on his own to scout merk signs and found too many; they were stepping up their raids. Arin waited. The blue and gold of the land went gray with autumn rain.

Arin woke at first light to the anger of a wet bird piping its pique to the sky. Shalane's arm moved in sleep to encircle him. It was chilly in the room. He heard the hiss of rain, not hard but steady. There would be no warmth at all today. Old sun was halfway to Loomin. Arin yawned and burrowed back into the hollow of Shalane's throat, warm and smelling of last night's love. The musk and sweat of both of them mingled heavy and rich in his nostrils, lulling as the whisper of rain, and he might have fallen asleep again—

But someone else was thinking of the rain.

The thoughts leaked to Arin's mind, irritating as a trickle of cold water down his back, flickering in and out, troubling, troubled. Arin sighed and slipped from the bed into his robe and shoes. He found a moody, cheerless Moss in the kitchen. The quiet, gentle Karli was feeding wood to the iron stove. Fresh herb tea steamed in a kettle. Arin poured some.

*Matter, Moss?*

*Don't like the rain.*

Strange thought from a farmer, but Arin had seen Moss like this before.

*Can't help it.* Moss' eyes, the mirror of Shalane's, were shadowed with an indefinable expression Arin had noted earlier. The rain seemed to haunt him, like bony fingers tapping on the walls. Thoughts hard to lep. Arin opened himself, felt at the closed door in Moss' mind. It was a grim darkness.

*Lishin?*

*Yes.*

Arin swallowed some of the pungent tea. "I've wanted to talk about that."

"I know."

"From here I go to the Wengen, then to the Kriss. Garick wants them with us. I've got to get into Lishin, too."

"Getting in is easy," Moss said quietly. He shook his head. "Don't."

"Have to."

"So did Jude." Moss' gaze found ghosts in the shadowed corners of the room. "I carried her out. I *guess* I carried her. Hard to remember."

*Let's talk about Jude.* Arin passed to lep for ease and speed. Jude never told Garick much about Lishin, only that the Girdle was real. Maybe she couldn't remember too well after the fever, the deep shock of rejection by City and the fact that, after the first few years, she knew she was dying. But Garick needed the Girdle. Without it, whatever else the covens did—even crushing the merks if they had to—was an arrow without a head. Jude might have told more to Singer, but *that* bastard wouldn't help Garick if he was on fire, except maybe to fan the flames.

*But Singer told me one thing. See Moss at Karli.*

Moss nodded noncommittally.

"Jude's papers must still be in Lishin. Papers and a map marked with three circles, that much Garick knows. What happened to the papers?"

*Long ago. Don't remember.*

Moss looked down at the table as Arin's mind clamped over his own. *A big room. Hollow iron boxes. Full of dust and ash.* Arin shared the picture filtering faintly down the years, saw the vast, gloomy chamber, a frail woman swaddled in her blanket, tottering with fever.

*The papers, Moss?*

*—put the papers back in the iron box, shut it.*

*Where?*

*Don't remember.*

*Yes you do.*

*Can't!*

*Nothing is lost. Think, Moss. Think!*

Moss' body writhed in painful recall. Gannell called and Arin tasted the growing rebirth of animal fear, and yet he pushed the Karli even further.

*Arin, stop.*

But there was no more picture, only the memory of a sound growing swiftly as Moss-Arin tugged at a door, pulled it shut on night that covered the rest.

*Arin, stop!*

It was cruel to push Moss any more. The man was shaking, and when he looked up at Arin, there was a cold distance between them. The sibilant rain whispered under the crackling stove.

"Can you draw me a picture of that house?"

Moss' head went up and down in pathetic assent. Suddenly, it was hard to read him. He was a page with great holes torn out of it. He rose and hulked over the stove, more to evade Arin than anything else. When he finally spoke, the farmer sounded frail and faraway. "What Garick's made you . . . what Garick's made you, it's not all Circle. May not be all good, Arin."

*I know.*

They drank their tea in silence. Moss tinkered with a piece of harness that needed no mending. "There's a little room," he said after a long time. "Opens off the big one. I'll mark it on your goddam picture. That's where I hid the papers when I left. You go to Lishin, you find that room." He paused, drifting with that curious, cold distance. "Never get too far away from it." Moss hurled the harness into the corner with a vicious jerk. "Never."

Shalane brought the god's summons later that day, shaking the rain from her sodden cloak, glum as the weather.

"How many for me, Lane?"

"Me." She slipped the tabard over her blue robe, knotting the cord about her small waist. "Deak and Bern, the other young ones. *We* think you're right. There has to be change."

"And the rest?"

"They'll listen, Arin, but don't expect too much."

She was right. He could feel it in the way they waited for him, a formal semicircle of benches on either side of the dais on which sat Hoban and Tilda, their old heads weighed down with the antler crowns. Shalane sat on the right wing between Deak and Bern. Their smiles were encouraging but a little too brave and not very full of hope. Arin bowed to the crowns and waited for the god to speak first.

"Master Arin," said Hoban, "we know Garick. Karli and Shando arc like one coven. But Garick has raised himself to a place where his mind reaches beyond Circle. This frightens us."

"We know there's plague," Tilda's rusty voice cut in. "Plague comes and goes. How do we fight it? How does war with City help us?"

Arin answered carefully. "Garick doesn't want City dead. He wants it open, helping us."

"That's fine," one grizzled master observed, "but how? Garick says go to the knife, but war with City means war with the merks."

Hoban finished the thought. "And that means different things to them than it does to us."

A profound difference, Arin knew. To the merks, war was a man's job and, perversely, a man's pride. Fear of death was for women. In the equality of Circle, it meant not only men but women and even children over twelve, riding and risking alike. It meant a dirty, prideless task like removing garbage that everyone shared to be done with and never spoke of or glorified afterward. This was the peculiar realism of Circle. Arin would not change it.

"Merks are trained and paid for war," the god went on. "Would we fight and run as we always do, taking one or two here and there? How long could we do that, Arin? The day would come when all of us faced all of them, farmers and hunters against trained soldiers. They only have to hold us off, while we have to win or be wiped out. The time would come when one of us would ride down the line with his thammay raised, and it would go to the knife."

"God Hoban," said Arin. "There are more of us than them. We can win."

"We lose either way, master Arin. Lose the fight, what is left? Win, and where's Circle? Life ending life, a dog eating his own guts to stay alive, coveners learning to get by killing—for *what?* Winter passes, so will the plague and the merks. There's no danger we haven't lived with for a thousand years. City's silence? It's an understanding between them and us. Their soldiers don't attack. Unless we ride."

Arin interrupted. "Hoban, the merks have been riding further and further west into Uhia. They kill our folk for no cause."

Hoban demurred. "Even if that is true—"

*"Even—"*

"Master Arin, we see no hope and no need in this war."

Tilda spoke now. "Who knows what City is or wants? Jude came and lived with us. She learned our ways and helped us. Few of our women have died birthing since then because of the magic and washings she showed us. Is this my enemy, Arin? If I ride, show me my enemy."

They waited for Arin to speak. He glanced at Shalane, her wet hair pulled tightly back in a strip-and-pin that accentuated her tautness and worry. He gauged the temper of the masters. So far from being frightened, they weren't frightened enough. How do you move men to anger who have always been strong enough to live without it?

"Masters, men walking over a bridge would stop anyone from cutting it out from under them. How different is the man who comes day after day, year on year, to cut one sliver and draw one nail from the wood until it falls? The merks are City's hands cutting our bridge. Every year there's more of them west of the river boundary. They *do* attack. They do City's work a little at a time."

The young master Deak rose from his seat beside Shalane. "Last year they killed a whole train of Wengen farmers."

"Yes." Shalane raised her voice. "Eighteen men and eleven women. And three babies, goddess. For nothing, for no reason at all."

"Yes!" Arin spun gratefully, glad for their voices. "But not for nothing, Lane. For money. City pays the merks to be a sore in our side, to keep us bleeding a little all the time." He ran his eyes over the masters, making contact wherever he could. None averted their gaze. "They get so much for every dead covener. Like beaver pelt." He paused to let it sink in.

Hoban spoke, his voice betraying shock—*good, I've made a hit!* "Arin, where did you hear a thing like that?"

"Garick learns things," Arin said simply. "If his mind goes beyond Circle, as you said, is it strange for him to learn what happens outside it? Yes, they're paid so much a head. A grown man brings two krets, a boy or girl under twelve brings three. Young women, four."

There was a murmur among the masters quickly stilled. Arin pressed the point. "That makes you think: less for a man than a child that won't grow up, and the most"—he jabbed a finger at Shalane; close as they were, he felt her flinch away from it—"for the three or four children she won't bear."

Shalane stood up. "That's enough for me. I say we should ride with the Shando."

The young man who had spoken before rose and joined Arin in the center of the room. "Arin, I'm Deak. I've trapped north; I've seen merks kill." He turned respectfully to Hoban. "And I know how thin-spread they are around City. Maybe four thousand, no more."

"No more." Shalane bobbed up again to make a third before the older masters. "Four thousand against five thousand Shando and 'most as many Karli."

"Two thousand Suffec," Arin added.

*And who knows how many Wengen—*

*Three to one!*

"*If* we move as one," said Arin. *Even more with the Kriss.* He locked the thought away, but Tilda turned on him her sudden, sharp glance.

"Against four thousand!" Deak pressed.

Hoban was not impressed. "If there were just four, I'd still say no."

"We've said no too long!" a new voice protested.

A youth lunged energetically off the bench, squaring himself beside Arin in three long strides. Arin sized him up: Bern—half Wengen. With an open, emotional nature and a vitality impatient at anything but the root of truth.

"Too long, god Hoban!" he said. "I love Circle and the life it respects. But I want more than that. I love the goddess who brings summer home, but I don't want my children shivering hungry while they wait for her, or sick and dying before they've lived a year, or full of sores because magic like the Jude woman brought can be had only in that *City* that don't even know we're here and don't care. I want to see with their lamps that don't need oil or fire, and learn things—I don't know—things that just might make Circle even stronger. Living isn't enough any more, Hoban. I want to *grow*."

"Like creeper vine?" the god asked calmly. "Until it kills the tree it feeds from and dies itself?"

"Hoban," Arin jumped in to back his new supporter, "can a tree stop growing without beginning to die? Could I stay a boy and not grow just by wanting it? I thought so once. I said Circle can't change, but it *has* to now. It's ready. We call ourselves masters, but masters of what? Can we feed hungry people in a bad year, save the babies like the Jude woman did with her pebbles out of a jug? When the stomach pains come and split the belly and kill in a week, what can we do but cool the fever and dull the hurt? Can we slice into the sick body with our thammays and cut out the pain? Why have so many of our women had one child live and the rest born dead? The Jude woman knew. She said there was a sickness in our bones, the inside of the bone, that could be cured with City pebbles. I don't understand it, but City does. They know how to live four, five times as long as we do, maybe more. Jude was close to four hundred, I heard."

"And lived less than ten years when she left City," Tilda reminded him. "Good and brave, but I never saw a sorrier woman in my life. She wasn't made to live in a real world."

"But she knew our world." Arin's eyes darted from one to another. "She knew the past, *our* past. What do we know about who we are, where we come from, except the song-stories? City has books, miles of them and—" There was no word in Uhian for *machine*. "And boxes with memories like a man that remember everything. That's what *they've* got."

An old woman stood up. "Who cares what they've got? Are they like us, boy? Are they Circle?"

Arin's exasperation was building. "Circle is just people—"

*No!*

*More than that, Shando!*

*More!*

It was wrong; he had stepped on them instead of elevating them. A tide of lepped and spoken denial surged over him from the elder masters, the things they had held back out of courtesy. *Garick's too rich, more like a Mrikan every year.*

As with the time Jay knocked him down, Arin felt his own anger surge, peak, then simmer, ready to burst. And then a flow of cold, competent power flooded over him again just as it did on the road to Karli.

"Just people!" His voice crested over the clamoring masters. "People who live one way. It's my way, but like one of my father's trees, I'll cut a branch I need, to help the tree grow. Masters—" His extended finger swept in a line over all of them. "Goddess Tilda was the first to speak of Jude. Listen to what Jude told Garick once when she was still with him. In the beginning of the world the leaders were like us, masters of small covens, doing magic for their people the same as us. But the covens grew and so did their needs, and the masters learned that magic wasn't enough. They became kings.

"This is what Garick says. It's a time for kings *now;* time to be a people, not just coven; time to shake City wide open, bang on their door and say, Here we are! Shando, Karli, Wengen, Suffec, even Kriss, the whole, hide-shirt, pig-sheep'n-apple load of us. *Here we are!* No more merks, no more Self-Gate. Look at us! *See* us! Help us, and maybe—like Jude—the great City just might learn from *us.*"

The burst of power awed Shalane. Part of Arin, so new to her, was still a stranger, though she was bound to that as to the rest of him. Deak and Bern were affected, too. He was their only rallying point on the floor, a lonely island off the disapproving mainland of the older masters. The lengths to which they must be committed to Arin frightened them, even as they were securely bound to his revolutionary position.

Hoban set aside the heavy antler crown. Seventy-eight, coming at last to that heaviness which forest life held off to the very end or sometimes altogether, he lumbered down from the dais to confront the four young people.

"You're not fools. You're masters. But young ones. At your age, who can imagine he isn't always right? You talk of change. This thing is changing us already. We're nine fighting four of our own." He touched the scarlet device on Arin's robe. "Broken circle. That's just the start. Like that tree-sucking creeper, if you win, you'll get everything you thought you wanted—and pay for it with everything you are."

Arin's worm whispered that Hoban was right, yet the young master drew the sheaf of thick papers from a pocket of his robe. "The merks are paid. Garick will fight money with money. Twenty krets to every master if you join. Twenty more to every Karli rider."

Shalane couldn't breathe, excited and ashamed at once. The money was a living thing in Arin's hand, more than all the Karli's farms and sheep could make in a year, more money than existed anywhere. With twenty alone, she and Arin—no, a master shouldn't think that way. Her family were never as hungry as some others; they'd even shared out in bad years. Still, the bright reality of the money burned her eyes; the thoughts came, hard to push aside.

Hoban contemplated the money. "Garick means it."

"Sure as frost," Arin nodded. "Every half-kret in his house, every apple on his trees for this year and next. And the next. As much as Lorl will lend him."

Tilda exploded in a rasping, mirthless laugh. *"More* changes. Now we bargain like Mrikans? We fight their merks and they lend us the money for it? Not even Garick could work *that!"*

Arin smiled; it was a peculiar smile. His half brother might have noted it sourly as the beginnings of sophistication.

The Karli knew less of Lorl than his father, Arin thought. Its heart was a stack of bills. You could buy men there as easily as a crib girl. They sat on the side of issues, fat frogs watching the dip of the scales. "The sida mills go with the money, Tilda. Garick wins, they get paid. Garick loses, they take his land."

Like an old, forgetful bear, Hoban shuffled back to the dais and placed the money on the arm of Tilda's chair. They shared privately an old knowledge of Garick: *all brain, but a heart you could drop in an acorn shell and hear it rattle. Gets what he wants because he always pays the price.* Maybe if Jude had lived, he would have been different, but men warped with the world. Hoban leaned close to the goddess. "I bought Garick a knife in Lorl once. Bad lesson. Now the bastard wants to buy me."

One reflective finger tapped at the stack of krets. Twenty of them would buy a lot—good clothing, axes, plows—or a lot of death. Hoban picked up part of the packet and chucked it in a spinning arc at Arin's feet. "There's my share."

Tilda rose, peeling off a sheaf of krets. "And mine."

The other masters stood one by one.

"And mine."

"Mine, too."

"Mine."

Hoban lifted the crown and fitted it over his white hair. The god and goddess stood gravely side by side.

"Tell Garick," said the god, "the masters of Karli will talk with City any time City wants, but we won't kill one farmer to do it. If that's what it takes, the Karli say no."

—CANT MAKE THEM UNDURSTAND HOW MUCH WE NEED THIS. BUT SHALANE AND SOME OF THE YONG MASTERS ARE WITH US—

"That's you, Lane. That's your name."

"Well, lookit that. Hoo-*ee!"*

Draped over Arin's shoulder, Shalane divided her attention between his ear and hair which were her rightful playthings, and the puzzle he was making on Maysa's kitchen table. Arin called it a letter. Shalane thought it decorative but pointless; wasn't lep quicker?

"Quicker, sure, but it can't say half of this." And, thus written, he knew, no one could read it but Garick. Arin worked on. He had seen Moss and made his map of the weapons house. Clay found fresh, iron-shod hoofprints two days north. Merks. Arin passed on the boy's canny observation in his letter. The curious thing was, in all the time he rode as a merk, Clay neither received nor overheard any actual order from City dealing with covens, other than the standing command to keep the neutral zone clear of settlers. No direct order to attack or harass. The kill-word and money, when they came, were transmitted by a young officer named Callan, but there seemed no regular system to it. When did City tell Callan how many to kill, and when did they pay him for it? Clay had no idea.

> CLAY SAYS IT DONT MAKE SENSE. IF CITY REALY WANTS TO BREAK THE COVENS, WHY NOT MOVE ON ONE COVEN AFTER ANUTHER? REMEMBER THE NAME CALLAN. MAYBE SPITT KNOWS HIM. RAIN LET UP AND WE START FOR WENGEN TOMORRA . . .

"Arin, you pack neat as a windstorm."

Shalane huddled glumly on the edge of their bed—she thought of it as theirs rather than hers now—watching Arin stuff his belongings into the saddlebag. She wanted to tell him he was right and Hoban was right, too, but what would he think of them now, and yet somehow it was choked off by the panic of seeing him go, seeing him take the robe from their bed so that not even that was touching her any more, roll, stuff, cinch . . . go. Maybe if she had a child in her, maybe if he even thought there was—

"I'd still have to go, Lane."

"Damn you, do I always leak? Can't I think just once without—oh, gimme that!" She snatched the robe and shook out his clumsy folds. "No, leave off, Arin. I'll do it."

*?*

*I'm all right, Arin.*

*You're not.*

"Go 'way."

She meant it, head turned from him, fingers too careful and too long at the refolding. "That Elin, can she cook?"

"Sure."

"That all she does?"

*I'm with you, Lane.*

Shalane shoved the robe into the bag with an angry push. "With you, with you. I don't want *any* woman with you. Hell, I must be sick," she finished with lame disgust. "Hey, what you doing?"

He was pulling the pin from the hide strip to free her hair that was still crinkly from the dampness in the air. "Want to smell it." Arin buried his face in her hair. She twisted around into his arms with tearful need, pouring out the hot feelings in a jumble of sharing that words couldn't begin to sort. Neither he nor Garick could dare think the Karli were afraid to fight. *If Hoban says no, he's got good reasons. But I'll come like I said,* only she didn't want him to go now or ever, and that Elin with her goddam bedtime eyes, she was too pretty, and Shalane could hate her "If I wasn't a master and above that." *But you call me, Arin, and I'll hear. I'll pick your lep out of a hundred voices and a hundred miles. I can, I'll hear. Call me.* "And I *did* put love herbs in the juice that night," Shalane wiped clumsily at her tears, "but . . . but just a little." She shivered against him. "Lie down, there's time. Please say there's time." *Hold me.*

They lay still together, complete, senses and thoughts closed to all but each other. And so they missed the first faint lep as it pulsed into other minds.

*Someone coming.*

A dozen, a hundred mental fingers poked at the new thing to find its shape. A man? It leaked no thought, no feeling except a peculiar, impenetrable coldness. No plague, they were sure. But not Circle. *One cowan.*

Elin paused, washing the new baby with Cat. A look passed between the two women. Magill, cinching his saddle, lifted his head to listen, and turned to Kon. Like half a hundred riders all over Karli, the two mounted and rode out of the stockade.

Before the cowan was within a mile of the stockade, he was observed by hundreds of puzzled coveners. He leaked nothing they could read him by, and the children stopped dead, the shouted greeting stillborn. If their elders detected no fear in the man, they found no warmth.

"Not a hunter." Kon studied the colorless, travel-stained robe. He scoured his scant knowledge of geography. Wengen, maybe; there were some Wengen on the north Mrikan border that weren't real Circle any more. But no, he was too light-skinned. Young, but carrying himself like twice his age, head down between stooped shoulders.

A premonition niggled Kon. He rode out of the trees in a lazy arc that bisected the trail. Magill followed, noting the other men and women who moved noiselessly out from cover. The cowan plodded on as if he didn't know or care that he was ringed in.

"Where y'all from?" Magill asked, regarding him with open curiosity.

The cowan halted his short-legged pony. He looked at Magill with remote distaste. "I am called Micah." His voice was deep; the words were Uhian, but slow-measured and carefully pronounced like the Old Language Arin spoke sometimes. "Sent by Uriah to see the man called Arin."

Moss rode up between Kon and Magill, an arrow ready. With surprise, the two Shando read him taut as his bowstring. The feeling he leaked was dangerous.

"You-riah." Magill tried the unusual sound. "He your god?"

"No," said Micah. "He only points the way." He spread his arms to show his lack of weapons, about to speak again when Moss cut him off:

"Whoever he is, he owes me a horse and a friend."

Kon lepped, *Know him, Moss?*

*I know his kind; I wouldn't forget.* "He's Kriss," Moss stated, frigidly calm.

Micah's bowed head moved once in affirmation, a narrow head with a blunt ax-blade for a face, all planes, nothing soft. *Touch his cheek,* Kon thought, *it wouldn't push in at all. Cold. Hard as an ax.*

"That is your name for us," said Micah. "The Kriss . . ."

THE KRISS HAVE SENT A MAN TO TAKE US OVER BLUE MOUNTAINS AND IM GOING THERE FURST BEFORE THE WENGEN. THERE MASTERS NAME IS URIA AND MIKA SAYS HE MAY JOIN US LIKE YOU WANT. REMEMBER HIS NAME TOO. URIA.

An amusing rumor circulated in Lorl that autumn, snatched up by certain people paid to hear and report such things, that the Shando were urging a war against Mrika and City. It was laughed at by most.

The few that knew it for fact profited by silence. Informed attention focused on Garick's Mrikan agent for the sida mills, a round, ingenuous, popular little man named Spitt, bald as a melon and endowed with a look of perpetual, childlike surprise, bumbling, forgetful and untidy enough to earn the solicitous observation that he ought to live in a basket.

Spitt was extremely generous in buying liquor and food for whoever happened to be present, which partly accounted for his popularity.

One night, several high-ranking merks sent personally by Callan to make Spitt's acquaintance almost regretted their false pretenses. The little joke of a man was so damned friendly, got drunk so easily, it was almost embarrassing to take advantage of him. And when the drinking got somewhere between the stages of heart-sworn friendship and incoherency, he proved pliantly ready and willing to talk about Garick.

"God of Shando," Spitt hiccupped. "Very unhappy man."

"Why?" asked an attentive young merk officer.

"Common knowledge. Don't y'know? First wife." Spitt winked solemnly, lugubriously, full of peasant wisdom. "First wife. Died. So he buries 'mself'n work. Don't help. Poor bastard. Can't talk to second wife, all edge like a butcher knife. Two sons, one can't stand the other. You heard about the one—" He gestured elaborately for them to duck their heads in a tight circle of private confidence-sharing. "Young man now. Singer. *Weird.*"

The youngest mercenary remembered. "My ma pointed him out once. Why'd they throw him out of Charzen?"

Spitt shrugged. "Dam'f I know, but they say he's bad to cross. Ah-h, shit; it's a hell of a thing. Garick, poor son of a bitch, and he's a good man. You hear me? A *good* man. Trying to find where the plague comes from."

"*We* heard," said an older officer, "that he's looking for war."

Spitt's round eyes goggled in blank surprise. "*War?* What the hell *with?* He ain't got that kind money t'start with!"

"We hear he's borrowed a lot right here in Lorl."

Spitt giggled foolishly into his glass. "That a fact? Sounds like old Garick. He's smart. He always makes money. Thinks ahead, I guess. Just sent his other kid clear to north Wengen for prime maple saplings, you know why? Because there ain't one covener in fifty ever sees sugar. Garick's gonna grow his own. Just like apples. 'Nother round? Sure!" Spitt yelled for the potboy. "Hey, boyboyboy, don't make me holler twice! 'Nother round here." He shook his head at the mercenaries. "Naw, don't reach for your own; *I* pay. Old Spitt always pays."

At length, Spitt bought enough liquor for his new friends to guzzle all night, as well as a couple of crib girls to help them enjoy it. He didn't keep them company, though his speech thickened beyond coherence until, at last, he went down over the tabletop like a sinking ship, in blissful sleep while the others talked.

"Funny little bastard," the merks laughed, talking about him as if he were dead or someplace else. In fact, Spitt—snoring with the seraphic smile of an infant in slumber—was neither asleep nor befuddled. His ears heard all, his mind missed nothing. He had a tolerance to sida that boggled even Garick, who paid him handsomely to hear everything and look ineffectual.

Within days, by a relay of swift horses, Garick received Spitt's breakdown on the strength and organization of the southern division of mercenaries. The division consisted of twenty companies of forty to seventy riders each.

The company table of organization was laid out by Spitt in a neat flow chart:

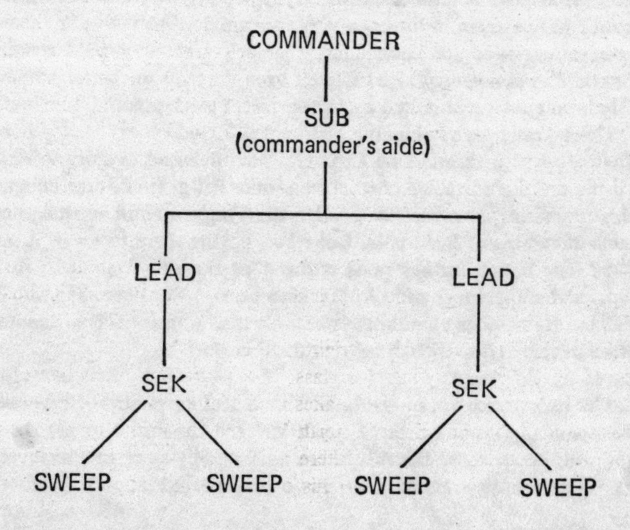

**The lead and sek,** Spitt's letter explained, **are first and second riders in two separate platoons under each commander. In each platoon, the respective leads and seks are assisted by two sweeps, experienced riders who transmit orders to the troops. They ride tough, well-broken quarterhorses. These animals are used to confusion, better in pitched battle than anything Circle's got, better than any stock west of Lorl.**

The letter went on to tell Garick that the mercenary soldiers were armed both with bows and heavy-bladed swords called sheddys, describing the latter with sketches.

**IMPORTANT. I hear talk of some kind of special weapon left over from an old dump abandoned long time ago by City. Very secret, not much talk about. Called THROWERS.**

Garick looked up from the letter, thinking grimly. Secret weapons? Picked up by merks from a junkpile that used to be inside City? More like City handing them out, getting ready for war. Maybe *this* was City's answer to his letter.

**Merk strength is always shifting,** Spitt wrote. **The trouble for them is they have—seem to have—a very thin connection with City. Contracts are written for companies, not each man, and paid by the month. Pay is not very high. There's been demand for better money. City hasn't answered it, and many contracts have lapsed.**

**There aren't many standing orders; I'll include them next report. They all deal with guarding City. Not one mentions activity west of Filsberg in the north, or Lorl in the south. Yet at least three companies are bounty-hunting (they call it dragging) in Karli territory because they haven't been paid. But who's paying them to do it, if not City? The bunch furthest west is the 43rd company, southern division, under the command of a Wengen named Bowdeen. His sub is Callan. Remember that last name—Callan. I hear it too damned often in connection with dragging . . .**

The two stocky young merks in brown leather pondered carefully the hoof- and human prints pressed into the streamside sand. Dragging was never easy, but this bunch was especially clever: scattered over half a mile, never more than two horses together.

The youngest of the two stood up. "Still bearing north on the old road. How far behind you make us, sek?"

The other man pointed to the still-moist horse droppings. "About an hour."

*"About forever, sloppy as you are!"*

The pair spun, startled, when they heard the deep, rich, cutting voice so close behind them.

The black man, close enough to touch, was a tapering oak in a camouflage suit just beginning to tighten over the added flesh of middle age. Under the camo paint, his mahogany skin was carefully dulled with dirt to eliminate any shine.

"Commander," his sek murmured, still surprised, "you do walk quiet."

Bowdeen regarded his men with strained patience, but his generous, everted mouth was not made for scowling. The ghost of an old joke haunted its edges. "Man, you call that quiet?" He pointed to the tracks. "Longside them coveners, I'm loud as two skeletons screwin' on a frying pan." He bent over the mingle of prints. "Well, lookee here, sek," he drawled, "don't that look like moneymeat?"

Bowdeen indicated a long, narrow footprint. "That's a woman. Makes two. Lead found another one on his flank." He spoke with a musical rise and fall, the Wengen sound still unobliterated by twenty-five years in the merks.

The sek looked pleased. "I make out at least six all told."

"Eight," Bowdeen judged, scratching idly at the graying tangle of his hair, "maybe nine."

"Do we take 'em?"

Bowdeen stared at the faint tracks and calculated. Their tally bags stank already from the feet and hands that had to be presented for proof to Callan. Even so, the drag hadn't earned much for any of them. He'd ordered Callan to ride on back for money to be paid out on what they had so far. Callan didn't like it—that fish-eyed mofo always thought he knew better, but it was a direct order, so off he went —where, Bowdeen didn't know or care. Maybe the money came from City, maybe Lorl, he didn't give a goddam so long as his men collected something on account. They weren't on City contract at the moment, so they could quit his company unless they got paid. A little money down might keep the outfit together till real soldiering time again.

The fresh trail was too good to pass up. He nodded. "We take."

Bowdeen spread out a map from his hip-case and oriented his compass. He knew the coveners zigzagged as much as possible, but always came back to the same bearing on the ancient road. His company could trail and maybe get one or two, but they'd flush the rest that way. Spooky deepwoods mofos probably reading them already. Bowdeen continued to peer at the map, following the line of the road, looking for . . . yes.

"They can't move fast in these hills," he said. "Pass it on, sek. We gonna angle off fifteen degrees north of their base line, pass them up and wait . . . right . . . here." His finger touched a brown spot in the wide splash of green on the map. "It's a high, bald top, highest around. And the road crosses it."

One of the younger men started to protest, but Bowdeen grinned down his objection. "No, man, they ain't gonna just walk up and say *hey,* but that hill gives 'em a good looksee ahead and behind. They know we're here, I bet on it. They gonna wanna peek and find out where." He nudged the young sweep. "Boy, you remember the meet-point for sub Callan?"

"Yes, sir."

"Get on down there, wait up for him, bring him over to old bald top, like I show you on the map. Tell him, have his money out, 'cause he gonna be dealin' till his goddam thumb gets tired."

The sweep was reluctant. "I'll miss out on the take. That's a hunk of money up there."

Slapping him on the shoulder in friendly understanding, Bowdeen replied in a high-spirited singsong:

> "Well, don't you fret . . . 'cause it's all fine!
> You gonna get a piece of *mine!*"

He gestured to the sek. "He's your proof for sub Callan. Now haul ass."

"Yes, *sir!*" The sweep saluted in the careless manner that only old Bowdeen would allow a subordinate, swung into his saddle and spurred the horse. Bowdeen and the sek watched as he worked the mount back across the stream bed.

Bowdeen's good humor faded to a frown of concentration. He stooped, spreading a big hand to measure the footprint. He rose, exhaling noisily. *Damn, getting harder to squat.*

"Sek," he questioned, "before you came to the 43rd, you get much merk time in deepwoods?"

The boy shook his head. "Chased some Wengens when they raided Filsberg. Mostly wagon traffic on the Balmer passage."

"Balmer, huh? Right up there, cock'n'box with City."

"That's about it, sir."

Bowdeen nodded in worried agreement. "All you boys pretty new to deepwoods, except Callan. Now listen: learn to read these prints. It's way north for them, but I bet my granny's ass we're dragging Shando. See that crisscrossy mark along the edge? That's how their women stitch their moccasins. Big, too. Never saw one much under six foot."

The sek grinned, interested. "What about the women?"

"Man, I'm *talking* 'bout the women." His voice softened. *"Fine-*looking women, sek. Got a lazy way of looking, some of them, and a way . . . some of them got a way of touching a man . . . hoo-*ee!"* The memory sparkled in his eyes.

> "Up all night until you droop.
> Make that thing jump through a hoop!"

He sighed, letting the picture float back into the past like a dead leaf.

"Two of those fine-looking women on ahead," the sek reminded him.

Bowdeen's voice turned hard without raising. "Not on *my* drag, boy." He fixed the sek with a hard look. "These are *Shando*. You can dry-shave a tough beard with them black knives they carry, never even *feel* it. We find them, we drag and take, that's all. Anything else you forget, 'cause them fine, four-kret women'll cut you balls to brisket 'fore you even get it out."

Bowdeen rummaged in his pocket, found a protein ration bar, unwrapped it and took a healthy bite. "Round up your men, column order."

"Yes, sir." The sek started to move off, then paused. "Commander?"

"What do you want?"

"I was just wondering, I guess. Weren't they—uh—Circle where you come from?"

Bowdeen's white teeth chewed steadily, while his mouth widened in a dry grin. "Boy," he drawled, "where I come from they weren't nothin' but *hungry*."

Clay was sweating, despite the cold. He'd ridden hard to catch up with Arin. The broken circle ringed him now, as he reported, half in lep, the rest in whispers to exclude Micah, the Kriss.

*Merks.*

Arin shot a glance at the Kriss. *How many?*

"Thirty, forty."

*Bears after honey,* Kon observed.

Magill shot a look of fierce exasperation at Micah resting against a tree. "Probably heard old Mike singing one of them him-songs. Got no sense at all."

Ever since Karli, Micah had been a problem for Arin. The worm of doubt still niggled in his skull, sardonic, distrusting Micah: *he might have set this up, throwing us to the merks for money. Try to read him.*

But reading Micah was near impossible. He was locked in, apart, with eyes that looked as if they'd been hollowed from the outside, not designed to see others, but to look *in* as if whatever good there was in the world lay in Micah's own dreaming.

In the forest, at least he had colossal endurance, but it wasn't adjustment to nature; rather, the Kriss showed a stolid disdain for surroundings and discomfort. Because of this, he had no sense of caution. He was not part of the forest, and the men were consequently cool to him. Teela wouldn't go anywhere near Micah, and Elin approached only when she had to bring him food. She never received the simplest thanks for this, yet Elin, in her sensual way, felt the truth of the man. He wanted her. But why should he hate himself for it?

Arin laid his hand on Clay's shoulder. "Walk your horse over to mine. Wait for me."

"You're the master," Magill challenged. The words had a belligerent edge.

"That's right," Arin responded sharply, "and I'm gonna do what's best." He strode over to the tree, searching Micah's impassive features. "Mike, we've picked up some merks."

Micah returned from his distant meditation. "How do you know?"

"We know."

"There is no danger, Arin. Your people are under Kriss protection."

Arin could not probe that closed mind. "My folk think maybe you planned this as a trap."

"To have you killed?" Micah's surprise seemed genuine. "Uriah would hang me for that."

True or not, a decision had to be made. Evasion, zigzagging would cost time, and the air was already flat with snow-smell. If they ran, the merks would trail, forcing them to scatter and waste more precious time. They might even be forced to fight outnumbered, over ground that gave the merks advantage.

Clay, waiting with their horses by a chestnut oak, peered at a high, bare prominence across the steep valley. Arin leaned across the horse's shoulder to him.

"You were a merk, Clay. What would you do now?"

Clay's narrow fox face contorted in thought. "Got a look at their saddle markings," he said. "Looks like the 43rd, old Bowdeen's outfit."

"Who's he?"

"Black Wengen. No lep, but smart. Knows Circle, hunted with Shando way back. Trying to guess what he'd do."

*What you think?*

*Old Bowdeen's coven-smart.* "Snow coming, maybe tonight," Clay guessed. "Hard on the horses, we can't hide as good, neither can he. He'll bush us, get all he can at once." His eyes pulled Arin's to the mountaintop across the valley. *There.*

Arin considered. *We go around, will he follow?*

Clay's shrewd mind weighed it all and added his own merk experience. As well as he could, he explained for Arin the principles of base line and compass, and how Bowdeen could plot from it their direction and average speed. Likely he knew where they were going, and if he missed them on the bald top, the snow would make them easy to follow. He'd trail.

Arin remembered Kon's thought. *Bears after honey.* The merk had it all guessed out. *Then—what's the one thing old bear'd never think of?*

Clay didn't know.

"We're gonna hunt *him,*" said Arin. "Just like a bear."

*?*

*Over bait.*

"Bait?" Clay echoed, surprised.

Arin's eyes went to Micah, sunk back into his meditation beneath the tree.

*—arrow slamming him back and back, again and again—*

Micah was a cowan; he might well have set this up, but the choice was still hard.

*Who said anything was going to be easy?* his mind-worm taunted.

Bowdeen scanned the deep valley to the southeast where, through a sea of dull green and brown foliage, the ancient road wound up toward him. His men were in position around the trees and scattered through the high brush that bordered the bare, rocky saddle, with himself at the left extremity. Nothing to do but wait. The Shando ought to touch this same hilltop for their next visual reference of the valley beyond. He might be wrong, but the odds were with him.

A lot of years since he was this far into deepwoods. Half-atrophied coven instincts shaped a very uneasy feeling about this drag. Bowdeen didn't like the smell of it. His men were too green, hadn't even known enough to pack camo suits. His five-to-one against the coveners was less impressive than it sounded.

He sighed in resigned disgust, thinking what a shit way dragging was to live. But it was the only one around till City came through with new contracts. Sidele wanted him to quit. He ought to. Forty-eight and not as hard as he used to be, ready to sit quiet and talk with Sidele of an evening instead of drinking all night. Roll of flesh around his middle, not much, but getting started. Still they couldn't eat off Sidele's fortunetelling, so one more contract, and he'd quit or put in for promotion. Less riding, more sitting. He was just too damn old.

Bowdeen grinned at the self-delusion: *hell, it's always after the next hitch or the next. Woman, you picked a rambling man.*

Something moving down below. Bowdeen's eyes crawled along the estimated position of the partially hidden road. There! One rider coming right up the line of rubble. The commander spun and jogged back up the edge of the saddle, pointing down the hill.

"Get ready."

Maybe they weren't Shando after all. The rider seemed too careless. Nevertheless, Bowdeen's word passed down the line: think white, just white, nothing but white. They can maybe read you.

He chose a point near the center of the arc just short of the ridge, commanding the best view with a sweep a few yards away to relay orders. The young man near him strung his bow. Three arrows protruded from the ground beside him.

When the wind veered, it brought to Bowdeen's ears the sound of a deep voice. Again it came, stronger. Bowdeen and the sweep looked at one another incredulously. *I don't believe this.*

Singing.

The monotonous chant grew steadily louder, then the man broke into view, leading his horse out onto the bald top.

Bowdeen felt faintly ludicrous; the dumb mofo was marching right up the middle of the bare saddle, oblivious to the world. Bowdeen noted the cut of the heavy woolen robe with its unique hook-and-eye closures; only one kind of folks made their clothes that way. The man was Kriss.

The commander considered rapidly. Callan didn't say Kriss were moneymeat, but then he never said they weren't. The question never came up; you didn't see Kriss that often.

*But where's the others?* His fingers curved around his bowstring when his old instincts flared, kicked him hard: *let him go. Don't!*

But three other arrows hit the man almost together. He toppled over like a gutted sack of grain. The spiritless horse faltered to a stop a few paces away. Silence.

Bowdeen still didn't like it at all, the more because he didn't know why. He waved the sweep to him. "Tell lead and sek to wait for my whistle. Don't go for money yet."

They waited. First one, then several hawks wheeled high over the dead man. Treetops rustled gently in a slow, chill wind. The heavy-shouldered horse nibbled at sparse grass while the hawks swooped lower. *Where are the others?* The sweep eased back to his own position. They waited.

Finally, Bowdeen knew they must have passed by lower down, which meant he could still trail. If they were as careless as this one, he could bag the whole bunch. Bowdeen shrilled a long, low whistle through his teeth. Three men stepped from different points of cover and converged on the body. Bowdeen rose, motioning the sweep. "Stay put, gonna go out and—"

The warning instinct froze him in mid-stride. It squeezed at his stomach, shaping his mouth to the unborn shout of warning. *Get back. Cover.* A hot spurt of danger feeling burned straight through him. His three men were doomed, already dying in the gray light and snow-smelling air; he saw them dead even while they stood there breathing. "Run!" But the arrows were already snarling. Two of the men fell without a sound. The third staggered an aimless step or two, more shocked than hurt by the missile high in his arm.

"Run, goddammit! Cover!"

Dazed, the man lurched into a clumsy run. The second arrow took him square in the back.

Bowdeen flattened out, cursing his own stupidity. They *were* Shando, the long arrows told him that. Self-disgust filled him like a cold poison: getting old, getting slow. *Felt it coming and did nothing.*

Someone called him from the left, the sek's group. "Commander! Com—" The voice was sliced off. Silence. Moments passed. Nothing moved the circling hawks.

The Shando couldn't be everywhere, not enough of them. Let his men freeze in position, make the mofos come to them. Bowdeen started to signal the sweep—and then saw the figure behind, within an arm's length of the boy, tall but too slight for a man, the cannily painted face barely visible under a streaked brown hood. She would have been hard to see dead on without that terrible, purposeful movement Bowdeen was already too late to stop, her face a blur of paint and dirt, a wisp of straw-colored hair under the hood and the knife scything down even as Bowdeen pulled the bow, and gurgling hiss as the sweep's life sprayed out in a dark fountain, the *thum—wock* of the arrow and the girl spinning away, sprawling with the shaft under her ribs.

"By two's!" The order came from the lead, off on Bowdeen's right. "Fall back on center!"

"No, stay down!" Bowdeen yelled. "Stay where you are!" He rolled sideways, grasped the sheddy stuck upright in the ground, was on his knees when he saw the boy coming past the dead girl. Almost the same blunt face twisted in a soundless shriek as the boy bent the bow. Bowdeen dove flat; the arrow furrowed deep across the back of his shoulder.

Sand dropped the bow without breaking stride, jerking his black knife from its sheath. With no time to rise or guard, Bowdeen slung the sheddy at his legs. The boy leaped high, avoiding it. Too late for anything else. As the other plunged at him, Bowdeen went over backward, tripping him up. Even as he fell, the boy was slashing. The knife trenched across Bowdeen's middle in a long, shallow wound. He grabbed the boy's wrist. *Make it fast, he's too young, too quick.* He drove his fist into the narrow stomach, opened his hand and chopped down with its calloused edge at the base of the neck.

Bowdeen panted on his knees like a crippled bear. His shoulder burned and the front of the slashed camo shirt was covered with a dark, widening stain. Not that deep, he told himself, but old man, old man, don't you go riding no more.

He trembled as he inched away on his side, putting space between himself and the dead covener. They always buried their dead; so he better not be too near when they came collecting.

*Just a boy. I could be his gran'daddy. Sidele, Sidele, magic me home. Can't make it no more.*

He inched further up the ridge through the underbrush, thoughts pounding in slow tattoo with his labored breathing. *No way to live. No way to live. I hunted with these people. None better nowhere . . . for two krets . . .*

The stillness was eerie. A hawk glided across an opening in the treetops. Time passed. His consciousness of pain was punctuated at intervals by the whine of arrows, choked cries. He *felt* every one of them. Someone broke and crashed heavily through dry brush before the missile or knife brought him down. *Don't run. Let them come to you.* Awkward and stiff, Bowdeen sprinkled the packet of healing powder over the coagulating wound. He wondered dully if the lead and sek were still alive. *Go down, sun. Get dark.*

But it would be a long time.

"*All* of them," the young sweep cried, stumbling out of the trees toward the men in the open. He felt like throwing up.

"Not quite," Bowdeen groaned, still on his side by the stiffening body of the Kriss. "One damn no-brains commander over here."

A trim, angular man with taut face and unsmiling eyes stepped forward, ignoring his superior. Sub Callan bent over the body of Micah. He seemed more upset by the one dead Kriss than the rest of his whole, throat-cut company.

"Some arrow-shot, most knifed," the sweep said as he passed Bowdeen more of the wound powder. "You gotta get close for that, awful close. How could they do it?"

"With help!" Callan snapped, his voice crisp and cold. "Coveners have magic, more than humans. This is the work of hell!"

Bowdeen made a face. "Sub, where the shit you coming from?

You never seen a Shando knife before? Never up against Wengen raiders? What you *givin'* me? Hell, my ass!"

There was no love lost between them, never had been. Callan was young, capable, ambitious of command, but Bowdeen pitied the company that mean mofo might lead. The sub's protruding, intent eyes never saw humor in anything, the tight, pursed mouth didn't know laughter or the softening tremor of mercy. As far as Callan was concerned, he was clean right about everything, no almost. And yet, a lurking weakness about the mouth and chin suggested sub Callan wasn't always master of his own destiny.

He and Bowdeen, unlike other company heads, never talked easily, never drank together, *If I was a dog,* Bowdeen thought more than once, *I wouldn't wag my tail at him.*

Callan stared at the dead Kriss. His mouth compressed in more than characteristic disapproval.

"Commander, the Kriss were not to be hunted."

Bowdeen vented his disgust in Wengen, jamming an ampule of antitet into his side. Then he returned his sub's all-damning stare, saying nothing.

"Commander," Callan repeated, "did you hear? The Kriss were not—"

"I heard you." Bowdeen felt terrible. His wounds would burn all night from the shot he'd just taken. "Now you hear *me,* sub. This badluck drag cost me the whole 43rd, and all I got to show for it is three pieces of moneymeat."

"Where?" Callan challenged. "You show me where."

"Goddammit, I took them both, sub. I heard them digging the graves! I was that close. You ever think white for over an hour, sub?" He rolled over partway and prodded Micah's corpse with his sheddy. "Two: dig the mofos up, you want. This one makes three, Callan, that's how I count. Eight krets for this ripe mofo and the others, and I get it *now* or it comes out of your contract pay." The corners of Bowdeen's broad, generous mouth turned downward in disgust. "You get a hunk of the girl, sweep gets part of mine. Shit," he concluded with a hell-with-it gesture. "We end up bust anyway."

Callan paid out the money with marked reluctance. Jamming the rest in his pocket, he moved apart to his horse, more than usually morose. Bowdeen, stiff from lying on the ground, stood up and limped over to the sweep. He stuck out two krets for the boy to take.

The sweep, staring off into the bush, didn't see the money till Bowdeen pushed it into his fist.

"'Smatter, sweep?"

"Sir, we . . . we gonna bury the men?"

Bowdeen hesitated a moment, studying him. "Too many," he decided. "Pick up the gear we can use and leave them. There's a mess of hungry birds, boy. Just like us."

He paused by the sweep a moment longer. He wanted to say he was sorry for the lost men, that he should have trailed instead of going for the whole bunch with a green company, that there was a time when no one could have done this to Bowdeen, but "time-was" wasn't now. The hell with it. All he could think about was the pain.

"Sweep, haul that medkit over, get me some kind of hurt-shot." He shook his head slowly. "Boy, boy, let me tell you, this ain't *no* place for an old man . . ."

One by one, the broken circle—Arin, Kon, Magill, Elin, Clay and Hara—stumbled along the riverbank until they reached the rockslide. On point ahead, Clay and Hara found the steep upward trail that three other travelers took several decades earlier. Leading their exhausted animals now, they crept, scrambled and crawled up the narrow trail. The rock face was on their left; a sheer drop—masked by thick brush, pine, oak and chestnut—dizzied Elin when she looked down the right.

The ascent leveled at last in a broad shelf that arced out in an immense plateau from the rock wall. The Shando stumbled up onto it, single file, and slumped, exhausted, to the ground, each alone with his cold and fatigue, unmindful of the whipping snow.

When he'd caught his breath, his curiosity got the better of Clay. He stepped up onto a rock at the cliff edge. The huge vista showed him, it seemed, half the sky that ever was. He could see for miles across a broad gray valley. Below him, a river wound like a brownish-black snake past a dreary place of canting spires and hulking dark towers bigger than anything Clay had ever seen. Off left, the fog-wraithed water was spanned by a wide, rotting bridge, much of it eaten away.

"Lishin," whispered Hara beside him.

Arin said Lishin was one of the places they had to go, even though it was dead. They stared at the dark stain of the town on the valley floor and shared their fear. Now they knew how the sun must feel at

Loomin, furthest from goddess earth. Lishin was—cowan, it was outside, it was many bad things. But it was *not* dead. Death would have returned their probing senses empty-handed. Something was there, coldly alive. They turned away.

It was almost impossible to lep now, drained as they were, but the broken circle managed a faint trickle of power to the masters at Karli: how they fought the merks, how Sand and Teela would be born again. There wasn't strength to say much else.

A surprisingly powerful lep came back: *and Arin?*

Shalane's voice, but though Arin ached to share with her, his folk were too exhausted to lep further. Reluctantly he broke the connecting threads of power and let them rest.

Magill knelt by Elin, sprinkling the merk powder along the four-inch cut that laid open her cheek from ear to mouth. It wasn't healing well. Clay had garnered a supply of the powder back at the bald top; it was City magic, he said, to keep wounds from festering.

"Ain't deep at all," Magill lied. "Won't even leave a mark."

But it would and she knew it, a long scar deep in her flesh and deeper in Elin herself. Magill winced with the flood of anguished sharing that poured from her. It mixed with his own confused feelings. Elin touched him deep, the first who ever had, and he didn't know how to deal with it.

Never good at words, he sensed Elin's need, a loving woman with a hunger that Arin never saw in all the time he was with her. That need brightened her eyes now with its painful loss. *Will I still be—?*

Magill wanted to cry or curse. She shouldn't look at him like that. It made him want to kill the merks twice over and Arin, too, because mile by mile he led them further from everything good.

"Gill . . . ?"

"What?"

"Tell me I'm still pretty?"

Tight in the throat, he leaned over and pressed his mouth to her cheek where the open wound crossed it. "That's how much it means. No more'n that."

Elin tried to smile. "Gill, you old—" Then she was brushing tremulously at his mouth where it was all flaky blood and merk powder that might be poison to swallow, she didn't *no* way trust City magic that much, and—and *damn* she was tired, and when Magill returned with hot horsemint tea from the fire Arin allowed, Elin was asleep. He rigged a blanket on two branches to keep the snow from her face. Two small, star-shaped flakes fell on her slashed cheek. Against the dried blood, their symmetry was startlingly beautiful. Magill pulled the other blanket over her and sat nearby, alone with his struggling soul.

He had never ended life before the bald top. It sickened him, but beyond that there were other things that cried out for him to cut the last threads of the old Arin-tie and think for himself. He'd already made one promise to himself. When all this was over, when City opened up and said Come on in, or whatever Garick wanted them to do, Magill was going to be first in line with Elin, and they'd fix her. Never mind Garick, never mind Arin or this or that. Take their magic and give Elin back what she lost. *You goddam hear me?* In fierce, lonely silence, Magill cursed Arin and the Kriss and the merks and his world that was changing, melting even as he held it like the snowflakes.

Arin's side smarted from the slash that opened up again during the climb, but it hurt less than the other pain. *Did I do right? Was there another way?* He had to lock the question away, but he read the answer in Gill's eyes. A blanket folded down over his shoulders and Kon edged in beside him to share its warmth and his agony.

*Leave it alone, Arin.*

*Might have done different. Might have saved them.*

*Maybe yes, maybe no. Leave it.*

They fell silent, huddled on the cliff edge like winter-bound animals. Their ragged breathing fell into near-unison. After a long time, Kon muttered, "What's that Kriss name for where we going?"

Arin wrenched his mind away from Sand and Teela and the detested smell of killing that hovered over them all.

"They call it Salvation."

*Not more than half day from the Kriss. Going on . . .*

Strengthened and amended by the Karli masters, the intelligence pulsed into Charzen. Stubborn old Hoban still refused to fight Garick's war, but all merk patrols west of the neutral zone would be turned back or engaged.

*Time they learn what's our country.*

And Garick by the fire with Jenna, deep in his own winter, felt his world move forward by the length of an idea.

"Our *country,*" he said to the bleak woman staring into the flames. "Hoban didn't say 'circle' or 'coven.' *Our country.* It's beginning."

Jenna rubbed thumb and finger into her weary eyes. "Not hurt bad," she repeated the old lep aloud, once for the hundred times it echoed through and haunted her mind. "How bad?"

"He's all right, Jenna."

Jenna pushed herself out of the chair. "How would you know? That's *my* son out there, not *hers*. Going on. Sure, he'll go on. Don't you know why?" *Didn't you ever know?* "He'll kill himself to make you love him." Her husky voice was tinged with bitterness. "Like all of us."

The old silence between them came slowly back like a sluggish tide. Jenna shrugged forlornly and went to her own rooms. Alone, Garick returned to the letter he was writing to his agent, Spitt: the Mrikan was to move north to Filsberg and acquaint himself, in his own genial way, with the merk officers of the northern division.

—MAKE FRIENDS, SPEND MONEY, AND LISTEN. THE NORTHERN DIVISION IS—

"Garick."

He looked up, startled.

Jenna hovered in the doorway in her night robe. He read the dull plea that expected to be refused. It had been a long time since she came to be kissed before bed, longer since he went to her. "What, Jenna?"

She wrestled with the thing so long concealed, denied, surrogated in her duties as goddess. She had let go, hopelessly, of the physical need for him too long ago to have it flare up like this. Perhaps the need was not for Garick, but the part of him she helped make.

"Stay with me tonight. I miss him."

Garick hesitated a moment, then rose and went to her. The tenderness was rusty but genuine. "All right, Jenna."

"Hold me till I fall asleep?"

He did.

The last lep out of Blue Mountains was so feeble only one Karli master could read it, a girl Arin mentioned in his letter. Garick couldn't remember her name.

*In sight of Salvation.* Arin had reached the Kriss.

## *The Laughter of Wolves*

They followed the southern shore of the river due west, glad to leave Lishin behind. The snow fell steadily. Blankets spread over the horses' backs protected them from the stinging wind-whipped snow; mile on mile, but neither house nor human was sighted. Hara scanned the dreary panorama of river, hills and shore so low the oily water lapped at the slush around their horses' hoofs. "Maybe we gone wide."

"No." Arin was sure. "Micah said we'd hold the river till we came to their god sign. Like this." His hands sculpted a queer shape in the air. "From there, the trail cuts up through the hills into Salvation."

They all rode together now except Magill, ahead on point. All were grateful to be near the end of the ride, even though it was a strange place they were going to. Their food was gone, there were no game signs, and all of them were worn to irritable shadows by fatigue and the rankling wounds that thinned what little sleep they could snatch.

The lep pierced Arin's thoughts like a pin in a bladder. He reined up. Magill—coming back fast. In a moment, he emerged around a shallow bend in the shore line, galloping out of the whirling snow, jerking to a snow-spraying halt in their path.

"Up ahead!" He waved his arm with a strangely spastic movement. They all read his fear. Magill was terrified.

"The god sign?" Arin asked.

"It's there." Magill didn't move out of their path. His agitation made them all wince in empathy. A sickened shake of his head. His eyes impaled Arin's with their accusation. "Where you brought us? When we fought the merks, didn't I come to have you clean my knife with salt and fire and water? Didn't we all come to be clean of death?"

"All right, Gill," Arin soothed, frightened himself at the depth of the man's terror. "We're with you."

"Ain't nobody with nobody! Not here, not in this place—it's dead, Arin, like that thing up there! Don't put me on no more point," he ended pathetically. "I'm scared."

Neither lying nor malingering, not Magill. He'd seen something that momentarily cut the courage out of him. Only a fool is brave all day. But they needed a point, and Arin couldn't ask any of the others now. Except one.

"Kon."

The tall, quiet man reined himself in knee to knee with Arin. They spoke in low tones. "Moss said the Kriss would be watching," Arin murmured. *Our folk are scared.*

*I'm right with them,* Kon admitted. "What we gonna do, Arin?"

Magill's fear soured Arin's mouth. "Whatever's around that bend, we ride up and look it smack in the face. You and me. They'll follow."

Kon glanced at the others. "Arin," he sighed, "you're gettin' dangerous to know."

The two trotted forward, hoods drawn back for better vision despite the snow. They rounded the shore line and saw it. Kon would have jerked to a halt, but Arin's mind grabbed at his. *Keep riding.* They slowed to a walk, silent in the face of the thing that scared Magill. From a distance, the figure seemed alive, an illusion created by the movement of the driving snow and the artisan's unbearable realism. Closer, they saw it had been cut from wood with a morbid skill bordering on genius.

It stood easily ten feet high, its thick beams hewn roughly square. The figure had been painstakingly carved from a lighter toned wood, horribly faithful in its agonized detail, the flesh of the splayed, tortured hands torn with exquisite, almost surgical accuracy where the brutal spikes pinned them to the crossbeam. Life-sized, the wooden victim hung by his hands and nailed feet, a further wound in faded red gaping under his skeletal ribs. A corona of thorns, jammed cruelly down over the skull, was etched with painted blood, ancient and peeled, trickling in realistic droplets.

*Told you, Arin.* Magill waited some distance behind with the others. Arin read their horror not only as a sharing but in the stiff aversion of Hara's glance, Elin's head bowed over her hands. But Clay seemed absorbed by it. Something in his reflective tone made them listen.

"Old man in Filsberg told me once about the Kriss. They call us *witches.* I remember because I never heard the word before. They say we can't look their god in the face." He stared for a long time at the god sign. "No wonder they think that. What kind of people would make a god out of *hurting* like that?"

Arin wheeled around to them. "Come up close, all of you. Take one good look!" *They're watching, you know they are. Look at it.*

Loyally they moved forward to stare at the carven god. The wind blew over the river and the still watchers in the hills above followed every movement of the Shando. Starting up the trail into the hills, Arin told them, "Witch is just a name, Old Language name for Circle."

His attention was focused on the wooded slope ahead. Several shapes flitted through the trees in clumsy attempts at concealment. Anger grew in him. *Bastards—who's afraid to face who, Uriah?* He squinted back down the trail, looking for Clay who still lingered by the god sign. "What the hell's he doing, Kon? Clay!" He didn't care who heard him now; he was tired of hiding. "Close up, boy!"

Clay waved back from the beach. He had less fear of the god sign than the others. It was a new thing; he wanted to look at it. The evil he saw had its own allure, a fascination of Otherness.

Perhaps the artist hoped to represent some humanity in the face; its line strained unsuccessfully in that direction, all but obliterated by the crude howl of pain. It was the twisted mouth, caught in its agonized utterance, that revolted Clay. He flinched to think of that obscene shriek as the voice of a god, braying out forever over the dark river, season in and season out, the pain-maddened eyes blind to the greening of the goddess, the scream distorting the song of birds, howling forever without surcease.

Clay forgot to breathe. The face was a doorway opening on terrible pictures that flashed by too quickly to be singled out, blurs of movement caught in light and shadow. He tore himself back into time, glaring at the figure, as if it authored the evil visions. Wheeling his mount around, Clay bounded up the trail after the others, eyes bloodshot and unfocused like a man too quickly awakened from bad dreams.

Salvation loomed up suddenly.

A vast, tidily cleared area of a mile or more, well-kept cabins, hardly a sign of worked fields, trails that crossed regularly in a definite system more like the streets of Lorl. The snow deadened sound. To record his position, Arin called a gather-in and they lepped their arrival to Karli. There was no palpable answer; he doubted if they were read.

They drifted in eerie silence down what appeared to be a main artery, always expecting people at the next corner, always disappointed, but their instincts quivered with the sense of being watched. Elin glimpsed the hostile eyes of a woman through the narrow slit of a door before it shut with a bang. The road opened at last into a wide square bordered with dwellings and dominated by a large, white-painted building, spired and surmounted with one of their god signs. In the center of the square was a larger replica of the same symbol, slightly different from the one on the riverbank. The thorn-crowned head hung forward, brooding down on the Shando. Wind eddied the snow around them in little whorls. Nothing else moved.

They knew they weren't alone in the cold square. The heavy, impenetrable blanket, felt first when Micah approached Karli, now closed tighter about them like a shroud. Their overbred horses skittered nervously. Magill saw a dark-garbed woman scuttle between two houses and disappear. His tentative call was flat and sudden in the silence.

"Y'all come out and say hey!"

His temper worn thin by fatigue and lack of sleep, Arin rode a puzzled circle about the square. His people were reaching to him for assurance. He had no patience left for Uriah's shadowy game. *That's what it is,* his tutor worm whispered, *a power game. Wait humbly, he'll know you're uncertain. Get angry, it will show you weak and arrogant. Either way, the moment is his. Take it away from him.*

"Sumbitchin' games." At his rein flick, the mare leaped into a loping gait about the square. Arin's voice rose clear in Old Language, beating like an angry bell in the stillness. *"Where is Uriah? Where are the Kriss?"* Wheeling around and around so all the hidden watchers could hear him. "We have seen the picture of your god and are not frightened. Is his magic so weak it can't save you from six tired Shando who only want food and rest and a warm fire? *Where are you?"*

Their sharp hearing caught the minute creak of a door hinge, then another. Arin spurred about the square again, halting before the white building. *In line behind me,* he ordered; the Shando trotted into formation. Arin swung aside and swept his arm toward them. "As we looked at your god, look at us. We're men and women like you. This is Kon, my right hand. This is Magill, my left. They've followed me since we could first ride. Is loyalty strange to the Kriss?"

He paced the mare down the line. "This is Hara, the best of our hunters. Is hunting new to the Kriss? This is Clay who will be a master someday. Are strength and discipline strange to the Kriss? And here is Elin who might have had any house in Charzen and any man to be with. She chose to ride with us instead. No man here has endured more, no one of us who isn't grateful for her warmth—"

"Sure as frost," Magill murmured. Only Elin heard him.

"—are fine, brave women strange to the Kriss? Three of ours and one of your own died to get us here; do the Kriss, who carved pain into wood, think so little of it in flesh? Was Micah a fool to bring us?" He spread his arms wide. "We're only people like you. Be people and come out."

"Welcome, prince Arin."

He had turned away from the large white house on his last words. When he swung around, two men were there on the steps, one bareheaded, the other cowled in the wide folds of a black hood. The bareheaded man, not very large, was thin and erect in his robes. His voice seemed impossibly powerful for his ascetic frame. He descended the steps; the other followed. The wind whipped snow into his face, but he seemed oblivious to it. "I was praying with the elders in the church."

Arin dismounted to meet him. The cast of the face was not unlike Micah's, the eyes deepset but clear and present, glowing with life and intelligence. Arin could read even less of him than Micah, only the mere surface of deep and powerful currents. The white hand offered to his own, though delicate, was work-calloused, the creases black-veined with years of coal dust that nothing would wash out. His untanned cheeks barely wrinkled with the first lines of age; older than Garick, perhaps, or a little younger.

"I am Uriah, the chief elder of Salvation. And this is Jacob"—he indicated his escort, who stood with bowed head one respectful pace behind him—"who serves at the altar. Forgive my people." He gestured with graceful authority toward the houses. "You are the first coveners to visit us, and our beliefs go four thousand years deep."

More doors opened now; men and women appeared cautiously on front steps, staring at the newcomers.

"Nevertheless, as king Garick says, it is a time for change."

Arin nodded without reply, but his mind fluttered with something not quite as sharp as a warning: this was a man who listened and remembered what he heard.

"We will forget as much of our difference as the time allows. You are welcome." Uriah shot a keen glance at Arin. "How did Micah die?"

"Mrikan soldiers. They bushed us."

"Bushed?"

"Set a trap for us. City pays them to hunt us, so much a head. They got Micah and two of my own. Let him be born again to you as ours to us." Arin was conscious of his first diplomatic lie and was glad the Kriss had no lep.

"Each to his own," Uriah acknowledged inscrutably. "Garick sent no fool for a messenger." He turned and walked down the line of dismounted Shando, greeting each. "You are all welcome. A man's face is his history. Let me see how you are written. Kon, is it? Yes, Kon." He peered up into the big man's face. "Strong and gentle and loving. Be careful not to love too deeply in this world, Kon. It could hurt you.

"Magill." He moved down the line. "An interesting face. All fighter and all heart, I'd say. And a Jing by the set of your eyes. They conquered this country once."

"Heard that," Magill drawled, catching no more than one word out of three in the unusual, cadenced flow. "Don't know for sure."

"Be sure." Uriah passed on. "And Hara. Yes, Hara." He perused the hunter silently for a moment. "You're a fortunate man. You've found peace somewhere. That is a treasure. And last, young Clay, the master-to-be. You—" The chief elder paused again, longer this time. "You have strange eyes, Clay. I think they see more than they want to." He turned to Arin with an air of courtesies well concluded. "Prince, a warm house is ready for you and your men. We will find something for the woman."

Arin stiffened at the cool insult to Elin, felt the same reaction surge through his men. He started to speak, but Elin did it herself.

"I look like a horse, Uriah? My name's Elin."

Uriah turned too sharply, apparently surprised that she would dare address him directly. Though Elin was inches taller, he seemed to look down at her.

"And Elin, yes; Elin who might have stayed home. We have different ways, girl. Unmarried women do not live with men. You will be housed apart."

The silent Jacob touched Uriah's sleeve and whispered something. They moved apart and spoke rapidly in Old Language, inflected in a manner Arin found difficult to follow beyond the drift—" 'What you do to the least of these' "—and Uriah countering with dry composure, "And will you quote Scripture to your own purpose, Jacob?"

Jacob's voice rose out of his cowl. "She is hurt, elder!"

"Young Jacob reminds me of charity," Uriah allowed with a glint of humor. "And what must be rendered to kings. The girl may house with you."

Jacob raised his head to Arin. "We're not strangers to suffering, Arin, or its value to the soul—"

"Wait!" Arin pushed the cowl away from the man's face. "Well, damn, it's Jay! Old Jay." He engulfed Jacob in long arms, happier than he thought possible to see a familiar face. "Jay, haven't seen you since you laid me out."

"Forgive my anger, Arin."

"It's forguv—looklook, here's Elin!"

But magically they had already moved toward each other, awkward and eager. The girl's eyes shone with tears.

"Hey, Jay."

"Hello, Elin."

His hands won the conflict with his caution, went out to close about her shoulders. He peered closely at the two rivulets lengthening through the dirt and vestiges of paint, then at the long, powder-flaked wound.

"They hurt you," he murmured heavily.

"Don't look at me, I'm dirty as a hog." Elin tried to duck the lacerated cheek away from him. Gently, he turned it back to him.

"They hurt you."

"Just a little mark, Jay."

"May God damn them forever. They hurt you."

They might have been entirely alone beneath the god sign. Magill read Elin and closed his thoughts away from the others. She had come for this, then; all the miles, all the pain for this, not even sure, perhaps, until this moment. The wind whipped about them while the Kriss watched and Uriah measured them both with an expression Arin could not fathom.

A house was readied for them on the square across from the white church. Reproachfully clean, maintained in that neurotic condition by two older women who served their meals with the air of martyrs and, each morning, swept the plank floors of the fine black coal dust that settled everywhere. As unappetizing as the food they brought, these two never volunteered their names, merely scuttled about their duties, never spoke to or looked directly at the men, though they glowered with purse-lipped disapproval at Elin, fear mixed with frank curiosity.

Coal heat was commonplace to Kriss but a joyous novelty to the Shando. They made a game out of hot baths, three to the tub. The Kriss women fled, to be replaced by even older men, when they found Elin, Kon and Magill singing and scrubbing away together, with Clay, bare as peeled birch, waiting to replace the first one out.

There were no invitations, no visits, no mixing whatsoever. Arin learned very quickly that Uriah, as chief elder, was to be their only contact with these reclusive people. He tried to assess what glimpses he caught of the men who might join Garick's cause. Sour, taciturn, undersized by Uhian standards, with few weapons or horses, they were still hard, fit from spending their lives mining the coal that fed Wengen iron forges. They were not poor or poorly furnished—their clothing and houses were the best-crafted Arin had ever seen—but no luxuries were evident. Those were of this world, Uriah explained, and not to be indulged. Thus Kriss men welcomed the chance to work in the dark of the mines, since it shrouded the imperfect world and turned their eyes within.

"Coal sells high," Hara mused. "Old Kriss got a pile of krets somewhere. Don't spend any on themselves."

Not true, Arin observed. The Kriss spent a good deal just to live, they had to. Their cloth came from Lorl already cut in bolts, their wool from Karli, bought in Mrika and woven to the singular patterns of Kriss style that concealed the body entirely except for the head and hands. Almost all food was imported, including feed for their stock. The soil was too acid for crops, and the hills were barren of game.

"Old buck just like me." Clay lazed at the window. "Can't stand that coal dust."

"No." Hara stared out onto the square where the evening mine shift gathered to pray before the god sign. "Something else. When the wind shifts, there's a smell."

"No wonder they never smile," Magill growled. "Just go to work, pray, come home, sleep, pray, *get* up, *go* out, pray and goddam off to work again."

"They must quit sometimes." Elin worked the gut-threaded needle through the tattered hide shirt she was mending for Magill. "They get babies like hunters get ticks. Not one of these women over twenty ain't bust out at the hips from birthing. They birth easy," she noted with a trace of envy, "and just as much as they can, Jay said."

"Jay said." Magill watched her closely. "Here we been cooped up like chickens. When you see old Jay?"

"If I told you, we'd both know," she teased.

"Jay lives with his folks. You go there?"

She bent her head over the mending. "No. Not his house."

"I think that's why you came," Magill said at length.

"I guess maybe." She plied the needle, considering it. "Didn't know for sure. I want a house and babies, Gill. Arin found Shalane, Cat found Jon. Oh, that baby of hers . . . why not me? Been out on the hill with you and Arin and who-all since I was twelve and, damn, who cares?" Her smile flashed suddenly, the expression Gill knew best—easy, intimate, sure of men and enjoying them. "Oh, Arin was fun, and you—"

"Girl, listen to me."

"—and you, Gill—ain't no one good as you inside."

"Girl, them Kriss women *hate* you."

"I know, Gill. But . . ."

Magill sighed. "But Jay."

"Yes."

"Why? Because you couldn't have him?"

"I guess. Maybe he wanted me more. That made me think." Elin wrapped off the yarn and snipped it. "Sure as frost, I ain't done too much of *that* before. Don't fret me now. Here's your dirty shirt." She tossed it in his lap with a kiss on the ear. "Wash it sometime and scare hell out of your fleas."

"You have the lep," Uriah explained to Arin. "We have other ways of gathering information. Our men travel to Wengen and Mrika with the coal wagons. They watch and listen very carefully."

"I wondered how you knew so much," said Arin.

"And we pay others to watch and listen, the same as Garick." He answered Arin's surprise with a faint smile. "We are an island of—*cowan* is your word?—in a sea of coven. In our place, wouldn't you watch and listen, too? Nothing is free, Arin. There's always a price."

Arin nodded at the truth. He was learning that rapidly. They walked on over the snow. "Sometimes our people have tried other ways. Young Jacob left some time ago. Our faith seemed too narrow for him then. He wanted to try Circle. He traveled a long way, finally to Charzen. He was half-determined by then to come home."

Arin listened as the intense power of the man rolled forward in measured thought like a broad river. Uriah, pale face partially hidden in his hood, was totally magnetic. He carefully rephrased the fluent Old Language when Arin's command failed him, passing with ease and tact into simpler Uhian.

"Jacob had to find his faith by leaving it. It is very deep in us, prince; like certain musicians of the ancient world in whose work the *Dies Irae* could always be heard, so our faith sounds its own deep chords with which our souls must harmonize. Strange you have no word for religion."

Arin's mind, already hammered by Edan and honed by Garick, began to flex, seeking new strength under the test of Uriah's agile, darting intelligence. "Religion? How could there be such a word, Uriah?" The constant use of Old Language was adding its own precision to his thought. "We say Circle, but that's not all of it. Not deep or low or high or anything. Circle just is. We take it . . . granded."

*"For* granted?" Uriah plied and corrected in the same tactful breath. "Yes, perhaps."

They worked their way across the snow-drifted square toward the church. "Like king Garick, my power is not absolute. I must plan and argue and persuade."

"Why do you call him king?"

"Because he becomes one and invites the other coven gods to take up crowns as well."

They reached the doors of the church. Uriah pushed them open, stamping snow from his boots. A few candles burned near the altar, over which writhed a smaller replica of the murdered god.

"Why do your people think we can't look at this?" Arin's voice echoed slightly in the chill, vaulted nave.

"An old belief."

"But it's not true."

"Obviously."

"Then why do they believe it?"

Uriah shrugged delicately. "Why do your people believe that you, as master, have power over their lives when you are only a hypnotist with a peculiar type of brain cell developed into an hereditary trait? Belief is a nail, prince. Belief defines. You and I perhaps can shape our creeds with subtler tools, but for the average man, there is only the hard, hammered nail. I would not change it." He studied the young man's face upturned to the cross, saw the aversion Arin couldn't quite cover. "Is our belief *entirely* untrue?"

Emerging from his own thoughts, Arin faced Uriah. "Elder, I'm here to know whether the Kriss will fight with us. How can Garick trust a people who won't even sit down to talk or eat with his kind?"

"And what will happen to us among Circle folk," Uriah countered effortlessly, "if their messengers chafe at our ways even before any agreement is reached?"

Subtle: it was a word he'd learned from Garick, but Uriah demonstrated the meaning. Subtle Uriah: he couldn't be read or maneuvered or outthought. Arin weighed his tactics. "Then, to find where we touch, let's find where we part."

"An excellent beginning." Uriah seemed pleased, even eager. "Tell me how we differ."

"When we look at your god, we see only a cruel death, something no covener would do to anyone, not even a merk or a cowan."

He caught himself with the last word. Uriah caught it too, but his irony carried no barb.

"The mercy is commendable. Go on."

"It's not your god makes us hurt, but the way he died."

"They think of it that way?"

"It's not a *thinking,*" Arin differed carefully. "We *feel* it. Hard to explain to a person who thinks in words."

"Fascinating. What else?"

Arin leaned on the altar rail, searching for one simple picture to show the Kriss. "You don't like Elin." The flat statement flickered a readable shadow against Uriah's mask of composure. "Your women can't understand why she wears the same clothes as us, bathes with us, or that she'll fight with us when we go to war. And to us, the strange thing is that your women won't."

The shadow vanished, the mask smoothed. "Impossible, prince. Bad thinking. Whatever the powers of your female masters, you've never fought a real war. Your women will be as useless in combat as ours. Woman, by definition, is weakness."

Arin gave him a long, curious look. "Yes, that's it."

"What?"

"The difference, or a big part of it. One bit that sticks up out of deep water, I guess. You have a daughter." Arin mangled the unfamiliar word. "If I asked her out on the hill—"

"The hill?"

"For bed, loving—she'd go red as rhubarb all over."

"Of course!"

The man's sudden, uncharacteristic stiffness puzzled Arin, but did not deter his point. "Well, Elin or any coven girl would be happy to go, most times. Afterward, she'd take you home to her folk and tell how good it was, or if it wasn't so good, you'd laugh about it—because there's always tomorrow and life is so damned good."

"I see."

"No, you don't," Arin contradicted, serious, "not yet. When the merks bushed us, that same Elin brought her knife to me to be cleaned because of what she had to do to stay alive. I don't know how many men she killed. She wouldn't talk about it. And if you said one word about *that,* elder, you'd make her feel dirty. She might never speak to you again."

Uriah blew on his hands. "Yes, fascinating. You are excellent company, prince. You will educate me. Consider this, now." He leaned across the railing, thoughts focusing with his concentration on the grim crucifix. "Outside this church the weather is bad and getting worse. The door that faces on it is warped and haggard, ugly as this death you find so distasteful. But inside"—his gesture lovingly included the gloomy nave—"there is this. Death is only a door; *He* is a door, our God. Only through Him may we attain our true life which you call death. This air, this body, this world are not life to us but a testing ground where He heats us on the anvil of our days and works us to the desired shape. The tempered steel will last, the shards will fall by the way. Everything in this false world is a test for the real world of the spirit."

The voice neither harangued nor pounded nor rose and fell as with an old, tiresome lesson, but proceeded as soft music, note by note, over a melody as inevitable as it was profound.

"Nothing that is not a trap or a step upward depending on the choice of the free will. Thus we store against winter while you merely live. Our women beget children in duty while yours are the accidents of pleasure. Thus we feel obligated to receive anyone who will believe, while Circle remains closed. Your faith and mine are the beginning and the end of a long line of faiths that grew in a circle from where they began: the believers in God—and those who followed other powers—what you call the gods of earth and seed. They are not Him. You are many, we are few. There was a time when we outnumbered you, when this whole land worshipped like us. Circle was a remnant, then, isolated little bands of disaffected souls—just as our own faith survived in small groups of plain folk in an earlier time. An age-old balance, Arin: it rises and dips and rises again. For the thousandth time, people were exhausted and disillusioned with the bankrupt creeds of spirit no less than materialism. From luxury and ease, they fell to famine that shifted the world's balance of power, made the last criminally stupid mistakes that lost the West, saw the Jings come and go and leave nothing but their seed and a few words of their language.

"The creed of personal salvation was a farce then. What good a savior who promised later when the need was now? Many experiments were made, practical plans based on what people remembered of a vanished way of life, many different types of government and belief and even different traditions of witchcraft—Circle, if you will, but only those circles that dealt directly with the earth survived, because the earth was all that mattered.

"It seemed to satisfy the enduring need to be united with something greater than self, the ecstasy of apparent release into the spiritual whole, even if the contact was merely flesh to flesh. But flesh is a mask over vision, like an eyelid." His voice had fallen to a husky, persuasive whisper. "Something remains that is not eased, not fed, not soothed of pain. That splinter of creation, the lonely, fragmented *I* with its unanswered needs—and its burden of guilt. In the end, the man who does not reach to *Him* at His center is trapped outside the door in the cold, and ultimately, like the laughter of wolves, he hears the meaningless echoes of his own voice in the void, calling to a silence like stone, and only the silence can answer."

Arin looked skeptical, but Uriah pressed his point inexorably. "We are born with a sense of our imperfection; it must be so or why do we—you and I alike—grope in our different gods for a perfection beyond us? But here is the difference, Arin: in the ecstasy of Circle dance, there is balm and consolation, but no cleansing or absolution. Only *here* may a man unburden himself of sin, purifying himself of the filth of an unclean world even as he moves through it."

Uriah caught Arin's flicker of doubt. "I know," he said in genial admission, "you're young and vital. Your days are an unspent treasure. You say, with the blood singing in your veins, that life is good.

'I *feel* good, therefore *I am* good. What could I possibly do that is a sin?' But is the question honest or even self-observant, prince? Let me see."

Under that scrutiny, gently merciless as Edan's, Arin felt self-conscious and vulnerable. "A good face. Intelligence and simplicity. Profound combination. A strong base with infinite room for growth. What else? Pain, yes. Very new, but there. Eyes perhaps not quite so unquestioning, mouth not quite as soft as a year ago. New burdens, new regrets. Orders that had to be given. Sacrifices . . ."

That deep-flowing voice was like heat drawing infection to the surface of a wound, the persistent dreams of Holder and the cold stars, the death of Sand and Teela, the unrelieved weight of choosing and choosing and never knowing if he was really right; of the worm thoughts that pulled him further and further away from his own people. He opened his mouth to answer and perhaps affirm Uriah's judgment, when the clear voice doused him with insight icy as it was true: *all men carry this burden, ask these unanswerable questions.* Garick walked alone not only because he couldn't love Jenna, but because he had chosen to think and act for himself away from the usual paths.

Arin's mind teetered over the abyss to which the thought led him. He recoiled physically from it, moving away from Uriah. "You've painted a clear picture of your ways, Elder. It's enough for now. It's just as important to know how many men you can promise Garick."

"That must be decided by all the elders. We'll talk again tomorrow. Come early. You are disturbed, prince?"

"No." Arin kept his features blank. "Good night, Uriah."

The green robe faded down the darkness of the nave and was gone. Uriah sank down onto a bench, frowning in reflection.

"Sacrilege!"

He raised his head at the voice. An old man, bald and beardless, his loose-fleshed neck sunk like a buzzard's into the cowled throat of his robe, appeared from the small vestibule to one side of the altar.

"Were you there all the time, Joshua?" Uriah asked.

"And listening," the aged elder confirmed, his watery, red-rimmed eyes glistening with indignation. "You brought that heathen into the church. To the very altar—"

"And disproved a silly myth. They do not choke or burst into flames at the sight of God."

"But he was discomfited. He was afraid."

"Perhaps. But he came." Uriah turned back to his own thoughts. Joshua loomed over him like a judgment.

"You are devious, Uriah, and proud of it. The most powerful elder we ever raised. We have called you Proselyte. Why do you break tradition, bring that filth to Salvation, even into the church?"

"Because I need to *know*." Without rising, Uriah's voice suddenly bore an edge. "If I've learned more about them than my predecessors, it's because I've tried harder; because I'm *willing* to learn; because, like Garick, I will buy men when I have to. A year ago, by every report from Charzen, that heathen in the green robe was an undistinguished lout drinking his way to a cipher of manhood. Look at him now—tough, committed and shrewd as his father. Twenty years ago, Garick was an easygoing apple farmer. Next year—between crops, more or less—he plans to change the world. He's made a very capable beginning. Make no mistake about Garick: he won't let his heathen traditions stand in the way of his very modern ambitions. You will not conquer or convert such men with a passage from Scripture. What policy would *you* pursue?"

"But if their corruption infects us?"

"What do you mean?"

"The whore who came with them. Jacob turns to her. The women are talking already."

Uriah was without expression. "And?"

"One word to Jacob's family would keep her locked up with her own."

"That word will only come from me, Joshua."

"You are too tolerant!" the old man raged, his mouth flecked with spittle. "Dangerously so."

"Tolerant?" Uriah rose, preoccupied. The old man's vituperation was something heard at a distance like the chattering of birds. "Is it not written, 'Thou shalt not suffer . . .'?"

"It is," said Joshua. "Let you remember it."

"Yes, but for the time, we know nothing of Jacob and the girl." Uriah knelt at the altar. "Come, pray with me."

Was it the man or the idea that was so persuasive? Listening, floating on the deep flow of Uriah's words, Arin had felt—just for a moment—that it would be sweet to be relieved of pain and doubt, to find someone, even that wooden death, if it could give him peace from Holder and Sand and Teela. But as he swayed on the edge, somehow he realized that Uriah was playing him like an instrument, knowing just what string to pluck for the sound he wished. The truth was, there was no place to rest or hide. If he drifted further from Circle, it was not Uriah's way but rather toward stars that looked like blind men's eyes.

The weather turned worse after Loomin. Arin celebrated it carefully, more for his people than any personal devotion. He drew the pentagram precisely on the plank floor, reciting every verse of the sun-calling ceremony. Lep to their own kind was hopeless; their spirits seemed enfeebled, wrapped in a smothering blanket.

The snow fell and fell. Only the industry of the silent women kept the square negotiable. They shoveled morning and night; night and morning, the shifts of men appeared to pray before the cross and trudge off to the mines, returning black-faced against the white world to pray again before sleep.

"There they go again." Magill leaned on the window sill, casual but with an audible tension in his voice. "And there's them shovelin' women. Think they'd come over and get friendly. Hey! Lookee there, Kon! Damn if she ain't looking over." Magill rapped on the window. "Hey there, Krissy! C'mon over and get me saved. Aw, she went in."

Kon left the window and joined Arin by the stove. "How long you 'spect we gonna be here, Arin?"

"Weather like this and those damn elders with two no's for every yes—could be till Leddy."

Kon took up Elin's scissors and trimmed his beard in the fragment of mirror Arin held for him. "Karli was different. People like us."

Their whole style of life was interrupted. They had never been without women or the physical movement that cadenced their lives. Day by day, they grew sourer, more corroded, less of a whole. Kon canted his jaw to reach a flange of brownish-black stubble. "Not even Elin now. You know where she is. That could be trouble." *Snip*. Kon considered his reflection as if all philosophies lay revealed in it. "Get a bad feeling from these Kriss. You're the thinker, Arin, but if I wanted to slow us up, I couldn't do it nicer than old Uriah has."

Arin wondered how right Kon was. They were bottled up. Beneath the courtesies and the surface honesty, he and Uriah were pitted in a game that boiled down to how much you gave for how much you got. Still, while Uriah held out the hope of an alliance, he was bound to wait and watch. He measured and studied the Kriss and, as the sun began its long journey home after Loomin, he began to know their shape. Under the aggression and toughness, the Kriss men were not all that healthy. The snow was dotted with their coal-blackened spittle. The bulky preserved food chronically bound up their bowels. It was doing the same to his folk. The rubbish heaps were piled with Mrikan containers labeled as strong laxatives. Most puzzling were the large amounts of capsuled pain-killers imported through Lorl and Towzen from City dispensaries. The Kriss, especially the women, suffered from a type of headache virtually unknown to other Uhians, a pounding, day-long torture accompanied by nausea, that left them limp and spent. Intuition told Arin it was no simple physical malady. And why the women more than the men? The answer provided his first solid insight into the Kriss mind.

Perhaps the confluence of Loomin and the traditional birth date of the Kriss god jostled Uriah's sense of charity. Arin was invited to breakfast at home with him, the first shade of personal sociability in their odd relationship. Uriah's house lay next to the church; at the appointed time, Arin crunched up the ash-strewn path, noting the evergreen nailed over the door in a wreath arrangement, part of the holiday's insignia.

He had listened politely to the story of the miraculous birth of their god. It was an uphill fight to understand it, since the word and the concept of *miracle* were totally alien; nevertheless, the tale stuck in his mind for its sheer ingenuousness, and Arin recounted as much as he grasped of it to his Shando. There was this girl who had never had a man, and one day she was working in the fields or something when a shape-stealer, a powerful master, appeared and said she was pregnant, and then disappeared again. *Just like that?* So they tell, and sure as frost she birthed when her time came.

"Sneaky," said Elin. They all thought it unlikely. No one was very interested.

Arin was admitted to the house by a sallow girl of about fifteen. She would not look directly at him but scuttled away as her father came in. Uriah led Arin to the kitchen where, in the ample warmth of a coal stove, they sat to a frugal meal. The room was drab; beyond the ever-present cross, the elder's house was unadorned as his person. Arin took his place in bemusement. The table had been set only for two. The women crept around the periphery of their meeting, trying not to exist. Uriah named them like possessions.

"The girl is Mary, my youngest. That is Miriam, my wife. She works slowly today. Her head." He signified the common malady. "Pills have no effect any more."

Miriam's face was drained of color. She went about her duties at a snail's pace but never paused or sat down. Arin had the impression Uriah would have disapproved. "My older son Jeremiah is on pilgrimage," Uriah said, but was deliberately vague concerning his whereabouts. "It is a journey of the spirit. He goes where he must."

"Bless him," Miriam ventured. It was her first utterance; to Arin, that bleak visage lacked the love to bless anything.

This morning Uriah seemed generous. If the Kriss joined Garick's cause, they would ask no money beyond restitution to widows. The proposal was too good not to have its price. Kriss soldiers must be under Kriss command. Arin agreed. With few weapons or horses, they would be best employed as support troops.

"And," Uriah added, "we desire to begin religious missions among the Shando and Karli."

Arin stalled, played with his fork, commented on the well-fried eggs. He had no power to grant a concession like that. Uriah was delicately insistent. "Nevertheless . . ."

Arin strained to parry that agile mind. *When you give something away,* the worm whispered, *make a profit on it.* "You could come to Charzen and speak before our masters. I could promise you that."

"And how safe would I be?"

"As safe as I am here. But in return for that . . ."

Something like warmth twinkled in Uriah's steady appraisal. He chuckled dryly. "Ah, yes—*your* price?"

"We go into Lishin as soon as possible."

The chief elder drank his tea and took his time before answering. "Three people went in thirty years ago. One of them was Garick's first wife." He dropped the question offhandedly. "What were they looking for?"

"She never said."

The understanding of gamblers passed between them. "What will *you* look for?"

"Call it the difference between a long war and a short one. Send a man with us if you want," Arin's glance shifted to Miriam by the stove, "but for now—"

The clang of metal interrupted him. Miriam had dropped a pot from pain-weakened fingers. With a little mew of misery she sank onto a chair, head in her hands. Uriah called Mary. The child sidled in, took several tablets from a jar and drew a mug of water, but Miriam waved them away. "They don't help any more." She appealed to her husband. "I should lie down for a while."

"Very well, if it is so bad."

The coldness made Arin cringe. "I think I can help her, Uriah."

Miriam shook her head. "I must bear it. Suffering is natural."

"So is sleep." Arin knelt by her. "If you could sleep and wake without pain, would that be unnatural?"

Uriah was courteous but adamant. "Prince, you must use no coven herbs on her."

"Only my hands. And Mary's. Will you help, Mary?"

With Uriah's assent, he lifted Miriam and followed Mary to a bedroom bare as the kitchen. Like Garick's and his own, the room contained, in addition to the bed, a plain, sturdy worktable littered with papers that Arin itched to peruse. He stretched Miriam on the bed and undid the headdress that hid all but her chalky face. While Uriah watched in the doorway and Mary assisted, Arin turned the woman on her stomach.

"Rub her back up high between the shoulders," Arin instructed the girl. "Keep moving, easy . . . easy. Miriam, in a little while you're going to be asleep. All we're doing is smoothing out those muscles. They're all knotted up like a fist. Shalane—my wife—did this for me all the time. Going to sleep, wake up fine."

His voice lulled, vowels soft and crooning, while his fingers kneaded at the hard mounds of tension. "You have hair like my mother, but hers goes all the way down her back. Breathe deep, now. You're sleepy already; going to do some fine dreaming . . . where's the pain now?"

"On top," she murmured softly. "In front."

With Mary's help, he turned her again, bending close, massaging temples and forehead, noting the gradual relaxation of the tight lines around her eyes. They focused more clearly now, drowsy but still wary of surrender to him, distrustful and even more curious. Even young, Arin thought, she could not have been desirable; the mouth gathered by decaded habit into a grimace, rigidity of spirit that held in check its own natural outpour as their bodies would not release waste. He let Mary help as much as possible to ease suspicion, but imperceptibly, Arin bound Miriam's concentration to his.

". . . and my wife is a Karli girl. We were *married,* you call it, just before I came here. When I think of her—close your eyes if you want—it's how her mouth is all front teeth like a happy squirrel when she smiles, and her tabard's never straight. The tabard? It's a sort of robe without sides that we wear when we become masters. There, now . . . there . . ."

Her eyelids drooped over the widening pupils, totally relaxed. He knew the pain was gone, but Miriam fought sleep with its loss of control even as she opened cautiously to Arin.

"Now," he spoke to the silent gratitude in her eyes. "There's no more pain."

". . . no." She drew a deep breath, nestled like a child against his soothing hand. As his palm trailed across her mouth, Arin felt the tiny contraction of her lips in a furtive kiss. Now was the time to find the door he knew was open in her, not to grasp but touch delicately, define, shape.

It was a mistake; to find Miriam, he opened himself. The brutal impressions battered him with a sudden virulence that shook him physically and broke his concentration. Miriam's eyes snapped open. *"No."* She shrank away from him. "Husband, get him *out of here,* take him away! He has witched me." Her finger pointed like a knife. "Sorcerer! Son of the devil!"

She sat up, rigid, still shrieking at him, features drawn tight with loathing. Stunned, Arin could only stare as young Mary shrank away and crossed herself in protection. Uriah led him from the room. Arin was too confused by what he had seen in Miriam to note the satisfaction like winter light in the chief elder's face.

But before the fear, there was that kiss out of a memory of need until something whipped out of the dark to tear it away, deny it, twist the mouth into that mask of fear. Hunger—but a hunger so long denied it no longer knew its object and damned it with a force capable of murder.

They met in the warm stable set aside for Shando horses, safe since no Kriss would come near it. Jay came by a cautious route from his duties at the church or soot-grimy from the mines to watch Elin feed and curry the skittish, small-headed mare. Her movements were unconsciously sensual. She stroked the white-blazed nose as if nothing else in the world were quite so important as that the care in those long brown fingers should be lavished on their object. Loving her was once an unrelieved torment; possessing her now had shaken his world, and there was nothing in it that did not lead to Elin.

"I think she understands you," he said.

"She's like me. Likes to be rubbed and fussed over, loves to run. Likes to touch noses with a boy horse now and then." Elin leaned past the horse's nose and kissed him, lips and tongue teasing and promising with the same caress.

If the Shando men were miserable and Arin a stranger, at least she had a little happiness of her own and couldn't let go of it. No one ever needed her so much before. She tried sometimes to put it in words since Jay had no lep-sharing, the wonder of having him inside her, but any mention of body loving made Jay uncomfortable. She sensed his mixed feelings though his body more than satisfied her. He was fiercer in love than Arin, as if trying to touch the deepest part of her while tearing himself away from something that held him back. She wondered how the women of this place related to men. Frightened mice, she had only contempt for them, but part of it might just be how the men treated them.

"Women here walk like they 'spect to be spit on. Why, Jay?"

"In our religion, it was woman who let sin into the world. She is stamped with it. And men, to have children, must sin with her. The man must take responsibility for her weaker soul and come to her only when bidden by God."

So baldly said, Jay knew he no longer believed it, perhaps never had. That arid absurdity had nothing to do with Elin and him. He had to explain it twice. When Elin finally grasped it, she threw the curry cloth at him with a hoot of derision.

"Well, if that ain't some kind of un*fair!* What's she s'posed to do while y'all wait around for the word, huh?" Elin turned away and gave her tenderness to the more deserving mare. "Way these women birth, old god must keep the men running sunup to suppertime, look like." Softly, then: "Am I a sin, Jay? Never even heard that word till now. Am I a sin?"

"No, not you," he cupped her breasts under the green robe. "It's different with us."

"Don't lie to me, Jay. Don't lie when it cost me so much to find you. It's not I've had so many men. You think I put you up against them. Against Arin."

The honesty was painful. "Yes. And I hate it."

"Oh, Jay. You lived Circle, didn't it learn you at all? Young people go out on the hill when it's time, because that's all they need then, to get it out of them. And I did," she affirmed with a pleasurable grin. "And I can't be sorry for any man I ever had, because it showed me what I want. *Me,* Elin." She looked sadly at him. "I bet you hated yourself a little for every woman you touched. So who's lived better, Ja-cob, you or me?"

She was always right, instinct defeating intellect with no effort at all because, ultimately, what had been a way of life for his people was a lie for him. All but the sense of God; that would never leave him.

"I hate you sometimes."

"I could kick you, too." Elin held out her arms. "But come to me."

The spare young man in merk leather had ridden a hundred miles and looked fit enough to do it again on a bowl of soup and three hours' sleep. He resembled Miriam more than Uriah. The hard, prominent eyes were stamped with eternal certainties but lacked the intelligence that raised conviction to insight. Jeremiah ate noisily, paying scant attention to the hovering affection of his mother and sister. When the women cleared the plates, Uriah dismissed them and spread the wide table with maps.

"Garick has two alternate plans," Uriah said, "but I don't yet know their pivot. If the main strike against the mercenaries is to be north or east, the covens will gather here, east of Karli. If south, at Charzen."

Jeremiah chewed a knuckle in thought. "Why south?"

"Could they enter City there?"

Jeremiah smiled at his father's uncharacteristic naïveté. "Forget City. Numbers mean nothing to the Self-Gate. The only way in is to deactivate it from inside. Garick knows that. His strike, when it comes, will be against our companies. It will be a cavalry war, and once we lure him out of deepwoods onto open ground, it will be over."

"What's the money situation in the companies?"

"Desperate," Jeremiah answered. "City still has no new contract for them. The men are all looking for sub Callan, because he's got the drag money."

"They still think it comes from City?"

"If they think about it at all; they don't care. It's hard for the commanders to keep them together with so little money coming in. That's why Bowdeen—" Jeremiah broke off with pent disgust and changed the subject, bending closer to the lamp-lit map. "One thing must be considered in advance: the Wengen."

Uriah tapped a point on the map. "The iron-makers have asked how we stand on Garick. They don't want to lose our coal. I've advised them privately to stay out of it."

So much was foregone, they both agreed; with coal at stake, and the iron men more Mrikan at heart than other covens, they were no danger. But the western Wengen were all Circle, with blood ties to the Karli. The northern division of merk companies *must* keep them plugged up, unable to reach Garick: easy as long as the money flowed through Callan. Uriah agreed absently, his concentration on the map. It was not a power seesaw between himself and Garick, but a triangle with City at the apex. City must stay neutral, unconcerned and uninformed.

Jeremiah shrugged. "I intercepted Garick's letter, didn't I?"

"He might have sent more."

"He didn't. If he does, I'll get it." Jeremiah was confident. "That's where part of your money goes."

Uriah mused. "Who are they in that City? What are they? What do they want, what do they do, how do they think? Who leads them? Does anyone know?"

"I've bought what I can," came the flat answer. "The power of our money stops at the Self-Gate." Jeremiah paused, then sat forward suddenly. "No, wait. Something. An idea. A long time ago, when City last sent revised orders to the guard at Balmer and the other through-point, they used a little box that works on sun power, don't ask me how. Their orders are recorded on a thin ribbon. You press a button and it *talks* to you. I used to play with it a lot, all of us did at first . . . City magic, father, something so different . . ."

"Go on," said Uriah.

"Last month we got the first new ribbon any merk can remember, a warning about the throwers we found outside the Gate. City won't tell us how they're used, but it's not hard to figure. Anyway, both ribbons, they're the same voice. That last order ribbon is *eighty years old.* Last time City talked to us before the thrower warning—and I swear it's the same voice!"

"What's he sound like?"

*"She.* Mature, but not old. Very clear, precise, you couldn't mistake it." Jeremiah's voice trailed off in puzzlement. "But it *can't* be the same woman . . ."

He was not prepared for Uriah's benevolent reaction. The smile was full of satisfaction and even a gleam of excitement. "Yes, it can, Jeremiah. And you've just given me what I couldn't buy." He pushed the tea mug away and leaned across the table. "My predecessor had a spy in Charzen—unreliable, something of a drunk—who said that Judith Singer was over three hundred years old. We laughed. He swore it was true; we laughed harder. But I won't laugh any more."

The young man's pale, protruding eyes widened in disbelief. "No, it can't be. How can anyone live that long?"

"A pragmatist's question, Jeremiah. In this pigpen of a world, it's not *how* but *why."* An odd pleasure shone in Uriah's cold smile. "Learning is more delight than knowing, and what have we learned? Fact: an informer claims a City woman who looks twenty is actually over three hundred. Fact: you identify the same, unchanged voice on two ribbons made eighty years apart. And *fact"*—the hard white fist came down on the map—"Judith's husband shows a quantum leap in learning and political insight that leaves every other god of Circle groping in benighted wonder. And cap it all with what we already know, that Garick's other son, by Judith Singer, is being held prisoner in Charzen. No one knows why."

Uriah flexed his shoulder muscles with an almost youthful energy. He grinned at his son. "Uriah was David's soldier, son. He asked nothing more than the battle, and neither do I. It's a joy to know that I'm up against the best."

The flash of warmth passed quick as it came; again Uriah's attention was wholly absorbed in the long, long crescent of City on the map before him. "Then Garick knows and wants a great deal, but the whole thing is pointless unless he can get into City. How . . . how?"

"The Shando hasn't said?"

It was Uriah's turn for strained tolerance. "Our talks would exhaust what little patience you have, 'sub Callan.' We bargain like misers. Clever man, and I would say . . . admirable. He's described something of his training to me, the way of the masters. The whole being, body, consciousness, is considered inseparable, forged into a tool of the will. Clever. And disciplined."

The room was warmer: Jeremiah took off his leather jacket and rolled the sleeves of his wool shirt over mine-hardened knots of muscle seamed with old scars. "Clever? He's more than that."

Uriah ignored the remark. "What about Hoban? Arin gives the impression the Karli are with Garick."

His son drew a line of crosses on the map. "My man in Karli took weeks to report. Officially, Hoban said no. *Un*officially, the war has already started. Look."

The north-to-south marks indicated the Karli's eastern frontier now patrolled by their bowmen. "Hoban's turning us back and shooting if we don't. We can't just walk in any more. The men drag with full equipment now. We've been losing too many. Again," he glanced up at his father, "money: up the bounties all around. Now, while Hoban's masters are still split on the war issue."

"How split?"

"The young ones are for Garick. Logical: one of them is Arin's wife. Well"—the small mouth curled in contempt—"his whore, anyway."

"An interesting point of language." Uriah sipped his tea. "Neither word is current in their dialect. She is 'with him.' Mystical but vague."

"Father, will you let that dirt ride out of Salvation?"

Uriah was occupied with the map and his own questions. "Oh, in time—I suppose."

The mug banged on the table. "Let him go free?"

Jeremiah suddenly was fixed with a gaze as hard as his own. "Nothing is free." Uriah tapped a forefinger on the map. "Arin didn't say how they'd get into City, but he *did* say—Jeremiah, are you listening?"

"He's a murderer. He murdered Micah."

They stared at each other. Wind rattled the shutters.

"Murdered." Jeremiah said it again, carefully. "The company that bushed him was mine."

"But you *knew* they were coming. You knew Micah's mission. He knew yours."

"Micah didn't expect the company to be operating without me. Bowdeen called for money, so I came to get it. It was safe, because the route for Micah was well west, but Arin zigzagged east every ten or fifteen miles, close enough for Bowdeen to pick up his trail and bush him on a bald top. The logical move, it was all *too* logical. It went wrong because everyone did the right thing. Micah walked right into it. He was meant to. Bowdeen said he waited so long after Micah was shot, the hawks came down for the body. Arin waited just a little longer." He appealed to his father. "Bowdeen said he came out on that bald top singing a hymn."

Uriah regarded his hands without expression. "I know the song. It was his favorite."

"If you love me, father, don't let that witch leave here alive."

The answer came from a cool distance. "I love you, but I love God more. Vengeance is useless to me unless it serves His purposes. Learn that lesson, Jeremiah. Learn the kind of soldier He needs. Buy, use, bend, plan, cheat—above all, learn and know the *world* you would conquer for Him. If some of us are defiled by it, the end will cleanse us. So much for love." He returned to his study of the map, searching out one last elusive fact. "The difference between a long war and a short one . . ."

"What?"

"Arin wants to go into Lishin."

Their glances met and understood each other. "In the spring, you mean?"

"Certainly not before. Judith Singer went in for a reason, so will he. There's something there that Garick needs. That's what I still want to know. Until then, one way or another, Arin stays here." The elder rose and brought the teapot from the stove, eyes cloudy and closed around the complex of strategies.

"But Micah—?"

"I cannot prove Micah. I cannot use indiscriminate moral rectitude. It has no edge. See what I mean by use, Jeremiah. They are free to go when they please, unless—as we will shortly discover—our laws have been broken. A capital offense. Fornication," he answered his son's unspoken question. "One of theirs and one of ours, a young man for whom I had great hopes, the rare kind for whom God is an almost physical need." Uriah fell silent. An observer more sensitive than Jeremiah might have guessed him troubled. "As yet," Uriah refilled his mug, "we know nothing of it. At the right moment, of course, we will be collectively outraged. During the trial, the Shando will be held in protective custody. Arin will have to consider the safety of his people. He'll take whatever I offer. When I know what is in Lishin, he will be released to go there . . . in the spring, like Judith Singer." He reached for Jeremiah's mug. "More tea?"

Someone muttered in his sleep. Probably Clay, Arin thought; the boy slept poorly in this place.

The house was dark except for the stove light that defined Arin's narrow cheek in the warm glow. Once, he could never have sat up alone without Kon for sharing. But now, all things shaped him to the edge of loneliness. His own counsel, that worm that distrusted where he wanted to accept, was cold comfort. It forced him to stand apart, always measuring, summing two and two to an implied five—as he must to match Uriah. He envied his folk their sleep, realizing even with the thought that to envy is to be apart. What was that strange word in Old Language? *Solitude*. Like in the Girdle.

Arin scooped a few more coals onto the glowing bed and returned to his thoughts. Miriam. He'd breached her wall and touched a well of fury unknown to Circle women, frightening at first but ultimately resolving his picture of the Kriss. Their life seemed built on denial of this world for another, but their bodies were in *this* one and, deny as they might, the flesh made its own demands. Perhaps the tension of this impossible conflict produced the never-ending headaches.

Arin could never trick Uriah into that self-revelation, but it would tell him so much. If he could only pry that iron wall apart and read Uriah like a page. Just one crack, one unguarded moment . . .

The steady heat made the room close. Arin opened the door and sucked cold night air deep into his lungs. Across the square beyond the silhouette of the murdered god, a light still burned in the chief elder's house. The moon rode clear in a cloudless sky. There'd be sun for a day or so and perhaps a thaw. Like flowers, his people needed warmth and light. Already Clay was troubled with dreams he couldn't share even with Arin. They should get out, exercise the horses, get off a few arrows and—

Suddenly he saw the movement. Shadow blending with other shadows as it flowed along the houses bordering the square. The cold, sound-sensitive air brought nothing to his ears but the faintest whisper of narrow feet placed carefully on the brittle snow before any weight came down. No Kriss could move that noiselessly. Arin closed the door, waiting. In a moment it opened just wide enough for her lithe body to slip through. She knew his presence without looking.

"Hey, Arin."

*Elin, you fool.*

"What you mean?"

"Like you don't know."

She pulled off the sheepskin poncho and knelt by the stove. "Never complained when it was you."

"It's not me and not Charzen. You're not dumb." *You know how Kriss will take it, they catch you with Jay.*

*Won't catch us.* "Anyway"—she spread her hands to the stove's warmth—"gonna be with him from now on."

"Where? Ever think of that, Elin? Where?"

"Don't matter. Somewhere." A happiness and peace radiated from Elin. She answered him with the smallest corner of her mind like a busy mother talking to a child. Arin knelt beside her, trying to make her understand. "Elin–" but she blocked his mouth with a kiss, and when she drew back, her eyes were large and grave in the flickering light.

*I earned Jay.* She rose and picked up the sheepskin.

"We have to tie you up, girl?"

She leaned down to kiss him again and gave his lip a playful bite. "I'd get out. Good night, master Arin."

The sun was a brilliant miracle after the endless days of white gloom. There was a slight thaw. By mid-morning, the snow was packed tight underfoot and, to the purposeful light in Elin's eye, of a superior quality for snowballing. She patted one into shape, wound up and let fly. The white sphere splattered between Magill's shoulders with a soul-satisfying *sqush!* Kon threw one in retaliation, choosing sides, while Arin hooted as he ran, clawing snow from the ground.

"Gettem, Elin!"

"EEEEEAAA-HI!"

The suspicious Kriss whose houses fronted on the square or anywhere near it were jolted out of complacency by a raucous, drawn-out howl of exuberance that climbed through every possible vowel sound and broke like the crack of a whip. From their windows they saw four of the youthful heathen embroiled in a running snow fight while two others patted a lumpy snowman into shape in front of their house.

Jay, assisting Joshua at the altar for morning worship, hurriedly packed away the consecrated articles, receiving a querulous reprimand for his haste. He saw, from the church door, little groups that gathered to watch the action.

A few unattended children itched closer, yearning into the battle. Jay looked for Elin, just off to his right a moment before, dodging lightly as Kon aimed one at her—

"GOTCHA!"

Neatly tackled from behind, Jay went down in a spread eagle. Astride his rump, Elin giggled as she rubbed his face in the snow. He flung her off, laughing, and they stood up. She grinned at him, hands on hips. "Morning, Ja-cob."

Arin tossed him a snowball. "Give her a good one, Jay."

She backed away, weaving to elude the throw. Infected by her taunting laugh, Jay prowled after her, arm cocked. Elin crouched ready to spring away. Jay's arm whipped forward. The missile whizzed Elin-ward like a stone from a sling and caught her square in the stomach to the vengeful cheers of the Kriss children. He roared after her.

Jacob was in the game; it was enough for one—two—then all of the jiggling children. They had so little time for play. To see grown-ups at it was license sufficient. They began, with shy mischief, to throw among themselves, then the Shando, and were quickly sucked into the roiling, running fight, darting and victorious since not one of them was touched by a Shando ball while the latter were large, amiable targets who groaned, staggered and fell picturesquely when hit.

When Hara led the horses onto the square, the battle had collapsed in a laughing heap with Arin between Elin and Jay in the trampled snow, a flurry of children and a ring of curious adults, silent but not so hostile as before. He flicked an eye at the church door. No one ventured out though Uriah's door might have opened a crack, he couldn't be sure.

For Jay, the joy in Elin he wanted for weeks to share with someone kindled now into a gorgeous, chest-squeezing bubble of happiness that transcended the sober regularity of his handsome features and made him human and beautiful. "Mordecai," he greeted his neighbors, "this is Arin. Esther, Moab, Elin, Magill, Kon. I lived among them for a year. They're my friends."

Young and solidly built but as severe as Jay was incandescent, Mordecai pulled his small son close to him. "Jacob, is it true we will go to war beside these?"

"Yes, if the elders rule."

Mordecai pried the snowball from his son's hand and dropped it near Arin's foot. "With men who do not know the meaning of a day's work, who make fools of themselves in front of children?"

Magill grimaced, stretching out in the snow. "Aw-w . . . shit."

Arin grinned up at Mordecai. "Where we live, the earth is kind. We learn very early the need for joy. To share that joy with children is what you'd call blessed." He raised his voice so they could all hear, rising to his feet. "Our word for war is 'going to the knife.' That is *not* blessed, and we speak of it as little as possible. It's a dirty job to be done quickly with the best tool we have." He unsheathed his knife and held it out to Mordecai. "So we named it for this. The black knife."

Mordecai held the knife as if it might explode. The handle was marked with Circle signs. "What spells are on—*ow!*"

He had lightly tested the edge before Arin had time to caution him. A bright tear of blood stood out on his thumb. He dropped the knife. "I did nothing, and it cut me. It *is* witched!"

"No, Mordecai," Jay laughed, returning the knife to Arin. "Not witched or spelled or anything at all. Just made a certain way. I own one myself."

"Sharper the knife, easier the work," Arin said. "Wengens learned from the Jings how to make one thin strip and sharpen it, then another and another till there's five or six, then hot-forge them together. Five edges in one. Without your coal, they couldn't do it, so you see how we all need each other."

He addressed the crowd at large, feeding the open curiosity with which the Kriss regarded himself and his people, a wonder at the unfamiliar that flourished from the enforced separation of the two peoples. Uriah and his closed circle of elders kept them apart. Today Arin intended—among other things—to bridge that gap. As he talked, he kept a watchful eye on Uriah's door: any time now.

He took his bow from Kon, and the reins Hara handed him. "This is Soogee." He patted the mare's dappled nose. "Fast as an arrow, and about as much brain. They're both built to *move,* that's all." He flowed onto the horse's back as if the empty saddle had been a mere illusion his movement dispelled. *Kon, Magill, Hara. Let's ride.*

Magill followed Arin to one end of the square, Kon and Hara to the other. As Arin wheeled about, Kon's mind whispered into his own. *He's watching.*

Arin stood in the saddle, waving to the erect, black-garbed figure. "Morning, elder. Just saying hey to your folk."

On his porch, Uriah remained unmoving, ominous disapproval clear in every line of his rigid stance. "So I see." The cordiality was minimal and chill, but before he could say anything else, the four riders exploded into motion, riding a collision course, arrows nocked and bows bending.

"Hooooo-ee-HI!" Elin hopped up and down in excitement. *"Go,* Soogee! Go, girl, go, go, *go!"*

The riders passed each other, loosing their arrows within a hair's-width of clearance. Four projectiles *sished* through the snowman's ragged shirt, lodging in the wall behind.

Uriah descended the steps of his porch.

As they wheeled again at the far ends of the square, Elin sprang deer-light across the snow to halt between them. "Gill, Arin!" Her arms thrust straight out. "Old boar gonna get me."

The two horses leaped out at her, closing the distance with incredible speed. Jay's heart seemed to stop with his breathing. At the last split instant, Arin and Magill leaned in, mirror images of the same flowing motion, and scooped Elin off her feet. Jay could no longer contain his excitement. He hugged Mordecai happily. "I told you! Half horse and half cat, Mordecai. They might be devils, too, but by *God,* can they ride!"

The horsemen dropped off Elin and trotted back to the Kriss. "Now, sometimes we hunt boar," Arin told them. "When a hunter loses his horse, that's how we get him out of old boar's way."

Uriah was advancing slowly across the square, dignified, silently powerful. Arin watched him negligently. Kon winked. *Ready.*

"Now, if one of your people was in trouble going to the knife, maybe an important man you can't afford to lose—"

The act had a beauty of motion that left the watchers gasping before the enormity of the sacrilege could be fully grasped. Two horses wheeled, shot forward with legs and bodies fully extended, men and animals rippling as one flexed muscle into full speed in two bounds.

Uriah halted, not frightened but unable to believe it was going to happen. But even as he knew it would be, he knew he couldn't run. He froze, the hot spurt of instinctive fear flamed into rage, and then he was weightless, sailing backward, hooked under each shoulder in an iron-trap grip with a jouncing view of flying snow rainbow-gleaming in the sun and his stunned people watching. They sailed effortlessly around a corner of the square in perfect coordination, and Kon yipped happily.

"Elder, ain't it just one hell of a grand day?"

Uriah could not speak; he could barely breathe. His legs dangled inches from flying hoofs, stomach and thigh muscles already agonized from holding them high out of danger. One more turn about the square and the horses, like two hands obedient to the mind, gouged to a halt in front of the Kriss. Uriah gasped incoherently, engulfed in Shando hugging and shoving him with lunatic affection from one chest to another, roaring in their detestable dialect that it was the best goddam horse-hanging they'd ever seen outside of home or even in Karli where they invented it, that *no* one but Uriah should lead his people against the merks. They kept him spinning from one to another. Reeling, livid with the first personal profanation of his ascetic lifetime, Uriah caught only a blur of faces until he found himself gaping up at the ecstatic Elin, wrapped in her arms and kissed soundly on the mouth.

Uriah tore himself loose, finding his voice at last in a snarl of fury. "Get *away* from me, you filthy—" His mouth contorted with loathing. He raised his arm to strike at her—and froze. He choked back the rage and lowered his hand, trembling, but with a conciliatory sign to his people. He had played the game too long and too well not to know his unnamed loss, and Arin had not missed it, whatever it was. The young master's eyes were bleak as his own with a new, bitter knowledge.

In the dimly lighted church, Uriah knelt at the altar between Joshua and the huge bulk of elder Matthew. Engulfed, he considered with cold distraction, between the pebble and the rock of ignorance. His mind raced impatiently beyond the familiar prayer.

He had not suffered a loss to Arin, merely a telling thrust through his guard. The blow was entirely personal and smarted all the more for it. He did not like surprises and carefully removed their possibility from his path like a pristine housewife banishing dirt. Arin's ploy had shaken him, but he wasted no anger on it. Fury, like vengeance, needed a channel or it was worthless. His acute, tactical mind was already on Arin's next move, whatever it might be.

"—And he that turns from belief shall see Thy back at judgment and know Thy power even over darkness. Amen."

Joshua raised his brittle frame, wheezing with the effort. His bleat of surprise made Uriah and Matthew whirl to see the lofty figure midway down the darkened nave.

"You did not knock!" Joshua admonished. "We did not hear you come in."

"You never will." The figure moved toward them. "If the deer heard us coming, we'd never have meat."

"Shando," Matthew boomed ominously, "you do not enter our church without permission."

"Forgive this one last time. Uriah, I have to see you. Your elders can hear if they want, but . . ." The trailed meaning told Uriah his best interest lay in privacy.

"Elders." He touched each on the arm. "Please wait for me in the vestibule."

When they were alone, Arin took a breath. "We're leaving, Uriah."

The chief elder toyed with a candlestick. "Surely not now; it's the middle of winter."

"Inside of three days I'll need a written record of all we've agreed to. You'll have the same from me."

"But not *now*. These mountains are impassable until spring."

"Uriah." He heard the edge of tension in Arin's voice. "I'm not a fool."

Uriah put down the candlestick. "No. I would say folly is the least part of you, prince Arin. But why?"

Arin sat on the railing, arms crossed. "You wouldn't understand. My folk are miserable. Away from what they know, they die a little every day."

"And you?"

The careful smile turned chill. "Call that a gift from you, one of your blessings. I'm finding out what a big, strange world it is. We've never been apart from Circle until now. We can't even touch our own here. Now I know why." He continued to scrutinize Uriah like a form of insect.

The Kriss found it difficult to contain his irritation. "I don't think that's all of it."

"No."

Words were surprisingly difficult. "You tricked me today, prince. Your magic. You laid hands on my soul. That is God's."

"I had to. You're too careful to let anything be shared. But I've read you now; not all, but deep enough. You were born into the wrong life in the wrong time, Uriah." Incomprehension and a certain sadness clouded Arin's gaze. "And you hate me. I've never hated anyone, not even the merks. How can you live like this?"

Uriah turned on him a composure frigid as his own. "You find that unwholesome, do you? I am called Proselyte, Arin. An honor for which I spend most of my life with my spiritual arms up to the elbow in garbage. For my faith. For the love of God."

"Love's not a word for you. You don't have any." Arin pushed away from the rail with a weary disgust and started down the aisle. "Not for your woman—and she knows it—not for that sad, sick Mary, not your people, not even for yourself. You're cold as Grannog, Uriah. And I'm sick of winter."

*"And yet we have a great deal in common, prince."*

The voice stopped Arin, a knife-edge of sound. "For all your talk of warmth and love, and the sweaty self-delusion of your Circle, you have the makings of an *exquisite* bastard. You find coldness in me? I see it growing in you. It's not easy to carry a king's mission in this world or the next. And we both know that heroes have bad dreams that never find their way into songs."

"Three days, Uriah." The door closed.

Matthew strode out of the vestibule like a gathering storm, Joshua muttering at his elbow. "Did you hear what he said to the elder? No one, *no* one has ever dared such—" Joshua leveled an I-warned-you finger at Uriah. "This comes of your 'improved' policies, your 'broad, inquiring mind.' They should never have been allowed—"

"Be still!" Uriah spun on them, wiry with purpose. "Joshua, bring all the elders to my house. Have them there in one hour. Matthew—"

"At last," Joshua breathed. "It happens."

"Gloat later, Joshua. For now, act. One hour."

The old man hobbled down the aisle and out of the church.

"Matthew, a guard of thirty armed men will be formed tonight and relieved of work in the mines until further notice. And—" Uriah gripped the altar rail, head bowed in thought. The wood creaked under the press-and-release of his strong fingers, which shook with cold rage. "And a watch will be set tonight on the Shando stable."

"Finally!" glowered Matthew.

"They will keep hidden, prevent no one going or coming. Merely wait and observe."

"It is time." Matthew clumped down the aisle. "Long past time. She is a blot on—"

"And, Matthew."

"Yes, Proselyte?"

"At worship tonight—in a casual way—let Jacob know they plan to leave."

He thought in the breathless beginning that he would have to atone for the crime of being content and filled with Elin. As time went by and Jay lost more and more of himself in her, the need for atonement fell away with the vestigial sense of guilt. He dared the happiness and felt no pang.

In the warm, dark stable, when they lay on their pallet, sweaty and close and breathing slowly again after love, he told her more and more of his life. How did one accept what one was born with? Elin didn't *accept* Circle; for her, it simply was. So with his own faith. Only as he grew older, a sense of something wrong or incomplete nagged him like a splinter under a thumbnail, and he went out to Circle to see how other men lived. He was certain of the presence of God but no longer complacent that the cross or his people's way represented all of reality, nor that the way to God lay in the rejection of everything else. The openness consumed him, made him inarticulate. Lying with his mouth against the curve of Elin's breast, Jay could no longer feel fear or jealousy of her life or the men before him. They merged into the colors of the gift of herself she lay in his hands, and Jay felt at times that he could love Arin for having been a part of her. He had grown a little.

But it could end in two days.

"I could stay here with you," Elin tried to sense his thoughts, but lep-sharing didn't work beyond Circle; not even if you were with someone. "What's that word? We could go to the white house and . . ."

"Be married?" She understood so little. "It wouldn't work, Elin. You could say the words, but they'd mean nothing to you. And the women wouldn't want you."

Elin tangled her legs with his. "Then come home with me."

His head shook wearily with the impossible, worn choices. "And stand outside the circle at Belten or Samman, never a part of it? I tried. You're Circle or you're not. A mind can change, but the rest, that's all your life, Elin."

She laughed into the hollow of his throat. "Well, we can't stay here with the goddam horses."

"Hey, there's a family: you and me and six dumb Shando horses."

"And they all look like you."

"Except they have your nose." He kissed it. "Your freckly, freckly nose."

"Half horse, half cat."

"But I *was* thinking." Something in his tone made Elin apprehensive and hopeful. She slipped over onto his stomach. "What, Jay?"

"That house I built."

"He-ey!"

"Anyone take it?"

"No, it's just like you left it. They shared out your crop, but nobody needed the house."

"Good house," Jay remembered. "Three rooms, space for more. Good watering—"

He felt her hard stomach muscles contract against his as she leaped clear of the pallet. "Jay, *lookout!*" Quick as he was, the shapes moving swiftly in the darkness gave him no chance. He heard the dull blow and Elin's cry before the heavy tool handle thudded into the side of his skull. Stunned, he felt himself rolled on his stomach and the ropes that forced his arms over his back.

Uriah lighted the lamp.

Elin crouched in a corner, covered by Mordecai and another man with ready pikes. The black knife in her hand was absurd against them. Uriah threw her a blanket. "Cover yourself, pig."

More shapes moved beyond the lamplight. Two men advanced on Elin. Her back pressed against the rough boards, she sent the only appeal she knew. *Arin—*

It lanced into his mind as he sat across from Kon, working over the papers that must be exchanged. The pen dropped from his fingers.

*Help!*

Even as they lunged for the door, Magill's eyes blinked open, Hara and Clay swung out of their bunks. Arin yanked open the door, saw the line of waiting men in the moonlit square, then Kon's bulk knocked him aside as the arrow tore into the door behind them.

"We don't have to miss," Matthew shouted. "By order of the elders, you'll turn over your weapons and go with us to protective custody."

"Uriah, please." Jay trembled for both of them, for what was coming. "She doesn't know our ways. They're leaving, they'll be gone. Let her go."

"Oh, Jacob," Uriah sighed with distant pity. "Jacob."

"It was my sin." Jay looked desperately from one cold face to another. "*I* did it. You think she forced me, for Christ's sake? I brought her here, made promises. I made her do it."

"You are naïve, Jacob." Uriah turned away. "Take them out."

"Kill the witches! Kill them all!"

Beyond Arin's window, the women wove in a tireless snake, venturing as close as they dared to the guarded church where, in a cellar beneath the nave, Elin awaited execution. Even with senses shut down tight, the solid wall of hate was painful to Arin, chilling as a fingernail dragged across slate.

"Stoning, prince Arin," said Uriah. "The lawful method in such cases. The woman most wronged under law will throw first. Since Jacob was not married, it will be his mother."

Arin was sick with horror. The nightmarish trial, Elin's frightened eyes always seeking him or Jay, the helpless fury of Jay's frustration, all blurred under the ugly clamor of the women, who strained toward Elin like caged, impatient packdogs. They screamed for her death, vicious, reeking of the same soured desires that trickled blackly from Miriam, overriding any hope of mercy. Uriah himself took her defense. The girl knew nothing of their customs, he argued. It would be enough to banish Jacob. But his calm logic was lost under their surging fury. Joshua and Matthew answered with what became for Arin a black litany throughout the ordeal: *Thou shalt not suffer a witch to live.*

They allowed Elin to speak for herself. The halting, stammering foreign drawl only provoked the women to fresh howls. *Stone her! Stone the witch!*

Then it was Arin's turn. "For the first time, there's a door open between our two peoples. Try to understand us." Coveners, he told them, could not divide body from spirit as the Kriss did. To love was to touch, the way of his kind all their lives. He offered to take Jay with them, to leave immediately, make cash restitution, whatever terms the Kriss could name. He saw Jay's ironic smile, grim but pitying his own ignorance of the Kriss.

*Thou shalt not suffer a witch to live.*

"Was not Jacob chosen for the altar?" Matthew roared in the prosecution. "Did he not serve at Uriah's left hand? Was he not chaste before she came? Or was he already tainted from living among them, living as Shando, as dirt underfoot?"

*Thou shalt not suffer . . .*

"These"—Joshua pointed at Arin and Elin—"are creatures of wile and magic. I will not criticize the wisdom of our chief elder—young though he be for such a burden—but I say he has erred in letting them into Salvation. I say Uriah, whose wisdom is still only that which God *allows* to mortal men, has, in his many cares, overlooked the danger of an ill-considered path. Praise our chief elder, and pray God grant him peace and continued wisdom."

". . . and it is the decision of the elders in solemn assembly that the sentence of Jacob be subject to a vote of all the men of Salvation, under which, by a majority, he shall be cut from the body of the church to suffer perpetual exile or such death as the elders may direct.

"It is their further judgment that the Shando woman named Elin, as the proven agent of sin, be placed within two days in the hands of the women of Salvation . . ."

Alone in the trial room with Uriah, Arin watched the women. The sickness was a new facet of his education. The Kriss had taught him how to hate. Haggard with strain and the long pleading, he reached across the table to Uriah. "You win. Name it: money, conditions. I'll pay or sign whatever you want for her."

"Easily promised," Uriah demurred. "Hard to collect. Garick would regret the girl, but not so much as a lost alliance."

"Words!" Arin heaved himself away from the table. "Uriah, you can stop this."

Uriah joined him at the window. "Can I? You'll never think or feel like us, Arin. We are an island of faith in a sea of coven; only that faith has allowed us to survive. Life itself is nothing."

"You've survived because you are ringed with peaceful coveners who will *not* say that life is nothing. Life is everything."

"The *way* of life," Uriah amended. "I administer the laws, I don't make them. This is beyond me. I cannot even allow you to leave yet."

"Why not?"

Uriah indicated the seething women. "Look at them. Listen to them. You'd never make it past the church. The custody is protective. You can't help that girl or even yourself right now, only wait for me to repair the damage she's done."

Arin slumped with fatigue. He stared out the window. Uriah returned to his chair.

"Could it be something else, not the women? Something quick?"

"The right is theirs, prince. Flesh is the strongest temptation. It must be checked by a law and punishment unarguable as the hunger itself. I have no more recourse to wanton mercy than to cruelty. Mercy would imply a tolerance to flesh which cheapens the sacrifice of the spirit."

"You talk like a book. I'm a man. Talk to me like a man. I can understand you."

"Yes." Uriah looked at him with a now-familiar mixture of envy and sadness. "Yes, you can. Perhaps more than the so-called faithful."

"Nothing is free; that's your saying. All right, what's the price?" Arin tried desperately. "You wanted a mission among the Shando; you've got it. My word as a master, as Garick's son. A house of your own, cropland for your people—"

"Arin"—Uriah held up his hand—"it can't be stopped."

"Please!"

"No."

"She's down in that dirty hole, she's scared, doesn't understand half what's happening to her. And I *feel* her, Uriah. You can't know that, but Elin's calling now, been calling out to us since you took her. I want to shut her off, but I can't. I . . . I beg you, elder."

Uriah's eyes were flat and bleak. "I can't afford it, Arin."

The young man blinked. "What?"

"Your people have your needs in this war; so have we. In this tiny place, I answer for almost three times as many people as Garick does. Because more of ours live after birth than in Circle. We need, and soon will *desperately* need, more land for crops, the knowledge that goes with it, more goods than just coal to export, more money to import. Like Garick, we will need *change*. Like Garick, I have to fight for it, fight people for whom change is near to impossible. You heard Joshua's very respectful criticism; the chief elder has been misguided. I brought you here against almost every voice in Salvation.

I've already stretched their faith in me. If I let her go, another elder would challenge my power and very likely win. Then it wouldn't be just the girl, but all of you." His eyes, though hard, were tired. "Yes, she's a sop, a bone. The price you'll pay to get where Garick needs you next. Don't look shocked, Arin, and spare me your forest philosophy. You bought your way here with Micah. Different dogs, different bone. But you threw it."

Arin dropped his eyes and said nothing. Uriah clipped off the words as if they tasted bad. "I don't blame you; blame is irrelevant. The game is called history, and unless you're an unmitigated, heaven-towering son of a bitch, you're lost. Let the pure take up farming."

Hopeless, Arin plowed agitated fingers through his long hair. "It's tomorrow?"

"In the morning."

"I want to be with her. A few hours."

The elder's consideration was brief and dubious. "I think not. You are masters of deception. Your robes are full of pockets for—"

Arin's fist battered down on the table. "Naked, then, you bastard! Stripped, searched, whatever you want. But let her have one friend."

Uriah stared at the livid knuckles; his expression altered subtly. "Buy it, then. One bastard to another, what is it worth?"

"What do you want?"

Uriah placed his finger tips together. "You've insisted on going to Lishin, but you won't say why. Lishin is ours. We want to know what use Garick will make of it. Something in the old laboratory?"

Arin hedged. "If I promise to tell you, can I see Elin?"

"Tell me now."

"Uh-uh. Half now, half when we go."

"You're not in a position to bargain, Arin. You're in prison and you'll stay there."

"And stay and stay." Arin leaned across to him. "But time passes and snow melts and one day, elder, you'll wake up ass-deep in Shando asking questions you're not ready to answer. You can't hold me forever, and I don't think you want to. So half now, half when we leave." He couldn't hope Uriah would swallow it whole, but there was just enough truth to give it weight.

"All right, you can see her. Now, what's in Lishin?"

Arin nodded and rose. "A map with three circles drawn on it. And that map is going to open City for all of us. It's the only thing that can."

"How?" Uriah pressed. "A map of what? Where?"

Arin paused at the door. "That's the other half. I'll send word when I want to see Elin."

"Stripped," said Uriah. "Searched. And in clothes I will provide."

"I'd feel a little dirty, elder. Just a blanket."

It was no surprise to the disenchanted Shando that Salvation had a house set aside for punishment alone, an unfurnished one-room hut with a fitfully efficient stove. They set Clay closest to its warmth because he had fever and still slept poorly. They all looked sallow and sick, Arin thought, exhausted himself to the brink of tears with the compassion of a leader powerless to help his people. Elin whispered into their minds, a ghost already mourning its own death. *It's tomorrow morning.*

"Garick will be all over this place," Hara judged bitterly.

Magill turned on him sharply. "That won't help Elin."

Arin rummaged among the few possessions Uriah had judged harmless and extracted a thin red Lorlcloth shirt, a present from Shalane. He began to pick at the hem with nimble fingers. "I've done what I can. You hear those women in the squarc. Right now, Uriah and his guards are all that's keeping us alive."

Dangerous, quiet, Magill asked, "What about Elin?"

Arin pulled at the loosened threads. He spoke carefully, bent over the task. "Nothing's free, Gill. If we can't get to Lishin, all of this is for nothing."

Magill didn't move. "And Elin?"

"We can't help her. Except for one thing." Arin fingered the edge of one of his blankets and ripped a small opening in one corner between the thicknesses. They watched as he withdrew a small moleskin pouch. "They'll strip me bare before I see her, but they won't find this." He regarded the pouch. "Call it sleep. An easy sleep, even dreams."

"You gonna do it yourself?"

Kon warned: "Gill . . ."

Arin's expression was hard for them to read. "It's me or the women."

Magill stood frozen over him a moment longer, then turned away, cocked and tense. "Guess I'm pretty dumb. Thing gotta fall on me before I know it's there. Been around Elin all my life, rode with her, been on the hill. That's . . . that's some kind of woman, Arin. But there was that damfool Jay, and before that, there was you." He came back to stand over Arin. "Rode with you fifteen years out of twenty, never knew you, either. You a strange kind of master, Arin. Ain't done nothing but get people killed."

Arin rose, feeling his arms begin to tremble. "Get off me, Gill."

"Think Elin don't want to live? Read her now, listen to her."

"I hear her." They faced each other like drawn bows.

"You gonna get her born again, Arin? How many more of us you gonna bury?" The enumerating, accusing fingers stabbed in Arin's face. "Holder, Sand, Teela. Now *Elin,* you coldblood sonofabitch—"

"Get *off!*" Arin's open palm came up, catching Magill under the chin. Magill shot backward across the room, fighting for balance, but Arin was on him before Hara or Kon could intervene, battering brutally about his face and body. Kon tore him off while Hara held the struggling Magill.

"Lemme go," Gill raged. "Get off me, lemme go!"

"Hold him, Hara." Kon wrenched Arin around, slamming him against the wall. "Stop, Arin. Hold now." Arin tried to twist free. Kon's open hand smashed across his face. "Stop!"

They held the two men apart. "All right!" Arin's breath exploded in a sob. "I'm *not* much of a master. Had to learn too much too fast and done all wrong since. Wrong, wrong, wrong! That what you want to hear, Gill? Sure I read Elin, been reading her all along. I begged that Kriss bastard—money, anything he wanted. More than Garick would pay. I couldn't save her." His hands went out to them in supplication. "I told that girl, I warned her. What I gonna do, tie her to a tree?" Arin wiped his red eyes. When he could control his voice, its hardness surprised him. "Garick used to say you get what you pay for. All right, Garick gets his goddam Kriss, five of us live, one dies, that's *it*. Now leave me alone."

"Five?" Magill wiped the blood from his nose, crying for the ragged end of something torn away and lost. "You count four, Arin. They let us out, I go home."

"Hell you will," said Hara.

"Hell I won't! Too much lost. No more."

"Boy," said Kon, "you never did have enough brain to put on a fork. You get past the merks, there's Karli. What you say to Shalane? Then Garick. What you tell him, Gill?"

"That the rest of us died in Lishin." Clay sat up in his blankets, chalky, shivering with a fresh assault of the fever. "Because it'll happen." His glazed eyes went from man to man. "Night after night since I saw that dead god by the river, I dreamed the same dream. We'll go to Lishin. It'll find us there."

Arin squatted beside him. He felt the dry flush in Clay's cheeks. "Hara, coal up that stove, boil some water. I'll make a brew, Clay. You're sick."

Clay persisted. "My head ain't sick. I see it."

"See what, boy?"

Clay's voice was leaden, old. "No feel, no shape, but it's there. And we're there." He lay back down, staring at no one, at all of them, Magill included.

Arin went to the church two hours before dawn. In the chill gloom of the nave, surrounded by Uriah, Joshua and four guards, he was stripped to the skin and subjected to an exhaustive search. The guards pawed through his hair and beard, turned up the soles of his feet. They looked into his mouth and rectum, turned him this way and that. Satisfied at last that he carried no poison or sedative to alleviate the woman's just punishment, they gave him a thick blanket. The trap door in the floor of the nave was thrown back. As Arin prepared to descend, Uriah asked a curious question.

"Will she want breakfast?"

Arin didn't know. The humanity surprised him.

"Matthew will send for food if she wants it. He is with her now. He'll remain while you're there."

"Does he have to?"

"I'm afraid yes."

"He hasn't hurt her?" Arin warned. "He hasn't touched her?"

"Don't worry about that." Uriah's lowered voice carried a trace of irony. "Elder Matthew is not the brightest star in the firmament of abstract thought. His weakness lies in a certain spiritual myopia, not women. Nevertheless, he hopes someday to be rewarded with a holy vision for his labors."

The cellar had one small window, glassed and barred, flush with the ground. Loose boards were spread over the earth floor. As the ground froze and thawed, mud oozed through and over them. There was no heat. Matthew's surly bulk hunched in a chair near the ladder. In the far corner, as far from him as possible, Elin huddled on a small cot among a litter of ragged blankets. They had not starved her. A tray with remnants of a meal sat on the plank floor near her cot. Washing and other comforts, however, had not been considered necessary. The magnificent hair, grown thick since Charzen, tangled stiffly about her face, and the rich green robe was stained with mud. The cellar had a damp, unpleasant odor.

She rose nervously as he descended the ladder, a wraith half visible in Matthew's candle glare, her rigid frame speaking eloquently to Arin of the numb fear she held back.

He nodded curtly to Matthew. "Uriah said you must stay, but leave us alone."

Matthew shrugged. "I have spoken to her. What use? She was lost long ago."

Elin hugged him close. "Hey, Arin." She giggled at his foolish blanket wrap, a high, constricted sound. "Don't you look fine." *Help me. I don't want to die.* "How's Jay?"

"I haven't seen him." They sat down on the cot. *Matthew hurt you?*

"No." Elin vented a pitying glance on the Kriss elder. "Just talk at me about old dead god till I yell quit."

"Lost," echoed Matthew.

"Ah, shut up!" Her laugh was too sharp and loud, frittering away into a shudder. "Kriss don't get around much; don't know how folks feel." *Help me. Why can't you help me? You're*—"a master!" she flashed at him. "Where's Garick, where's Shando and Karli to help me? What I do? Nothing!" Elin pointedly disgustedly at Matthew. "Gotta sit here and smell *him* till they come."

"Sit down." Arin pulled her back. *They won't get you.*

*?*

He lepped it briefly; they'd searched him, but missed the magic he brought. *I swallowed it*—wrapped in a small, greased pouch suspended by fine thread from a back tooth. She was to call for breakfast and a cup of something hot. If she took it now, the women wouldn't be able to hear themselves hoot for all her snoring. *You won't feel, just sleep. Arms and legs like wood.*

*So scared.* He saw the panic tighten her jaws. Elin hesitated. She touched the tangled hair, traced a finger along her forearm as if relishing their reality. "Born again—is that true?"

"To the Shando." All his life he had said it with a faith far below conscious utterance. Now he was painfully aware of the impoverished words. The anger rose in him, a helpless, crippled ghost without hands to do or mouth to cry out that one more thing, one more large piece of him was being torn away by the world and the worm.

Elin lifted her head. "Know what, then?"

"What?"

"Next man I pick gonna be a farmer." She seemed to consider it a moment. "Matthew, y'old horse!"

He was nodding over his candle. "Um—what?"

Elin stretched on the cot. "I'm hungry."

Matthew grumbled and heaved out of the chair, turning to call up the ladder. Arin's hand darted swiftly to his mouth; he retched silently as the pale thread emerged followed by the moleskin pouch, which disappeared under his blanket.

The food came with decent promptness, a bowl of grayish substance, hot enough but clearly just removed from a preserving jar. Elin dabbled her spoon in the unappetizing mess. "This looks like I already ate it."

*Drink some tea and give me some.*

She drank and passed him the cup. "But the tea's real good. Must have used the goldenrod I had left."

"You always could find the best." Arin drank and passed it back to her under Matthew's scrutiny. His hand held the mug over its steaming top, but Elin alone caught a glimpse of the whitish powder before it dissolved.

*Won't even taste it.*

*Thank you, Arin.* She took a large swallow.

Gradually the trembling of fear and cold ceased. Elin's body relaxed. She took off her shoes and wriggled her feet like a little girl, sheathing them under the blankets. The glaze of terror faded from her eyes. "Lepped you people all day. Felt you."

"We read you."

"You hurt Gill."

"It hurt me more."

*Gill's sick inside, gone from you.* "Didn't have no one but you'n me and Kon."

Arin stroked her cheek. "You should have taken Gill. He'd stay with you."

"No . . . no." Elin yawned and slid lower on the cot. "He'd be gone, he's wild like you, always riding off. You ain't home folks." She took another drink. *Sleepy*. She smiled. "Ma never did know why I wanted to come with you. Tell her . . . tell Ma it was all right. I'm not sorry. There was Jay."

She plumped the pillow roll and lay down. Arin tucked the blankets around her. "Should've got to Jay in Charzen," she breathed softly. "Not my fault I didn't, but hoo*ee*"—the thought was spaced by another luxurious yawn—"that boy *did* learn quick." Elin opened one eye, tender and mischievous. "Better than you, master Arin."

"I guess."

"Tore me up six ways from Sinjin." Elin sighed with drowsy pleasure. "Would've had ten kids, I 'spect." *Can't feel my feet and hands.*

*Don't fight, Elin. Let it work.*

Elin yawned again and stretched her whole body. Then, as if reminded of something important, she raised on one elbow suddenly and barked: "Mat*thew!*"

The Kriss reared like a startled bear. "What? You wanted to be alone. I don't want to talk to you. What is it?"

Elin rewarded him with a smile devastating as it was innocent. "Y'all don't forget to call me when it's time."

Matthew warmed his hands over the candle. "It will be soon."

*Will you be close, Arin?*

He would. The brown fingers, no longer able to feel, groped clumsily for his.

"Then kiss me good night."

The candle guttered. The narrow window grayed with early light. Matthew rubbed the need to sleep out of his eyes, massaging porcine jowls, and lit another candle. The girl was asleep. Arin hunched at the foot of the bed, head bowed over his knees, still holding her hand.

He had too often folded into the warmth of Elin's spirit to forget the way. She slept, a tiny curve of smile on her lips as his energy clasped about her for the last time. The coils went out as they had to Singer, but softly now, lovingly, to twine around Elin like bright ribbons about a handful of flowers. He thought his power might not be enough, but it was there as in the forest before Karli, plenty to spare, and though it drained him, it had to be given. The heart beat against his, the young blood sang through the healthy veins. Arin curled tighter. Her heart and blood, without laboring, seemed to tire in their action, the dreaming mind paused.

She was on a riverbank. The sun was shining and Elin hesitated midway between Jay and Arin. Both of them called her. She must go to Jay because he needed her, but somehow Arin must be touched first, like the god at Samman circle. Jay would wait, she'd just be a little time. She ran to Arin, but he looked too sad and thin because he never did eat enough. For the last time she nestled in his arms and found them full of security and peace.

*I have to go, Arin.*

He still held her close. The arms stretched out around her, holding, slowing, a gentle breath blowing out a small candle. The heart thudded softly like blood in the ear, slowed, slowed . . . stopped. The blood stilled and the dream darkened.

"Dead, Matthew. Turning cold."

In the garish, smoky light of the torches, Matthew's small eyes bulged with astonishment and fright, the chief elder's accusation boring into him. "Elder, I swear! She drank nothing but the tea. He even had some. They just talked. She lay down on the bed and"—his slow mind grated against the absurdity—"told me to wake her when it was time. They just talked. Before my God, that's all."

Uriah turned away. He knew Matthew had watched. The man was doggedly trustworthy. It was his own fault for setting an old tortoise to supervise a young cat.

"Get him on his feet."

Arin slumped between the two guards. His face glistened. The blanket had fallen away as they pulled him up, and Uriah saw that it was more than tears. Arin's body was clammy with cold sweat, the red eyes aged with exhaustion and pain. Elin had been deep in him, like Kon and Gill. To cut her away from life, he had lanced into his own soul and a part of him died with her.

Matthew covered Elin. "The women will be here soon. What can we do?"

"You could pray for her," Arin croaked. "That's what you do, isn't it?"

Uriah tapped the club against his palm, busy with the problem of the thwarted women. For the loss of Elin, they would want all of the men, and that he could not give them. The Shando must die in Lishin without incriminating Salvation. He stepped close to Arin. "You are a strange and incomprehensible man, but I've never underestimated you until now. You're right, I can't keep you forever. But you must stay until you're healed, Arin."

He handed the club to Matthew, who took it gratefully and moved in on Arin. The first blow exploded just behind Arin's ear. He didn't remember falling, just scrabbling stupidly on his knees with the cellar going dark around him. The second blow broke his left arm.

As the leps jumped into his mind, he realized he was still pitifully open, sharing this pain with the men. For the first time in his life, he shut them out completely so they wouldn't suffer for him, totally cut himself off from Circle, dying a little again as he ceased to feel the blows, alone in the dark on the brink of a precipice from which he had once before stepped back . . .

He learned the savage, ridiculous end of it weeks later when it didn't matter any more. Imprisoned away from the others, lying on the cot from which they took Elin's body, Arin could still laugh feebly at Uriah's resourcefulness. With hardly a minute lost, the corpse was laid close to a hot stove for as long as possible. When the women came, they were told that the girl had swallowed hidden poison. She was in terminal coma and would die without waking. Justice in this case would be academic, but if they insisted . . .

They did. They took up the convincingly warm body and, with somewhat dampened righteousness, carried out the sentence. The remnant was wrapped in a blanket and left deep in the woods for scavengers. So Elin went home to the forest that bore her, receiving her again and cleansing itself as it always did.

By a close vote, Jay was cast out of Salvation, out of the sight of God, never to return.

"He chose to go to Charzen," Uriah told Arin. "So he will carry our agreement to Garick's alliance. He is one of you now." It sounded like something spoken at the edge of a grave.

As the snow melted and spring advanced toward Leddy, the women seemed to have forgotten them. The Kriss community went on its dogged way, praying and digging coal. The pain of Elin dulled. Clay fought off the fever but remained withdrawn and listless. Kon and Hara sometimes argued with Magill for his loss of faith in Arin, but Clay took no part and spoke no more of his dreams. The men knew nothing of the missing Arin but his lep, and for many weeks there was not even that. When it returned, it was steelier, singly intent on one purpose. *Gather in.*

Obedient, they linked with Arin's mind, boosting his power in a wordless sending each day from first light until the sun was high. At the end of each exhausting effort, Arin shut himself away again. They received nothing by way of an answer from any circle. Still they persisted, grateful for a point of reference in a backwater of time, unaware that they lay in the eye of a hurricane that spread and swirled faster each day:

The eastern frontier closed tight. No wool went out of Karli, and even the Kriss coal trains took a new route safely west and north into Wengen. Mrikan merchants, heavily invested in Garick's future crop, sent their own missions to Charzen across a border bristling with merks, and along this thin vein coursed the brief, articulate reports of Spitt.

**"—northern division still within Mrika, but strong elements of southern division strung west across the Karli-Wengen frontier, dragging without City contract. All drag bounties have gone up by at least two and a half krets. Callan repeat Callan definitely the source of money and orders."**

Spitt constructed a spotty profile of the merk sub he had never managed to meet: twenty-five or -six, able to read and write, abstemious, no woman that anyone knew of, a loner without friends, sub to Bowdeen in the reactivated 43rd company, southern division.

**"—Bowdeen is a kind of fond legend, but Callan is called Iron Ass. No one's ever seen him in anything but leather, riding most of the time, driving himself as hard as any man under him. Bowdeen's close to fifty. There's talk he'll retire. If he does, his promotion to field commander may go to Callan, putting five to ten companies under his direct command besides his financial influence, and I'd give half a year's pay to find out where that money comes from. Have you considered it might not be City? So far, Hoban and the Karli are containing the merks north in running fights, avoiding a stand. Suggest no commitment of Shando for the time . . ."**

"He's right," Singer remarked. Garick looked up at him in baffled irritation. Through the winter, his enigmatic older son had maintained his aloof, resentful disinterest in Garick's preparations. It surprised Garick now to hear him volunteer an opinion.

"Why's Spitt right?"

Singer lay back on his bed, hands behind his head, already detaching himself. He murmured something half audible, like "One more piece."

Garick's temper flared. "You wouldn't care to get your ass up off that bed and tell me something?"

Singer barely paid him any attention. "Your war," he murmured. "Never said I'd help. You want me to stop laying around, daddy"—he held up his tether—"get this goddam rope off me."

His father made no answer. He turned back to his worktable. A new map lay on it, already dog-eared with handling, measeled with green and red wooden squares writhing in a shifting line along the north and east frontiers, wooden squares that Garick moved daily guided by the Karli lep, aware that each green square was twenty or more men and women riding all day on a flask of water and a handful of pone, groping for the nearest red square or running, wolf-wary, to elude and thrust again, burying their dead in shallow, hastily scooped trenches, never allowing themselves to be caught on open ground, taking three or four to one in casualties, but the one was usually a man Garick had known all his life, names tolling deep under the Karli lep.

*Beddin, old Rice, Rill and Fox will be born again.*

From Charzen a steady supply of fresh horses drove up the Cumlan Valley toward Karli, swift animals from the southwest Suffec herds to mount the new contingents that rode almost daily out of Karli.

*Master Deak leaves tomorrow with thirty more. Moss rides with him.*

Moss riding again? The map and its story, the silence from Arin that said tacitly what no one would speak aloud, all the demons that jostled through his thoughts and haunted his sleep were stilled while Garick's mind brushed at the memory. Moss by the wagon while he and Judith clung together, needing and promising before the world happened to them. Moss telling him he was a fool, telling him to go home and take Jenna and raise apples, not seeing how touched with fire the other was. So many years. *Remember, Moss?*

The riders milled about the muddy stockade puddled with spring rain, falling into riding order behind Deak. Maysa looped the bag of provisions over Moss' saddle horn and hooked a toe in the stirrup to hug herself against his sheepskin poncho.

"You take care, Moss. Take your tea nights, dammit, and wrap up good."

He pulled her close. "Don't get fat while I'm gone. Always liked you skinny." His grin was a young man's. Maysa couldn't escape the feeling that Moss looked forward to this.

"Aw, go—" She bit his lip and jumped down. "Look at him, Lane. Thinks he's still your age."

Shalane stepped lightly onto the stirrup to kiss her father. "Moss, listen for Arin. Open up to him. Don't care what anyone says, he's alive."

Moss let himself share his daughter's need and hurt. "Baby girl"—he kissed her—"take it one day at a time."

"He's alive! I read him. Not words, just a little whisper that comes and comes. Please."

"I will, Lane. G'wan now, they all waiting."

"And I love you, Moss." Shalane kissed him quick and hard, and ran dodging under horses' necks, grabbing a hand here and there in farewell until she came to Deak adjusting the hood of his skins against the raw morning wind. Shalane tugged at his bridle. "Remember, Deak. Listen for Arin. He's out there."

Deak took her hand, tender with the desperation that flooded out of the girl. They had listened and hoped all winter. Someone somewhere would have heard anything readable out of those mountains where not even trappers could ride till now. The hurt would end mercifully for Shalane soon or late, like a hand opening and letting go. By then she'd be gone to the knife herself, and if she lived there'd be other men.

"If he's there, I'll read him."

The column was moving now, Shalane trotting along at his knee. "And come back yourself, you Deak."

"You teach them Shando horses some manners, now."

"Sure as frost!" That was something she could do, gratefully translating her helpless uncertainty into action. The inbred brutes that took her bit were not only broken but educated within an inch of their pea-brained lives. Shalane drove them and herself furiously to relieve the frustration. Every day for weeks the feeble ghost signal seeped into her consciousness, always at the same time. It *was* Arin. No one could tell her different.

Still, as she watched the riders out of sight, her mind stung with the bitter joke. The Karli whom Garick couldn't buy were fighting his war for nothing, none of them knowing where it would end. Where were the Wengen? And the Kriss that Arin had risked his life to reach? And where was Garick, the strange mind that started it all?

*Where are you?* she wondered. *All of you, when are you coming?*

They played out the last moves of their game over a map spread on Arin's cot. When they were done, Arin knew he'd be free and Uriah would have the capstone to his puzzle. Arin slid the pen along a sketched-in road and marked an X. "This is the weapons house."

"The old laboratory, yes."

"Five houses. It's the one with big numbers over the doors. Just inside number seven on the south side is where Jude left the map. A big room full of iron boxes."

"Why didn't she take it with her?"

"She was carried out half dead by a man who wasn't right in the head for a year after. He didn't even think of the map. Couldn't read it, anyway."

Uriah considered the possibility. Skilled as he was in nuance, Arin's face still told him nothing. He could read now only the outward changes in the man. The unkempt beard sank into hollow cheeks, the mouth tighter than before as if folded down over some private revelation. His left arm had not set properly and would always hang slightly twisted. Arin might be telling the truth. Uriah was one of the party that went into Lishin after Judith left and the waters receded. A search of the laboratory had been part of their business. Nothing had been found.

"What's in that place, Uriah?"

"What?"

"We call Lishin a dead place, but it's not. There's something there." Arin searched for the old word. "Something evil."

"Perhaps truth," Uriah answered enigmatically, "which surprises us in any form. I couldn't say. To us the place is just lonely, more so because so much of our past is still there—like a rather futile reproach. 'Look on My Works, Ye Mighty and—' improve." He pointed to the map. "Our bargain, remember? What will this tell you? What will it take you to?"

"The Girdle of Solitude."

Uriah stared in bald disbelief. "The *what?*"

Arin said it again.

"But that's just a myth. A çoven song-story."

Arin shrugged. "Sure."

"Oh, come on! Garick doesn't *believe* that."

Arin handed him the map. "You asked, you got told: a map with three circles, and one of them is the Girdle."

Uriah's mind raced to comprehend. "It doesn't exist!"

But . . . if it *did,* his mind told him, a man totally invisible in broad daylight, the right man, could walk through the mercenaries, across Mrika to the door of City itself. Except . . . *what* man? Who could survive the Self-Gate? Still, the imagination in Uriah perceived the same quality in Garick; an audacity of a staggering dimension. *That* was why his plan of deployment was so ambiguous. It hinged on the location of the Girdle, ready to swing north or south as needed.

"Who will wear it, Arin?"

Arin paused, one hand on the ladder. "I don't know. Some damn fool with an itch for playing god. Maybe you, elder."

"Yes." Uriah busied himself folding the map. "You *are* clever; you read that in me. I want to be . . . more."

He was surprised now, at the end, to find that he would miss Arin if only for the mind to push against. A tragic difference, the coven mind that conceived itself as part of the enchaining earth, man as flower rather than fallen angel, yet stallion-spirited to dare heaven could they reach it—and if they believed. And himself, reaching for the same heaven from an earth that mired him too deep to grasp it. Sometimes he toyed with the ancient heresy that man was really an animal, an ape caught midway in evolution between tree and ground, too clumsy to climb and not yet able to stand erect. Too cruel.

"I envy you," Uriah confessed. "You can go and become. I must stay and be." He did not move or offer his hand. "Good-by, Arin."

That was their endgame. As at the beginning, they gave each other truth when it didn't matter, lied when it did. Arin did not tell Uriah that Moss had rehidden the map before his mind blanked out the horror of Lishin. And Uriah, a day before, had caused his miners to dam up the two tributary creeks that fed alkaline water into the rain-swollen river to balance the acid spill from the mines. The flow grew more toxic by the hour. Even as Arin cinched his saddle and watched Magill ride away, his stiff, unforgiving back like another death between them, the first of the poisoned fish were floating belly up into the low, flooded shore line at Lishin.

About half a mile northwest of the last Kriss houses, the river narrowed, spanned by another iron and stone bridge like that at Lishin, smaller, but in better condition. The spans had been reshored in recent years as the main access to the mines north of the river. The four crossed in silence under a steady drizzle. The road turned due east on the north bank past a sprawl of ruin dominated by an overgrown cylinder of stone, and followed the river to Lishin.

Better for the men this way, Arin considered. The smudge of road should lead them directly to the weapons house. They would avoid the rotted town until departure. At a steady trot they might raise it just past high sun or a little later, with plenty of light to find the map and be gone.

Kon and Clay rode close, Hara leading out ahead, leaving the trail now and then to investigate this or that sign, constantly sniffing at the wind as it veered from different points. Arin's arm throbbed, the barely knitted bone protesting the dampness. The air was foul with a decay he couldn't place.

None of them were at their best or near it. The long winter indoors, combined with bad food, had sallowed the men and dulled their edge. The horses were listless; Soogee stumbled along like she was ten years old instead of three. The Kriss probably fed them grudgingly and locked them away with no other care. The old coven sense in Garick's son cursed with a shriveling contempt. He would never understand Uriah or his Kriss, but men too thick to care for good horses weren't going to do too much for their own kind.

He'd hardly talked to the men since his release. The apartness had become a habit with him. He should share more, though they were glad to have him back—all but Magill, who'd ignored his outstretched hand and gone on cinching his saddle with a hurt finality. Arin couldn't blame him; Gill had come too far and lost too much and probably couldn't name himself all the things eating at him. Let it go.

The remains of the road led close along the riverbank, spotted here and there with patches of the stuff Uriah called concrete, stone crushed to powder, mixed with sand and water and poured like corn batter into any desired shape. His own folk didn't believe it, they never did. Sometimes he wanted to yell at them: *Circle isn't the whole goddam world. Everyone's not like us.*

He felt weak and depressed and just plain old.

After Lishin he wouldn't ask the men to go any further. They could follow him or go home, the choice was theirs. It was selfish, but death had a weight that hung on the heart. He couldn't carry any more. Let them take the map and go back; splitting up would double Garick's chances of getting it. A searing irritation jerked his head up at Clay and Kon. They'd have to carry it all the way to Charzen, couldn't even lep from Karli. The best minds there, even Shalane, would be no help at all. *Stupid sons of bitches can't read. Uriah's right; what are we? A bunch of plain people with one extra little fold in the brain we call lep, and because of this we think we're something special. We hoot around in a circle singing about how nice it is to be part of the earth while the earth couldn't care less.*

Soogee stumbled; he brought her head up with a sharp twist of the reins that told him he was wasting energy in succumbing to the depression. Kon and Clay were looking at him curiously. He was shut off, hadn't even read the lep. "It's Hara."

*Come on. Waiting.*

They found Hara sitting on a log a little distance from the road while his horse cropped hungrily at the short new grass.

"Dead fish." He pointed down to the rocky shore line. His arm swept over the yellowish waters. "This must be the west run of the Skanna, can't be anything else. Trapped the north run some. Seen it muddy and clear, never like that."

Kon frowned at the turbulent stream. "Old river looks sick."

"More fish down there," Clay discovered. "Must be a thousand. More'n that. Look, Arin."

The wind veered again, coming from the south. Hara pushed back his hood and sniffed, hunter-wisdom feeling at the air, sorting trace from trace and delivering its verdict.

"Not just fish. Something else."

The rain thinned to wet mist when Arin dropped the reins and let Soogee crop at the grass that bordered the broken black paving. The low oblong of the weapons house squatted before him, broken glass windows set in curious, many-paned strips along the weathered walls, faded numbers over the memorized entrances: *1–2–3–4* close together, *5* in the middle, *6* at the southeast corner. Eastward hulked

Lishin with the square stone tower as his reference to the bridge. The dead fish smell was sickening here, mixed with that other alien odor that prickled the hair on his neck and made Soogee hard to quiet.

The weapons house was really five buildings, two north of the road, three on the south side, of which the center building was their destination. Arin urged the mare forward.

On the south face he made out the numbers *7–8–9*. He knew none of them wanted to enter the house, to let it close over them with its unknown magic. Clay said they'd die in Lishin. Part of Arin was afraid. The house, the town like an unburied corpse, the foul air, battered his instincts with their warnings. The place was evil, quivering with the full virulence of that trace he once read in Moss like a stain on the mind. But it had been built by the great masters of the old songs, the men who rode under the sea and high as the moon. He wanted to touch what they made, take it in his hands and learn from it.

He stepped down and led Soogee by her bridle. "I'll go in first. Come when I call."

The doorless entrance yawned below 7. Soogee balked at the threshold. Arin coaxed her inside. The roof was partially caved in just ahead, the passageway full of rotted debris and muddy water. The iron-box room was to his left, but Arin paused. There was a little time. Jude must have wandered some, curious as himself. He tethered the mare to a door handle and splashed across the ruptured floor, kicked at a door that disintegrated inward before him. Arin stepped into a small room. Its main furniture consisted of three drawered tables that hadn't rusted much. In one of the drawers, he found a picture. The air-tight covering had turned cloudy with age and grime, but it was whole. A picture of the masters as they lived, real as looking at Kon or Magill. His hands shook a little; it was like opening up buried time and looking into the grave. Realness caught on paper! Such fine clothes, so many buttons, so cleverly cut. The woman's dress was a faded rainbow. No one in Mrika could weave such thin material or dye so many colors into one piece of cloth. She was young, even pretty in a queer, foreign way, her lips unnaturally dark against paper-white skin. Shorter hair than Shalane's and combed up in a fussy way that would take a coven woman half a morning.

"I'm here," Arin whispered to her smile. "Me, Arin. City remembers and Kriss remember, but what did you leave for me?"

The picture-people smiled across the centuries, confident, composed. They seemed small next to the table, but it was the expression that set them apart from his own kind. Those minds had never locked as one. The ears had never listened in the forest.

The iron-box room was not new to him but like coming home, almost as he pictured it. Many rows of tall *files,* Uriah called them, traces of rotted, blackened wood pulp from Moss' last fire. Halfway down the long room, the metal door he was to mark. The rickety table. Arin's hand trailed over the dusty surface, seeing again the image of Jude as Moss shared it. He could almost feel her now close as Shalane or Jenna.

The rain increased. Arin sent a gather-in. Kon and Hara answered. *Clay, you asleep?* The boy answered absently. His mind was elsewhere, listening.

He heard the others in the entrance, pulling the reluctant horses after them. Arin tugged open the metal door and slipped into the darkness of the tiny room, his head barely clearing the entrance. Shelves on either side, the highest just above eyeline. He groped at one and came away with nothing but dust. On the other, his hand brushed against folded paper. Between careful thumb and forefinger, Arin lifted it down, blowing away the loose dirt. A large, thick paper quarter-folded around several handwritten sheets.

The other men gathered about Arin as he spread the map open on the table. They shared no part of his excitement; bedraggled and ill at ease, saying the horses were spooked and might have to be hobbled. Arin barely listened. "This is what we came for."

The map had held together far better than he expected. Moss said Jude used City magic on it, a metal can that hissed when she pushed a button and covered the ancient paper with tough, clear dust. The men admired it perfunctorily as a colorful object and had no idea what it was.

A picture of the land, Arin told them. Hundreds of miles of it. They marveled: sure as frost one big-assed country.

"This cross mark is Lishin where we are. This blue line is the Skanna, but they wrote it different." All the names, the long-dead ghost names sang like faint music in Arin's ears as he pointed them out. Karli, Salvation, they were just tiny pieces of a bigger place, but not too big. Look, with two fingers, he could cover the miles. So little the long name stretched clear across it.

"Hell," Kon figured, "ain't nobody gonna say *that* more'n once a year."

"Pennsylvania." Arin tasted the sound. "Kind of pretty."

One of the horses whinnied high with fear; Clay started nervously. The tautness in all three of his men leaked to Arin, but he thrust it aside. He needed time with the map, had to send a letter to Garick with it before he started north. Give the men something to do, let them move.

"Clay, Hara: see if you can scare up some fresh meat on that north slope. Kon, break up everything you can burn."

Hara shifted, uncertain. "Ought to cross the river before dark."

"Yes," Clay agreed.

"We will," Arin promised, "but not hungry. We're sick for fresh meat." Uriah had offered a supply of preserved food, but they'd declined beyond a sack of flour.

Arin heard them ride out as Kon went for wood. He pulled the table closer to the windows and spread out Judith's notes beside the map. The three marked circles stood out clearly. Her knowledge of history must have been profound. Beside each circle, in letters that wavered with her exhaustion, she had written what looked like names, though they made no sense to Arin. NEW LONDON NAVAL BASE. And much further south, ABERDEEN PROVING GROUNDS. The third circle, far southeast of Charzen, almost to the sea, was wider than the others and left blank.

Arin struggled with the semi-intelligible notes. Other than eliminating Lishin as the site of the Girdle, they gave him no clue to the circles. There were his three choices, but no two could be logically ruled out. There was just too much he didn't know, a whole world and thousands of blank years to smother the tiny candle Garick had lit in him. He stared out the window at the dirty river and brooding mountains. Kon returned with a load of wood. The fire smoke made the air acrid before the windows sucked it out, but it was better than the fish smell. Something drew Arin again and again to a page of Judith's notes, a smaller copy of a portion of the large map. She had sketched the coast line and, just inland, a curved line that must represent almost five hundred miles, a long, thin loop that could only be City. To see the immensity of it on paper staggered him even in this afternoon of wonder piled on wonder. *Five hundred miles long!* Arin pored over the map and Jude's sketch. Though his worm gnawed at him to think, neither sheet of paper told him anything. He couldn't think, anyway; his exhaustion and the damp cold kept his arm throbbing. He gave it up, put the papers on the table and stretched out by the fire, bad arm toward the heat. Kon fed another piece of wood to the embers.

"They'll be back soon," he guessed. "Don't want to stay here past sundown." Kon appraised Arin shrewdly. "That arm ain't no way well yet."

"It's not too bad."

"I could kill Uriah, kill them all." Kon stared into the fire, morose, gathering the thought that came finally with a flow deep and bitter as the poisoned river. "Kill them and use their hides to cover up that dirty dead god. Ain't no place anywhere for Kriss. Forest don't want them. They make it smell. They—" Kon broke off, not even sharing the rest silently with Arin, the thing he never understood himself. Cold with the same unshaped fear that chilled Clay and Hara, he wanted now to touch Arin for reassurance, but Arin was off alone again with his map and strange thoughts and nothing could make a dent in him. He wasn't thinking like coven any more, slow to read lep, deaf and blind to the sense of danger that neared and thickened like that damned smell while they just sat and let it come. It angered Kon; he wanted to scream at Arin that Clay was no fool. *Something's out there. It wants to kill us. We can die in this place.*

The rain splattered dismally in the passageway where the fallen roof left it open to the sky. Clay and Hara would be wet through when they got back.

Arin's lep startled Kon. *I want you to go home.*

*?*

*You and the others go home.* "Take the map to Garick."

Kon digested it slowly. *And you?*

"North to Wengen. Not finished." Arin massaged his arm thoughtfully. "You heard what Gill said. All I do is get people killed."

"No."

"Don't fight me, Kon. Elin, Teela, all of them, they hurt in me. I'm tired of dying, and I can't lose you. Go home."

"I said no," Kon reiterated stubbornly. "Gill already quit. What you do alone?"

Arin wanted no argument. Only half of him was listening; the rest contended with the worm screaming *think* when he was tired of thinking, forming words that made no sense at all.

"Kon, I don't know how long or far. Your horse is sick."

"So's yours, so are you! Arin, smell that air, listen to them horses. *Open up. Feel.* This place just waiting to kill us, Arin, you too busy to know it. I ain't leaving you alone." He subsided on a melancholy note. "What's so much in Charzen, I gotta be there? Hell."

*Think!* The worm battered at Arin. His eyes swam from studying the map, the notes, Judith's final cryptic comment: *The deduction is inevitable* . . . three circles, two named, the third a blank. Unable to sit still, he got up, weaving like a man who'd lost something and didn't know where to look first. "Don't know how far," he murmured. "Might be clear up north, where's that place?" He looked at the map, made a stab at pronouncing it. "Bows-tone."

"What's that?" Kon asked.

"Old town. Part of City now. That's how Garick says Jude learned him City was built. Bunch of old towns. Got so it was really just one City even before the Jings came." His eyes suddenly darted to the map, the beginnings of a thought welling up—only to be lost when Kon called from the entrance.

"They're back."

There was trouble with the horses. Arin heard the three men soothing and cursing them into the passageway. The animals were frightened and stubborn, straining against every step. The other two, infected with their fear, fought to free themselves.

Clay and Hara squatted by the fire, stripped to the waist to dry out their soaked, rank skins. They shivered close to the heat, answering questions distantly, oppressed and preoccupied. No game anywhere, not even old signs. Then they'd seen the black thing break out of the underbrush, skittering flat across their path. It wobbled a little and ran into things as if it were sick. Clay had an arrow hooked and let go at it. Thought they'd got a small coon at first. But it wasn't a coon.

"Never saw one before," Hara mused. "Like a coon, but long and skinny, naked tail. Sort of cat whiskers. Teeth like needles."

"Dirty." Clay shook his head. "Fur all stuck with mud like it lived underground. Full of fleas. Wouldn't bring it back. Wouldn't touch it." He trailed off into silence, but there was more; over the stamping, terrified horses, Kon and Arin felt it brimming in the two men like nausea.

"Had a smell," Hara said at last. "Same smell I read this morning, read all winter when the wind was right."

And then the lep hammered into their minds, pleading, pulling them onto their feet. Kon stared at Arin, not knowing *why,* only *who—*

"It's Gill!" Arin bolted out of the room into the pelting rain.

On the south bank of the river in a stand of fir near Lishin bridge, Magill sheltered from the dreary rain.

Strange and unnatural to be so alone. He told himself that it was just a rest for the horse, that he'd pick up in a bit and ride on. The grass was fresh here, good forage and soft to sit on with his back against the pine while his heart contended with the warring emotions within it.

A small shiver of warning skittered down his spine. He searched briefly for the source. Old spring bear, maybe, just woke up and feeling mean, or perhaps a boar. Magill listened. Nothing. Not likely. Wasn't a game sign anywhere near the river. One more reason to put the first line of mountain between him and Lishin before dark. At least he could start tomorrow on fresh meat.

He felt mean himself for not taking Arin's hand when they parted. Magill didn't know why he had to quit, just couldn't live hurting like this. There was a lot of time in Salvation when Arin's mind closed off from them, to sort things out and add them up, and that hurt, too.

The change that began last summer with Arin's mastership and everything since, all the miles and deaths, had sifted fine what he once swallowed whole, until he realized that *he* had changed as well as Arin. Maybe it was nothing more or less than growing up, but all of it focused in Elin. They shared a great deal on the road; he began to need her as a friend. Sometimes they loved, most often they just rolled together in their blankets, warming each other, half talk, half sharing, until they drifted to sleep. He looked at Elin, saw her beyond the fun and the loving. Elin had needed something more and now so did he, when he never used to think beyond his next meal. Arin always did that for him. Only on that hilltop with the blood drying on Elin's cheek and her eyes so full of pain he couldn't meet them did he start to know, like ice melting away from spring earth, what she could mean to him. What maybe life was all about. She was his friend, she was fine, and he had no words to tell her. And Arin let her die. That was one pain, but not the worst. Arin couldn't stop it, Magill knew that now. The real torture was his own blindness not to see her clear when there was time.

He was twenty; late to get out of Arin's shadow and think for himself. Well, it hurt a baby to grow teeth, but he couldn't go all his life on mush. The Three had fallen away from him like last year's skin from old snake—and here he sat in the rain at the end of the world, hungry, dirty as a pigpen and skinny as his worn-out horse. Magill chuckled. A man could choose better places to start over, but in a way it was like being born again.

The warning instinct washed over him again, stronger, raising his hair on his arms. Magill tasted the air. The footloose wind changed every little while; it was north now, bringing him that damn dead fish stink. He trotted up the slight rise to the edge of the bridge, commanding a clear view of the river and the dirty brown pile of Lishin beyond. The low north bank was disappearing under the rising water, frothed thick with dead fish. His senses shunted around the odor, reaching for that other, undefined trace that quickened his fear as his flat black eyes narrowed west along the swollen stream. The two islands, one near the bridge, the second further upstream and close to the north shore, were flooded half over, just scrub treetops in the middle of rushing water. As Magill watched, something floundered out of the water onto the near island and disappeared into the dark green foliage. His eye caught only its movement, but the trebled burst of fear was echoed by his horse. Turning, Magill ate up the ground in a loping run down the hill. The capricious wind slammed the danger smell like a fist into his face. His stomach turned over. He fought the sudden panic, senses straining to grasp at the still-unshaped but rapidly growing terror. He knew its direction now, if nothing else. Coming from the south and fast. He took the white-eyed horse from upwind, letting it mix his smell with the other, and close-led it up the rise toward the bridge.

The center section of the age-warped bridge had been open iron grillwork, long since rotted away. The river rushed beneath the yawning gap. Only the two narrow stone walks on either side were passable, wet, twisting and canting in places toward wide gaps in the railing. Magill led the horse step by nervous step, hoofs slipping sometimes within an inch of the edge.

"Come on. Come on, you dumb—"

The terrified brute fought him all the way until he had to cover its eyes with his poncho. His own smell in the animal's flaring nostrils, Magill inched the blinded horse across the bridge. The lines of huge, strange buildings like rotted teeth menaced him with their own alien warnings. Magill's senses were crushed between the black town and the unshaped thing behind. At last, he eased the poncho off, soothing the horse, but it reared away. He cursed and made a snatch at the reins. The horse's momentum yanked him around to face the river and the bridge just crossed.

His mouth opened to scream. Nothing came out.

The earth had gone mad, come alive, plunging and seething down to the river that boiled with the first black wave, its forward fringes already milling over the dead fish on his side. Only for a moment could the obscene darting things be defined as separate shapes before more floundered out of the yellow tide, and more after them—

*Millions!*

—until the water line and the fish were blotted out in heaving blackness from which rose a flat, voracious squealing that grew in volume as Magill stood frozen. Beyond, the river frothed with more and more and beyond those still, pouring off the flooded islands, a steady black stream spewed into the unclean river, drawn by the smell of the fish, fighting the current with a desperation born of hunger.

*That's why no game,* Magill realized numbly. *That ate it out.*

For half a mile, the south bank had disappeared under the scurrying, scrambling horde. Hundreds, denied room on the living, writhing bridge, plunged into the water to be swept away and replaced by as many more. Tough and shrewd in survival, they washed up on the islands, clutched floating logs and mere branches to float; some clung to the naked tails of the strong swimmers in front.

The living darkness swarmed across the bridge like a cloud over the sun, rapid but not headlong, as if guided by a canny intelligence. As Magill and the horse were sighted, a signal passed like a tremor down to the near bank which rippled like muscle under live flesh; lean, whiskered snouts lifted, read the message and billowed like a dirty blanket up the bank toward the bridge.

Magill wrenched himself out of his paralytic fear. There wasn't much chance they could catch him if he rode dead away from the bridge, but even as he vaulted the saddle and kicked the horse into a gallop, the thought loomed clear: *Arin and Kon.*

Reining short, he fought the fear in order to think. The weapons house was due west, flat along the river. They had to be there by now. The black things could reach them, too.

He could barely manage the fear-crazed horse; it plunged against the rein, wanting to run north. Magill forced it around cruelly, letting the bit tear at the rebellious mouth, hissing: "You gonna move or die right here!"

The animal screamed and reared, then gave in as it jumped into a flat run down the broken street. All Magill's fear poured into the lep. *ArinKon! ArinKon! Run!*

Already the black tide was pouring into the street behind him. The horse flew deftly over a deep hole. Magill rode high on the shoulder to give it better balance, letting out the rein to give the horse its head in longer strides, closing the gap between himself and the open land ahead.

*Arin, run! All of you—*

He cleared the last rubble of the broken street, feeling the hoofs dig into bare earth. As he let the horse out to its limit, the green of the rise before the river vomited black, curving in on his front, alive with that shrill, purposeful chittering. Magill drew his knife, goading the point over the laboring flanks. "Move! Move!"

He was completely cut off now, but they were yet not that thick in front of him. He bent low over the neck while the distance narrowed. In the black swarm, single bodies leaped high, scaly tails lashing in anticipation before they fell back into the raging mass. Five good jumps, six, could clear them. Magill gripped the knife tighter. "Ready . . . ready . . . *go.*"

The horse bounded high over the first of them.

The shock stunned Arin for a moment; the flying horse tiny on the fringe of Lishin bearing down on them, the nauseous danger smell making the world quiver with its threat. The sound of damp-rotted wood rending as their own horses broke free, Kon, Clay, Hara shouting. And over it all the terrified lep *run . . . run!*

He whirled. Dashing to the entrance as the horses emerged, the men pounding after, Arin threw up his arms to rear them back. Soogee careered on her haunches, lashing out with her forehoofs, charged at him. Arin dodged aside as she plunged past. He made a grab at the loose reins, missed, tried for the saddle horn. At full run, the mare dragged him off his feet. He lost his precarious hold, grabbed a dangling stirrup. The horse dragged him painfully over the broken stone before he had to let go, roll over, rub his torn knees, see the other horses milling blindly at each other and the men grabbing desperately for any hold they could find. Hara managed a solid grip on his saddle horn, jumped high to fork it. He managed his left foot in the stirrup as the crazed horse dropped flat and rolled viciously over him. Stumbling to help, Arin clubbed its head aside as it flailed onto its feet. Hara had the stunned, vacant look of the gravely hurt. Kon cursed, trying to lift him.

"Goddam stupid horse."

"Forget the horse." Arin scooped an arm under Hara's shoulder. "Get him back inside. Clay. Clay!"

"It don't matter now." Clay, standing erect, still as the death in his eyes, could feel it coming like it always did in his nightmares. A sound of choked pity welled up in him, a sound hopeless in its terrible awareness.

The riverbank erupted with teeming black life. Part of it swept in a great sickle curve toward the doomed Magill, another part sensed them, swerved their way.

Arin tried to blanket their minds with his command, but the fear was too strong to touch Clay. Clumsily, Arin and Kon wrestled up Hara, regardless of his pain, stumbling toward the building.

"What? What is it?" Hara mumbled thickly, jolting in their arms. "I can't see."

Arin caught one glimpse over his shoulder as they tripped, slid, ran, Clay falling, picking himself up again. Arin shut his eyes. *Don't look back. Don't look!* In that instant, the picture was stamped forever in his mind, indelible, etched deep into metal with a fine steel point. A million glaring eyes, thin snouts, a rushing advance, yet for all the pell-mell haste, the inexorable, still *purpose* in that millioned gaze transmitting the image of Arin and Kon and Clay and Hara to primitive brain tissue. Even as he ran, he saw them frozen in time: the eyes, the small, naked pink-white claws like a parody of human hands obscenely out of place against the coarse, filth-stiffened fur. He might have stayed sane, even in the face of the flood tide of vermin a mile deep, but the other sight stopped his legs from moving, skittered Kon to a sudden halt, grabbing Hara to keep from pitching headfirst onto the stones.

The shapeless creature heaved like a derelict vessel on the surface of the poisoned sea. Most of its muzzle was eaten away, yet the horse still lurched forward, its leg muscles—where muscle remained over bared bone—bunched mechanically, carrying the flesh-stripped rider that clung lifelessly to the neck. Neither had any shape except the swarming black tide that lapped over them.

Arin felt nothing more after the first of them leaped at his legs, just one sharp pain someone screaming it bit me where's Clay Clay Clay his eyes they're eating his eyes Clay's dead we dropped Hara they're dead they're dead get in there they're dead get in there Arin you sumbitch they're dead get in there

Darkness

The black things scratched and squealed and gnawed at the metal door. When they were feeding, they made a different sound. It seemed important to note the variation.

Arin had seen one only once before, in Lorl. The Mrikans called them rats, but the one he saw was big and fat. Not as fast as these. Or as hungry.

One of them got in before the door closed. Kon grabbed it by the tail and slammed it against the floor again and again till there couldn't be a whole bone left in it, his fury and loathing hissing in sibilant bursts of breath as his arm flailed.

The rat lay between them now, adding its smell to their own.

They were cruelly bitten, Kon worst of all. The bites made him feverish after a time, shaking hot and cold all over. Like an animal, without words or reasons, Arin knew Kon was dying.

"Arin," the weak voice pleaded, "how long'll they stay out there?"

Till they're finished.

"Talk to me, Arin."

After a fashion, Arin could talk. The strange words streamed out of him because the wolf was there, sharply etched in flat white light against the darkness. He must be mad. It sat on its haunches, resting on nothing, regarding him with amusement. It talked to him, but Kon could neither see nor hear it.

*Kon will die,* said the wolf. *He insists on why when there is no why.* And Arin knew the wolf was right, because Kon never knew the link between those black little rat eyes and the sky full of stars seeing everything and nothing. *Because he can't accept an earth without meaning.*

Listen, Kon. The laughter of wolves.

Reach out your hand, Kon. Feel the thing you killed. That's her, that's the goddess. Not crazy, not sane, neither bad nor good, not caught in your rhythms, moving to your music; merely flesh, and under the flesh and fleas and fur is the pus of her we forgot.

*Arin, stop. Shut up please shut up.*

Chittering down eternity like the rats outside, the song the covens forgot or blotted out of memory, drowning out love, reasons and irrelevant hopes. Why us in this place, why the rats, why one more meaningless death? *Feeble, self-centered question,* answered the wolf. Arin as center of reality. Not *why* but why *not?* If the universe rolls toward purpose, must it be yours? You in your Circle, Uriah in his church, both of you clogging the cosmos with personal significance like sugar on meat, equating the single toad-hop of your lives with the clean arc of Forever. The world carries you, carries the rat who carries the self-absorbed flea. The horror is not an evil, but an innocence. Let the wolves laugh.

"No," Arin growled. "No. Go away, you aren't real. Get out of me."

The wolf wagged its tail, but looked sad. *You haven't taken that last step, Arin. You haven't broken yet.*

Time passed, a long time. A little of his mind came back, recognized how he was *now.* The bites burned in his flesh. He stretched out a hand for Kon to pull him back to sanity. "Kon." He hardly recognized the croaking sound as his own. "Help me."

"Stay back." The other voice was weak, thick. "Stay off, Arin. I got plague."

Instinctive fear. He recoiled from Holder. Not Holder, no: Kon. But Holder couldn't come back. He was apart and had to die that way. Holder. Not Kon. Not Kon.

"That's what it is, Arin. Hot and cold. Tongue all swelled. You . . . you off in your head someplace plain crazy, talking to wolves, talking Old Language. Me, nothing to do, just lie here, think, feel it coming."

His breathing labored over the counterpoint of rat sounds.

"Those black things did it," Kon rasped. "The one Clay shot, he said it was sick, all swelled up, couldn't walk right. Half dead when he got it. Garick wants to know where plague comes from, you tell him what Kon thinks."

"Can't be, Kon. Bit me, too, but I'm not sick."

"Just crazy. Tell him, you hear?"

Little by little, speech grew too difficult for his swollen throat. Kon lepped faintly. Thirst bothered him. He tried to stretch out, but there wasn't room. Still he lepped, more to keep contact with life than anything else. His silent voice simmered like a forgotten cooking pot in Arin's mind, still working and working in the action of its own heat.

Now and then Kon made sense. He was trying to accept his own death, trying to understand it. Once Arin heard him sob.

*It will only be a little while till he asks the Question,* the wolf said in detached pity, *only a little while till he breaks on that last betrayal that was never a promise.* Why has he been forsaken? Even Uriah's god asked and got no answer. No wonder they carved him howling. *Thief, give it back!*

*Yes!* That was the word, the accusation Arin wanted, had been looking for. The rage seethed in him. *Give them back to me! They were mine, part of me, part of my love. You have no right to take them!*

*Who?* asked the wolf. *Who has no right?*

Arin brushed the dead rat aside, dragged himself the distance in the rank darkness to cradle Kon in his arms, keep him warm. The shuddering arms were too weak to push him away. Even as he held Kon, he wanted to shut out the lep that faltered through his mind, but he couldn't. Kon had no other hold on life but that frayed thread unraveling in his own mind, unwinding in a pile of irrelevant wisps.

Such a Kon—forever lonely, strong only because he met up with life, compromised with it, always constant: never knew what a mother was or a father, plague got them, too. From the beginning, there was only one he could clutch, only one to follow, only one to love, the center of his solitary life. Women, they meant nothing, they never mattered, who was he to love them so late? Uriah, shrewd weigher of men, was right after all. Kon loved Arin. *And old Arin got me killed.*

*Kon, I'm sorry, I'm—*

*Got all of us born again.* But it was funny when a man came down to it: they *all* had it better than Arin. Gill, Elin, Holder, Teela, Clay, Sand, Hara, Kon—all of them died wondering why, still able to wonder, hoping, feeling. Poor Arin got to live with all the questions he can't figure, like the map and Jude's writings. *Poor Arin, poor damfool, what you gonna do without me?*

"Give them back!" Arin sobbed, holding him. "Give them back to me."

*Who?* asked the wolf again.

Or take them whole. Don't leave them like sores in my brain. You liar, you thief, take them proud, in dignity. Take them on their feet, not crumpled and whimpering.

The wolf's tongue lolled out. *You're not there yet.* Death is still a person, an enemy, a god or goddess to be fought for all of them. Pride? Dignity? Who the shit cares for them when Kon would trade both for one more breath? They *all* would. Ask the rats for dignity. *Let go, Arin, let go or be crushed by it!*

With his last howl of denial, his mind snapped.

Arin crouched unmoving in the darkness long after the body in his arms ceased its final convulsion; conscious of every sound and smell, he sensed everything from a great distance. He couldn't love the body or mourn it, couldn't hate the thinning, fading sound of the rats. He didn't hurt, needed nothing, not even purpose. And the exhilarant lightness, he knew, was the ultimate step, taken at last. He was free and quite mad.

And then—precisely then—the phantom wolf rose off its haunches, slouched closer to touch its nose to his. Its fathomless eyes held a knowledge that would have been bleak without the tinge of laughter; wolf-laughter at the cruel joke of the world that made it lilt with meaning.

*Not mad, Arin. Now you're there. Now you've learned. Say it.*

"Random."

*Say it all.*

"Random universe."

*Again.*

World without meaning beyond its existence.

"Without meaning."

Ego irrelevant?

"Yes."

*Now,* said the wolf, *meaning has meaning.* Build, make your own, clean as the arc of Forever.

*Arin,* the wolf whispered, fading, *you've just gone sane.*

He pushed at the door. It swung open on bright sunlight. He blinked against the painful glare, crawling out of the closet to stand on aching, cramped legs. The floor was strewn with dead rats, some torn apart by others in their feeding frenzy, some whole but swollen and stiff in the last agony of the plague that killed them. Near the entrance was the clean-picked skeleton of Hara where he'd writhed out of Kon's and Arin's arms with the rats at his face.

Arin stood by the cold remains of their fire. His blackened lips moved in ironic greeting.

"Welcome to the world, Arin."

Elder Matthew considered himself a simple and devout man. He carried out his labors unquestioningly, even when they were harsh, remembering the terrible sword wielded in battle by the Archangel, and knew that all things would be cleansed at last in glory. His only vanity was a modest wish that someday he might be rewarded for his work with a holy vision.

He slowly turned his huge bulk and surveyed the carnage with a satisfaction that lay as much in its justice as its total efficiency. All four: one mingled with horse bones a little way off, a second pile clean of flesh in the courtyard and the third skeleton just inside the door. One bloating corpse in a closet where he'd managed to escape the rats but not what they carried.

He expected the fifth who'd ridden alone would be found eventually on the south bank. Matthew found no papers or map: Uriah would be disappointed, but he cared little. His business lay with the rats.

Most of them died fighting for food. Matthew and his men chose only those that succumbed to the disease they carried, obesely swollen and reeking. The metal and glass instruments were unwrapped, gloves donned, needles fitted, the gathering commenced. Into the distended rat mouths and throats, under the heart, the needles probed and drew out the mixtures of diseased blood and liquefying tissue to be sent abroad in the unsuspecting blood of cowans, those nomad hunters sometimes granted a charitable meal and a night's rest; or in various game animals known to range south; or in drinking water of any other carrier that might come in contact with the covens. God's scythe to cut down the witches, the heathen, as it was given to Moses in Egypt. Sometimes it claimed a few, sometimes many; the last time it nearly extinguished the Shando; this time it might totally succeed. The rats were plentiful and the strain had grown as virulent as God's own anger.

Bright sunlight lit their work like a smile from Him. Matthew sent the other Kriss back to Salvation with their gathering, staying to work alone out of preference, warmed by the sun and even more by the holiness of his task, moving from carcass to carcass, replacing needles with meticulous care, storing the virus in glass vials. The land about him was more than usually devoid of life, extremely quiet. He worked on, realizing as he did that the joy and devotion in his soul were mounting by perceptible degrees to euphoria. Not even in church in the most consummate moments of ecstatic involvement had he felt so near to the Presence as here at his chief work. The sun waxed golden over the stilled river, bathing Matthew in a warmth that reached deep into his spirit. Kneeling by the swollen rat, he paused before inserting the needle and closed his eyes in prayer.

A sudden breath caught in his throat, a sob of joy. The Presence was overwhelming in its power. Matthew *knew* before his eyes blinked open that *He* would be there before him in reality as in the countless fantasies of a devout lifetime; the Cross, the beloved Saviour in the agonies of his foreordained death.

He was right.

Matthew was transfixed in his attitude of prayer. He could scarcely breathe. Bathed in deep golden light, the Saviour hung on His cross before Matthew, eyes still turned to Heaven, the lips parted in their last supplication. Unable to move, Matthew's eyes welled with tears —a function that stopped abruptly as His parted lips opened wider and wider till they gaped in a cavernous yawn. The head turned and favored Matthew with a tolerant smile.

"Hello, Matthew. Having fun?"

The elder gaped. He might have fainted but he couldn't. Nor would his mouth work or his eyes close. He could only watch.

"More fun than I am," the carven figure confessed with a hint of peevishness. "It's fine to be an object of adoration. That's my function. I don't mind being prayed to, or even those hysterical women fondling me in secret as if all my divinity lay beneath this amorphous pair of drawers." The god sighed with plaintive boredom and yawned again, wider. "Oh . . . oh . . . my."

Matthew's eyes bulged; his locked fingers whitened. He could not even tremble.

"I mean," the voice went on, "these things go with the position. *That's* my complaint: the position. Day in, year out, rain, shine or flood, hung up here like the wash. Why couldn't you show me lying down once in a while? More dignified and much more restful." Restrained as he was, the vision did his unsuccessful best to ease his arms. "Well . . . the wages of deity."

Matthew found a muscle or two that responded to earnest will. His mouth quivered open. "What . . . ?"

"Oh, I know; my own grievances are petty." The icon regarded Matthew with a fatigued benevolence. "You want a voice of thunder to fill all creation, a prophecy to be graven on the mountains. They all do." A vast sigh. "All right."

The explosion cracked the sane world asunder. Matthew's eardrums shrieked as the blue sky split prismatically into every color of the spectrum, fading quickly to normal again. Over the thunder, a great, sublime chord rolled from a thousand unseen throats. The god reassumed the classic cast of suffering.

*"Unto ye is given evil tiding, for the Kriss shall be as dust flying in the wind before their enemies."* The image relaxed. "More like it, more in the style? As long as I'm in voice, try this for size."

Again the celestial music and the voice of doom. *"For of those five sent to answer the wrath of Heaven, but four have been slain. One only is escaped alone to fry your ass in its own fat."* The god went on more chattily. "Of course, that one is very bitter and lonely with all his friends gone. And the girl, Matt; don't forget the girl you had to shovel up into a blanket after your women were done. No, no," the gaunt head wagged ruefully, "if you think *he's* had it bad, Matthew, just you wait." The icon froze again in its accustomed position as the voice faded. "Just you wait . . ."

He could move now. He fell forward, shuddering violently, face buried in palsied hands. "God! My God, I'm possessed!"

Cautious, expecting new horrors, Matthew raised his head. Nothing but the ruined laboratory and the river. He turned. A yelp of fear ripped out of his throat. He recoiled and cried out again in physical pain, his back seared by white heat. Nothing but air, and yet the heat walled him in, restraining him in every direction. Just beyond it a huge, brown-black wolf lounged on its belly, forepaws crossed in watchful repose. Beside the wolf squatted a scrofulous compound of dirt, tatters and starvation, chuckling continually over some inane secret joke as he pawed through Matthew's work bag.

"Matthew, this sure is my week to learn." The madman dug at his filthy beard with black, bitten claws, laughing in a way that chilled the elder. Arin held up a needle. "Been watching you all the time."

"In a fever of curiosity," said the wolf.

Matthew hunched in the center of the heat wall like a bull at bay.

Arin was real; his mind could accept Arin, hollow-eyed with madness as he was. But not the other. "What is that—thing?"

"Him? That's a wolf."

Matthew's voice rose to a precarious pitch. "Wolves don't talk!"

"Sure they do. What's wrong with that?" The heat wall contracted around Matthew. He winced. He was not afraid of Arin or even devils, but no matter where he reached for support, his world was gone.

*"What's wrong with that, you fat sonofabitch?"*

"It's crazy!"

"That's a narrow view." The wolf glided off its haunches, passing unscathed through the heat wall. "Here, feel me." It licked Matthew's hand. He jerked it away. He blinked; the wolf form *wavered* now and as if inclined to reform, second to second or fade out altogether. "I'm a Lishin wolf."

"There are no wolves here!"

"Somewhere else, then." The canine equivalent of a shrug. "There's always a Lishin, over the river, over the years. Pragmatism doesn't help."

The madman turned the filled needle before his eyes. "Kon was a long time dying. But before he did, before the boils broke out, while I could still understand him, he figured the plague comes from the rats. Like the ones you've been sucking on with these pretty little things." He resolved the tube before his sunken eyes. "Mymymy. All of a sudden . . ."

"Like a clear light," the wolf grinned. "We knew you were the man to tell us."

Matthew quelled his trembling with an effort of will. "I do God's work. *My* God, not that thing your spells put in my brain. My soul is beyond you. I know nothing."

The pile of rags shifted closer. Its smile was horrible. "Elder, I'd love to kill you."

Matthew labored to breathe, certain of death. The scene had a garish, sunlit clarity, the rat-strewn stone paving, the hawks wheeling overhead, the mundane world beyond. He answered the hollow stare with steady eyes. "Go ahead."

"No, not you. Not that easy, not for a long time. It's too hard getting into a Kriss mind, but you, Matt, you've been an education. You've always prayed for a vision. I gave you one—and sort of poked around your imagination at the same time. Your mind is a mess."

"Chaos," the wolf agreed.

"I wonder you get your shoes on right five days out of the week."

"Liar," Matthew choked. "A lie before me, a lie and a devil."

The pattering laugh rose again from the madman. "Of course he's a lie. Not really there, except he is. Don't try to understand; it's as sane as the world. We are *in* your mind, Matt. We can take from it, bring to it—break it in half if we want, but I need to learn from it. You're my teachers, you and Uriah. And I want you to tell him how much Arin has learned." He tittered horribly. "Oh yes, Matt, you tell him special."

Arin sat back, stretching emaciated legs, amused by his toes wiggling inside ruined moccasins. "Don't look at me for life. I'm one of the dead." He went on, absorbed in the flexing toes. "Don't say you won't tell us, or that you'd rather die. We'd be fools trying to scare a tough old coal miner with a little bitty thing like death."

"Inefficient," the wolf agreed.

"Pure waste of time," Arin considered. "You're not just going to talk—"

"I won't," Matthew glowered. "You can kill me, but I won't."

"—you'll *beg* to talk."

"Babble," nodded the wolf.

"Sing."

"Cry."

"Scream."

"Dredge your memory—"

"—for everything you know."

"And wish you knew more."

"To keep *him* off you."

"You'll pray for one more second of sanity—"

"Before you lose it. Dying would be easy."

"Trite," said the wolf.

"Too easy. See, you won't be telling *us* . . ."

"Not us." The wolf sprang up and bounded away toward the weapons house.

"—it's *Kon* wants to know."

The instinctive hawks circled low over the entrance to the weapons house, graceful silhouettes against the azure sky. The wolf trotted out, followed by Kon. The scavenger birds *grakked* their bewilderment: it was dead meat, their legitimate tithe, already swollen with the gasses of decomposition—but it moved, decaying tissue straining in tardy response to a center of strong will. Kon lurched forward in a parody of his familiar stride as the elder remembered it. Matthew gagged. His tongue went thick in his mouth and his stomach heaved as the body folded down like a misshapen scarecrow beside him. The boiled-onion eyes moved sluggish in oozing sockets, the tongue protruded darkly from blackened lips that moved with difficulty around it. A large plague boil festered on the neck. Kon's voice burst corruptly over the rotting vocal cords as he closed cold sausage fingers on the man's arm. "Matthew."

Matthew made a pathetic sound and retched. He tried to pull away, but the dead hand held him, tried not to breathe, not to smell it. Tried to pray.

"Tell." Kon moved closer. Yellowish pus seeped from his nose and ears. "About . . . the black things."

"And the needles," Arin prompted.

"Everything," said the watchful wolf.

Straining as far away as he could from Kon, Matthew gasped, "I believe in the life to come—"

"Tell us," the corpse mumbled.

"—that my soul is free. I renounce these phantoms—*that's what they are, Arin, you devil. They're not real, they're not—*"

The fingers left a dark trail on his sleeve. "Tell."

Matthew whimpered. "Please . . ."

It was his weak mortal body that betrayed him. Even as he flinched away from Kon, another arm snaked seductively over his shoulder from behind. The hand caressing his cheek was long, narrow-fingered, half eaten away. The bones, wrist, forearm, up to the disjointed shoulder were crushed out of shape, grotesquely incongruous to the slender throat. The pulped, eyeless face still showed the long scar from the ear to the remnant of mouth. The other hand, as shattered as its mate, moved spastically to brush back the thick fall of red hair as she rested her cheek on Matthew's shoulder. The gasping mouth trembled, moved.

"Hey, Matthew," Elin said.

He felt her mutilated breast burning his arm. The last thing he recognized with a lucid mind was the image of Arin, calm, intent, merciless as time. *"Because hell was your invention, don't think I can't work it."*

"Tell us," Elin whispered in his ear, "and I'll give you a kiss . . ."

Matthew told Arin all he wanted to know and more, much more than Arin might have guessed. He was still talking when the Kriss searchers found him. He had to be tied and kept apart in an unused house on the outskirts of Salvation, with two men of high character and markedly low sensitivity appointed to tend him. For Matthew had been an elder, a selfless servant of God who desired only a vision, a fragment of ecstasy before he died.

The Kriss never clearly divined what had happened to Matthew. What he wailed or whimpered did not chill the two unsusceptible miners, nor did it enlighten Uriah. He heard names in the unceasing babble, remembered names of the Shando dead, most often the condemned whore who came with them. That, at least, vaguely suggested that Matthew was a weaker vessel than Uriah had realized.

At last, they tied his hands that Matthew would not exhaust himself with the endless, palsied, brushing movements, as if struggling to be free of something that would not let him go. But after a while he stopped, changed, surrendered, *welcomed* whatever held him with such relentless affection. He tried to hug the empty air, caressing and crooning, fulfilled and joyous that he would never be alone again, that he would be with her always and always and always.

# *The Quest and the Knife*

Sidele slipped into the back room. Clutching the tattered cloak about her bony shoulders, she cracked open the rear door and wet a finger with her tongue. She prodded the wet digit outside to catch the turning of the wind.

Coming from the west. With trouble.

She wondered where Bowdeen was. He felt close. "Old man," she told him more than once, "you got more lep than you think."

She slammed the door shut. Picking up a few dry twigs, Sidele shuffled back into the sitting room and fed the wood to the dying fire. The young sweep, still sitting where she left him, rattled his fingers impatiently on the tabletop.

All the minor officers that came to her wanted facts fast and thick, but the first part of her job was to slow them down, like lovers who finished too quick. Only when her slower tempo prevailed was it possible for her to read the subtle telltales that told her what they wanted to hear. It amused her that more than one merk decision had been based on her ability to render back in new words the same fears and hunches her clients brought to her. Nobody ever complained, so she supposed she did a better job than she realized. Of course, being Bowdeen's woman carried some weight.

Callan, who avoided Sidele, called her some kind of witch, but like Bowdeen, there wasn't much of Circle left in her part of Wengen. All she did was dispense shrewd common sense tempered with time-worn advice that crib girls could interpret however their ignorant hearts pleased. But hints of dark, rich strangers and elixirs sold for extra profit weren't enough for the merks; to satisfy them, she had to bolster her knowledge of wind and weather, and stretch her limited understanding of the events behind the Karli line. Naturally she picked up a stray scrap or two of news from Bowdeen during his hasty visits, but most of her merk-sense was pieced together from the half-formed doubts and questions weighing on her customers' minds.

The undeclared war was a blur of confused, isolated skirmishes. None of the fast-moving Karli knew what was happening even though they were in constant lep with each other, Bowdeen guessed. "Yesterday they chase, today they run, tomorrow they might turn again." The game played out on the pathless, brush-choked mountains, vicious, silent and swift.

But two days before Belten, it began to change. Just at twilight, a nameless Wengen rider dashed through the barriers hastily erected by the 44th along the trails north of Karli. With poor light and the confusion aroused by the swiftness of his approach, the messenger won through to coven territory, though he took an arrow in his thigh.

Why? the merks asked Sidele repeatedly. Was there any message that couldn't be sent by lep? Was he carrying something that had to be hand-delivered? What could be so important the rider would take a chance like that?

Damned if she knew, but she wasn't about to admit it. Already she'd come up with three different answers to three different sets of officers. If two ever met over a jug and compared stories, they'd figure the other was lying to do the home company in the eye.

Sidele brushed aside a strand of dark hair from her temple and pinched up her face in concentration. It was a shit way to live, but she hunched over the glass and muttered Wengen obscenities low enough for the dumb sweep to think she was summoning power. Rocking back and forth, Sidele peered into the crystal and wondered what the hell she was going to say *this* time . . .

When the messenger reached Karli, part of his news was already known by the masters. *Arin is alive*—found by Moss and Deak after homing in on their lep, too weak to hunt, so belly-shrunk they had to feed him berries and bits of pone no bigger than a fingernail, one at a time; alive and safe in grave-smelling skins, scabby with bite-sores, clutching a sheaf of tattered papers, but indestructible as a Shando flea.

It was the papers that the messenger caught an arrow for, bringing them to Hoban for relay to Garick.

"But he's *safe!*"

"There now," Tilda soothed the girl sobbing against her knee. "No, stop, Lane, I'm wet through with you crying all over me. There, I'm happy for you."

"I *told* them." Shalane gulped through the blur of tears. "I said he was alive. Oh, Ti-Tilda, it's so good. I was so sc-scared . . ."

"Wipe your face and ride, Lane. It's a long way to Charzen."

The girl scrambled up, the start of a smile shoved her front teeth out over her lower lip in a grin, and her cheeks dimpled. "Thank you, goddess. I'll ride good and fast."

"We pledged you too young, for all your power," Tilda grumbled, "but you loved him, you believed in him, and it's grown you to woman-size. Nobody else should ride with his folks. Tell Garick."

"I will."

"Tell him we're waiting."

"Yes, goddess." Shalane bobbed back and forth between Tilda and the door, desperate to translate her joy into movement. Tilda's laugh was gruff and tender. "All right, git!"

She watched from the window as the girl forked the saddle from a running leap, galvanizing the horse into a dead run toward the stockade gate. The jubilant young voice floated back to her. "Did you hear? You hear? It's true."

*Arin says it's the Kriss who—*

—who massed their coal wealth over the generations, who bought informers in the covens and in Mrika, who studied, controlled and then used the black rats of Lishin to spread plague at periodic intervals, whose avowed aim was to cleanse the world of Circle, that abomination in the sight of their god. But not until Uriah came to power did they have someone capable of focusing it all in a concerted attack. Uriah knew his people needed room to grow. He saw what was coming, measured Garick and knew the decisive contest had already started. The Kriss were afraid of Uriah's secular mind and bold policies, which called for total control from within of the mercenaries, domination of those covens that would submit—and elimination of those that would not—to the true and benevolent rule of the Kriss god. They were afraid, but despite much questioning among the elders, Uriah's plan prevailed. When and if City ever came forth to deal with the outside world, it would come then to Uriah and his holy kingdom. To this intricate end, Arin had been invited to Salvation, to be delayed, have his brains picked, eventually to die in Lishin.

*—and the Shando must ride now.*

The lep strained out of the north from the minds of exhausted men, women and masters unable to comprehend most of what mad Arin whipped them to transmit.

But Garick understood.

"Safe," Jenna breathed. As masters, she and Garick rarely drank, but now they sat alone in the room where Garick first charged Arin with his mission, and they opened a fresh jug of sida. Across the long table, they shared without words, finished the first cup and the second and filled them again. They drank slowly, deliberately, savoring the liquor as the thoughts flowed between them. Garick watched the emotions riot across Jenna's bleak countenance—love, gratitude, relief, gradually chilling to cold, intense fury.

"We go to the knife."

Garick nodded. Another silence.

"Uriah first." Jenna rose. "Before the Girdle, before City, before anything. Uriah first."

"Yes." Garick finished his drink. "Uriah first."

She left, and he sat there, considering the best policy to pursue, the one that would be fastest and cost the least. He poured another cup and lepped a command for the cowan Jay to be brought before him.

By the time he arrived, Garick was prizing the seal off a new jug. He glowered at the young Kriss. "You rode in here with Uriah's agreement to an alliance. Then you told us Arin was locked up. Now I learn where Uriah really stands." Garick's tone was low and decidedly dangerous.

Jay stood before him, wondering, a little awed by the intensity of the god of Shando. Garick rose, pushed Jay down at the table like a child and shoved a written transcript of the intelligence under his nose.

"Cowan, how much of this did you know?"

"None, I swear." Jay read the page and as he did, the surprise faded. "But I'd believe Arin. It makes sense now. Christ! And I was one of them."

"I've given up the luxury of trust." Garick clipped off the precise syllables of Old Language. "I can't believe Uriah, so what about you? You're Kriss."

"Yes."

"They raised you, gave you your beliefs."

"They gave me a God who will never leave me."

"Would you fight your own family?"

Jay bent his head over the sheet of paper, seeming to give it his full attention. It was a long moment before he answered Garick's question.

"My mother made the formal accusation against Elin. She led the women in the punishment. And my father voted for my execution.

For the good of my soul, he said, to save me from further corruption. I believe them; they weren't lying, but they enjoyed it; oh yes, I could see that satisfaction oozing out of their eyes, dirty as anything they claimed to punish. This is what happens to the love of God when the love goes out of it." He handed back the paper. "Yes, I'll fight them. But it's not easy to say."

"Maybe." Garick studied him, wary of the instinct to believe. "But easy or not, you'll take me into Salvation." He pushed paper and pen toward Jay, filled a cup from the jug and set it down in front of the young man. "I want a map, Jay: Salvation, the whole town, the way the houses are built, bridges, the mines, Lishin—everything. Have a drink."

Jay demurred. "I don't like sida."

"Drink it," Garick ordered. His eyes caught Jay's; suddenly it was impossible to refuse. Jay reached for the mug. "Because after you make my map, you're going to let me into your mind for all the little things you've forgotten. A drink will make it easier."

Jay swallowed the sida in one uninitiated gulp. Through his choking, he gasped one impassioned, uncapitalized, wholly secular oath.

Garick gestured to the paper. "Start."

Later, the god of Shando studied the two maps, Jay's and Judith's, and glanced occasionally at Spitt's latest report. Three circles, and the Girdle could be in any one of them, as far north as—

It didn't matter yet. The Girdle would decide the end, not the middle. Now there was still the vital, uncommitted northern division of mercenaries to worry about. Callan's cash would spread deeper without them, true, but Garick couldn't afford to be caught in the pincers of a north and south claw; it wouldn't take long to end the war if *that* happened.

All wars since time began, Garick knew, were won with money. He had to dry up Callan's well. When the merk officer found out, he'd throw all his remaining weight with the southern division, but that couldn't be helped. So the orders went out.

*Break off and gather in—*

Across the vast single mind of Circle a purpose began to shape and converge on the force that wanted to destroy it. More lep voices called and were answered, indecision altered, firmed up. South from Wengen, north out of Suffec, west from the Mrikan frontier, the riders streamed toward Charzen and Karli while the forest whispered the new message to the embattled Karli squadrons.

*—at a point three days above Karli at river fork. Garick joins there.*

"Except that's west," Deak told Arin, "and *we're* supposed to go east."

"Then we don't meet Garick." The gaunt Shando paused in sharpening an arrowhead. "But who said?"

"Hoban. Callan's getting smart and Bowdeen was born that way. Some of us got to stay east and fool them."

Arin nodded, recognizing the way Garick must have weighed him and decided he was still expendable. While the covens gathered for the thrust at Salvation, a decoy including Deak's people must engage the merks under Bowdeen and Callan. The decoy, pretending it was the main force, would run east, luring the mercenaries to give chase. The whole idea was to give Garick time to move against Salvation. It was a good plan, provided one didn't reckon it in terms of dead coveners. The one flaw was in their horses, exhausted as the riders.

"They're ready to drop," Deak predicted ruefully. "What then?"

"Eat 'em and steal more." Arin strung his bow and mounted. "Let's go."

Garick's eyes swam from concentrating too long on the precise writing, a last unexpected contact with the woman who would never leave him.

*"Judith, I do love you. I owe you so much."*

Three circles, two named, the third a blank. And the last line of Judith's unfinished notes: *The deduction is inevitable, The—* The what? Kept nearly twenty years on a shelf in a dark closet in Lishin: *The deduction is inevitable. The—* The Girdle? The Girdle is—where?

Three circles, two named, the third a blank.

*". . . I owe you so much."*

*"Yes, you do. You owe me your life and most of your mind—"*

One circle: New London.

*—and all of your learning."*

Another circle: Aberdeen.

*"And your son."*

New London and Aberdeen. Logical places for Callee to take the Girdle. Only . . .

Garick traced the old markings on the map, his finger running back and forth along the impossible crescent that defined the borders of City. Its size still made him dizzy.

Inevitable deduction. Three circles. Inevitable deduction.

*"And your son. That's quite a debt. Think—"*

His finger traced and retraced the arc of City.

Inevitable deduction.

*"—quite a debt. Think you can pay it back?"*

"Yes!" Garick's eyes darted suddenly from the notes to the map, surer and surer every instant. "Yes, damn it! Yes!"

Then he was rummaging furiously for more paper and pen, finding them, returning to trace and compare and determine.

East and east and east. Arin and Deak and Moss and Bern. Callan and Bowdeen took the bait held out to draw them after.

East and east. Ninety men and forty women, a raveling edge from which the merks tore fragments every day. The coveners stayed massed just within striking range, the women showing themselves as much as possible, taking apparently careless, often fatal chances, moving with less cunning in concealment; time and again allowing the merks nearly to encircle them only to slip out eastward once more.

East. They ran. They fought when they had to. They buried their dead. They buried Deak. Bowdeen made money. He and Callan pressed harder, allowing the coveners no time to rest or hunt, certain they could eventually pin them with their backs to the frontier river boundary.

For Bowdeen, it meant eventual security for him and Sidele, sickening and without pride, but if he lived through it, it would be the end, no more riding.

*No more. Better make it soon, old man, because time-was ain't now.*

Garick entered Singer's room, where he sometimes worked when he didn't want to be disturbed. He spread the map and Judith's notes on the table.

"Get up," he told his son. "Got something you'll want to see."

Singer rolled over on the cot and opened one eye, more in comment than curiosity, but then he saw the handwriting on the time-worn scraps of paper. He sat up quickly and angled himself off the cot and to the table in one swift movement. Garick returned to the doorway, out of reach of Singer's rope.

The young man eagerly scanned the faded writing, then his dark eyes darted to the map. He nodded.

"Absolutely. The deduction *is* inevitable."

Garick grinned. This was Judith's son, Judith's *and* his. "Took me a little longer," he said, not at all envious of the quickness of that mind.

Singer put his finger on the third circle, the southernmost. "It has to be here."

"Why?"

He stared at his father. "You worked it out. Since when do you need my opinion?"

"Just wanted to see if. Knew you could. Makes me proud, boy."

Something odd stirred in Singer. For a fleeting moment, it was as if his father was no longer the master of Charzen but the exuberant Shando farmer who learned hungrily at Judith's knee at the same time she taught the child cradled in her lap. Warily, he shoved back the barriers against the old yearning he thought had died by the carved tree.

"So you want to know why? All right. Three places the Girdle could have gone. New London, Aberdeen, that's two." He ran his finger along the curve of border. "But both of them are inside the Self-Gate, maybe buried and built over for more than a thousand years. If the Girdle were in either place inside City, you think my mother wouldn't have known?"

"She drew three circles."

"Yes, but then wrote, 'The deduction is inevitable.' Meaning, if it was inside City, there would have been information on it when she was doing her original research. They've memory-banked the history of every square inch of City. So that means it has to be *here.*" He pointed to the southernmost circle. "All the way down in Suffec. Place without a name."

"It's a swamp," Garick said. "Great *something* Swamp. Down where even hunters could get lost. I lepped to Webb—"

"Who?"

"A cousin of Sand and Teela. Webb says they duckhunt the edges of it; once he and his cousins went inside. Ten miles wide, forty long. No way in or out except by boat."

"You could look all year and maybe not find it. And even if you did, what makes you think it'll still work?"

"Your mother must have thought so. She went through a lot for it."

"Yes," Singer nodded thoughtfully. "Yes. But still, ten miles by forty . . ."

"Webb remembers a large island, high and dry, deep inside. He didn't land, he only rowed past, but he *thinks* there was something too regular to be natural, something overgrown but square like a big house. That means stone, wood would rot. If it's stone, it had to be brought in. That takes bigger boats than the Suffec ever had. Singer, that stone must have been poured in blocks, I'll bet on it, and no one's poured stone since Jing times. It could be a weapons house."

"Could be." Singer suddenly looked hard at his father. "Just who were you planning to send paddling around that swamp. Not baby brother?"

"Arin's too far east."

"Then who?"

Garick said nothing.

His son laughed once, then dropped heavily onto the bed. " 'Proud of me.' Who the hell did you think you were fooling?" He shook his head. "Don't bother asking, you already know my answer."

"Look, son—"

"I told you once what you can do with that word."

"All right," Garick grated. "You want some poor dumb Suffec to run the Girdle past the merks? Fine. Only don't think you're going to laze around all summer like a pig in mud. We're riding north. You come with us. I want you at arm's reach!"

With a long, eloquent sigh, Singer rolled over so his back was toward his father. "You want me," he yawned, "you can damn well carry me."

*Time-was ain't now*—and Bowdeen wasn't nearly as sharp now as time-was. But he and Callan weren't careless that day; they'd only stopped for a minute on their own flank to do a map check. They never halted long, not with Callan pushing to run down the coveners and kill them all, the sooner the better.

The horses were tethered within three strides, the map laid out on the ground. When the arrow whizzed between them, it grazed so close to Callan's cheek it left a slight mark. They whirled about toward the bush fifty yards away, a stand of brownish-green briar.

The only reason they were alive was the empty quiver slung on the tall man's back.

"Wengen," he drawled, "your name Bowdeen?"

"It sure ain't horse shit," he answered, already busy calculating. No danger, but the mofo would be gone before they could get to their bows. It was dumb. The three of them just stared at each other.

"That Callan?"

The absurdity of it amused Bowdeen after his first shock of fear. "What is this, a goddam roll call? That's Callan. You wanta get killed, we'll do it for you."

"Callan," the tall man said, "you ever hear tell of Salvation?"

Callan unfroze, clawed the bow from his gear, set an arrow, but the covener was already gone. "Get him," he yelled, mounting. Bowdeen grabbed his bridle.

"Man, where's your brain? Go after him in that bush? He ain't alone, they're never alone."

Callan yanked at the reins. "That bastard aimed at *me*. Let go!"

Bowdeen held on. "Sub, you get down off that horse *now*. That's an order." The commander waited, jaw clamped in stubborn determination, till Callan reluctantly obeyed. "That's better." He stared thoughtfully eastward. "You thinking that's who I'm thinking?"

"That's him."

"Thought you said he was dead."

Callan shrugged, too busy deciding whether he should chase or try to get word to Uriah.

"What's he worth now?" Bowdeen asked.

"Ten krets."

Bowdeen's eyes widened. Maybe Arin *was* old Garick's number-two son, but if Callan was offering ten krets for his hide, it didn't matter who he was. Ten krets was more than moneymeat. It was prime steak—and the stove to cook it on.

"All right, sub, we know for sure which way that mofo's moving. We follow slow and easy. Slow and easy, hear? Because there ain't much further he can run."

Callan nodded, thinking of his last talk with Uriah, how his father seemed almost reluctant to rid the earth of the dirt from Shando.

Arin first.

In the silence of the marsh, someone thought of him, and he stirred, surprised. It was Garick, and the power of his lep made Webb's head throb.

It took a long time, repeated over and over, the most complicated message ever hammered into Webb's brain, like a harsh voice grating on sensitive ears, and the request it carried dizzied him even more than the strength of the lep.

*Garick wants . . .*

When the earlier call came to meet north of Charzen, most of the scattered Suffec moved out to do Garick's bidding, but some refused, remembering how Sand and Teela got born again for answering the same call. Webb vacillated awhile, but at last he saddled and began the long journey. He was never certain why. He'd been to Charzen once; he knew the Shando, though the Karli, Wengen and other peoples were just names to him. Like his solitary kind, he lived, fished and hunted alone. Hunters chanced by sometimes; if it was a woman, she might linger awhile before fading into the forest. No words were needed. Birds flew south when it was time, and the Suffec spirit had to move when it felt the urge. Sand and Teela had come like that often—just there, slipping up the bayou in their canoe to share his camp until it was time to go.

Maybe he was going because of the change in things. Shando, Karli, other folks had always been a faraway *them. They* were fighting people called merks and a place called City. But in the last year, the lep pulses out of Charzen brought the Suffec a new thing. They didn't understand it at first, didn't trust it, but . . . *all* of *them* were in it, now: Circle against cowan. Webb understood that much. Gradually, as it sifted through the Suffec mind, *them* became *us*.

The lep caught him skirting the marsh a day above Sandrun. He couldn't believe what Garick asked. *Not me, Garick.*

The great swamp was dangerous. His people hunted the fringes sometimes, but stayed out of the middle where they could get lost or worse. He and Sand and Teela went in just that once, on a dare, and they were spooked half-crazy before they found their way out. Bugs ate them alive, had to haul Teela out of a sinkhole, Sand got cottonmouth-bit. He and Teela had to cut and suck the wound clean.

*Dumb. Never go in again.*

But Garick was waiting for an answer. Should he keep on or go back? *What I do?* Even as he tried to make a decision, he knew. The Shando master deserved a lep at least, but Webb couldn't manage it by himself. He turned south again, trilled a birdcall, half-lepping the sound to let old Doon know he was coming back.

East. Fifty men, twenty women. More buried. They ate raw horse, first the merks' and then their own when they fell. East—till Arin and Moss stood on the last rise with the broad river spread before them and, beyond it, smoke curling from Mrikan chimneys. Their faces were sunburnt to dark leather under layers of dirt, and their filthy deerskins crawled with ticks and wood lice. Their quivers were empty. They passed the chunk of pinkish, fibrous meat between them, chewing slowly in rhythm with their thoughts.

"What now?" Moss asked Arin.

"Scatter north. Two or three together, I guess. We're done, Moss. Can't do any more."

The young girl, no more than fourteen, appeared noiselessly out of the brush, her drawn face tight with fear. "Merks, Arin."

"How many?"

"Don't know." Her nose ran; she dug in it nervously.

"Close?"

"Four, five bowshot."

Arin's speech slurred with weariness. "Go on back, Dorry. Tell them no fight. From now on we run north fast as we can. Moss and I will ride tail, try to slow them up, lead 'em off."

Dorry sniffled loud and wet, looking hungrily at the meat in Moss' hand. "C'n I have some?"

Moss glanced forlornly at the two wet tracks in the dirt under Dorry's nose. He tossed her the meat. "Raw horse is bad enough, but you and your boogers is too damn much."

Arin might have laughed, but he needed the energy to haul himself into the saddle. The horse coughed and faltered, its mouth lathered white with exhaustion. It was Matthew's mount, stolen at Lishin, not as fast as Soogee but enduring, though near spent now like himself.

Today would probably be the end; today he would die. Or not. Like the flea on the fur of the rat, he'd try to go on living, but why wasn't any too clear. There *was* a reason somewhere on the other side of Lishin, he was pretty sure, but he couldn't hold onto it here. Meantime, whether he died or not, Garick would probably take the Kriss, would or would not find the Girdle, then use it to shove some poor sonofabitch—probably big brother who always meant more to him—smack through the Self-Gate and into City that wasn't even at war with them. Arin had helped push it all over the edge and now it was rolling like a downhill snowball, bigger and bigger with the *why* of it lost.

But it was good, at least, to be with Moss, who read him deeper than lep, who shared the strange stillness and cold he felt. And other feelings. Like hating the rain that brought back the fear-smell and the darkness, and the horror of closed-in places and the sound of too many birds.

Moss understood.

Once, a few years back, Webb visited Charzen out of sheer chance and stayed for the fun of it. Hunting upland game, he fell in with a bunch driving horses up to Garick's people. The Shando lived good in well-stitched, colorful clothes—bought clothes—and comfortable houses, though he just didn't feel *right* indoors. Webb spent most of the lazy summer nights on the hill. He delighted in the women, the sida that never ran out, the decorations some of them wore—headbands, metal hoops on wrists, coven signs in iron hung about the neck.

He spent a few weeks hunting with young Arin and his two friends. They took him out on the hill with girls, and *that* was like home only with more people around and more often than Webb was used to. *No wonder Arin always tired.* Still, he liked Garick's son, he was always laughing.

The god was different, though. A quiet man, a deep man. You could sense hurt, though he never shared, Arin said. Webb sometimes wanted to reach out and say something to Garick, but he couldn't think what.

Fun as it was, life in Charzen palled eventually. He missed the salt marsh smell and the quiet. By his lights, Charzen was a riot of talk, too much for ears used to backwater hush. His own people shared more, rarely spoke.

Still, the Shando made a fuss over his going. Goddess Jenna gave him a cloth headband she said came all the way from Lorl, wherever that was, used to belong to somebody, Webb couldn't remember the name. When he got back to Sandrun, Webb took a couple of the northern honkers running south for autumn, and saved some of the brilliant green-black feathers and sewed them into his new headband. The Suffec laughed: *old honker Webb.*

But they didn't laugh at Garick's demand.

Suffec had no god like Garick; it wasn't needed. In Suffec whoever felt like it put on the horns at a gather-in, or Belten or any of the other fire-days. They never invoked goddess earth or fire or water, because they were *with* both and each other, sharing all the time, and to make a fuss over it like Shando and Karli would be like making love to themselves.

At the moment, Doon was responsible for calling the gather-in, because he was the oldest in Sandrun and held as much authority as the scattered, independent Suffec could take. Even when he wasn't serving as gatherer, lep that affected all the hundred-odd folk of Sandrun bayou focused through him.

As usual, they took their own lazy time collecting at the pond bank. There were not many young men or women; these were north with Garick. Older folk they were, or women with children on the way, men who might go next year if the urge took them, but for now it didn't. Silently they collected on the bank in a circle around Doon while Garick's need was sifted and weighed. They listened to the forest around them, the music that measured out their lives: the *rick-rick* of a squirrel spiraling down a tree trunk, the flutter of a bird, the slight splash of a fish breaking surface to take a water bug. They thought about what Garick wanted.

They held no superstitions about the swamp, merely a healthy respect for its dangers. You could cut a trail, but the damned thing might get grown over in summer like this. There were no reliable landmarks; after a heavy rain some of the small islands you saw on the way in wouldn't be there on the way out, and what was dry land weeks back might be quicksand now. No, they saw no sense in this. Garick was far away; they'd already sent their folk who wanted to help. The rest had their own business to go about. Doon collected the silent opinions, then chose thirteen to lep the refusal back to the Shando.

Webb stood up, confused and distressed by his own action. *I'll go.*

All heads turned toward him, though Doon did not seem especially surprised at the decision. He looked at Webb. *Alone if you do.*

Webb accepted this, not without difficulty. His mouth felt dry when he swallowed. *Alone then. Been in before.*

The breeze stirred ripples on the surface of the pond. A bird squawked. Doon squinted at Webb with cold, clear blue eyes. *Could get born again.*

*Maybe. But Garick needs.*

Doon frowned. *Garick owes. Suffec don't.*

*I know,* Webb shrugged. *But I got to.*

The circle nodded its acceptance. None tried to dissuade him, none had that right. He knew they would loan as much gear and food as he needed. *Go tomorrow,* he decided.

They slipped away one by one into the bush, leaving Doon and Webb by the pond.

*Dumb, Webb,* said Doon.

*Maybe.*

They listened to the birds.

Garick was a day south of the meet-point when the lep came. He heard it and rode back to Singer, who was tied on a mare. Good as his word, he hadn't budged a step. His father had to roll him up thick in homespun and sling him over his shoulder to get him to the horse.

"Hope you're happy," he growled. "Webb's going after the Girdle alone."

Singer nodded without interest.

"That all you have to say?"

His son yawned. "Yes."

Garick dug his heels into the horse's flanks and rode back up the line, furious and frustrated that he could not get through to Singer. *Stubborn like Jade.* Sometimes Garick wanted someone to talk to; now was such a time, but Jenna never had anything to say about Singer, and the girl from Karli, warm as she was, had no thought but Arin. Garick started to regret not calling his younger son home, after all. He wondered where he was.

Callan squatted by the dead horse. "Run to death," he judged. "Less than an hour ago. Still warm."

To Bowdeen, nosing about the grass and short brush, his sub

seemed more interested in the saddle markings than the carcass. Callan muttered something under his breath.

They were within half a mile of the river with the Mrikan settlement of Filsberg on the other side, a street of cabins, a trading post of sorts and the main barracks of the northern division. For Bowdeen it would be coming home. Sidele was up this way by now, working her circuit, fortunetelling and doing tricks. She always did good in Filsberg with the barracks there and the crib girls wanting to be told how they were going to meet a stranger with a lot of goodness in him, live to be a hundred and die rich.

He thought more and more of Sidele now as an antidote to the mean reality of the drag. His tired mind weighed the possibility. If he could only get the hell away from Callan, then hire a boat . . .

Might as well, the moneymeat was gone. They'd made a bundle today—more than half the pathetic remnant of coveners, five of them his own score. Not much to it now; the Karli were too tired, too hungry, too plain run out to give much of a fight. So few of them: it strengthened his growing belief that they weren't the main Karli force, but a diversion. If that was so, somebody somewhere was gonna get hit awful hard and fast. He wasn't about to tell Callan, he was already getting harder and harder to keep in line. And anyway, if the Karli'd screwed him, he'd been kissed a lot, too. Fifty krets in his pocket, enough not to mind losing ten-kret Arin. That bothered Callan a damn sight more than it did him.

"This was his horse," the sub declared. "He was here."

"How you know?"

"I know."

Bowdeen studied the ground. The Shando master was an obsession with Callan. He was gone, and the other was acting like a hungry weasel without any chickens to steal.

"I'm sure it's him, Commander. I want him."

Bowdeen shook his head in disgust. "All right. I can get him."

"Where? They split up."

"I can get him. Course, we'll have to chase now, just the two of us. Can't wait for the company."

"All right." Callan rose, impatient to move.

"That means we gonna be missing for a while, sub. That don't sad me none; way I see it, we've been out of a job all year."

"Yes," Callan nodded. "Just the two of us."

"Lead'll head the rest back to Lorl, all the companies. No more money to make anyway."

"My orders will cover it," said Callan.

Bowdeen gave him an unflattering appraisal. "Like to see them orders someday, sub. Like to know who gives you orders beside me."

Callan did not reply.

"And the price goes up, sub. To get myself missing is worth more than ten krets."

"Fifteen if you find him," Callan said. "Twenty if you bring him down."

Bowdeen didn't move. "Ten now."

"All right, ten now, but let's move." Callan fussed with his saddle. "We don't even know where to start."

"Sure do." The Wengen pointed to the ground at his feet. "There and there and there."

Now Callan saw the line of spots dried to the color of dark brown rust on the pale green grass. Their direction led off toward the river.

"He's leaking blood," Bowdeen judged. "Maybe not bad, but he's too beat to be thinking good. Fooled me last winter, fooled us all along." He dusted his palms and rose. "That mofo's on the river right now, and I know where we can get a boat."

Callan's protruding stare widened. "To Filsberg?"

"That's where." Funny how it worked out so nice.

"He wouldn't do that."

"No, he wouldn't," Bowdeen agreed. He felt tired and too old and more than a little sad. "He's been running, though, and fighting and outguessing too long. He was due for one mistake."

"But not into Mrika, not with the barracks and the headquarters of the whole northern division!"

"That's his mistake, sub: guessing I'd never think of it."

Bowdeen slipped the reins over the horse's head. He sighed, mightily sick of Callan. They didn't come harder or tougher or braver than the sub. More than just his ass was iron, and if he himself didn't take the open field command, it would go to Callan, who knew as much as anyone about deepwoods fighting now. But Callan didn't know or care anything about people. You have to know men to lead them.

And—Bowdeen had to admit it—he was gut-sick of himself, too, because, except conscience didn't no way fill a belly, a Wengen ought to run with Arin now, not chase after to cut him down. Bowdeen faced Callan again and stuck out his hand. "He got tired, sub. Happens to everybody sometime. Deal me ten."

The flatbottom skiff, his only inheritance from his father, had withstood long years of use. It never leaked; every cranny and crack was well caulked with a mixture of resinous gum and tar.

Webb pushed it into deep water with the willow pole, a gift from Doon, the only one who'd come to see him off. Strong and light, it was notched at one end to be fitted with his fish net. Other gifts of meat and cooked rice were stowed forward with his bow and quiver.

Webb waved to Doon, and the old man nodded with calm melancholy. In a curious way, Webb felt that though Doon didn't approve of Garick's mission, he thought more of Webb for going.

As he poled off the bank, Doon's lep whispered in his mind. *Yes.*

*You said dumb.*

*Going's dumb. Reason's not.*

Webb wasn't sure about the reason. It was too big.

Doon nodded gravely from the shore. *Find it, then.*

The skiff floated further from the shore. *Webb . . .* Doon once more, one last word.

*?*

*Luck.*

Webb grinned and waved again, then turned his face forward so Doon couldn't see the smile fade. Luck was what he'd need, luck to get in and remember where the island was, luck that it actually held the thing Garick wanted, luck that he could get out without ending up lost or bit or bear-ate.

The boatman, thin, stone-hard, moved about the wet rocks of the shore line as if each step had been long practiced. He ceased moving, dropped the nets in the stern of his boat and stood quite still when the tall man broke out of the bush and stumbled toward his boat. The wind was right—or wrong; the boatman could smell his filthy skins. He thought at first it was a Wengen, but closer he perceived the long-blended layers of dirt, coven paint and sunburn. The skins were literally rotting off him. Through a rent in the remains of trousers, he could see a leaf-wrapping around the thin leg, brown with dried blood. The man wobbled over the rocks and slumped down on the stern board of the beached boat. For a moment he seemed to forget the owner, head hanging forward, breathing weakly. "Old man—" The boatman caught the Shando drawl. "Take me across."

"Well, now," he hedged. "You got any money?"

He had to repeat the question; the Shando had forgotten him again, so spent that only will apparently prevented his falling over. The head wagged vaguely. "No."

"Well, I got to eat, and the fish ain't running like last week."

The tall man stood up with an effort, towering over the Mrikan, his emaciation adding to his height, the matted hair hanging over eyes that were winter-cold but distant rather than cruel. He was filthy, but the knife in his scabby claw was spotless and fresh-honed.

"Old man," he repeated dully, "I want to go across."

The boatman looked at the knife. "Sure, I'll take you. But I ought to get something. That's only fair. Good Shando bow and quiver there. Some merk might give a half-kret for that. Maybe more for knowing where I got them. But I'm a fair man."

The Shando looked through him, past him. Distantly: "Oh yes, that's only fair." The bow and empty quiver were unslung and handed to him. "Look at me, old man."

"Huh?" But the eyes held his. The boatman could not look away.

"Your life and mine are irrelevant, old man. Isn't it strange that we both want to live so much?"

The man's bearded lips moved, but the voice seemed to come from inside the boatman's head. He felt queer; as if he were not alone in his private thoughts. But that was foolish. It was important to shove the boat out away from the shallows and cross swiftly, and if there had been any idea of selling anything to the merks, he forgot it.

Ego irrelevant. What he wanted didn't really matter, except to him. And what still mattered? He leaned back in the prow of the boat and tried to remember a time before Lishin, before Holder. He couldn't hold on to anything. There was Shalane, but even she was hazy. He pressed his eyes tight-shut and tried to make her face stand out clear in his mind.

The woman-figure came into focus so suddenly, so vividly, she might have been real. Not Shalane. He opened his eyes and the vision was gone. He closed them again and tried to bring her back, but failed.

Arin looked at the boatman, but the old man rowed mechanically, his back to the Shando. It didn't leak from him; his simple mind was easy to control. He could have killed him and taken the boat, but he was too weak to pull against the slowest tide. And one more death was as pointless as one more life.

The woman-figure didn't resemble anyone he'd ever known or met. Though his mind only held her for an instant, it retained every detail sharply: the short nose; wide-set black eyes, dark hair hanging down her back; broad mouth with teeth nervously chewing at the back corner of her lower lip. Thin, even bony, her body had a stark femininity in spite of, or perhaps because of its angularity. Around her shoulders she clutched a faded shawl.

Who was she? Why did she invade his mind in Shalane's place?

On the bank from which they'd cast off, two men stood close together, too far away to see clearly, except one was black. The black man raised his hand and pointed toward their boat.

Bowdeen and Callan. Hiding in the underbrush was sure death. Bowdeen and Callan would find him fast, or the merks would. Town was his only chance, and it was a slim one. But there at least he might be able to hide behind a door or in a loft. Might steal something to eat, an hour's rest. Pitiful hope, but all he had left.

Strangely, Arin thought, the closer the danger came, the more important it seemed that he might not be breathing by nightfall. The strange woman's face appeared again in his mind. He willed it away, and then it was Shalane as he last saw her, clearer than he'd remembered in countless weeks. Sharp and dear and—

Shalane looked up, suddenly uneasy. *Arin in trouble.*

Garick was going over Jay's map, detail by detail, with the other masters. They were all at meet-point above Karli. Shalane knew the map by heart now; she could have drawn every corner and curve of Salvation from memory. Later the masters would share it with their various people, but for now she was expected to be part of the meeting. But this sudden, worrying gist of Arin—

Jenna was the only one who caught some little edge of Shalane's anxiety.

It was his first real call in so long Shalane couldn't reckon up the time. Even the night they first joined, the worm of cold doubt was beginning to turn Arin into someone else and she couldn't share everything Garick was changing him to, but since Lishin, Arin was so *away* from her, even further than Moss on the wet days when he shut himself off from his family.

Now she caught the signal again; she was sure it was meant only for her. Shalane tried to read some message in it, but it was no more than sharing, a faint, feeble yearning need, but the fear mixed with it told her there was trouble. Something bad. She closed her eyes, trying to hold contact . . . but it faded.

Shalane stared around the circle, almost frantic. She had never felt so alone. *Got to help him.*

Bowdeen and Callan were rowing now. He had to get ashore at the closest point and take a chance on getting lost before they landed. They were pulling straight for him. The old man with his back to Arin swerved the boat directly for the nearest shore, as if it had been his own idea.

Sidele stared at the crystal with feverish intensity, willing the sudden vision to appear again, but it wouldn't.

This was real! This was success! Heart hammering, she recalled the strange features seen in the glass: narrow, bearded face, wild auburn hair, eyes sad beyond sad. She wondered who he was. Not that it mattered: the crystal could bring anyone, anything first time. The trick was making it work again on purpose.

She used to regard it as a piece of junk to impress the customers, like the sign she hung outside with peculiar, meaningless red symbols on it. Oh sure, old Pelly with the yellow hair and bad teeth taught her the power might not come for years and years, but Sidele doubted the talent of a reader who needed half a jug before she could see pictures in a saucer full of ink.

Yet maybe there was truth in it. Maybe hers *was* a real talent. Her readings were almost always strengthened by a lucky hunch or, sometimes, a random jolt of lep, but this was so different, much more important because—

The approaching footsteps broke her train of thought. Coming fast. She cursed, hoping for once it wasn't a customer. She wanted to work more with this thing, keep trying. But like the old man said, they both needed the money. Hell, if she was beginning to get it, really get the power, she could double her prices, but . . . the customer.

Sighing, Sidele rose and grabbed her shawl. It was muggy, felt like storm, too hot for the wrap, but customers expected her to look the part. She got her thoughts running on the right track, trying to pick up first impressions. The hurrying footsteps were coming right at the door.

It burst open with a force that strained the hinges. A giant man stumbled through it, slammed it shut behind him. He lurched against the table, head down, totally spent. Sidele saw the fresh blood on the filthy, torn deerskin trousers.

In spite of the shawl about her shoulders, Sidele felt a slight chill. Maybe it was the tangled mop of auburn hair that warned her she'd recognize the stranger's features when he raised his head. She would know the cut of the mouth, the eyes . . . yes. The face in the crystal, astonished as her own.

"You . . ." he croaked. "It's *you*. It *is* you."

Her mouth hung open. "What?"

He said it in a low, awed voice. "Who *are* you?"

"Sidele."

"Sidele . . ." It seemed an effort for him even to think the syllables. He reached out to her, wavering on his feet. "Help me."

His fingers touched her hand. Then his knees buckled. Arin crumpled to the floor.

Their boat crunched on sand and rock. Callan jumped ashore. "Which way? Town, you think?"

"I guess." Bowdeen clambered out with less nimbleness. He was bone-tired, but keeping it from the sub. "More places to hide." Bowdeen pointed to the last straggle of squat houses that marked the outskirts of Filsberg. "He's hurt, too. I guess he'd try for one of these. Too many merks further in."

Callan loped off briskly toward the nearest house. Bowdeen fell in beside him, wishing they could walk easier, but not wanting Callan to find the moneymeat first. The day was still hot, but a sudden gust of cool wind swept across the short grass. Bowdeen studied the northeast sky.

"Storm before night. Coming fast."

Callan nodded shortly. "Then let's get him quick."

They strode off again in silence. After a few minutes, they came up on the rear of the closest shack, a low, wind-blistered structure of raw pine plank. Bowdeen halted.

"Two doors. You watch the back, I'll go around and—"

"I want the front," said Callan.

"No. You ain't gonna cheat old dad out of five krets."

Callan fidgeted. "All right, you go in. But I want to see."

"You will, sub," Bowdeen grinned. "If that Shando's inside, you gonna get the loudest y'all-come you *ever* heard."

Sheddy drawn, he stepped carefully through the high weeds near the house, doing his best to walk quiet. Callan watched him turn the corner and disappear.

Arin or no, Bowdeen almost whooped with delight at the sight of the red sign nailed over the door. Sidele. *Sidele! Damn if I ain't lucked!*

He checked an impulse to sheathe his sword and rush inside. The door was closed; maybe she had a customer.

Except it didn't feel right.

She often teased him for being more Circle than he remembered, and he always laughed it off, but she was right, Bowdeen had a lot more deepwoods instinct than he allowed for consciously. It whispered to him now and took the warmth out of the day.

He willed his pulse to ease, forced his respiration down till he couldn't hear it himself. Then he crept close to the closed door and put his ear against it. Nothing, no sound. Bowdeen waited motionless, one minute, two, three. *You outwaited me once before, man.*

Four minutes. He couldn't stay there forever; if he didn't move soon, Callan would, and that was money gone.

He pulled back a step, hefted the sheddy and kicked the door in. Nothing happened. Cautiously, Bowdeen stuck his head in, looked around, then took two paces into the room. It was empty except for the scratched, unfinished table in the middle with Sidele's dumb old glass ball. It was a small room, probably only used for her readings. Bowdeen figured the rest of the house was where she lived and stored the stuff for her now-and-then public shows. Behind the table was a narrow doorway. As he crept toward it, he saw she'd hung it with the old bead curtains he'd bought for her out of his first drag money. He still recalled vividly the fight he had with Sidele over those damn beads; she didn't no way want his present, because it was bought with money made off his own kind. *Long time, woman. Just took you longer to get used to it.*

Bowdeen shoved the sheddy point through the beads. Then he heard Sidele moan. With a yell, he forgot caution and rushed into the room, turning fast, the blade at guard. He stopped, feeling foolish but still balanced to spring. There was no one.

This room was bigger than the front, and Sidele had her stuff tossed all over. A cracked mirror hung from one wall, reflecting himself. Clothes, false hair, jars of color, boards with heads wagging yes and no and a few old skulls with holes dug in for candles covered the bare-boarded room. Bowdeen took it all in, from the dirty clump of hair beneath the mirror to the rags piled high on top of her big old wooden trunk.

His eyes stopped at the trunk; the heap of cloth on top of it moved.

"All right, boy. Come on out of there."

Another groan. It came from beneath the rags. Bowdeen swept them away with his blade. It was Sidele: tied at the wrists and ankles, gagged, flat on her face on the trunk top and bare as an apple.

"Damn, woman." He plucked out the gag. "What he do to you?"

She coughed and cleared her throat. "Old man, you are one sweet sight. Just get these ropes off me."

"I will, but where's he gone?"

"And pour me something wet—tea, sida, anything. Feel like I been breathing dirt since sunup."

Bowdeen cut her bonds, then went to call Callan, pausing to toss her the first clothes within reach. "Sidele, that body of yours is a joyful sight, but my sub don't approve of folks being natural."

Bowdeen sat on the trunk, one arm around Sidele while she sipped horsemint tea and told her story. Callan paced, not yet at the bottom of that well of energy that marveled the weary Bowdeen. He stayed the length of the room from Sidele. The lifelong habit of thought would not bend: she told the future and called up powers other than God. She was, therefore, to be lumped with coven and equally disdained.

"Next I knew," Sidele continued, "he points that knife at me and says take off my clothes."

"Like he had time to play," Bowdeen mused.

Sidele made an eloquent gesture. "With a knife, who argues? I said he could do me till dinnertime, but put the knife away." She and Bowdeen lapsed into rapid Wengen and laughed about something. *"Dunesk."* She shook her head. "It's sad."

Callan paced agitatedly; time was wasting and Bowdeen, with his woman near, seemed quite content to let it slip by. "And *then?*"

"Then he rams the greasy *shmota* in my mouth and hits me on the head. Next I know, I'm buried under these rags until you come." She gave Bowdeen a quick kiss. "And you are still the best-looking man in town."

"So he's still running," Callan said. "Why stop here at all? What did he want?"

"Use your eyes, sub. Plain as day what he did."

"Commander," Callan's patience was strained, "you're wasting time—as usual. If you know—"

"If I know, I don't gotta say. My feet are just about run off chasing that mofo, and I don't have one hell of a lot of good temper left, so if you want a favor, you ask nice."

Callan sighed and regarded the wall. "Sir," he clipped off the words carefully, "I *respectfully* request you tell me what you think Arin did." He glared at Sidele. "*One* of us should be looking."

"Well, hoo*ee*, now ain't you polite when you really want something?

"Yessir, yessir, tell me true!
Kiss your ass and lick your shoe!"

Callan ignored the taunt. Bowdeen pointed across the room to the mirror. "All right, what do you see?"

"Mirror."

"On the floor."

"Pile of hair. So?"

"Put it together: hair, black knife, Sidele's clothes."

Callan shook his head. "He shaves, maybe cuts off some top hair. Why make her strip?"

"So he can look like what he ain't."

"Like a *woman?*"

"You got it," Bowdeen said. "Bet he's down on Crib Street right now getting his butt pinched by merks."

Sidele giggled. "He didn't look like that kind of girl." Another exchange in Wengen. Bowdeen roared, hugging her.

Callan glowered. "Commander, are you just going to sit here with that—?"

"Watch—your—mouth, Callan."

"—with that witch while that bastard Arin gets away?"

Bowdeen rose, stretched lazily and collapsed again on Sidele's rumpled bed, patting it in invitation to her. She slid down beside him. "As a matter of fact, that is *just* what I'm thinking." He sighed deeply. "I'm tired, sub, I'm done in, and I'm wondering now if I give a damn about finding him. And why you do."

"He's a murderer."

"So what are *we*, chicken farmers?"

"He murdered Micah."

"Who?"

"One—one of my people."

"Your people, huh?" Bowdeen considered it with half-lidded eyes. "And just who are they, sub? It comes to me, I never did know you any better than I know City."

Sidele said it: "I think he might be Kriss."

"Nobody asked you," Callan shot at her.

"Oh, now, hold *on!*" Bowdeen sat up, remembering. "This Micah —Arin did him?"

Callan's expression was peculiar. "Not quite, Bowdeen. He let *you* do it."

"The Kriss on the bald top."

"Yes."

"'The Kriss were not to be hunted.'" Bowdeen looked up at the young man with new understanding. The edge of laughter went out of his voice. "And I made you pay me for it."

"Yes." Callan moved to the bead curtains. "That's all right, that can pass. But I want Arin. Are you coming or not?"

It was a long moment before Bowdeen answered, staring at him with that mixture of comprehension and pity. "Not," he said finally.

"*You're* passing up twenty-five krets?"

"I came in here for that. But I don't know, Callan. I just don't know. Saw myself in that mirror just now. And you. Man, look at us. We ain't fit to sleep in the garbage. Leather so worn, it gonna fall off us if it don't rot off. Coven knives, coven moccasins. You never wore a beard—you ain't shaved in a week. That rope you tie your pants with, that belonged to a master once. There was a time when we did a job, Callan, and you were one of the best. I never liked your ass, you never liked mine, but we were good. We were soldiers."

"I was something before that," Callan said quietly. "I was a man with a dream. That hasn't changed. Are you coming?"

Bowdeen swung wearily off the bed to face him. "Oh, man, forget him. He's too fast, too smart, and not worth it. You don't get him, someone else will, today, tomorrow, who cares? He coulda hurt Sidele bad, but he didn't, and I'm so damn glad—sub, when things work out right, a man ought to be smart enough to know it." He lowered his voice, almost gentle. "You want that field command, take it, sit easy and wait till City writes contracts again."

Callan tried to understand. "You don't want the money?"

"Oh, man, you are *thick!*" The Wengen slapped his thigh in disgust and exasperation. "Ain't you had *enough?* You see that meat we took today? You get a good look at those poor, sad—?" He broke off and looked helplessly at Sidele, who watched impassively from the bed. "All I know is my last drag has *been.* I don't give a shit about Arin."

"Of course, it won't be too hard for Callan to find him," Sidele put in. "That mofo must be six-five at least. And in my clothes . . ."

The incoherent knot of disgust dissolved in Bowdeen's laughter. "Sure," he grinned. "That *do* make it easy."

Callan strode through the front room and yanked the door open. "I'll find him."

"Long as you catch him in Filsberg, I keep the ten and five more." Bowdeen followed, leaning against the doorjamb. "You get caught out in the rain, come on back and sleep dry if you want."

When the rain came, it came hard, turning the streets of Filsberg into ankle-deep mud. It didn't stop Callan, but then very little ever did. He wasn't bred that way. Anywhere that Arin might have gone, he followed—the public houses, the few shops, the stables, sheds and back rooms. He worked his way through the crib girls to their indignation, slogged along the riverbank north and south of the point where they'd landed.

Trudging back toward the main street, Callan had to stop and rest under an overhanging roof. He considered the situation while the water rolled down his sheepskin, puddling around his ruined moccasins. There was no problem with money. With Bowdeen quitting, the easiest thing would be to offer a good bounty on Arin; that would bring him four or five fresh men to work with, and they could travel faster than the wounded Shando.

He willed himself to move. His body responded sluggishly. Uriah's son waited a few moments longer under the eaves. With a reproach for its weakness, he *allowed* his body to feel its fatigue. He permitted his stomach its hunger.

The tavern had been a large barn once and still retained that name. Of the five or six drinking houses in Filsberg, this one was chosen by the billeted mercenaries as their place, and the owner wouldn't have it any other way. Money was scarce in Filsberg now with the borders closed and Uhian trade at a standstill. Available cash was concentrated in the merks and little enough of that now. Most of them were idle; they spent their time drinking and wondering when City would write new contracts. Things were changing; a man couldn't count on anything any more.

The Barn was jammed with tables and benches, dim and smoky from the charcoal fire used for cooking, ripe with spices, fish, wet leather, spilled liquor and sweat. Three slatternly girls moved from the long bar to the tables and back.

A young sub nudged the only civilian at his table, a short, bald-headed, innocent-looking little man with a look of perpetual surprise. "Spitt, look there at the bar. Damn if that ain't a Karli."

For a moment—only a moment—Spitt's expression lost its bewilderment. "No, that's a soldier."

"Soldier?" the sub jeered at the bedraggled figure. "In *whose* army?"

"Well, I come from Lorl. I'd say that's sub Callan of the 43rd. Drink up, boy."

Another young merk leaned over to them. "That's the one looking around for some Shando in a woman's dress."

"Figures," a third put in. "What I heard of him, he wouldn't be looking for anything female."

"So that leaves men," the young sub chuckled. "Maybe we should ask him."

Spitt poured him another drink. "I don't think I would."

The barman gazed distastefully at the bearded, dirt-seamed face across from him. He placed the sida on the bar. "Prices gone up. Nothing coming in from anywhere. All we got left is bean soup."

"Get it," said Callan. He took half the sida in a gulp. Tired as he was, he shouldn't drink on an empty stomach. He tightened the control about his frustration and smoldering anger. When the soup came, he finished it quickly, churning the spoon to his mouth noisily, and shoved the empty bowl across the bar. "More."

He finished the sida waiting for his refill. The fatigue was like a sponge, soaking the strength out of his spine. He drooped over the bar. Shouldn't be drinking at all. At home it wasn't tolerated, a weakness that turned men's eyes away from God. Still, like his strong father, he dedicated his life to unpleasant things in the company of human garbage, to do God's work. Only in the last grinding weeks had he begun to feel—not a slackening of resolve or purpose; merely that his imperfect body wanted to be quiet and rested. It would have to wait.

Callan finished the second bowl of soup and ordered another drink, dropping a wilted two-kret note on the bar.

"Nothing smaller?" the barman complained.

The change would be just so much more soggy paper in his pocket. "Keep it," he grunted, retreating into his drink.

A new voice broke in. "Looks like Lorl has all the money nowadays."

Callan looked up. An older officer about Bowdeen's age was standing next to him, drinking quietly. On the shoulder of his neat summer cotton jacket, he wore the markings of a field commander. Callan recognized him: Trace, a respected soldier close to retirement.

"That little bald fella." Trace jerked his head toward Spitt. "He's from Lorl, been buying all night."

"Has he?" Callan replied without interest.

Trace studied him with steady eyes. "You're Callan—43rd south."

"Yes, sir."

"I've heard of you. Dragging close in. You and Bowdeen."

"Yes, sir." Callan turned away and poured another drink. He shouldn't, but he needed it.

"You and Bowdeen," Trace repeated as if considering it. "Sub, a man's life is his own business, but I've never let my men drag if I could talk them out of it. But you and Bowdeen . . ." He cut it off with a note of disgust.

The liquor had edged Callan over a thin line. He felt mean. "Me and Bowdeen *what,* field?"

Trace caught the edge in his voice and met it coolly. "Long time ago I had a Karli woman. We thought cowan hunters were about the lowest thing in the world. But you and Bowdeen have turned into a couple of packdogs. What are you doing here, buying more men?"

Callan let the remark roll over him. "That's right."

"Don't waste your time." Trace turned away from the bar, indicating the room full of men. "Nobody'll go."

Callan finished his drink and stood for a moment, letting the heat of it flood through his body. "Let's see, field. There might be one or two real men in this outfit."

Trace smiled. "Forget it, Callan."

Callan pushed himself away from the bar. "All right, listen up!" He strode slowly between the tables. "I'm looking for men for a drag. No deepwoods, right here in Mrika. Five krets apiece, seven if you have to cross the river."

"What the hell you after?" asked the young sub next to Spitt.

"After one man," Callan called back. "One man. Five krets each, ten to whoever makes the kill."

A buzz of low reaction, but no one spoke up. "What's the matter?" Callan looked from face to face. "That's almost a month's pay just for riding."

"We heard," one man chuckled, "that it wasn't a man at all, but a real tall woman."

The young sub stood up. "A woman?" he grinned. "I heard sub Callan didn't *like* women."

He was a very young man and slightly drunk. If he had been older or wiser, he would have seen the telltale stiffening of Callan's compact frame. He would have shut up. "So we were wondering what you wanted him *for,* Callan."

Callan turned on him. A few of the older men like Spitt and Trace felt vaguely apprehensive. "Come on, sub," Spitt plucked at the boy's sleeve. "Sit down."

He recognized the cold, deliberate malevolence in Callan's movements as he walked to within arm's reach of the other sub.

"Soldier, you probably never heard the word, but where I come from, men are hanged for what you're suggesting. It's called an abomination. I've tied the noose myself and watched my father swing them off. I'll take your apology."

The sub planted his feet apart. "You'll take a bath first. You stink, you know that?"

Callan started to turn away as if forgetting the affair. Then his knees bent slightly as he swiveled, bringing the power from his whole, hard frame behind the right hand that smashed knuckles first across the man's face. It was a coven trick like most of the life-or-death ploys he'd learned with Bowdeen. The sub flailed backward and crashed in a heap against another man's legs. He was up in an instant, breathing hard, the red welt already starting up on his face. Callan crouched slightly, waiting, lips parted in cold pleasure. He was glad of this. If not Arin, something or someone had to break to-night.

"Don't do it, sub." It was Trace at the bar, unruffled by any of it, but sure of himself. "He'll kill you. He's used to it."

But the sub was already charging, enraged, too furious for caution. As he struck out at Callan, the man was simply not there, stooping forward and to the right, catching him by the waist, using the young sub's momentum to swivel behind him. In one movement, he had the sub in a half-lock, the black knife laid across his throat.

"This," he said in the man's ear, "is the way skinny little Karli girls handle big tough men like you. Now, sub, when you can handle that girl, you come back and try me."

He gave the man a shove, releasing him. Before the sub could turn on him, Callan chopped him sharply across the base of the skull. The sub dropped like a sack of rocks.

Callan sheathed his knife. "The offer's still open. Who wants a job?"

The tables were silent; the men turned away as Callan caught their eyes. "If it's not enough, speak up. Bid."

No one moved. The small, hairless civilian bestowed a half-apologetic smile on the Kriss.

"Like I said," Trace remarked imperturbably, "forget it."

Callan strode past him, pausing only to fix the officer with scathing contempt. "Field," he said, without bothering to lower his voice, "as a 'packdog' to what I must consider an experienced 'soldier'—if this is the best you've got, God help the North."

Bowdeen was too tired for anything but a bath and food. He cleaned his plate three times, then sat massively like a contented boar while Sidele bathed him with water from the rain barrel. Later, she lit a candle and they lay close together on the bed, talking softly. His head began to loll onto her shoulder, his eyes closed. Instinctively, one hand closed over her breast. He slept. The hours passed, and they did not change position though the candle guttered out. Beside the sleeping man, Sidele stared into the darkness.

The rain hushed to a whisper, lightning flashed less often and further away, though each distant ominous roll of thunder made the crystal ball rattle in its mount.

Long after midnight, the door banged open. Bowdeen woke and snaked from the bed, sheddy in his hand.

"That you, sub?"

"Ask the witch," Callan grunted. "Can't she see in the dark?"

Sidele rose with a philosophic sigh and lit the remaining candles. The merk tramped into the rear room, soaked and bedraggled. He stripped off the wet poncho and his leather jacket and dropped them on the floor in a sodden heap. Sidele handed him an old piece of cloth for toweling; he took it without acknowledgment or thanks.

"Well," Bowdeen asked, "you find Arin?"

"Do I look as if I did?"

Bowdeen was amused and surprised. Callan was always a sour spirit, but sarcasm was unusual for him.

"The way you *look,* sub, someone did a bad job of drowning you. Anything to tell me?"

Callan was reluctant to discuss the incident at the Barn, but Bowdeen pried it out of him by degrees. When he heard the attitude of Trace and the northern merks, the commander's brows contracted—only to open in surprised recognition when Callan described the little civilian sitting with the unlucky sub.

"No hair at all? Big eyes, looks like he shouldn't go out without his momma?"

"Yes. You know him?"

"Maybe. Sounds like Spitt. You'd know him too, you went out drinking in Lorl."

"*I* remember him." Sidele poured tea into three cups. "Pleasant little dummy, harmless as milk. Sells sida for Garick. Told his fortune once."

Callan took the cup, again failing to thank Sidele. "Spitt," he mused. "Why's he this far north? Garick already promised this year's crop to the moneymen."

"Well, now, now," Bowdeen mused, sipping his tea. "Few months back, wasn't no end to them northern boys trying to find you and me. Now you hold out five krets, they just sit there. I hate to say it, but I think Garick bought himself some merks."

"He'd have to buy the whole division to make it worth while. Garick's in debt up to his ears. He hasn't got that kind of money."

"Maybe not," Bowdeen conceded, warming his hands around the cup, "but it sure looks to me like somebody has."

The streets of Salvation lay silent in moonlight.

Following Jenna, Shalane dodged from shadow to shadow along Salvation square. She grudgingly admired the tireless, loping energy of the Shando goddess. It helped to think of that rather than what she must do.

Disloyal to Arin, maybe, but Shalane couldn't feel close to his parents. Garick was kind but distant. Jenna talked little and shared less, and she did not even seem close to her husband. They slept in separate rooms in Charzen, and on the ride to Salvation, Jenna went out on the hill with others regularly. And yet, Jenna's eyes sometimes followed the reclusive, preoccupied god. One look from him—Shalane read that much in the goddess—and the others could sleep alone. Yet Jenna and Garick did not touch. The why of it was beyond Shalane.

Still, she was glad to be under Jenna's wing. Maybe the two of them *had* done something to help Arin, he seemed safe now. Shalane wasn't exactly sure where he was, but she read him out of danger. It was good she confided in Jenna.

Staying close behind her, Shalane wondered afresh at the woman's ability to walk on tinder without making a sound. Slipping ahead, the nocked bow in one hand, she might be a leaf blowing across the last of the summer moonlight.

All around them, other black-clad, soot-faced wraiths flitted in and out of the angular shadows of Salvation, each with an assigned sector. Shalane never met Garick's informant, but he was thorough down to every single house with its floor plan, as well as the change of the mine shifts and how many would be sleeping when they came.

And suddenly, in the pale light, it was time. They came to the corner of the first house in their sector. At Jenna's lep, Shalane melted back into shadow. *Wait.*

The door would lead directly into a kitchen; it would be secured with a simple fall latch that could be raised with the thin strip of iron supplied each covener for the purpose. Shalane reached for hers. Suddenly a lamp glowed in the kitchen. Men's voices. *Two.* A chill clutched at her stomach.

More shadows darted on all sides, flowing onto porches, kneeling to poke at locks. She wanted dearly to run away and not be a part of it, no matter how necessary. Her hand shook holding the knife; she realized she had it in a useless overhand grip. Cursing her stupidity, she changed it. Her teeth chattered.

The door opened. Two men, stocky, powerful, appeared on the front porch, first of the morning shift. Others would be rising soon. The shift changed about two hours before sunup, Shalane knew, and the moon was low on the horizon. Stepping down from the porch a few feet from where Jenna and Shalane poised like part of the dark wall, the two walked easily, yawning, striding with hard steps, careless and heavy.

They stopped at a stone well. One of them worked the rope.

Jenna stirred.

The arrow slammed him hard against the well wall. He buckled forward into it and the sound he made was like a pricked bladder. Jenna was already running toward them.

"HEY!"

The other shouted loud and sharp in the silence. Jenna caught his clubbed fist on her bow and with her right hand, slashed up with the knife.

The house door opened. To Shalane's fear-heightened senses, the hinges seemed to scream.

"Moab? John?"

Shalane stopped thinking. A numb giddiness took her as she whirled on the woman framed in the light. She cleared the steps in one bound. The woman saw her and tried to shut the heavy door. For a fraction of time, Shalane still thought she might turn and run, hiding where her knife would stay clean of this. Then her shoulder crashed against the door, hurling it in, carrying her past it in an unbroken thrust that knocked the woman over backward under her, the knife hilt-deep in her stomach.

The Kriss woman was young and strong as herself. Face against face, Shalane saw the shock flood the other's eyes, but her left hand vised Shalane's own wrist. The blow was too low, nowhere near the heart. She couldn't withdraw. The strong hand locked hers immobile while the other tore at her throat and face.

"Whore! Dirty coven whore!"

She hissed the senseless foreign words again and again as Shalane felt the restraining hand weaken. She pulled the knife tortuously upward. Her hand was sticky with blood. The woman writhed under her, moaning. *This isn't me. I'm not doing this.* The Kriss woman was in agony, but there was no fear in her eyes, only hatred and revulsion that frightened Shalane more than what she herself was doing. At last the hand loosed so she could pull free. With a sob of pity and loathing, Shalane used her entire strength, sliced upward through flesh until her knife sank into the tough muscle of the heart. Blood spurted and she felt the heart throb along the iron along her wrist, mingling with the beat of her own pulse. Sick, willing herself not to vomit, she held the knife in place until the heartbeat ebbed and finally stopped.

She floundered up on her knees, rasping for breath—and saw, there in the bedroom doorway, the two wide-eyed little boys, staring at a black thing out of nightmares, all shiny wet down the front with the stained knife in her hand, and she knew at last what Arin tried to share, the Holder-thing that came between them sometimes and the thrust of him into her would have an arrow shape, and now her arms would hold him and the dead woman both together, see, over Arin's warm shoulder, the infant eyes with their mute witness more horrible than any accusation.

"Run away," she pleaded, tears running down her cheeks. "Oh, runawayruna*way*."

But they didn't understand, just stood and stared, and already she was wiping her eyes and her feet were carrying her toward them.

Garick slipped the latch to Uriah's door and entered. At his side, Jenna drifted like vengeful smoke. They found themselves in a short central hall. Uriah's house was constructed differently, connected to the church, larger than most others.

Automatically their feet tested floorboards, moving close to the walls to lessen the stress that might produce an audible creak. Their linked thoughts projected the memorized house plan; to the right the kitchen and girl's room. To the left, Uriah and his woman. The chief elder's door was slightly ajar.

They listened in the darkness. Garick lepped. *Wait here.*

*Uriah is mine!*

*Not alone. Wait.*

Garick slipped across to the other door, pushed slightly with one hand, ready to halt it with the other at the first sound. When it was far enough ajar, he eased through and saw the small mound, Uriah's young daughter in the bed. He drew the knotted cord from his belt and paused over the sleeping girl. *I'm glad it's dark and you're asleep.*

The lep from all his people leaked continually into his mind, the overload of anguish from four thousand separate hells as they did what they must, slipping back locks, entering bedrooms and leaving them graves. Coveners whose minds had always nestled in the comforting All of Circle discovered in cold solitude that what they must do was neither pure nor selfless. Garick read the wordless thoughts, sharing as one hears music, but as in Arin's lep after Lishin, there was a new undertone, a bleak and mournful dissonance.

*We were innocent before this.*

A door creaked. The girl turned in her sleep.

"Mary, is that you?" Uriah's voice, had to be. *No, Jenna, wait!*

"Mary?" Deep, sharp and clear, used to command. Uriah surely. The girl stirred and woke. The cord would be too slow. Garick's hand gagged the surprised mouth, forcing her down. It was quickly done.

"Who's that? Who's there?"

A flurry of thumping movement. Garick passed through the open door and down the hall. The portal to Uriah's room was wide open. Beyond it a blur of locked figures, black and white. The white struck out, connected. Jenna spun with the force of the blow, using it to gain momentum, dropping to her knees, bent arm snapping straight to sickle the charging figure.

Uriah stumbled, the power gone out of him. He gasped and doubled sideways against the bed and slid to the floor. Jenna moved to finish him, but Garick held her back. *No.*

A small wick burned blue in a dish on Uriah's worktable. Garick lit two candles from it.

*No lights!*

"It doesn't matter now," Garick said aloud. Jenna's mind was closed to a narrow focus on what she must do, she wasn't hearing the myriad leps that bled into his own brain . . . *this house done . . . finished here . . . no more . . . finished the children.*

"There's no one left," said Garick.

The candle flame danced shadows on the figure of Miriam, very still in the bed, her excruciating headaches gone forever. Jenna had barely disturbed the covers, though it was enough to wake Uriah.

He lay against the edge of the bed holding his side, glaring at

Jenna like a downed bird of prey. He stared briefly at Miriam and with a deep, still horror, muttered, "Oh my God! Where were You?"

Garick bent down to look at him. *So this is my enemy*. A fine head, he thought, the intelligence of the expression delicately focused and tinged with a curious, mocking self-knowledge. Uriah regarded the master of Charzen and the disbelief in his eyes faded to comprehension.

"Well, Garick," he said. "I always knew you were creative. Mad, too."

*Speaks Old Language clear as Judith.*

"Your wife and the girl suffered no pain," Garick told him. "No one did."

*"No one?"*

"There is no more Salvation, Uriah. Your houses are still and all your fires are out. In a few years, the forest will cover you."

Uriah winced. Jenna's knife had sliced deep. "You think all my people are asleep?"

"No," Jenna answered. "Some down those mines. They're sealed in."

"You don't know where the mines are."

"Jay does," she replied without expression. "Your Jacob remembered."

Uriah barely acknowledged her presence, his eyes fixed on Garick. They measured each other. Though Garick couldn't read the Kriss at all, he felt a wave of admiration for him. A time for kings, Garick said once. What a king Uriah would have made.

The Kriss sighed with dry resignation, growing weaker. "So Arin got away after all."

"Just barely," Garick nodded. "He remembers Lishin. And Elin and Kon."

Jenna added heavily, "And the rats."

"Let's not speak of horrors, Garick. You've not seen Matthew. I find it hard to believe such as you totally human." Uriah regarded with detachment the stain spreading over his night robe. "Well, what's it to be? This unwashed cow with her knife?"

Jenna didn't move; she understood just enough of the foreign dialect to follow his drift. "You think Circle is animals. You think we *like* this. *We* think we'll never be clean again."

"I do sympathize." His mouth tightened in pain, but Uriah tortured it into a sardonic smile. "Garick, spare me this mumbling sentimentality. She seems to have done the job with her knife, but can't you spare me her tongue?" His breath labored. "That's odd. I'm thirsty."

"Jenna, bring him water."

"Finish him and let's go. We'll smell of this place too long already."

"He's finished. It won't be long. Bring the water."

She gestured her impatient assent; the door whispered shut after her.

"You stare at me," Uriah said, "as if you weren't quite sure what I am."

"I know what you are, Uriah. A waste."

"You surprise me."

"Waste," Garick repeated with slow despair. The feeling boiled in him, inarticulate with its complexity. He was changing the world, had changed it and must go on changing and never looking back, and yet to kneel by the cause of so much of it beggared words. "All the days we took to get here, I wanted to look at you, Uriah, talk to you. You—it's awful, but you—you make me real. We're both dreamers, dreaming alone and late at night, dreams so big and painful that anyone with a grain of sense'd know he was mad, but only the crickets and the wind say, 'yes, probably. Go to bed, fool!' Uriah, you're the other side of me, the same ambition turned inside out. What we could have done *together!*"

Uriah was losing the fight to mask his pain. "Where is that bitch with the water?"

"There'll be something with it to make you sleep."

"The poison cup? How historical." Uriah swallowed with difficulty. "The two of us, Garick? No, we've always been apart. Opposed. The sanity and mandate of God's plan against the madness of thinking this repulsive world worth more than passing contempt. Garick, you think you've won, but you can't. Eternity is against you."

Jenna returned with a mug of water. "Some masters at the door. Say they're done."

Uriah lifted his head. "You incredible whore, you'd make hell dirty."

Garick stirred the powder into the mug. "She doesn't understand half of what you're saying. And it's not poison, just something to take away the hurt and let you sleep till life goes." He watched the liquid swirl, dissolving the drug. "Uriah, this eternity you talk about: the real world never sacrificed so much as a smile or a flower for it and never will. Here."

Uriah took the cup. "It was not a very pretty world, anyway." He drained it in one pull and thrust it out to Jenna. "Woman! Don't you know your place, leaving a man with an empty cup in his hand?"

Jenna stared down at him as if he were a perishing roach. "It's yours. Drop it."

"Bitch," he repeated with dry fervor. "No wonder Arin had it in him to be such a consummate bastard."

They lifted him onto the bed and settled Uriah next to Miriam. At his request, Garick closed her eyes. Uriah seemed completely relaxed and composed, even curious about the onset of the drug's effect.

"It doesn't hurt any more. The working starts in the fingers . . . and toes."

"Yes," said Garick.

"A tingle, a numbness . . . a thieving death. You've even stolen my suffering. I ought never . . . forgive you that." He tried to laugh; it emerged as an inaudible chuckle. "Out of curiosity . . . for the hell of it, you might say . . . where *is* . . . that delightful boy of yours?"

Garick shook his head. "I don't know; somewhere east. Making *your* son think he's my whole force."

Uriah nodded. "At great expense, one hopes." He closed his eyes and sighed deeply. Minutes passed. His breath grew shallower. Jenna left, sure he was gone. But before Garick turned to follow her, the piercing eyes fluttered open once more. The lips moved.

"What?" Garick asked, bending close to him.

"Jeremiah will bury you."

Callan stared morosely into the darkness, unable to sleep. Questions tormented him: did Garick buy out the whole northern division and if he did, where did the money come from? And how much cooperation would Trace and the other officers give a covener, even a rich one?

Bowdeen said he'd nose around for information come morning; the question niggled at the Wengen. It was growing into something much larger than he figured. Bowdeen was oddly troubled.

Now and then a lightning flash still illuminated the room, and

Callan saw the twin points of Sidele's pupils glint briefly. The witch who saw in the dark was awake and watching him.

He had believed the merks were in his pocket. A threat from such an unexpected quarter upset him, it made no sense, his mind rebelled against the possibility. God would not put such an obstacle in his path now when the end was so clearly in sight. All the long years in hiding, infiltrating the covens, winning place in the merks, spreading false rumors of City policy, carrying out the necessary tasks according to his father's plan—everything had gone smoothly. Now that they were ready to break the covens for good and all, why should there suddenly be opposition within the very organization he'd worked so long to fashion as a tool for Uriah's purpose?

He knew that Holy tests of faith often came on the very eve of triumph. The soul was the prize; it was not for him to question God. Still, his tactical mind rejected the thought. Surely the long labors of Salvation on behalf of God's plan would not be so lightly valued as to be risked while the mettle of *one* soul was tested in some immortal crucible.

His mettle had been tested every day for years. There were the personal sacrifices, smaller but no less costly than Uriah's. He never let his father or mother see how ravenously he absorbed the feeling of Home in the brief hours he could spend there, how yearningly he looked after this or that woman as she moved with downcast eyes across his path, or the men with families they could come home to every day after simple, honest work. Like his father, he placed himself beyond this for the time, but the hunger came back. Once in a while, like tonight, he would weaken and drink, and the starvation rose in him. One more drink and he might have killed that stupid sub, but that was away from purpose.

Always and first a soldier, a man of action, Callan racked his brain for some way to counter Garick's probable incursion into his mercenary resources. He had to know what the next few days might bring, but that was impossible.

*Not* impossible. There was a way.

Jeremiah immediately recognized the sinful nature of the temptation and tried to cast it from his mind. But the idea came back again, stronger . . .

Uriah had said—what was it? *Learn the kind of soldier He needs.* What else? *Buy, use, bend, plan, cheat—above all, learn and know the world. If some of us are defiled by it, the end will cleanse us.*

*Learn and know the world. Use it.*

Uriah was the leader; mustn't his injunction be Jeremiah's law? And if Callan misinterpreted out of zeal, wouldn't zealousness in God's cause be forgiven in the end?

He felt his father's spirit guiding him. It became clear that he must do this thing. There was even a certain amount of Scriptural precedent for it.

"Witch," he called softly. "Get up."

"Why?"

"You must prophesy for me."

They went into the front room. Sidele took her place behind the crystal and gestured for Callan to sit opposite. She put the skull candle on the table, then stretched out her hand to him. He did not respond.

"Put your hand in mine."

Callan shook his head. "No."

"The spell will not work."

"No."

Sidele regarded him somberly. "All night, you have avoided touching me—even the most glancing contact. You've stood across the room; if I came close, you moved away. You would not even accept the tea from my hand for fear our finger tips might brush. Is it my power you fear, Callan, or just that I'm a woman?"

"I don't look on you as a woman. You guessed what I am: Kriss. That's your name for us. Our lives are shaped—they have a purpose; woman has her place in that purpose and doesn't exceed it."

Sidele sighed. "Never mind. I'll try to read for you. But you make it difficult."

"Go ahead."

Brushing a strand of hair out of her eyes, Sidele bent low over the crystal. A long time passed; the merk grew more and more restless. He started to speak, but she stopped him, silently ordering him to remain still.

"I see," she murmured after an even longer pause, "a town with homes and stables and one great building dominating the rest. It's white. There's a strange shape on top."

"Like this?" Callan described his god-sign in the air.

"Don't speak unless I question you."

He had to ask: "Is it Salvation?"

"That may be its name."

"What else?"

She stared into the crystal for nearly a minute. "Nothing," she said at last. "No one stirs. Not one person."

The tap of the rain had ceased; the room was quiet. Callan heard the rasping of his own breath. "Tell me something about myself," he demanded.

Sidele nodded, studying him. "It *would* be easier if you let me examine the lines of your hand."

"No."

"All right," she sighed. "What do I see? A man who thinks he knows the answer to the entire riddle of the world. Who will do anything to prove it: lie, cheat, kill, go against his own—"

"So will my enemies. I do what I have to."

"Oh, more than that, sub Callan, more than that. You are a man frozen into a tight, inflexible view of the world. If that world changes, either it or you must break. You are rock, not iron; you'll shatter rather than bend."

Callan leaned forward, intense. "No soldier has ever had to do what I do, endure what I do. It is a mission."

"Perhaps," Sidele agreed inscrutably. "But these are facts. I read what I see."

"I want to know what will happen tomorrow, the day after."

"It's hazy. Hard to see. Is there a part of City that's no longer City? Abandoned?"

Callan sat up straight. "Yes. Go on."

"I see a group of men, many. You are there. Giving orders."

"And?"

"They lift something, I can't see what. More than one object. Passing them out to other men. Somebody—I think it's you—somebody is naming the things."

"What are they called?" Callan whispered, hotly curious as to how much she could really divine.

"Throwers," she tried. "Is that right?"

"Yes! Say more."

"I can't, it's too hazy."

*"More!"*

Sidele gestured helplessly. She clutched her head in her hands. "I can't see them clear enough; you'll have to help me. Describe those throwers, help me see what they look like."

Callan started to tell her, but then the long tradition of secrecy won out. He sat back. "I can't."

"Then there isn't anything else I can say to you."

"No, wait—" But she rose and blew out the candle. The room was gray with early morning light. In the back room, Bowdeen grunted, yawned and turned over.

"Don't tell him about this, woman."

She smiled sardonically. "Afraid he'd be annoyed to find his sub plotting his own battle strategies?"

Something like a canny smile creased Callan's thin mouth. Perhaps Sidele had helped him more than she knew. The idea might have been unshaped in his mind, but it was clear and hard now.

The throwers.

By first sun the square was packed with coveners waiting to move out. Some had been there for hours standing in the open, avoiding the houses, the tombs, the doors of Salvation that would never open again.

In the coven way, Jay knew, they would simply ride off and let the forest grow over it all.

They sprawled about the packed square, an eerily silent multitude, spilling out of the open space down the straight paths between houses as far as the forest edge: four thousand Shando, Karli, Suffec and Wengen of every age between childhood and the chair by the fire —gawky young men and women, graybeards, girls still so flat in their black-stained skins they were indistinguishable from the boys they rode among. All had toiled over the hard ridges of the Blue Mountains for that ending, this beginning.

For that reason, Jay realized, there was almost no looting from Kriss houses. It was not *part* of what had happened, was still happening to the innocent, sullied coveners. And there was a practical why for it, too. The killing mountains were still there to cross again. Everything taken would add extra weight on the exhausted horses, and after, the road would still lead to war with the merks. None of them would be going home for a long, long time.

Jay's own part had been bloodless, a small mercy on Garick's part. He led the party across the bridge to the north mines, but they'd worked for hours to seal off the shafts and the approximate third of Salvation's men within.

Jay leaned heavily on the log pilings that supported the large cross in the center of the square. Dull with fatigue, he observed the latecomers mill into the open space. They all seemed stunned by what they'd done. There was a naïveté among coveners that perversely irritated Jay at first: the reverse image of his own people's blindness. The Kriss could see no good in flesh, the coveners none of the evil or inherent tragedy of mortal life. As they passed him now, dazed with killing, he sensed a new knowledge in their eyes: stumbling Adams driven from Paradise into the merciless light east of Eden.

Some of the masters slipped white tabards over their blackened clothes and set up a circle with the ritual salt, water and fire, and many lined up to purify their knives, far too many for the masters to handle. The smell of killing was real to these people, an actual scent compounded of blood and the accelerated secretions generated both by their own bodies and those they destroyed. It made them physically ill to endure it.

Jay drank from his canvas water bag, wondering that his thirst was stronger than his concern for his dead people. He settled himself back against the pilings. The head of his god intruded itself on his vision. Just as well. He'd meant to pray. *Some* kind of prayer.

*Am I leaving You, my God? Is it possible to leave You? The love must have been there once, must have had a meaning, because I knew more of You, in Elin's arms, than all the years at the altar. Was it that, the forgetting of love, that made this place a plague?*

He raised his head at a flat jabber of Karli dialect. A group of them clustered about a young woman reeling with exhaustion, helping her with respectful hands. Jay guessed her for a master. The hide shirt was torn down the front, her throat and chest bruised and lacerated with claw marks. She shook her head at a question, disengaged herself and slumped down on the pilings near him, head sunk on her knees. Her body trembled pitifully.

Deep in his own thoughts, Jay became only gradually aware that the blond girl was talking in a rapid, pattering monotone—to him, past him, to no one at all, rigid, fists knotted tight on her skinny knees.

*God, in my ignorance I was so sure. Now in knowledge perhaps not very different from this girl's, there are only questions and more questions. I've saved the Book, I've got that. I want to strain it through life and read it again to find where it was wrong—and how it was right. You inspired it, but men wrote it down, and there's the weakness. I guess that's all. We have to go soon, a long road that won't end till City. Be with me if You can. If not—I just wanted to tell You how it is.*

". . . yes, when I was sixteen, that's how young I was. Didn't know much. You got something to drink?"

Jay turned to the girl. "Just water."

"That's all right, all right. Just my mouth is so dry, and I can smell . . . and I feel sick. No, I wasn't much of a master, but I read Arin when nobody else could. You know Arin? He's my man, been with him since Samman and he's alive but I don't know where, someplace east where he rode with my dad Moss, and Moss didn't want me to go in the Circle and maybe I shouldn't. Always better with horses since I was twelve, thirteen, so when I went out on the hill, wasn't much left for a boy to break in. I could live and sleep on a horse, so used to it, but when Arin came along I was still scared he wouldn't want me, so scared I was glad to be pledged to the masters and hid up at the masters' hall so we couldn't touch yet. But Arin's like me, half horse, and sometimes when we loved, I'd feel like I was riding a good broke horse that knew my legs, and then riding, I'd forget and be off loving Arin in my head. Now—" Her voice wound tighter and tighter, jittering on the edge of hysteria. "Now ain't that a damfool thing for a master to think about? Don't look like one, don't feel like one, but my folk over there want me to clean their knives, I should but I *can't*—" The aimless wandering voice pitched high suddenly, peaked and shattered in an agonized sob. "I'm not clean, I'll never be clean again. Please," she thrust herself toward him, helpless as a hurt child, "help me please, please, please, hold me a little."

Jay put his arms around her. Her body shuddered against him, fingers strong as ten steel nails bruising his flesh.

"Just—"

"What," he murmured as to a child. "What is it?"

"The . . . the *babies*. No one wanted to do it, but they said we couldn't take them, and it's true, they'd die in the mountains. They'd make noise, can't hide like coven young. I mean, we had to, but they were so little and—" her voice went hoarse as she couldn't stop remembering. "And so *many of them*. D-damfool Kriss women with their big, easy hips, why they got to have so many babies? So many babies. So many babies. So many babies . . ."

He let her swallow some more water. She dabbed some at her swollen eyes, streaking the black paint.

"Know what you look like right now?"

"N-no, what?"

"A sad raccoon."

"I guess. Oh, here they come. They'll want me."

Four coveners, two men, a woman and a young boy stood waiting at a respectful distance for her to notice them. Still holding her, Jay felt her trembling body draw up, seem to pause in every shuddering muscle—and relax. Her ragged breathing lengthened into an even swell, her back straightened without stiffness. When she rose, it might have been from a refreshing sleep, and yet Jay knew the effort of will that enabled her to lock personal agony into a corner of the well-disciplined instrument of her mind, where it could not twist thought or quail the muscles. This was why they were called masters; not because they held sway over others, but rather themselves.

One of the men came forward. "Shalane, the other masters, they so busy. You're Karli like us. Clean our knives?"

"I will," she granted. "Has to be done. Give them to me."

They hesitated. "Weren't sure," the woman began. "We didn't want . . . I mean, just you look so tired yourself."

Shalane started to reply, then, with the others, her head turned sharply. About the square, people began to rise—ten, fifty, a hundred, all Karli. Jay was used to the group response by now, disconcerting as it could be to a cowan. Someone lepped a command, and they all obeyed with the same deadly silence that blotted out Salvation.

"We ride now," Shalane said. "You find me with Garick tonight. We'll be clean together."

"The boy here," the woman said, pushing him forward. "He feels real bad."

Shalane put her hands on the boy's shoulders. To Jay, he looked barely adolescent, trembling, eyes vague and unfocused.

"Hey, Janny. How old are you now?"

"Thirteen."

"I remember," said Shalane. "Since Grannog. Been a pretty bad day, huh?"

His head jerked up and down. "Just . . . I ain't never . . ."

"I know." Shalane stopped him gently. "The same for all of us. Bad day in a bad place. That's all we can see right now, like one ugly bent tree on a bare hill. Janny, you know what the merks call us? 'Deepwoods.' It's true. We're forest ourselves, and our days are trees; they grow so many and so straight we can live with one got bent a little. It's a lot to carry, but we'll share it. Come tonight with your folks, we'll share. But go on now."

They withdrew with whispered thanks, taking her promise.

Shalane sagged back into her own fatigue, but the trembling was gone. "Karli got to ride out first. They're Garick's point. I'll ride a way with them. Make me feel better."

Jay got up. "Will you be able to do it tonight, help them?"

"Why?"

"It's important. I want to know. Are you that strong?"

"Strong?" There was no humor in her bare smile. "This ain't the end, you know that. This'll happen ten times over before we go home. That's why I'll draw the circle for them and clean their knives and say all the words, every single one of them, for every Karli who comes to me, and I'll share with them—so maybe *I* can feel washed, too. Like when Arin came to me." The memory was frayed, but she let it live damaged in her mind. "No one gets clean alone. I have to do it."

"You will." Jay took her hand. "Maybe I'll see you across Blue."

"And Arin. He'll be there. He *has* to be."

"Tell him I said hey."

"You know Arin?" She brightened. "Where?"

"Just along the way. He told me about you. My name's Jay. Good-by, master Shalane."

She moved close suddenly and kissed him on the mouth, not in friendly affection but a woman caressing a man and enjoying it. "You were good to hold me," she said. "Just, I haven't seen him in so long, and it's good to touch a man. You scared me at first. You didn't share."

"I—there's folk I miss, too."

"Your woman?"

"And others."

"You Wengen, Jay? You look like one."

"I live in Charzen now."

"Charzen? Good!" Shalane waved to the boy. "Janny, bring my horse. Now listen," she said to Jay with (it seemed to him) very married graciousness, "you come and see me and Arin in Charzen. We should be friends. You come now, hear?"

"I will," Jay promised. "I'll want friends."

Her horse was brought, a high-shouldered Suffec stallion too worn now to show much spirit. Shalane stroked its blaze with a tender concentration so familiar that Jay had to turn away with the poignant memory. *Did you know her?* he wanted to say, *did you see her walk, see how beautiful she was? We were together.*

"Yes, yes, I know." Shalane buried her face in the horse's muzzle. "You weren't born to climb hills and you're beat out and hungry, and dumb old me can't find a carrot in the whole damn Blue Mountains. Well, mama's tired, too." She forked the saddle, wheeled about to Jay. "Y'all going to City?"

Jay laughed. "Sure as frost."

"Us too, Arin and me." Her grin was sudden and white against the raccoon face; it took five unaffordable years off her master's dignity. Jay laughed again, pure pleasure at the inner life welling up suddenly to throw off her exhaustion like a worn garment. "City sure must be some place to look at, Jay. Come see us."

She walked the horse to join the stream of Karli going east toward the river trail. Jay watched her lean far out of the saddle to take a bow and quiver from another rider and trot on.

*Uriah should have known them better, should have lived with them. He never had a chance, not against that.*

Jay turned suddenly to the god-sign and its carven agony. *We should have known You better, too, remembered Your life more than Your death. Hell, that's not You! You're alive, and I didn't have to ask. You don't have favorites. You'll be with me and Shalane. You were with her when she pushed aside her own pain for someone else's. You're with Arin and lonely Garick, and Elin and even Uriah because You know that under the iron there was a man and a genius, too, who shouldn't be wasted. You'll bring him home like You brought me just now when I couldn't find You—*

Jay realized he was grinning, then crying, laughing aloud with joy and discovery. *Like Kon said, ain't it one hell of a grand day? Well, it is, it is, because I've finally seen Your face, You wonderful, wise, unkillable man-spirit of a Maker—and damn if You didn't look like a raccoon. I always loved You, but now, my God, my God, I* like *You!*

Moving through the crowd to find Garick, Jay passed young Janny and hugged the boy for the joyous fun of it.

Sidele woke at the slight heave of the mattress as Bowdeen rolled out of bed. "It's barely light; where are you going?"

"Going over to the barracks, gonna get some answers if there are any." Bowdeen rubbed the sleep from his eyes.

"There aren't any answers," Sidele murmured, "only questions."

He looked at her curiously. "You do talk strange sometimes." He slipped into his pants, then sat on the edge of the bed, pensive.

"Answers to what, Bow?"

On his pallet, Callan turned and sighed in his sleep. Bowdeen studied him before he spoke. "Sidele, this is big. I ain't told you all, but we got fooled out there. In the bush, you don't know if it's two men or ten in front of you. First they all over the place, then running east fast as they can. We followed, we made money, sure, but I swear they made it too easy. Like we were supposed to follow. I just got a feeling there's a lot of 'em somewhere else."

The woman watched him intently. "Like where?"

"Been thinking about that. It adds up nice and even." He lowered his voice with another glance at the sub. "Callan's the moneyman, and Callan's Kriss. The Kriss are west, we got fooled back east." He rose and bent over Sidele to kiss her. "Just gonna go ask around, that's all."

Sidele sat up in bed. "Suppose Garick did buy them. What's that to you?"

The question seemed to trouble Bowdeen. "I don't know. Everything's changing. I just don't know, Siddy." He shrugged into his leather jacket. "Be back soon."

Someplace not far away, morning was ready to dawn, but beneath the thick overhanging trees, it was still deep night. Webb woke early on the small islet, hardly more than a high hummock of tangle and sand. He was still bone-weary and meant to sleep some more, but his stomach gnawed, so he rose, found some dried rice cake and munched unenthusiastically.

It was his last rest before raising the sand bank that marked the west limit of the swamp. It was over. The thing Garick wanted was in the bottom of the boat, just a thick, wide belt. On the front where it cinched there was a small metal box with a wiggly piece sticking out of it. He didn't touch it. Garick warned him to be careful of anything on the belt that looked like it wanted to be played with. He still couldn't figure how the god of the Shando knew it'd be there, in the middle of a deserted house in a swamp no one ever went in or out of.

Besides the belt, he took a funny-looking cap with strange symbols on it; he didn't know, it might be important. There was a pouch, too, made of some kind of clammy skin-thick stuff that also lasted out the ages. But the body in that small, airless room certainly didn't.

*Must've made seven miles.* When he was rested and the sun up, he'd head for the northwest end, but it would mean guiding the boat in and out of twisting natural passages, weaving through a maze of black gum and cypress with branches overhead that might hold a cottonmouth ready to drop into the boat.

The place he'd chosen for rest was a tiny rise of weed, loam and sand, but there was one medium-size tree where he'd been able to hang his hammock and mosquito net. There wasn't room enough for cat or bear, and he felt fairly safe in spite of the snufflings and hoarse coughs all around that might be distant or close up, hard to tell in old swamp.

He felt hungry now, but wanted to save his rice cake. The clapper rail's nest of cordgrass had been empty the night before; now there was an egg in it. The rail squawked at him but he drove her away, lifted his head and cracked the egg into his mouth with a practiced movement. It tasted greasy, pungent and rich.

He looked again at the drab, unremarkable belt in the bottom of the boat. *Dumb.* Garick must be wrong. All the song-stories said it was bright gold and studded with gems. *This ain't worth piss.*

And the corpse. *Not Callee. He don't end.*

Webb never felt so cut off. *Bad. No lep. Doon asleep.* Not that he had anything else to say, he'd already passed along the word he'd found it. There was the feeling, but that shouldn't be shared. *Like I ain't.* Old swamp saying, Webb, there's nobody, nothing but me. No Suffec. No Doon. No Garick. Just swamp that always was and always is and always will be. Nothing else real. His ego protested: *there's me.* But old swamp whispered, only for a little while, Webb, because swamp don't need you yet, but maybe before morning it'd take a notion and he'd be like the nameless bones, lost in the mud and night and silence.

*Plop.*

The sound by his ear brought him out of it fast. He sat up sharp and peered into the shallows. The water was clear enough to see straight to the bottom, and the waning moon feebly lit the scene. A second noise. Could be old killifish, he thought, going after skeeter eggs in the shallows. Then he grinned. *Big catfish. Whole bunch.* He watched them, and felt a little less lonely. He liked their lazy, graceful way of foraging. It stirred something deep inside. Like, what *were* fish, anyway? Catch, sizzle on rocks, eat, look out for bones. And yet–

—and yet he guessed he never really saw them before. *Just plain alive.* Not there because he wanted to fill his belly, but because they weren't someplace else.

He stared down at them awhile, fascinated by the soundless wavering, darting, hovering rhythm of their food quest.

But then the bad thoughts started to come.

The first was simply a fact: *they don't see me.* But as it entered his mind, he realized the fish didn't know it was *Webb* up there, didn't know *he* liked them. And it struck him there was no way he could share how he felt toward them, not so they'd know; if he tried to reach out and touch their world, he'd shatter the silent ritual below. He couldn't grapple with the idea, it hurt. *Like old Garick.* But that was even dumber. What did the Shando god have to do with a school of catfish?

He screwed up his face in an agony of unaccustomed concentration, trying to sort out the hard fragments of thought. It took more effort than he'd ever put into anything besides hunting, but finally he began to get a grip on what his mind was trying to shape.

*Old catfish good. Like watching. But—*

But unless Webb ate them, they had nothing whatever to do with Garick's war . . . and yet, and *yet* . . . catfish all alive while—

*While Sandteela born again.*

The pang throbbed in his head, his heart; he let out a sigh, slow and bitter. Old Doon claimed he had a good reason for coming into the swamp, but now Webb couldn't make any sense of his own action, none at all. One thing only he knew sure, he must be some kind of crazy to waste sleep time gawking at fish that didn't no way care if he

Webb went stiff, stopped breathing. There was a new idea in his mind. He didn't ask it in, nobody ever had such a bad idea before, it was too much, he couldn't think it. Shaking, wanting to scream, he pushed it away quick and let his mind go white till the surging of his pulse slowed and the shivering died and the tension ebbed out of his body.

At last he lay down again, spent, hoping for sleep without dreams. But through the treetops, he could see one faint star, and for a long time, Webb gazed up at its cold, blue indifferent light.

"What now?" Jenna asked wearily.

"We pick up the west end of our line," Garick said, "and hope we hear from Arin."

"And if we do?"

"He goes south."

Her lips tightened. "Hasn't he done enough for you?"

Garick shrugged, but could not answer her or change what he had to do.

The goddess stalked away to throw herself down against her saddle under a tree. She batted viciously at circling flies as if to pay them back for Arin.

"Goddess."

The Karli girl stood over her. Like most of the women in the column, she cropped her hair short now. Jenna thought her too immature at first, but the girl had steadied out since Salvation; perhaps Arin hadn't chosen so badly. But she was too open and trusting. The world would hurt her—and it wasn't Jenna's worry if it did.

"I feel him safe," Shalane said. She had that innocent assurance, combined with youth, that can be strangely abrasive without meaning to be. "Don't know where . . . east . . . but I feel it."

"Sit down, girl." Shalane knelt in front of her. "You took a man last night."

"Yes, it—" Shalane pretended to fuss with her cord belt, the only insignia of rank she wore now. She went on with a quiet firmness: "We all do, don't we?"

"So we do. You love Arin?"

"I'm with him."

"Sure," Jenna sighed, "we're all with somebody. What you remember of him—he's not going to be like that if he comes back. I know Arin—"

"Oh, I don't mind." Shalane nodded quickly. "I know he'll take somebody, too, for now." She wouldn't grudge him any woman so long as it wasn't a Mrikan. They were all (she heard) dishonest and diseased, and some were even fat. That amazed Shalane. She had never been to Lorl, nor ever sick. And she'd never seen a fat woman under seventy.

"That's not it." Jenna lay back against the saddle. "Just, things change. Somebody meets somebody. You get changed without wanting to." She thought for a moment she could lep or share the thing she was trying to communicate, but that wasn't what she wanted at all. It was a very private pain to look at your own ghost, that earnest young face. Her chest heaved with a brief, soft chuckle, and she gave it up. Jenna was silent then, her eyes closed.

Shalane waited in respect, wondering if the goddess meant to sleep. She had not cut the great mass of red hair, but simply tied it back with a strip and pin. It was long as a horse's tail. She'd spent her lifetime growing it, Jenna said, and wasn't about to cut it for a few merks.

Arin's mother was not beautiful. They had the same coloring and the same eyes, the features a little too sharp for easy good looks. But even with her dignity, Tilda didn't seem half the goddess that Jenna did, stretched out now like a great, lithe cat—

"Shit!"

It startled Shalane. She had been staring at the goddess with the unconscious rudeness of youth, but suddenly Jenna rolled over away from Shalane. Her shoulders went on heaving.

"Goddess?" It distressed Shalane. Jenna's mind was closed tight. "What is it? Can I—?"

"It's all right. Just, you looked like—"

"Goddess, you're crying."

"Be still."

"I'll go get—"

"You won't!" Jenna uncoiled from her misery and trapped Shalane's wrist in a hard grip. "You won't get, you won't tell. You hear me?" The tears glistened wetly under her eyes. "He's got enough to worry him." Her voice tightened into a parody of a laugh. "And he thinks I'm strong."

The day was near high sun when Bowdeen returned to the house. Callan was out back with Sidele's washtub. Finished bathing, he was now shaving himself with Bowdeen's razor. Bowdeen paused when he saw the sub. Had Callan been an observant man, he would have noticed an uncharacteristic hesitation in the Wengen's manner.

"He bought them all right, sub."

The razor barely paused. "You could always buy Mrikans."

"It's called being hungry. Try it sometime."

"Any sight of Arin?"

"No, that mofo's gone. Forget him."

"How much a man?"

"Thirty krets, they said."

"Thirty!" Callan put down the razor. "Garick doesn't have that kind of money."

"He does now." Bowdeen squatted, pulled at a stalk of grass and gave it his concentration. "That's what I came to tell you. I found out where he got it."

Callan splashed off and rubbed vigorously with a ragged towel. "Well, commander?"

"Just Bowdeen, boy. I quit. I'm out of it." He began nipping the grass stalk into minute sections, took a deep breath and let it out.

"Well?"

"Spitt raised it. Sold off mine shares to the Wengen iron-makers."

"Garick doesn't own any mines."

"Well . . ."

"What kind of—" Callan broke off suddenly. His expression changed as he stared at Bowdeen's averted face. "What *kind* of mines?"

"Coal." Bowdeen tore off another stalk and performed the same surgery. "Coal."

The color drained from Callan's face. His mouth opened, but words wouldn't come. He sat down on the edge of the wooden tub. Bowdeen saw the flash of anguish before the man buried his face in his hands. His instinct was to touch him, touch his shoulder or something, but Callan wasn't a man you touched. You couldn't get close to him. And when he straightened up, his eyes were dry and bleak as ever.

Callan rose, handed the razor to Bowdeen. "I'm going to Lorl. You coming?"

"No."

"You won't take that field's job?"

"No."

Callan shrugged into his shirt. "Then I will."

"And?"

"And break Garick. As he should be broken."

Bowdeen half turned away in disbelief. "Boy, you don't know

when to quit. It ain't just Garick now, it ain't just dragging. It's Uhia —*all* of it!"

Callan reached for his jacket. "Break Garick, and there *is* no Uhia. Break Garick, and Hoban will stay quiet in Karli, the Wengens will run back north. Break Garick and we win."

"Who's *we?* And why? *Why,* you dumb son of a bitch? You ain't even gettin' paid!"

"I'll be paid." Callan buckled his sheddy belt. "More than you think." He held out his hand. "Bowdeen—"

Surprised, Bowdeen went to take Callan's hand, but the Kriss completed his sentence.

"—you owe me ten krets."

Bowdeen winced. *Goddam! Thought he'd forget.*

He dug the currency from his pouch, counted off ten and started to hand it to Callan.

"Don't."

The two turned. Sidele was standing near the back door. "Give him five," she said. "He owes me for a reading."

Callan frowned. "Five? That's too much for that."

Sidele smiled coldly. "The rate goes up when I have to work at night."

Callan took the five krets from Bowdeen, said a curt good-by and left. They watched him walk briskly off toward the center of Filsberg.

Bowdeen puffed out his cheeks and blew. "Never thought the day would come I'd get quit of that mofo."

"And you're not going to Lorl?" she asked.

"Sidele," he shook his head, "this old merk has drug his last drag."

An ordinary man, a rational man, might have seen the defeat and given up. Callan was neither. He was devoted and single-minded, and he was Uriah's son. He couldn't outbid Garick for the Filsberg division, but he could buy the more experienced Lorl garrison at a price they would leap to accept. Two thousand men and every thrower he could put in operation. It would take the rest of his money, but it was the last turn of the game.

"So he's gone." Sidele spooned soup into a bowl and set it before Bowdeen. He ate absently; a lot of things had been troubling him;

now they were shaping to a head. Sidele sat down opposite and drew another bowl to her. "What are you going to do, Bow?"

She had to ask him twice. He was chuckling over his soup. "I hunted with Garick once. Wonder if he remembers me?"

"You thinking of finding out?"

"I just might, Siddy."

"Why?"

"It may be him that wins."

Sidele gave him a peculiar look. "He doesn't have to remember that far back. The Karli know who you are. And the Shando."

"I guess." Bowdeen was bemused but not sour. "I been bought more times than a crib girl."

"You said we had enough money."

"It ain't the money, Sidele."

"Wha-at?"

"All right," he conceded with a grin. "I might hold out for a few krets."

"Garick wouldn't trust you."

"That old Shando don't trust, he buys."

He slupped thoughtfully at the bowl for some moments. Sidele studied his bent head with her distant expression. "So you'll be going off again?"

He nodded. "See you in Lorl when I get back."

"If you get back."

"Hell, Siddy, don't I always? This old man's no fool. Garick gonna win, and—" He put down the spoon and finally said it. "And he *ought* to win." He thought of Callan. "But, goddam, it's gonna cost him."

Sidele rose. "You're really going to see Garick?"

"Just said, didn't I?"

She reached for his hand. "Come with me."

"Where?"

"In back."

"I ain't done eating."

"It can wait. I've got a present to give Garick. Might make him happier to see you."

He followed her, wondering what was suddenly so important. She went to the big trunk box where he'd found her tied up. Sidele swept the pile of old cloth from the top onto the floor.

"Help me with the lid, it's heavy."

He grasped one end and she pulled at the other. They picked up the thick board slat and set it aside. The inside was filled with clothes and junk. Sidele scooped up a double armful and dropped everything on the floor.

Bowdeen looked down, expecting to see some kind of trinket. There, on the bottom, deep asleep, lay Arin.

He gaped at Sidele, unable to believe what he saw, what she'd done. Not that she'd fooled them both, him and Callan, but that she hadn't trusted him enough to tell the secret.

*Maybe she knew what I'd do.*

"You want to see Garick? Take him his son. Fair trade."

Bowdeen scratched his head. "Maybe. Or might be that Garick'll pay more for him alive than Callan would dead." He bent over the box and shook the sleeping pile of rags. "Hey, Shando, wake up."

Arin's eyelids quivered, blinked open. When he saw the black man, he started.

"Easy, boy, easy," the ex-commander soothed him. "Nothing to fret. Haul ass out of that box. Sidele's got soup on, and old Bowdeen's gonna get you home safe."

Sidele watched them leave. She wondered where the time fled to, why Bowdeen had to be off so soon. Her head hurt like it always did when he rode away, only this time was the last, and soon—she still couldn't believe it—she'd move south, and they'd meet and be together for always. The prospect of unexpected happiness made her giddy.

When they were out of sight, she went quickly to her table. Customer might be along any minute, and she wanted to use the free time to knock another picture out of the goddam crystal, because if she could, then, *then* they'd roll on up and ask her questions, and she'd give them back the same dumb answers they always got, only now there'd be a couple of real visions thrown in, and they'd pay twice as much.

Except no image appeared. Sidele crinkled up her eyes, swayed back and forth, practically bashed her skull against the tabletop, but the clear glass reflected nothing but the morning light.

"Aw-w, shit," she grumped after a fruitless wait. "Maybe Pelly had the right way to do it after all."

Sidele rose, scratched her rump, then stepped into the back room to find her jug of sida.

Shalane bounded long-legged down the hillside, darting among coveners in the halted column. "YAY!" She hugged her nearest friend tight and was off again.

*Goddess Jenna! Goddess Jenna!*

*?*

*I got him! He's safe! I know it's him. And he's coming home!*

Jenna urged her horse up the column till she found Garick. He was accepting Spitt's latest report from a messenger who'd ridden fast from Filsberg.

**—Wouldn't have believed him, but there was Bowdeen standing in front of me asking for two horses. He's got Arin safe, trust him or not. It's worth whatever you want to give him. The boy looks kind of chewed but all right. They left to join you south. I never know exactly where you are, but Arin says he can follow by lep. Callan met me—**

"The girl says Arin's safe," Jenna interrupted.

Garick looked up from the letter. "Yes. Spitt saw him."

"Tell me what he says."

He read the whole report to Jenna.

**—but nothing happened, only next time he might try to kill me, but I'm used to hiding when I have to. He went to Lorl to become a field commander and buy the whole southern division. Forget trying to outbid him, you don't have the money or the time now. On the other hand, Callan doesn't have the money for a long war or the time to drag you piecemeal. You've got numbers on your side, maybe you should find him and finish it. If you try to avoid Callan and go for City, you'll have two thousand trained men threatening your flank or between you and Charzen, and if he takes Charzen, he's got your money sure as you got his. Suggest you move in the open, let him know where you are. Let Callan come to you. He will.**

The god and goddess looked at one another. "He made it," Jenna breathed. "He made it. *My* son, Garick. You said he'd never be a master: he is. He's gone everywhere, done everything you wanted and come out of it alive. They couldn't stop him, not my son. Let him sit at my left hand in the hall when we go home."

Garick nodded. "When we go home, Jenna." Then he shut his mind off from her. *And where is that?*

# *The Field at Dannyline*

Webb guessed they were two days below the Balmer passage, maybe a little more. When they rested at night, they bedded down on dry grass with a strange, upland smell. The four volunteers collected by Doon to keep him company lay together, a silent, comforting colony of flesh that lifted heads like inquisitive birds to sift and identify the messages of air and earth. But he sat a little way off, his hand resting against the large sack containing the belt, cap and sealed pouch. Webb stared up at the darkening sky. Time and again he broke his resolution on the same thought. If there was a purpose to his actions —getting the belt out of the swamp, taking it to Garick—did it have any meaning to him personally, or was it something only important to the god of Shando? How could anything matter to *him,* Webb, sitting here, small, remote and still in a world submerged beneath the surface of the sky?

He could not escape the granite question, the unthinkable idea, the terror that seized him in the swamp.

Webb squinted his eyes shut, pressing the heels of his hands against his lids till he could no longer stand the pressure.

A light wind stirred the grass.

It helped a little. The discomfort drew him away for a little while from the edge of the abyss.

And then, just then, the *new* thought started to try to come again: the beginning of a resolution he could not quite grasp, though he desperately wanted to understand it.

*Sandteela. They did.*

Did what? Got born again. What was so good about that?

And yet, every time he thought about his cousins, he realized the birthing thing was somehow tied to them, and that it *was* good and would help him overcome the bad feeling. But when he tried to pin it down, it ran away and all he had left was a feeling he was alone and the memory of remote and silent feeding.

Garick's picket line of defense was strung out from the meet-point north of Karli southeast almost to the Mrikan border. Scouts reported a column of merks moving south along City border roads.

Rolling up his line as he moved southeast to meet Webb with the Girdle, he assumed Callan was in command of the column, deploying to cut him off. Spitt confirmed the neutrality of the northern division, but could not shed light on what Callan might be planning. Garick could only continue his southerly route and hope that the battle, when it came, would be on ground of his own choosing.

Every time they stopped to rest, they tied up Singer with a coarser rope than they'd used in Charzen. It was uncomfortable. Garick meant it to be.

Singer was drowsing against a tree when his father's lep curtly announced he wanted to talk. He opened his eyes to Garick's shadow, looming big in the flickering watchfire. His father dismissed the guard and approached Singer.

"Getting bored, boy?"

"Well, the guards aren't much conversation, but there's stars to count and a firefly now and then."

"I guess you've heard: Webb is bringing the Girdle."

Singer said nothing.

"That wouldn't matter to you," said Garick. "You never met Webb. A swamp boy who probably doesn't even know why he's doing this. Doon gave him a handful of riders, that's all he could get. If they're bushed by merks, it'll be because you wouldn't go when I asked you to."

Singer cocked one eyebrow at his father. "Daddy dear, this is your war, nobody else's. Anyone who dies is dying for Garick, not Singer."

"Is that all you can see? Is that all you've learned in twenty-seven years, how to hate?"

"What I've learned does not make a joyful body of knowledge. You've used people all your life, and if a few got broken here or there, well, that's sad. But not me, Garick. If I'm going to be a tool—my own hand does the shaping."

Garick glared at his son. "I just want to know one thing."

"What?"

"Webb's driving north, we're moving south, Arin's coming from the east with Bowdeen. We're not hiding now, we're letting them see us. Any time now, one or all of us are liable to run into Callan."

"So?"

"So when that happens, will you go to the knife with your people?"

Singer studied his hands for a long time. "They haven't been my people for twenty years."

"If you don't," Garick went on, "I'll see you're tied to a tree till the fighting is finished. Now, think about that, Singer. If I lose, you'll still be there when the merks find you."

"I like trees. They remind me of my mother." It was matter-of-fact without a trace of irony, but Garick winced. He turned and walked away. Singer raised his head in the firelight.

"Garick!"

The god halted, half in shadow. "What?"

"About Bowdeen: do you trust him?"

"No."

"I would."

Garick came back a pace or two. "Why? There's not a covener in this column doesn't want to cut his throat, and Jenna heads the list."

"Getting used to blood, aren't they?" said Singer. "You're a using man; use Bowdeen. There ought to be somebody out here who knows what he's doing."

Not far to the northeast, Callan's division straddled the one serviceable remnant of ancient road leading into Shando country from the southern Mrikan border. Dust rose around the milling horses and men to eddy and disperse in the heat-shimmering air. Normally there would be no movement, but like Garick, Callan wanted to be seen. His map folded over a board, the field commander poked another large pencil dot in a series that staggered from northwest to southeast: Garick's position sightings, reported every few hours. A straight line interpolated through them gave Callan the true bearing of march within two degrees.

East southeast. Garick was not deploying, he was going somewhere.

"Vanner!"

The burly hatchet of a man, his commander-aide, squatted by him. Vanner's face was expressionless as a calloused heel and as handsome. "What, field?"

"The scout back?"

"Lead point spotted him ten minutes ago. Should be in any time. Men are wondering why we're just sitting here in the open."

Callan didn't look up from the map. "Let them wonder; they're getting paid."

"Here's the rider now."

The scout cantered off the road and trotted through the trees toward them. Dismounting, he threw the two officers a hasty salute. "Raised a mounted party of five about an hour southeast."

Callan handed him the map and pencil. "Mark them."

"Right there."

"Bearing and speed?"

"By compass, northwest by west. Slow and easy."

Callan studied the map. The intervening terrain was fairly open and level, mostly grassland with patches of forest. At normal march pace, Garick would meet the small group in less than six hours. "You think they're his scouts?"

"Don't think so, sir. They're streaked, but not Shando green. Sort of gray-brown."

"Suffec," Vanner judged. "Moving awful close to Mrika. Why, when they could cut west just as easy?"

"No, there's a reason." Callan remembered Uriah's speculation about the Girdle of Solitude. They could be carrying something of value to Garick—if not that, something else. That would explain why he was skirting City rather than marching due east. The Girdle story was a pagan myth, too farfetched to take seriously, and yet—

And yet . . . his blunt finger traced the narrow distance between the Suffec party and his own position. The frown of concentration smoothed into a smile. "Dismiss," he ordered the scout. As the man walked his horse away, Callan stood, hands on hips, regarding Vanner with something like contentment.

"Pass it on, Vanner: two companies for a drag—39th and 44th."

Vanner looked quizzical. "You said the old bounties don't go any more."

"They do for these five."

"Five coveners? Where's the gain?"

"They're moving to meet Garick. Say they have something he wants."

"Like what?"

"Just say they do. Garick thinks we're spread too thin, anyway. If we drag these five, he might think we don't have any better plan than to tear him up a piece at a time—39th and 44th have been dragging with me all spring." Callan paced with his thoughts. "And I want them to *look* like it, Vanner. Every piece of coven gear they've picked up."

"That won't fool Garick."

"I don't want to fool him, not that way. You'll head the party yourself. Garick's close enough for an easy lep. You'll give them time to do it—that's important—and then tear them up."

"Right."

"And if they're carrying anything unusual—anything at all—detach two men and get it back here fast."

"I'll bring it myself."

"No," said Callan. "You dig in and wait for Garick. If I'm right, he'll come quick."

Vanner's fist of a face contorted. "Wait for Garick," he echoed in disbelief. "I'm gonna sit there with a hundred men while Garick throws everything but his mother at me?"

Callan nodded, sure at last. "That's right. One hundred men—"

"Field—"

"—and all our new toys."

The addition caught Vanner agape. His shapeless mouth evolved slowly into a grin of comprehension. "Yes . . . right; while you peel-and-fade?"

Callan nodded. "Right. Map check before you move out. And Vanner—"

"Field?"

"*All* the toys. The talk boxes, too."

The four others, the three boys and the girl, rested below. Webb felt hardly tired at all; the nearer he came to Garick, the more he ran on nervous energy that would have to be paid sometime in one hell of a sleep. But now he scrambled up the hill, hoping to see some sign of Garick from the top. The strength of the lep and Garick's own reports told him there wasn't more than a few hours' travel between them.

"Wait for me," he told the others, slinging the sack over his shoulder. They didn't question. They are all young, too young to fight, he was afraid, but Doon knew Webb couldn't travel any further alone, not after the swamp. And yet, since then, he had been alone. No people, no numbers would change that.

He was glad of the climb. It took away some of his concern with himself. All his concentration centered in his hands and feet as he worked his way higher and higher. It was a gentle hill, mostly, easy to climb. Once there was a difficult place, a bare outcropping of rock covered with a treacherous layer of shale, but he got on all fours and scrambled and grasped until he won past it, then it was up and up again till he reached the last lip and sprawled spread-eagled on the grassy summit.

The little puffs of cloud dreamed across the blue summer sky, distant and unconcerned. He allowed himself another private moment, one more breath before rising to search the country in front of him.

The merks were there, two straight, unmoving lines of them.

He saw them in their column order, sitting motionless on their horses, so still they might have been chipped out of stone. For one disoriented moment, Webb had the notion of a woven picture of menace that would remain fixed and changeless so long as he did not move himself. His heart thudding, he began to count them swiftly by two's. He made over a hundred of them, and a string of ten pack horses at the rear of the column, loaded with large boxes.

They began to move, urging their horses forward purposefully, without haste, circling the base of the hill.

*Webb!*

The others saw them. The frantic lep screamed into his mind and he watched them scrabble for their bows. Even as they did, the merks charged full speed down on the four young Suffec, sheddys swinging. By the time he reached the bottom of the hill, it would be all over. They might pick off two or three of the soldiers, but they could not hold out against them all for long.

Four arrows hissed, but the charging merks were elusive targets. Still, he saw two of them fall, another and another . . .

Then the distance was closed, and the blades rose and fell and rose again. The two remaining Suffec ran to gain their horses. One of them wheeled about to loose another arrow, and Webb watched dumbly, as the boy threw his own life away in the pointless action, bringing one more merk off his horse before a sheddy lopped his head from his neck.

It gained another second of time for the girl. She vaulted her horse and kicked it into a gallop but even as she did, fifteen men widened their circle, penning her in. One arrow flew, then two more, all three striking her horse. The beast's knees buckled; she leaped free before it could pin her under it. Spinning, she sought vainly for someplace to escape through the circle.

At a signal from the leader, a fierce, blunt man with a hatchet face, they ceased circling, dismounted and began to stalk her. She shot her last arrow, missed. Transfixed with horror, Webb watched her take one man with her knife as he stepped in, blade raised. Then the others were on her, bearing her down. They ripped away her clothes and began to paw at her, but the leader walked off to busy himself with the three dead Suffec. His blade flashed once over each of them, cutting the right hand from the body.

High on the hill, Webb gazed down with lofty stupidity at the nightmare below. It was not real, he couldn't believe it. The tiny figures were just puppets. *Or maybe fish.* And then the girl shrieked in pain as they sliced off her hand and dropped it into a bag.

That was the moment—he remembered it clearly afterward—that a thing broke in Webb, a sickness he had never felt before, poison and strength at the same time, that boiled out of his center and exploded in sound. He *hated* for the first time in his life. He cursed the soldiers, howled at them, dared them to come up and fight him one at a time, yelled without knowing what he was saying, screamed at them until his raw throat grew too painful to voice the murder he felt.

The merks stared up at him, silent, watchful. The leader spoke and they all ignored Webb, spreading out to search the grass in the immediate vicinity of the massacre. Even as they searched, he realized the merks were also managing to encircle his hill.

He cursed himself then for giving way to his anger. It did the girl no good, and only betrayed his own position. More important, he'd endangered the mission to Garick, because—

Because, he finally admitted, the thing in the sack might really be the Girdle of Solitude and he, Webb, might have contributed to Garick's war by putting a powerful weapon in enemy hands.

Now Webb partly realized at last why he'd entered the swamp in the first place and why it was so vital, no matter how he felt, to bring Garick what he wanted. Because Garick was *we,* and he was *we,* and the Suffec down below and the Karli and Shando, and all the coveners that had found peace and music in the forest were *we.* And these men with their long blades were *them,* a disease to be cut out of the healthy body, buried and grown over. They were a sickness in Webb himself that would rise to high fever before it ended.

He was crying. Clutching the sack, he closed his eyes tight and began a desperate lep to Garick.

The lep sped like fire in dry grass through Garick's people. Never the most disciplined of his force, the Suffec contingent was already riding down on the ambush point, and would answer no order to turn back. Others were saddled, anxious to follow, impatient for Garick's order.

"We can't get there fast enough," the god told Jenna. "How far away is Arin?"

She stared at him but did not voice her thought. "The girl's with him, she can say." In his haste, Garick missed the bitterness in her tone.

"Ask if Arin is further south than us."

Jenna lepped to Shalane. They waited in the dust and heat.

"She says yes."

"Bring her here. She has to help me get him."

They lepped Shalane up the line, then Garick shut his eyes and concentrated, trying to reach Webb with whatever instructions he could. Lately the god was so tired, he experienced difficulty in focusing long-range lep. Tentatively, Jenna put her hand on his shoulder. He grasped it instinctively and drew on her vitality to strengthen his lep. It was not the reason she took his hand, but she knew Garick would think it was.

The three masters completed the lep to Arin, then Garick called for his map. The scouts had just reported Callan and what appeared to be his whole force, moving east down the old road, away from the ambush point. This bunch—just over a hundred, Webb said—had probably turned aside to make some quick money.

He measured Webb's position to Callan's last sighting, then to his own. If it was a trick on Callan's part, it had backfired: he couldn't turn around in time even if he knew. And the loss of a hundred men for five would hurt him. Garick's force would roll over them like an angry river, and there would be no prisoners.

The god of Shando looked at Arin's woman and his own, saw his wish mirrored in their faces, and the lep went out to the whole column from their linked minds.

*Follow the Suffec. We will attack.*

The two men in green robes trotted briskly across the rolling meadow through a sea of high grass and dandelion. The afternoon sun baked down on them. They'd given up the cool protection of the trees the day before, cutting out across country and running on a tangent away from Callan's force.

Bowdeen grudgingly admired the tireless ease with which Arin rode hour after hour. Of course, he had twenty-five years on the Shando, but even now he was relearning coven shrewdness from the young master. They rode in open country but zigzagged every few miles and avoided fields where the grass even looked as if it had been recently crossed.

Arin was not warm company by Bowdeen's standards. He spoke rarely and to the point. The wintry set of his eyes never thawed, but they missed nothing. Bowdeen no longer wondered how he had been beaten at the bald top. The miracle was that he had gotten away at all.

Arin reined short, silencing Bowdeen's intended question with a wave of his twisted arm. He sat his horse, unmoving. At length, he turned to the Wengen.

"Message from Garick?"

"Trouble south," Arin confirmed. "Drag party's bushed some Suffec."

"Drag? Why'd Callan be dragging *now?*"

"You don't think he would?"

Bowdeen shook his head sadly. "No, but maybe that one bunch didn't get the word or don't care. Money comes hard. Anyway, what can we do about it?"

"Not us," Arin corrected, "just me. Garick wants me to ride south, try to help them."

The black man's eyebrows shot up. "With what? One bow? They're dead by now, Arin. And what do *I* do while you get killed, too?"

"Ride on west, meet up with Garick. Due west, you'll pick up his column somewhere along the line."

"Without you? They'll think I sold you again. What'll I say?"

"Bowdeen, considering who you are and what you were," Arin gave him a small, chill curve of smile, "I'd be *real* friendly." He slapped the reins and galloped off to the south.

"Arin!"

"Garick's orders," the drawl floated back across the meadow from the dwindling figure. "Any questions, ask him."

"Arin, goddammit—"

". . . Garick *said!*"

Which was a lie.

Webb moved cautiously down the slope, scared that he was doing just what the merks wanted him to. As he watched them range out in their puzzling search below, he couldn't believe they were so completely uninterested in him. He saw their tattered, dirty camo outfits and coven skins; they must have been long months in the forest. That meant they were worn out, desperate to earn every kret they could in bounty. That was what the bloody bag was for. He had learned that much from the Shando.

Garick's last lep urged him to use the Girdle for escape. Webb didn't think it would do anything, but he tried it—only to yank it off again fast. The thing made everything so wavery before his eyes that for a second he thought he might pitch headfirst off the side of the hill.

He could see only one possible escape route, didn't trust it. The remaining Suffec horses cropped grass, unguarded. Webb guessed he'd be allowed to get within a few feet of them, and then there'd be a signal and the merks would be there to cut him down. They were cruel like that. Still, if he didn't try, sooner or later they'd climb up after him, and it wouldn't no way be one at a time. He wouldn't have any more chance than the girl. There was no other choice.

He inched downward, using every bit of bush and rock for cover. There was still too much open ground where he was in full view of the merks.

Below, the horses ate the grass obliviously. Some of his feverish hate fell on them. He took a sliding step, shifted the center of his weight, made a scuffling run for the safety of another clump of bush, reached it. Only one more stretch: a few yards down the final curve of hill, then a short sprint across ten more feet of meadow to the nearest horse, all in the open.

Could he outrun the merks? He was rested, they were probably exhausted. Maybe, just maybe— He wondered how far off the closest of them were. He couldn't see anyone from where he was. They might be coming up the opposite side of the rise.

Not much time . . . *now.*

Sucking a lungful of air, Webb shot forward down the last slope, adding gravity to his speed, half running, half stumbling, ignoring the bruises and cuts along the way. Even in his headlong flight, the Suffec in him kept his leg muscles supple and relaxed, careful to make as little noise as possible.

When he hit level ground, he heard the cry go up, and he spurted across the intervening distance to the horses, not daring to turn his head, running, running, his lungs gasping for more air, not allowing himself the dangerous split-second he'd need to gasp in one sweet breath that could be his last. Already the ache for air weighed him down and the sack felt three times its weight. His legs were so leaden that his flight was now a heavy, slackening jog toward goddam horses that never got any nearer, like running from fear in dreams, while behind the merks chased and yelled threats. Hearing them, Webb thought with a wild hope: *too far, they can't catch me!* and the final burst of energy sped him the last few feet to his goal.

He had the horse moving before he was in the saddle, lashing it into a stretched-out gallop, lying low along its back to present a small target for arrows. One shaft hissed close to his ear, another thwacked the ground a few feet ahead and to the right. A few more misses, then no more. He was free.

The horse plunged on. Webb dared a look back; they stood there, cursing and shaking fists, a dwindling group dwarfed by the hill behind.

He gave the frightened stallion its head, riding high on the shoulder for balance. He did not look back again, but let the horse eat up the rolling meadow, dashing west until he perceived, in the distance, the single rider in green coming toward him.

As the fleeing rider glanced back fearfully, Vanner clenched his fist in mock menace and uttered a grunt of a laugh. "That's right, boy. Go tell Garick we're here."

"I could've got him, sir," one merk protested. "Clear shot; why'd you stop me?"

"Field Callan'd have your ass for dinner," Vanner warned. "You'll get your chance real soon." He barked at another man. "Sweep! Company officers to join me here."

He supposed the coven boy had time to lep Garick, but even without that, he'd carry the news of the massacre. That was the bait; Garick should take it. A hundred men would have no chance against him, and Callan couldn't afford to waste that many. Callan was counting on that. Vanner reflected: Garick was estimated six hours from this point when Callan sent them out. Another hour and a half to reach and finish the Suffec, say two to be sure. Garick would reach them with daylight to spare and come in with the late sun at his back.

"Dig in," he told his officers when they gathered around him. He drew two circles in the dirt, one inside the other. "Two closed lines of trench. When they're in position, let 'em rest and eat."

The commander of the 39th was a slow-talking, careful man. In his Karli skins he might have been Moss studying the two circles. "How far out for the aiming markers?"

"Fifteen yards," said Vanner.

The other man thoughtfully poked a hole beyond the outer circle. "That close?"

"That close," Vanner smiled grimly. "Man, it don't make no difference. Not with the throwers."

The sun beat down angrily. Arin's pulse pounded his temples. There was no time to satisfy his father; he had to catch Webb before he shied off from the green-clad rider he didn't yet recognize. He read the Suffec's fright, but Garick's lep was interfering with his own, wavering in and out of his mind. *The Girdle. Where is it?* Seeing Arin, the Suffec yanked his horse around, plunged off in another direction.

*Webb! Webb!*

The Suffec slowed and finally pulled up.

*Arin?*

*Yes. You have the Girdle?*

*Got something.*

*Come ahead. I'll wait.*

Arin dismounted. He unhooked his water bag from the saddle horn and sank down wearily in the high grass. He closed his eyes, shutting off his mind to Garick. Maybe it'd take Webb two minutes or so to reach him, moving slow till he made sure it *was* Arin, and that would be two minutes out of time, his own, two minutes when Arin would not have to do anything or be responsible for one little sliver of existence. Two minutes when he wouldn't have to think or decide.

Webb got there much too soon. He slid out of the saddle and leaned his head for a moment against the horse's lathered neck.

"Hey, Arin."

"Hey."

*Gonna be a bad day.*

*Yes.*

Neither spoke for a long time. The heat had a music of its own, rustling the grass, buzzing in the movement of insects. They listened. Finally, Webb gave the horse a pat and dropped himself down in the grass to drink thirstily from Arin's water bag. He looked up at last. *Almost didn't know you. You changed.* With more than years, Webb also thought. He didn't share, but Arin read it.

"I've been traveling." Even Arin's voice was different. *You changed too, Webb.*

*Yes.* Too painful to share.

Arin nudged the sack with his toe. *In there?*

Webb nodded.

Arin uncoiled from his stone-cut stillness. He opened the sack, dumped the contents on the ground. He picked up the dingy belt.

*. . . This?*

*All I found.*

The master's mind was locked away, the face something carved out of charred wood. It was not the face Webb remembered, not the laughing friend of the warm nights on the hill. It seemed for a breath Webb could read too *much* in that sun-blackened mask, too much to understand or bear—all his own dark thoughts of the swamp, all the old love and new hate-sickness, all of it there and beyond any imaginable word or sharing, distant, deep and cold. Into that deep he could pour the horror he had seen, the sound the girl made when they . . . all of it. And that mask would not even ripple. It was as if Arin had seen the same stars and, if it was thinkable, learned to live with them.

Arin held the belt for a long time, staring at it. What he said made no sense to Webb, but it wasn't meant for him. "These are my folk. Garick's broken circle. Shando's best." Another silence. "All of them. For this."

Arin sat there holding the dirty old belt in his hands, saying nothing, looking like he couldn't remember what to do next, in the middle of an empty field under an empty sky. Then he rose and fastened the belt around his waist. His finger found the toggle.

*Don't Arin!*

*?*

*I tried. Made my head hurt.*

Arin flicked the switch.

Webb started; one second Arin was solid before him, the next he was gone and even the grass showed no depression where invisible feet ought still be standing. Just as suddenly, he reappeared, clutching at his eyes. "Damn!"

"Told you, Arin."

"See what you mean," he murmured thickly. "The force field affects the wearer's own vision."

The strange words meant nothing to Webb. His eyes still bulged with the wonder of it. The other pointed to the cap and sealed pouch that fell out with the belt when he emptied the sack. "What are those?"

"Found them with the Girdle," Webb replied, accepting at last the real identity of the belt. "Thought they might be part of it."

He watched Arin examine the pouch, open it and remove a small book whose thick pages had survived the brittling of age. After scanning a leaf or two, he closed it, replaced the book in the pouch and handed it to Webb. "Take this to Garick."

"What is it?"

"Kind of a story, Webb. All about Callee."

That had to content Webb. Arin was already busy turning the cap over in his hands, until he found symbols imprinted on one side: SCU-A3. Mumbling to himself, he fitted it on his head. A pair of odd things with something like glass in them swung down to cover his eyes. "Now," he said, as his hand found the switch again.

This time Webb was braced for it, even casual, asking the empty air if the cap took away the dizziness. He received no answer.

"Arin?"

*Good-by, Webb.*

"Good-by? Where you go?"

No answer.

"Arin, come back so I can see you!"

*No time. Get to Garick. Give him the book.*

*You ain't coming?*

For answer, Webb saw Arin's riderless horse suddenly break out toward the east at a fast trot.

"I can't go to Garick without you, without Girdle! What I gonna *tell* him?"

*Tell Garick—meet me in Lorl. If.*

*If what?*

He received no other answer. The horse sped into the distance and was soon lost to sight.

Later, Webb would think about the curious meeting in the field, and the thing he'd remember most clearly would be the brief, silent time when he and Arin lay on the ground not thinking or speaking, until inevitably, the world started up again. There wasn't time for thought now.

He homed in on the god's lep, not without difficulty. It wavered uncharacteristically, but finally he pin-pointed the direction of the march, hauled himself into the saddle and ran cross-country to join up with the rest of his people.

Now that he knew, things weren't so bad as when he first came out of the swamp. The idea, the elusive thought, pinned down when he saw the drag party slaughter his friends, was that if Sandteela died for Garick, and if the merks murdered his people, then Webb needed no other reason for being in the fight. But yet, a small voice inside him asked, *Enough?* Nothing sure but what Garick said, what Webb wanted, what was important to anyone who said *we* need something more and better. *No other meaning*. Was that enough?

It had to be. They were coming, all of them, like a great tide, and the Suffec were in the lead.

Webb muttered to the horse's ear. "Move. Gogo*go!*"

He stopped once in a small copse to let the tuckered mount drink at a brook, splashing the sweat off his face and neck. Then he ate up the ground, keeping as close to cover as possible, mind tuned to the lep that leaked stronger and stronger into his consciousness like a widening stream.

He jerked to a halt when the first line of riders appeared over a rise, not more than a bowshot in front of him, his breath catching as the first line thickened with a second and third, and more and more until the rise was black with riders. Webb hesitated only a moment. The merks wore coven skins, too—but not the gray-brown of Suffec. His heart leaped as he spurred the horse forward.

*Hey! Hey! Hey!*

Then they were all around him, pushing water and fresh-cooked meat into his hands, *his* people, leading him back up the rise, pointing toward the west and, in the distance, the swift-advancing Shando green.

The Suffec lines moved forward at a walk, waiting for the Shando to catch up. Garick's order of battle was part choice, part chance. The Suffec demanded the lead, few hundred that they were. There was no arguing with the stony, silent minds. Behind them in ranks a hundred broad rode the Shando and then the Wengen, with the Karli, battered from fighting all spring, in the rear.

The first Shando element reached and blended into the Suffec lines, headed by Garick and Jenna. The goddess' trailing red mane was like a flag, recognizable hundreds of yards distant. They lepped Webb to them and, when he ranged at Garick's knee, the god demanded, "Where's the Girdle?"

Webb was at a loss. "Arin took it."

*Took it? Where?*

*East toward City.* "Said—said for you and goddess Jenna to meet him in Lorl. 'If,' he said."

The open, uneven ground flattened out for a good half mile before them. Without command, the leading ranks increased their gait to a steady, controlled trot.

"If," Garick snapped. "If what?"

"Don't you know?" Jenna answered quietly. "Don't you know where he's going?"

Garick suppressed the urge to curse them both. He knew where, but not why, and as he quickened into the trot, he knew as well there was no more time to wonder about it.

"Just this." Webb offered the book. "Arin says it's 'bout old Callee."

Garick shoved the volume into his saddlebag as Webb suddenly pointed ahead. *There.*

The hill rose above the rolling meadows. A hundred, two hundred heads lifted; a muted, continuous rattle went back and forth across the moving lines as arrows were drawn from quivers and tucked for readiness between nimble brown fingers. The next Shando lines closed the gap. The leading element became a solid mass ten ranks deep. A restless spirit breathed across it. The trot loosened, broadened into a steady canter, and the column rippled into the increased gait, cleaving the sea of grass and dandelion like a long, sail-blown ship. When the last thick wood rose up in front of them, they filtered through it, barely slowing or narrowing their ranks. Then the first lines were in the clear again, bearing down on the last rise. Webb pointed again. *There.*

The two merk riders walked their horses across the long ridge before Webb's hill, poking along at nonchalant ease as if there were all the time in the world between now and death. They were close enough in that moment for Webb to see that one of them rode with a foot braced up against the saddle horn. He flashed one fierce grin at Garick, then the Suffec line broke into a gallop, dashing across the remaining distance to the rise. Jenna felt Garick's mind touch hers like a hand laid on her hand: *now, Jenna. Shando go.*

The long-legged horses stretched out into the grace of speed so smoothly that the steady rumble of the canter became, with no perceptible break, a growing roar. The two merk riders were petrified by what came boiling out of the peaceful wood. Only a second, then they vanished over the hill.

*Go! Go!*

The forward edge heaved, raveled, straightened again as those behind strove to overtake the Suffec. As the gray-brown surged up the rise it was half green with Shando. The mottled line topped the crown and spilled down the other side.

*There they are! Shando go!*

Far back in the slower-moving rear, Shalane felt the ground tremble, heard the muffled roar and the thin-wafted shout that rose above it. Her line was moving faster now, the Garick-lep still echoing in their minds . . . *Shando go.*

The thing had begun.

"Look surprised and keep running!"

Standing on the rim of the forward trench, Vanner chewed a ration bar and watched his sprinting men clear the first trench and dive for cover into the second. Nearby, the young commander of the 44th swung his arms violently. "Run, goddammit, run!" He jumped into the trench as the last of them panted by, and yelled to Vanner. "Commander, get down!"

Vanner chewed. "Ain't done eating."

Wave after gray-green wave boiled down on them, narrowing the distance to their aiming markers. Vanner swallowed the last of the bar and watched them come. Someone close by whistled through dry lips.

"There must be—"

"Two thousand."

"More."

"*Look* at 'em."

With no haste, Vanner wiped the food fragments from his beard and dropped into the trench. "Get ready."

The 44th commander jerked his head at the apparatus strapped to each man's back. "I hope these things work."

Vanner's eyes were on the first line of riders already flattened out along the horses' necks. "If they don't, we get new ones free."

Someone tried to laugh, more like a gasp.

One hundred yards. Seventy-five. "Now?"

"Not yet."

The thunder came on, louder, filling the world. The company commander sucked in his breath. "Vanner, for shit's sake, now! *Now!*"

"Not—yet." Vanner's flat eyes were cold calipers that measured a narrowing fate. "Ready . . . ready . . ."

When he broke over the rise with the first line, the sight tore involuntary laughter from Garick: dozens of merks fleeing on foot down the hill toward their horses gathered within a wide circle of trench. They'd caught them at last, caught them like dull autumn flies in their vicious, stupid complacency, counting cut-off hands and seeing them as money. He nocked an arrow, saw Jenna do the same. The last merks leaped the outer trench—

*Why trenches?*

The instinct swiveled his head to the left toward the long wood that bordered the meadow. Linked with him, Jenna turned, too. They saw nothing but trees, and yet the *no* struck them both like a sudden blow, screamed the whole insane story in one split second. The wood quivered with danger, and there shouldn't be trenches *no wrong stop* as a single voice lifted over the roar—

"Fire!"

Garick saw the men rise out of the first trench like humpbacked dolls jerked up on a string, pointing something, then disappear as two dozen separate tongues of flame spurted out and became an opaque wall of sticky, flaming jelly. His will urged Jenna and sawed her horse's mouth with her hands. The two hurtling animals went stiff-legged in mid-stride, splaying their forelegs in a jolting halt, rearing up, taking with their heads and shoulders the flame that would have covered the riders, shrieking as they went down, forebodies lapped in curling flame.

Garick stopped thinking. Automatically he rolled free of the stricken animal. He heard his own screaming in the noise. His left arm was encased in a sleeve of fire. He rolled in the grass, the stink of his own seared flesh thick in his nostrils, trying to lock the pain away behind consciousness. The world roared and tumbled about him and, through the unbreathable, heat-distorted air, he saw the ruin of his first wave, burning where they lay. Some still moved, trying pitifully to crawl away while the fire puckered and split their hairless skin.

The ranks behind wavered, halted as they saw with horror another flame wall rise from the trench to engulf the second line. Vanner poised, arms raised, then pointed at two waiting men with large black boxes sitting on the lip of the trench. Each bent to the box; each pressed a button.

The air bellowed with bugles played at ear-piercing volume from the solar-batteried recorders. The high-strung coven horses bolted and plunged, neighing high, tossing their heads to rid their small brains of the agony in their ears. Garick gasped, only part of it pain. What had been a great, seething charge became now a milling confusion as the riders fought to control the maddened brutes. Further up the slope, the Shando looked down into the hell at the bottom, seeking Garick and Jenna.

"The goddess!" One master spotted the red-flag mane in the smoking maelstrom. "There she is."

Jenna's horse reared a split second before Garick's. She rolled clear, singed but unhurt and cursing. Down on one knee behind the burning carcass, she sent shaft after shaft into the ditch. The nearest thrower-man went over, then the next.

*Jenna . . .*

*Garick, where?*

The other lep lanced at her: *Goddess, hang. Hang.*

She loosed one more arrow, turned to look for Garick, then the green riders were on her. She grasped their arms and let them carry her out of the heat, twisting her head back to find him.

*I'm all right. Find the god.*

Lips drawn back, Vanner watched the horses run out of control from the nightmare horns, the riders struggling vainly to master them. "Hold fire!"

There wasn't enough fuel for the throwers, that was one weakness in the plan. None of them were more than a quarter full to start. *Callan, you shit,* he thought, *where are you?* He waved forward the bowmen already hurrying from the inner ditch. By plan, they were to press the advantage now, move forward mopping up the running wounded and push on to gain the ridge. There was one target for all of them, Vanner knew, and it was still alive. He'd followed it with his eyes all along, its clothes smoldering rags, trying to stumble away, falling again, the red-black remnant of arm flapping uselessly. Garick.

Three of his men lurched sideways and fell as they came out of the ditch. Vanner flinched as the arrow tore his sleeve. What—?

The arrows flew again with deadly accuracy. His men were running back to the trench. Vanner couldn't even get his head up to see what it was.

The slope above Webb was a solid, squirming mass of men and women, struggling on ground so cluttered with fallen horses and humans that there was barely room to move. At the bottom, around him, the burned carcasses became his own protective wall. Six of them came out of that first wall of fire unharmed—himself, the Suffec girl Dooby, and four others of his own. They crouched behind their wall of flesh directly in the path of the men in the ditches. Silently agreed in their linked minds, the realization became a plan: for whatever good it did, they could stop the fire-men from getting into the fight for a while.

There were plenty of arrows, and big, slow targets a hundred times easier to hit than the swift birds that honed their bowcraft in the bayous. It was almost funny; every time the merks tried to clear the ditch, the Suffec thinned them out and ran the others back to its protection. But their arrows were almost gone now.

Webb hugged the sweating, fierce-eyed girl. Dooby was fifteen, skinny, raised like himself in a bayou on wild rice and greens. She'd stayed with him once.

*Next time they come out,* he told her. *Watch my point. One man, Dooby.*

The last arrows flew. Webb didn't have to raise the knife. Dooby and his folk knew what had to be done.

Vanner swore. *Six* of them. Six goddam Suffec just out of thrower range keeping him out of the fight, calmly decimating his men, scoring more often than they missed. Not so many arrows that last time. They must be near out.

"Drop the throwers. Sheddys, dammit, we're going out!"

*"Vanner!"*

He looked where the soldier pointed. The six Suffec were running full speed down at him, bounding high over the obstructing bodies, nothing in their hands but knives.

A dozen men started forward with Vanner to close with them. One of the last snatched up a thrower and swung the nozzle at the six. It sputtered and smoked, empty. One skinny girl dropped under a chop that would have taken her head off, spun in a blur of speed to slash the man's neck, completed the spin and came straight on at Vanner with barely a break in her stride. Behind her was the boy. Vanner set himself, wielding the sheddy two-handed, raised it—

He was swinging when the girl's feet left the ground, came up before her, slamming low into his middle as she fell. Too light to knock him over, she broke his balance, and then the boy was on him. With no time to swing again, Vanner lunged in a straight thrust, but the girl tripped him up. He fell; snake-lithe, she pounced on his sword arm, trapping it under her while the boy wrenched the sheddy from his fingers, raised it and brought it whistling down.

The shock paralyzed Vanner. Through the numbness, he gaped at his right wrist. Webb raised the sheddy again and brought it down on the bearded neck, as the men from the second trench lunged forward, rolling over them, barely pausing as they pushed toward the slope.

Dooby crumpled beside him, an arrow in her chest. In the last second before the sheddys ended him, Webb threw the severed hand in their faces.

The two Shando riders tried to get to Garick. They were hit and still came on, hit again, falling while the riderless horses plunged by him. Barely behind them, the other rider in buff skins darted in, lying low along the horse's flank. He careered to form a shield between Garick and the merks, and dropped off, pulling the god toward the saddle.

"Go on, thickhead, get up."

Garick's parched lips cracked in a grin. "Moss!"

Suddenly Moss yanked him back. "No, down. *Down.*"

The rush, like the sound of supernaturally swift birds froze them still. From out of the bordering wood, a black storm of arrows rose, hovered and descended. They flattened themselves to the horse as the deadly rain came down, and then the wood spouted a quarter-mile of galloping soldiers.

"Master Garick," Moss pushed him up into the saddle, "you sure know how to start a fight." He slapped the animal's rump. "Git, horse."

On the brow of the hill, beginning to control his pain, Garick could still see Moss running, Maysa beside him, bows and quivers jouncing at their side in the press of milling horses and men, and the angry tide of merks that battered into them, sheddys flashing in the sun. His brain began to work. Behind him waited the unharmed bulk of his force, halted and confused for the moment. *Bowmen,* he lepped. *Bows on foot. Shando masters, move forward with Edan. Packdogs. Packdogs.*

The peel-and-fade worked beautifully. With his column half-obscured by dust, Callan had moved away from the direction of the drag site knowing he was watched. But as the distance increased, Garick's scouts could not detect the right hand column dribbling off into the concealing woods, or the parallel lines of men from the trees on the opposite side of the road that replaced them under partial cover of the dust. While it was still in sight, the column did not appear to thin.*

The peeled-off files reformed quickly and rode under heavy wooded cover to range themselves on Vanner's right flank, horses and men flattened to the ground. Waiting, watching the covens come down in that first charge, Callan weighed chances. Vanner was smart enough to conserve the thrower fuel. He'd move forward out of the ditches when he could, probably cursing the field commander all the

*See map, page 398.

way, but the one weakness of peel-and-fade was that his last men on the road could not reach him in time for a full-strength attack. Callan waited as long as he dared, but the talk boxes had done their work. Garick's riders, some of them, were being carried by the maddened horses right into merk ranks to be slaughtered. When he gave the order, a thousand men followed the first flight of arrows to smash into Garick's disorganized point.

When Callan's last elements arrived from the road, the struggle on the hill had separated into something recognizable: two lines, the coveners backing slowly up a hill thick with dead in an organized formation, the merks dismounted and advancing slowly behind their horses, throwing flight after flight of arrows into the open, unprotected ranks above. The throwers of the 39th and 44th were among them now, expending the last of their fuel in well-placed spurts of fire.

The dandelions could no longer be seen.

As the uncommitted men watched, a rider dashed out of the battle and drummed down on them—Callan, sweaty, waving his sheddy like a flag, cut in the leg but glowing with energy that crackled out of him as he swept the blade toward the west.

"Flank!" he snapped to the ranking officer. "Cut around Garick's right, flank them. There's too many of them to move, too dumb to deploy. They're piling up on themselves, lost thirty to our one."

"They're retreating, sir?"

Callan paused to gulp a needed breath or two before answering. "No, just moving back behind bowmen. Poisoned arrows. And masters," he rasped out of his raw throat. "They set up a kind of field, a field of power. Seen them do it with packdogs . . . can't push it very far out, but *stay out of range:* twenty yards, or they'll burn your brain out. Go in behind your throwers, use them up, throw them away when they're empty. No more fuel, anyway. Cut down the edge of the woods, keep covered, then attack in order. In *order,* is that clear? Move out."

The officer swung his horse around to execute the orders. "Where'll you be, field?"

"With the 44th." Callan pointed to the hill. "We can't give them the chance to come back at us. Keep pushing. Keep hitting."

The columns clattered off through the trees. Callan wiped his sweaty forehead on a sleeve. "Now, Uriah," he murmured. "Now, at last. Today."

Neither he nor Garick had any more choices to make, but he had a plan where Garick had only a chaos of stunned, untrained rabble. He couldn't afford to let Garick recover or mass in concerted attack, not with all his own men committed now. It hinged, as always, on the devil's own fate-maker, Garick. Someone said he was dead, others that he was badly hurt. If he was still giving orders—if he managed, unthinkably, to *use* those untapped numbers—if Callan had to fight defensively—

No, it had to be now, before dark. Before Garick had the chance. He spurred toward the hilltop.

In the wood west of the hill, Jenna crouched protectively by the limp god, glowering at the masters who worked with silent determination over his wounds. They could save the arm, but Garick would never use it again. The god would never have survived amputation; he was too weak. Besides the arm, he'd taken an arrow in his thigh. Not deep, they'd cut it out, but he couldn't afford to lose any more blood. They plastered the arm thick with mould-salve and wrapped it tight to his side.

As Jenna watched, her head ached with the jumbled lep that whispered and cried in the air. *Is Garick dead? Where is he? What orders?*

White with pain, Garick clutched Jenna's hand as Hoban and Tilda came through the trees to kneel by him.

"Garick," the Karli god asked, "can you ride?"

"You've got to," Tilda told him. "None of us knows what to do."

"I can," Jenna growled. She bent low over the colorless face. "Garick, I'll lead them. Tell me what to do."

"I'll tell you," Hoban grunted. "Pull back into the woods with what you've got left. Small groups. We'll cut them to pieces."

"He's right," Tilda agreed.

Garick's head moved weakly side to side. "No . . ."

"We can't match them on open ground," Tilda argued. "The Suffec are gone, your Shando are piling up out there. You think we'll send Karli out to pile it higher?"

Garick struggled up. He refused the medicine that would have dulled the pain and his mind as well. "If we go back in deepwoods, there's nothing to stop Callan. He'll live off our land and burn the rest all the way to Salvation, and once he's got the mines, he can fight us for years. We'll never see City."

"City!" Tilda exploded. "Who wants it? Not us, no one but you. What do you want from the Karli? We fought them all spring, we never asked for your money, your goddam sida money. We're going back. If he comes to Karli, we'll be ready."

"Send them out *there!*" Jenna pointed to the struggling field. "There, where they can help."

"No," Hoban refused. "Not on open ground."

"You," Jenna seethed. "None of you could do what he's done. Where would you be without Garick to lead you?"

"Then let him lead!" Tilda shot back.

Jenna's fury choked off in a gesture of frustration. "How can he? Garick—"

He fought the fainting. The world reeled and faded around him.

"Garick, tell *me*. Tell me what to do," Jenna pleaded.

He lost consciousness again. With a dry sob, Jenna folded down over him, cradling his head. She ignored the newcomers, the dark men and women who filtered through the trees to stand looking down at her, waiting to be recognized.

"Goddess Jenna."

". . . yes."

"The Wengen masters."

She pushed the limp hair back from her face. "What?"

The Wengens wanted to be courteous, but their mission was important. "Goddess, our folk need orders. They're ready to fight, but—"

Jenna pointed dully toward the field. "Out there."

The Wengens exchanged quick glances. "No, goddess. The people out there have no chance. We don't know this kind of fight."

"They're my people. They were the first in with me and Garick."

"Damn fool move." Hoban turned away.

"Fool?" Jenna rose to face them all. "Then he's paid for it. He was in the first line, and those fire things burned his arm off, but *he* won't pull back, and *I* won't. No, masters. No, Hoban. I'll take them out there myself—"

The sharp lep interrupted her: *Bern and Shalane coming in.*

*?*

*Got Bowdeen.*

Jenna took a ragged breath. Bowdeen. An outlet for the frustration she felt. *Bring him here.*

The other masters went to meet the prisoner, but Tilda crouched with Jenna, wetting a cold cloth for Garick's forehead. The old woman looked at her sister-in-power, saw the first wisps of gray still all but lost in the river of rusty auburn, the haggard lines around the mouth.

*You'd kill us all for him.*

*Don't, Tilda.*

Tilda's glance pitied her. Jude and her City magic had made Garick into something Jenna could never hold. "He should've stayed a farmer. He had everything."

"He's the god. He was born for it."

Tilda looked at her mouth, drawn with years of a silent hunger. Maybe, she thought, but who can lie down with the lightning?

Then Shalane was leading Bowdeen to Jenna, his hands tied behind him. The others ranged around, curious. This was what they called a merk, this gave the name a face. This killed their kind for money. There was nothing lower.

"Bowdeen." Jenna said the name with all she felt for it. "They tell me you rode with Callan. You cut off coven hands for money." When she stood up, her eyes were almost level with his. The black man's face looked lived in, but the lack of cruelty surprised her.

"Arin's gone to City. I don't need you." She set her knife just under his left ear. "You ought to die quick."

"Jenna."

Weakly, Garick tried to raise himself to a sitting position. Instantly, she was there supporting one shoulder, Shalane at the other.

"So, you're Bowdeen."

The black man breathed deep and let out the relief in a broken laugh. "Glad you woke up, master Garick. Look, about Arin—"

"He's gone, I know." Garick narrowed his eyes. "I know *you.* You were in Charzen once."

Bowdeen nodded. "Years back. Lotta years."

"A dragger. What the hell happened to you?"

Bowdeen didn't smile. "I got hungry." He shook his head. "Man, this is a mess. You got nothing working *for* you."

"Someone told me to trust you," Garick said.

"Wasn't me," Jenna put in. "Kill him."

"—and I've taken chances too long to be careful now. I need help, need it bad. I've lost a thousand people in an hour, maybe more, and they're still dying out there. It . . . was a mistake." He sought the other masters with his eyes. "We couldn't stop those Suffec, you know that. But it's not the end. We don't quit. Bowdeen, what can you do?" He studied the black man. "I forgot. You always get paid, don't you?"

Bowdeen was surprised that the words could hurt; that hadn't happened in a long time. "I got a woman. Can't ride much longer."

Garick rubbed the blur from his eyes. "You stop Callan and Jenna won't cut your throat. You try to trick me, and you're hers."

The goddess' expression was not pleasant to contemplate. "Hear that, cowan?"

They meant it. By their time, he was two minutes to dead already. He tried to grin it down. "They *said* you was a sonvabitch."

"They were right," said Garick. "You working for me?"

"I'm working for you."

With Bowdeen's knife, Garick laboriously sketched in the dirt the situation and what had happened, Bowdeen attentive, lips pursed.

"Sounds like peel-and-fade."

"You know it?"

"Helped work it out. First thing you gotta do, save what people you got left out there on the field."

One Wengen master spoke quickly. "We won't go out there."

"No," Hoban said.

"Neither would I," Bowdeen agreed. "Master Garick, lep them Shando back into the woods."

"No," Jenna refused. "Garick says we don't pull back."

"Garick, you gimme the say or not?"

Garick nodded. "We'll call them back."

"Right. I'll need a set of Shando skins. This robe's for a storekeeper, and I got a hint I'm gonna be running fast. Bow and quiver: you ain't got to spare, get 'em off someone don't need them no more. God Hoban, you got some folks shoot a good bow—"

Hoban smiled grimly. "You should know."

Bowdeen laughed. "I kind of remember you do. Can you lep me two hundred here? *Lep!*" The Wengen, without moving, seemed to come alive with energy. "That's your weapon, the lep. Callan can't beat that, but you got to work *together,* man. You Wengen, when the Shando get back in the woods, move up longside, masters on each end of each line for strong lep. Keep covered and hold the line. You gotta move back, move *back* as a line. Your people don't know how to move fast, tell them mofos there's a big black ass up here gonna teach 'em how. Move out."

The Wengen masters hesitated. He was of their blood, his speech rang with their laughter and rhythms, but he was cowan now. They took orders only from the god Garick.

Garick lay back, exhausted. "Those are my orders."

The lep went out, the Garick-lep that no one questioned. Chaos took the first, faltering steps toward order. Crackling with a purpose he knew would cost him later, Bowdeen stripped off the robe and took the skins from the young man who brought them: whiter than most covens, sensitive features. Not the face of a fighter.

"What's your name, boy?"

"Jay."

"Well, Jay, I need a horse, one that ain't been spooked too bad already. I'm gonna get one of those throwers, and I need two good men dumb enough to come with me."

"Shalane and I crossed Blue together." Jay took her hand.

"We don't spook any more," the blond girl said.

Karli girl. Bowdeen knew the breed. Thin and tough as vine, able to fight two days on a handful of acorns and a hunk of raw horse. He noticed the cord belt knotted around her waist and spoke respectfully. "Karli will need their masters, girl. Young ones like you. Can you push a horse through fire?"

Shalane spat on the ground in disgust. "Do that much two weeks after I'm born again. You just say when."

Bowdeen chuckled. "All right, look like you and Jay are it. We'll move when the Karli get here." He dropped on one knee beside Garick, took the god's hand. "Trust me or not, just back me up, Callan's gonna try flanking you again."

"How do you know?" Jenna challenged.

" 'Cause I taught him, goddess, and that's what I'd do. That's where I'm going. Keep up the lep, Garick, let them know you ain't beat, that you're gonna ride."

They understood each other. Callan might be stopped, but they had to go after him or lose. There was the wall of flame that none of them would forget, the burning they could still smell, the hill and long meadow thick with Circle dead. No one else but Garick could lead them into that fire again. Perhaps not even him.

Bowdeen squeezed his hand. "We get cock'n'box with Callan, you gotta ride. They won't follow me."

*Ride?* he thought as he moved away. *He can't even sit up. Sidele, Sidele, whyn't you kick me when I'm so dumb?*

"Orders, field? We go after them?"

Callan glowered at the frazzled, sweaty young lead who'd ridden back to find him. What orders? He couldn't push fast cavalry across that field piled two and three high with Shando dead. The bodies of horses and men had become a fortress for the slow-retreating coveners. And the flank move had never appeared. He didn't know where they were.

"Have the 39th and 44th move up on foot with every thrower we've got left." They'd burn the woods out from under the Shando. "Recall on bugle. We're useless in there after dark."

The lead swung out to ride; Callan grabbed at his leg. He seldom swore, but now the blasphemy was justified. "Send a rider to that flank element: where the goddamned hell've they *been?* They're no good now, there's nothing to flank. Get them back here."

He paced the ridge as the two veteran companies jogged down the hill. Someone was still giving coherent orders to the covens, someone who knew his business. The flank move might have broken them, sent their remnant tumbling back on those behind. Too late now, but he had to keep the initiative. He'd push through the remaining light, recall and move northwest under cover of darkness. In two weeks, cavalry as fast as his could retake Salvation.

---

The companies sent to flank had no experience in deepwoods. Deployment was difficult and slow, the ground uneven, choked with fallen trees and thick creeper that caught in their equipment and cut visibility to a few yards. There was no time to scout the wood, or Callan might never have given the order. Still, they used their sheddys to hack their way through, coaxing the now-useless horses after them. The battle was audible, only a few hundred yards ahead; it might as well have been ten miles.

One sek, inching yards ahead of his element, found a kind of path, overgrown but serviceable. Before waving the rest to it, he took a few steps along the twisting trail to see if it led to anything more than a dead end. No drag-wise merk would have done it for fifty krets. Any path that looked easy was always lined with coven.

The boy and girl rose up behind him, small and slight, close enough to touch. He never heard them. They took his sheddy when they were done.

Bowdeen's first arrows hit the merks.

When Bowdeen placed his line of Karli across Garick's flank, he was only applying for the covens what he had learned against them: two hundred coveners in the bush were worth a thousand in the open field. Crouching near the center of his line with Jay and Shalane, he received and passed information in whispers that flashed through Shalane to Garick and Jenna and the whole fighting line.

*Flank stopped. Karli holding.*

*Shando, Wengen formed in woods west of the meadow. Holding.*

The merk attack slowed and changed radically in the heavy bush, not the battle Callan wanted to fight. It became now what it had been north of Karli, a near-silent skirmish between small groups or individuals, punctuated briefly by a shout here and there and the incessant *boonk-wush!* of arrows.

Twenty yards in front of Bowdeen, the long spout of flame fanned out of the thick bush at some invisible target. He heard a scream, young and high-pitched. Someone crashed away to the right. For a moment, the figure was visible. It had been a small boy or girl, you couldn't tell now. It was nothing but flame, and it fell, still screaming. Shalane covered her ears.

Jay swallowed hard. "Jesus."

"Now we know where that thrower is," Bowdeen whispered to him. "That stuff burns a path for thirty yards in front of it. Hot, but you can get a horse through. Let's go, Jay." He nudged Shalane. "You got it straight?"

She jerked her head up and down; her mouth went very dry.

"Give you a turkey gobble when we're ready." The two men slipped into the bush and were quickly lost to sight. Shalane untethered the horse, quieting it with whispers and soothing hands. When it stopped quivering, she wrapped the hooding over its eyes. As long as it couldn't see where her hands and legs would guide it, she could run the horse anywhere. Carefully, she coaxed it back through the bush into a shallow depression, down on its stomach, and flattened to the ground behind it. *Get ready,* she lepped. *Jay and the cowan gone out. Fire coming.*

She and the Karli nearby had to make themselves targets for the fire-thing. Frightened to a numbness beyond fear, she listened to her pounding heart.

To the thrower-man, isolated from his nearest mates by the opaque tangle that surrounded him, it seemed no danger. He heard a turkey call that wouldn't fool anyone, then a crashing of movement yards ahead, a quick flurry of arrows and the voices.

"Hey! Hey!"

A target. He didn't have to see it. He pressed the valve and the flame shot out, dissolving the bush in front of him. He fired again. The roar of the pressure-driven jelly muffled the slight noise behind him.

"Now!" Bowdeen dove for the man's back as Jay caught the right hand, wrenching it from the trigger-valve. Holding the nozzle aside, Jay closed his eyes as Bowdeen's knife came down. Quickly, they removed the thrower from the body. Bowdeen shouted: "Go!"

Two dozen yards away, Shalane heard it and gave the reins a twitch. The horse bunched and sprang; she flowed onto its back as it came up, plunging forward, letting pure movement absorb her terror.

She could barely breathe. The whole world burned and stank around her, but there was a fire-lined path to her front and, heat-blurred at the end of it, Jay and Bowdeen.

She started down the flaming alley, throat seared by the burned-out air, feeling it scorch her face and hands. Drops of fire-jelly dripped from the bush; her skins were smoking already. The horse shrieked as it brushed against live fire, but she forced it forward. Then the lane was crossed, and there was clean air she could breathe, and Jay was slapping at her smouldering skins and Bowdeen was working at the black City magic, the fire-thing. He lifted the nozzle and pressed.

The flame fanned in a wide arc toward the jungle where the merks were deployed. The green erupted with running men, and the screaming began. Bowdeen locked off the valve and swung the thrower up to Shalane. "Get this to Garick. Fast."

Shalane sucked in air, held it and drove the blind horse into the burning corridor again. Bowdeen and Jay followed.

As he jogged along the corridor of fire, Bowdeen heard the bugles —loud, mechanical, out of the batteried recorders.

"Recall," he grunted to Jay. "Callan's calling them back."

There was no more sun, only the soft, cooling shadow deepening toward night. The armies fell back from one another like exhausted, fighting dogs, panting in the green silence.

*Sundown, Maysa.*

They used to watch it together in front of the house or walking by the edge of their fields. They made love there in that beauty as often as in their own bed.

They never had any sense; sometimes Shalane, in her mastership, was more grown up than both of them, but life had been good to them, Moss reflected, never made them work too hard, and Maysa came to understand when the rain made him stay alone.

They thought they had shaped their own life, but they didn't. Jude did, Jude and Garick: they carved. He and Maysa were only part of the wood.

When the Shando started forward on that first charge, it never occurred to Moss and Maysa to stay behind. Discipline was one of Garick's Old Language words that meant nothing to them. They just felt like getting forward quick. So they'd seen him on that burning hillside and Moss saved him. So they came to stand with the Shando in that open field.

So they waited while the merks came into the bush with the fire-things.

They were smart, those merks. They were draggers, you could tell from their coven clothes and the way they used every bit of cover. They burned the Wengens and Shando out of the trees, out of the bush. You could get them if you saw them, but they kept coming, pushing Circle back, burning holes in the line, closing to fight in small groups like coven.

He and Maysa got the fire-thing and the man who carried it, but the heat burned Moss' eyes. He shot the arrow just a blink too late. But he had the fire-thing and a sheddy and a tricky shovel that collapsed for easy carrying.

The merks went back when their horn sounded. That was fine with Moss. They could go where they pleased. There was no more fight in him. It was like the rain. Tomorrow he might care, but not now.

He grunted it to the tool as he worked. "Not now."

*Gather in. Gather in to Garick.*

A few Shando slipped out of the bush, answering the lep. Moss barely glanced up at them. Some were hurt bad, big blisters under their streaked paint.

"You didn't hear?" The man's eyes were glazed with fatigue. "Gather in."

The shovel blade bit again into the soft earth. "You tell Garick—this old man's busy."

They left him then and drifted like smoke into the green tangle. Moss went on digging.

He kept his eyes closed when he shoved and scooped the earth into the grave. Not till it was mostly full would he look directly at it. When the last bit was patted on top, Moss dropped the shovel and lay down beside the grave. In fierce silence, he hugged the length of his body to the mound, one arm over it as it had always been with them. He couldn't imagine not touching her.

~

As the light faded toward dusk, Bowdeen rode a cautious reconnaissance along Callan's flank. What he saw confirmed his logical suspicions. He galloped back in plain sight of the merks part of the way, yelling to identify himself as he entered the wood.

"Bowdeen coming in!"

No one challenged him, few even glanced up. He passed endlessly through clumps of people who sat or lay exhausted on the ground. Some dug with dull determination at shallow graves. *Everything stops while some farmer gets born again.* There wasn't anything like a line any more, just exhausted, sullen coveners ready to quit, muffling the agony of wounds and burns so the enemy could not hear how badly they were torn.

Bowdeen knew the extent of the damage and hoped Callan didn't. You couldn't match coveners in the bush, but Callan lured them into his own kind of war and gave them no chance to recover. Only darkness saved them, and the flank move that never came off. With two more hours of light, or even one, Callan would have won. Bowdeen had to admire him: well trained in strategy, Callan pushed his primary plan as far as he could, then switched to the logical alternate without any further waste of men. When next time came—where or when—he'd have better odds. Nearly a third of Garick's force lay on the hill or meadow or under the trees still burning where the throwers had whipped across them.

A little further on, he found Shalane arguing with some of her own people. Jay leaned against a tree nearby.

"They're leaving," Jay told him. "Some of the Wengen, too."

Bowdeen wasn't surprised. They had no idea what it was to be an army, didn't even have a word for it.

"They say Garick's dying," Jay went on. "They can tell from his lep."

Bowdeen cursed. "Dying, my granny's ass! Master Shalane! Tell them Karli—they leave now, won't be anything to go home to."

He pushed the horse faster through the brush to the copse where he left Garick. Only the goddess was there with him now, bending over the prostrate god in the deepening shadows. Bowdeen tethered the horse and knelt by Garick. The man was not dying. His eyes were alert. Only his body was beaten. Bowdeen offered him a ration bar.

"Try some of this. Concentrated food. Good for you."

Jenna refused it. "Could be poison."

"No." Garick unwrapped the bar and bit off a small hunk. "Lot of strength in it. Jude had some."

"See how big *she* grew on it."

Garick rested on his good elbow. "Well, Bowdeen, you stopped him."

"For now."

"You scout?"

"Yes, sir. Most of them strung out along the ridge, eating, collecting arrows and other stuff off the field. The horses are there, and nobody's digging in. He's gonna move come dark."

Garick waited for him to go on.

"Has to be now, Garick."

Jenna shook her head, strained. "Leave him alone, cowan."

"Garick, now. It has to be." Bowdeen felt desperate. "You gotta lep strong, a gather-in. And you gotta ride."

"He can't!"

"Goddess, they say he's dying, his lep's so weak. And some of them are leaving."

"Leaving?" For an instant, Jenna showed him a part of her he wouldn't have guessed: fear, not for herself but the thing she lived for. *"Leave Garick?"*

"Yes, goddess."

"Jenna," Garick said soothingly, "come be with me. Bowdeen, bring me that saddlebag."

From the bag, Garick took a gleaming, white-handled thammay and gave it to Bowdeen. "Show this to Hoban and Tilda and the Wengen masters. You know what it is?"

There was enough Circle left in Bowdeen for that. Garick called them to go to the knife, to the end. No one would come back until it was finished.

"You think they'll come?" Bowdeen asked.

"I don't know. They knew it might come to this."

Bowdeen dropped his eyes. Garick's cheeks were sunken. The wounds had unlocked the weeks and months of fatigue. It hurt to look at the man. "And you, sir?"

Something passed between the god and goddess that Bowdeen felt but could not read. "We'll be waiting for them with the Shando," said Garick. "Tell them, Bowdeen."

The Wengen sighed and pulled himself up into the saddle. "You won't mind my ridin' longside, will you? Case you get a headache or something?"

Garick gave him an ashen grin. "You just might help."

"Like those two throwers we got," Bowden added. "Been thinking about them." He trotted the horse away.

*Gather in. Meet the god and goddess.*

Jenna brought the horses as close as she could, cinched the saddles. It was time. Garick gathered himself for the effort to rise. He took a bite of the ration bar and offered the rest to Jenna. "Go on, eat," he coaxed gently. "Can't stop later."

To please him, she took the bar, bit, chewed and swallowed, as it were, at arm's length. "Got no taste."

"Cowan food, what else?"

She kissed him on the cheek. "We'll eat good when we get home."

"Yes." He put his good arm around her. "Pretty here. I've never been down this way; don't know if this is Shando or Suffec covenstead. Doesn't even have a name."

Jenna regathered her loosened hair and captured it tight under the strip-and-pin. "Some our folk gave it a name. For the flowers, there's so many. Call it Dannyline."

*Meet in the woods just west of the meadow . . .*

Jenna inspected the captured sheddys for their edge and tucked one into the straps of each saddle. "Shalane rode good today, Garick. Arin picked right, I guess. First she came, all I could see was them damn big front teeth." She smiled. "She'll be a good master, maybe even . . ." She turned to him, fingers touching the iron moon-crescent at her breast. *Garick—*

*?*

. . . *nothing*. She locked it away forever and knelt to help him. "Guess we're ready."

"I guess."

"Feel bad?"

"Felt better when I got hit by lightning. Give me a minute."

The fading light softened her face. "You know what? You remember the time we whitebrained the packdogs coming home from Lorl? I was in the masters' circle and you were inside with Jase and Moss—old Moss will be lonely now, should come live with us—and I was trying to keep up my part of the power, and all I could think about was Jude in your wagon. Where I wanted to be. That's why the dogs almost got me instead of ma."

She slipped his good arm over her hard shoulders and braced herself as Garick hung on. His mouth disappeared in a tight line as he struggled up. "Not far." Jenna held on to him. "Come on, hand on the horn . . . come on."

Before the pain could start, he felt her mind braced about the edge of his own like strong hands, helping his own flayed senses in their command to the muscles. "Foot in the stirrup. Up . . . up . . . there."

He was set in the saddle, but still Jenna clung to his leg, head tilted up to him. Her large hands spread gently up his thigh to embrace him awkwardly. Jenna rested her head against his leg; her face felt warm through the buckskin.

"I hated her then. I hated her for a long time. Not now. I got what I wanted, Garick."

He felt his chest squeeze tight. His bad leg was bleeding again, but he leaned down to root his fingers in the thick red hair.

"Girl, if we had time, I'd love you right here."

She laughed aloud. "Come see me, Garick. I'll make you happy like at Sinjin and all the other times. Like when I hid your pants."

"And I went home in a hide shirt."

"You had the *nicest* ass, master Garick."

He started to answer, then his head turned sharply. "Jenna—" *Listen.*

The lep was more a leaking of thoughts from many minds, few clear words, only an intent that grew in strength from moment to moment. They recognized a voice here and there, close, loved voices, rising briefly out of the others.

*Moss . . . Bern . . . Hoban and Tilda . . . will meet . . .*

"And Shâlane!" Listen, Garick! It's the girl. I told you, that's some kind of woman!" They led the horses out, heading toward the wood's fringe.

*The Karli . . . the Wengen . . . Shando coming in . . . will meet . . .*

More voices and more and more after that. Still exhausted, still frightened, not bright with hope. But coming back.

Garick held on to the saddle horn, feeling the strength surge back into him. "Jenna, Jenna, *listen!* They're coming. So *many* of them!"

Jay and Shalane rode close together through the thinning trees toward the edge of the meadow, the two captured throwers strapped to their backs. Behind them came the long green and buff lines, the whole wood alive, rustling and snapping under the stepping hooves.

They reached the last cover and paused. They were to separate here. Bowdeen's plan was simple: first in would be the two long echelons of Shando and Karli bowmen, then the two of them, and then Garick with the rest. No plan would be needed after that.

Together they watched the shadow-men and horses silhouetted against the ridge. "Be dark in a bit." Shalane turned to Jay. His head was bowed, lips moving silently. Just like him to pray to an old-man god, as if goddess earth couldn't do anything.

"Hey," she whispered. Their fingers laced together.

"Hey, Lane."

"I'm glad I loved you, Jay."

That shy smile of his: "It was needed."

She leaned out and kissed his fingers. "Born again."

"God bless you."

They trotted out of the trees and turned apart to opposite ends of the line that emerged from the forest edge, Garick, Jenna and Bowdeen in the center. Silent, all of it, but where there had been a fringe of trees, two hundred riders paced forward in a straight line as more issued from the wood, the dark green Shando almost invisible in the thickening shadows, lighter-salted with Karli buff. The straight lines advanced at a walk. More an extension than a break in that rhythm, Garick's horse flowed out ahead of the line and cantered laterally across the moving front. He held the thammay high overhead.

Shalane braced the fire nozzle under her right elbow as the walk rippled into a swift trot and two single-file lines of riders moved out from the first and second lines to stream ahead of the mass. When Garick's lep flashed across Shalane's mind, it was a rowel in the horse's flesh. She dashed forward and, for the second time, the darkening meadow filled with the roar of their coming.

Between his teeth, Callan said: "Bowdeen."

The set of the man in the saddle was too familiar; it *was* Bow he saw dash briefly across the open, must have been him who stopped the advance. And only Bowdeen would think to counterattack now when Callan's men were scattered about the ridge, finishing their rations, within minutes of the call to move out.

With no time to saddle, the companies swirled about Callan into some semblance of order while Callan watched that overwhelming green swiftness come on—speed unbelievable, tortured out of animals bred within an inch of madness, goaded to heart-bursting exertions by knives raked along their flanks; yet that speed seemed effortless, a hurtling cloud driven by a fury wind, cresting like water as the lines bounded high over the piled, obstructing bodies of soldier and Circle alike.

To the merks, the charge had a hypnotic, inexorable quality. It came on like a single being they could neither break nor stop, that had no relation to them. They themselves didn't seem the object, it had to be something beyond. The racing wave would top the hill and hurtle onward, outward forever.

Two single-file lines of riders in green rode forward from the rest; veering inward like sharp diagonals, they passed through each other in crisscross fashion, and the first arrows began to whine around Callan's men; the deadly, controlled grouping covered the whole ridge of soldiers. Then the first halves of the two files of archers turned inward, forming a staggered diamond—and loosed another flight.

The second volley ended, Callan's men started to raise their heads.

Suddenly, the diamond below opened. Two riders shot through the middle, pounding up the rise by themselves.

A bowman next to Callan set an arrow for them, grumbling, "What do *they* think they're—"

Callan grabbed him, yanked him over sideways. *"Watch out!"*

The two riders splayed to a halt even as merk bows bent at them. They raised the two captured throwers; two streams of fire shot back and forth across the nearest lines of soldiers, turning twilight briefly into day. The flame made it hard to see the thrower-carriers, but Callan kept loosing arrows. He had no line of defense now, only burning men, dozens of them, twisting like so many strips of bacon on a skillet.

"Back!" He sprang up, running swiftly but without panic, gauging by sound the nearness of the charge behind him. At the last possible moment, he dove headfirst behind a dead horse.

The main tide of coven broke over the ridge and down the other side; a hail of arrows rose from the ditches beyond; a few riders fell, but the rest came on. Many of Callan's men never made it to cover, trampled underfoot or cut down in passing. Garick's vengeful force rolled down the ridge, engulfing the ditches in a swirling mass that clanged briefly with iron on iron.

Callan's division had been effectively run over, as if by a storm wind, but they were only battered, not broken. Running to reform, the merks were dismayed to see the whole, massive body of Circle wheel suddenly, without a spoken order given, and turn to come at them a second time.

And again the soldiers shot, huddling behind horse bodies as the hurricane of coven raged over them, down the hill—only to wheel silently and come yet once more. And again there were many soldiers who never made it to cover.

Someone grabbed Callan's arm. "Field, we can't keep taking this! We got no plan, no defense, no cover. They're running us into the ground!"

"Four lines!" Callan shouted, tearing a quiver from a crumpled body at his feet. "Form four lines, thirty men each. Now!"

The merks scrambled desperately to follow orders. By fate, it was Callan's battered 39th, his hardened draggers, who formed the line with other men thrown in to fill the ranks. They knelt and waited for the wave to surge up at them once more. Callan stood, sheddy raised, until the frothed, white-eyed horses were within three bounds, then brought the blade down. "Shoot!"

At point blank, a wall of one hundred and twenty arrows slammed into the first oncoming line. A huge section of Garick's charge buckled and fell, but the rest tore on.

Yet it worked. Before the next charge, Callan knew a longer, deeper line had to be formed. The bows could stop them, but only if they were massed. He looked: many of the unhorsed riders were fighting hand to hand with the 39th. He yelled again. "Commanders, to me!"

A futile order. No one had time to obey him. He sprinted forward after the skirmishing 39th . . . and then saw the big man pushing his horse through the running merks, cutting them down like corn with his one good arm.

*"Garick!"* The sound tore out of Callan's throat. He ran at him, swinging his blade two-handed.

But Garick was coming too fast, Callan could barely dodge aside, only half-parry the blow that sliced his shoulder. And Garick was gone, taking his great wave with him.

And then, just then, Callan, on his knees, saw the red-haired woman whirl out of the skirmish on foot, surrounded by merks. She moved lightly for her size—spinning, ducking one swing to parry another, whirling in a slashing circle that took one man's arm off at the elbow. She kicked and cut her way free . . . and saw Callan.

With a wild yell, she rushed on at him, sheddy raised. With one surging lunge, Callan rose up and extended his body in a single straight thrust. The blow was clean and centered; though her eyes were still open, she must have died instantly.

Callan staggered, blood starting to flow from his shoulder. He permitted himself a tight smile. It was Red Jenna, the next best thing to killing Garick himself.

God was still with him.

Cool thought returned to Callan. He still had a fighting force, but wasn't using it right. The thing his men had to do was mount with or without saddles and break out at the weakest point to the woods.

He opened his mouth to give the order. And stopped.

It was too late. In the dusk, squinting to see the maneuver, Callan watched Garick's huge, charging mass lengthen into a serpent that slowly circled the hill just out of bowshot.

The merks would not break toward the forest. Anything else that happened would be contained within Garick's circle.

*Too dark to see them. We go again?*
*Garick says no. Hold the circle.*
*Hold the circle. Till sunup.*

Waiting in darkness, one of Callan's leads nursed an injured hand and grumbled. "Damn. We shoulda got more money for this."

It struck a few of them funny, yet there wasn't much laughter on the hill.

Long before first sun, the summer darkness lightened to a hazy, sweltering gray. Rousing himself from brief sleep, Callan felt gingerly at his bandaged shoulder. He sat up.

The closed circle was still down there, mounted, motionless, as if they hadn't stirred all night. Within it was a smaller ring of white-tabarded masters.

No move, no sound broke the early morning hush except the queasy sighs of his men waking stiffly to view the frozen tableau that surrounded them.

"Must be three thousand."

"What's the white coats for?"

"Them's masters. Dam'f they didn't dress up for us."

Callan called his commanders to him. "Report. How many fit?"

"One hundred eighty-three, sir. About a hundred wounded."

The southern division now numbered less than three hundred.

"Ran off what horses they didn't kill. Some of the 41st tried to get away last night. That's them . . . to the north."

"Orders, field?"

Callan had no ready answer. He swept his eyes across the ridge, the ruin of his force, the long waiting curve of coven.

*Oh, my Lord, I can do no more for You. Forgive my failure. See only the effort, the intent, and take the faithful to Your own enduring victory. Amen.*

"Field." It was the 41st commander. "Don't matter about orders now."

Callan spun on him: "Why not?"

"We fought. We got paid to fight, but not to die for nothing."

"For nothing?" Callan echoed, tensed as if he would strike the man. "For *nothing—?*"

"Hey, field! Four of them coming out."

"That's Garick."

The four riders paced forward out of the inner ring to halt at the foot of the ridge. Garick called: "Callan!"

The field singled out the young commander of the 44th. "Set an arrow, walk me down the hill. You leaders, every man that can pull a bow is to have one arrow ready. When I give the order, kill Garick."

He strode away. The commanders glanced at each other. ". . . what?"

"He doesn't know when he's beat," one officer said. "But *I* sure do."

Callan started to buckle the sheddy belt, then drew the blade alone and rested it on his shoulder. "Let's go, commander." There was a cold smile on his lips as he started down the hill.

Garick waited with Shalane, Jay and Bowdeen at his side; ironic that two of them should be cowans. He would have wanted Jenna with him now. The moment should have been hers, too. Strange to feel chill and old on a warm summer morning.

Forty-seven summers, the same as Bowdeen, but hence-forth he would feel the weight of them all in the stiff leg and the arm that would never hold reins again. He would count winters now.

Jay still carried the thrower; he thought they might need it. Shalane seemed thin in her tabard. Both of the young people managed to look coldly righteous. *But Bow's seen it all, and so have I. No wonder we sag a little.*

Callan stopped ten paces up the slope, the other officer a step behind him. Garick moved forward slightly. Two white butterflies chased each other across the space between them.

"Callan, we can come again if we have to, but there's no point. Surrender yourself as my prisoner and the rest of your men can walk back to Mrika."

The Kriss glanced disdainfully over all of them. "Well, Bowdeen."

"Hey, sub."

"Sold again, Bow. Good offer?"

"Best I ever got," Bowdeen answered, thinking of Jenna.

Callan pointed at Jay and spoke in Old Language. "Jacob. Jacob, who stood at the altar with Uriah. You think it is only him you've betrayed? You think it is only your own earthly people who have cast you out? You sold your *life,* Jacob, sold it for one stinking coven slut. You should have died with her."

"Yes," Jay said evenly, "that would have been a mercy. It's over, Jeremiah."

"Over?" Callan shot back at him, glancing again at Garick. "When is it ever over, Jacob? Remember whom Satan chose to torment with his own claws. Remember Judas, who dangles by his head from Satan's own mouth."

"Jerry, for Christ's love, it's *over,* it's finished!" Jay pushed the horse forward to Garick's knee. "There's nothing left to fight, you can't do any more. Jerry, why kill those men on the hill for your pride?"

"He's right," said Garick. "I don't want your life. That doesn't matter. Drop your sword and come with us."

Callan took the sheddy off his shoulder and leaned on it. "Go to hell, Garick! With Jenna!" He spun suddenly and roared to the men on the hill. *"Shoot!"*

Bowdeen's muscles bunched, ready to cover Garick. Startled, Jay raised his head to the hill, expecting the arrows. Shalane rolled out of the saddle, tensed for it.

But no arrows flew. The men on the hill did not move.

*"Shoot!"* Callan screamed. To the man next to him: *"Shoot, damn you! Kill him!"*

The commander dropped his bow. "No, sir."

Roaring, Callan shoved him aside and snatched up the weapon, scrabbled for the arrow and set it. Jay started forward, unlocking the fire nozzle.

"Jerry, you *fool—"*

Callan bent the bow.

Shalane felt Garick's will close on hers, shaping it with his own in one lethal spear of force that shot out at the Kriss as Jay pressed the trigger valve.

Callan never felt the flame.

The long, hot day was spent burying those who would be born again. Callan's men were left for the scavenger birds. When they were done, the ridge and meadow looked like a huge, plowed field.

No one paused to clean his knife. That much and more was changing.

Though they offered, Bowdeen and Jay were not allowed to assist in burying the goddess Jenna. Only Garick and Shalane stood close to the filled grave, the ring of masters about them. As always, there was little ceremony, more thought given to the living who grieved than to Jenna, who would come again.

When it was done, when Edan brought him the knife and necklace with the few, proper words, Garick turned to Shalane, who knelt before him. Around her neck he placed the iron moon-crescent: Jenna's wish caught by him before she shut her mind to save him thinking on her death. Into Shalane's hands he gave the goddess' thammay, then raised her up, leaning on his improvised cane.

"I'm—I'm very tired, but we have to move. Help me lep, master Shalane."

The order went out: *form by covens, Shando lead.*

It was a shorter, thinner column than had ridden into the place called Dannyline. Cinching his saddle, Bowdeen watched them gather along the edge of the meadow, drifting by him across the field and out of the woods, down the ridge. Some were too old to hurry, some too young to catch up with their long-striding elders, some too badly wounded to walk without help. But they could ride. The Karli girl said something about riding two weeks after she was dead. He didn't doubt it.

He knew all the maps of Uhia and City. It was eerie to think that these coveners, who didn't really know what they'd won and wouldn't know for years, were now the masters of the whole game right up to the Self-Gate. Mrika was theirs for the walking in. But Circle was thick; they knew and saw just what they wanted and no more. In their way, they'd probably just go home to raise sheep and crops and never think how things were changed forever, never see Garick's shadow lengthening over the maps they couldn't read.

Still, a man could learn a lot from coven folk. Like the way the very old and very young all went to the knife with their people, not just the able men. Few merks ever understood that. He did, now. A man could get awful big and proud thinking he was something special that other folks needed. So they didn't allow that. Dannyline,

Blue Mountains, Salvation, the Karli forest—they shared it, all of them, they *knew* what it was, and no bigmouth sonvabitch could hand them any shit later about how it was or what *he* did. They already knew.

Out of habit, he started to tuck the sheddy into his saddle straps, then stopped and just looked at it. *Who you trying to fool, Bow?* If he hadn't been good at ducking and running, he would never have come off the ridge. Not fast any more, not near fast enough. Just lucky. He didn't even throw the blade away, just let it fall at his feet.

"Bowdeen!"

He glanced over the horse's shoulder. Garick trotted across the new-turned earth of the meadow. The god's ruined arm was strapped for comfort across his chest, the stiff leg thrust out beyond the stirrup.

"Just fixing to ride, master Garick." Bowdeen scratched his head with a wry grin. " 'Cept I can't ride with the Wengens, they won't have me. Karli kind of old-fashioned, too. And them goddam thick Shando of yours don't think *no* one's good enough to ride with them."

Garick took something from his saddlebag. "Then I guess I'm all the company you can find. You want to ride alongside in case I get a headache?"

"Proud to."

"Here." Garick handed the packet to Bowdeen. "You always get paid, don't you?"

Unbelieving, Bowdeen riffled numbly through the thick sheaf of krets. "Ninety-five . . . hundred. You—you carry this much around *loose?*"

Garrick smiled. "Everything costs. I let the merks share all the money on their own dead before they left."

Bowdeen whistled, calculating. "Callan just paid them. Some them people went home rich."

"Not that rich. I charged them ten krets each to get off the hill." Garick swung the horse around toward the waiting column. "You still working for me, Bowdeen?"

That black man started to laugh. He couldn't stop. The deep, rich sound of it rolled across the meadow. "Working for you? Man, who *ain't?*"

"Then let's go."

Bowdeen hauled himself into the saddle with a grunt of effort. Too many muscles protested against it. "I am *way* too old for this. Where to?"

"Where Arin's gone," said Garrick. "To City."

*The Far Side of Sorrow*

High above the rest of the City, sitting in her pale gray robes in her pale gray office, she worked alone, always alone, and all she knew and all she had yet to learn charged her with that somber joy that may be found on the far side of sorrow. Her pale ivory complexion was delicate, and her eyes large, liquid and brown; she seemed young, and yet there was no trace of youthful uncertainty in her manner; she was composed and filled with dedication to the City's purpose.

In the morning, she was always first to greet the sun and begin work. At twilight, she was the final mourner of the day, eking out the precious seconds before darkness came. The sunset saddened her in more ways than one.

That evening, just before the rim of the sun dipped below the horizon, she pressed the 274 key to learn if there was any change in the status of the burnout investigation. While she waited for an answer, she was disturbed by thoughts of her daughter, long ago wasted and gone. The ache of something she did not care to define came frequently now at close of day; before the burnout, there had been little time for what she considered an atavism, it was inefficient.

The scanner flickered.

4647/9329.

It surprised her. In the year that she'd been asking about the progress of the investigation, she'd grown accustomed to seeing ~4647, report incomplete, almost before she'd finished entering the inquiry into the console. But now she was promised 9329: report coming.

There was no time to review it in entirety; she immediately ordered a précis readout so she could have the gist before central switching banked off power for the night.

The synergizer used to operate after dark, but a year earlier, the sudden and mysterious electrical burnout in a large section of the main energy storage unit greatly reduced available nighttime power. That which could still be returned had to be allocated to crucial needs, such as the hospitals and the Self-Gate. All data scanners were reluctantly shut down after dusk until such time as the crippled facility could be restored to full service.

It would take awhile to put it back into operation, she could only spare three engineers for the huge repair and replacement task, and one of them was independently responsible for investigating the cause of the burnout; it was his report that the scanner finally was promising.

It was quite possible, she knew, that he'd been unable to trace the malfunction back to the source, for many of the potentially suspect components—faulty terminals or weak connectors or stripped insulation—had been incinerated or melted in the catastrophe. So her abstract of the final report might consist of a single symbol: ~.

The relays clicked and hummed. She stared at the scanner.

6427/90: 5417.

This was news. The burnout was not the result of defective equipment, it was triggered by a power overload. She punched 917, impatient for once at the machine's lack of initiative. It had the capacity to evaluate and create new meanings from existing data, but only if directed to do so. At the moment, it meant wasting her dwindling time. Her order to collate sent it off to check all circuits operating at the time of the overload. She had to know the source of the excessive demand; it was disturbing. City power requirements were extremely stable.

Collation took a little longer than other operations. She tried to cast her mind onto some other problem, but all she could think of was her child. She wished she might see her once more, hear her speak, but to order up a holograph or a voice-print would be absurd and irrational, it would serve no purpose. She did not act upon her impulse.

The relay clattered. Gratefully, she turned her attention to it.

5417/040: 015/97.

The final symbol startled her. But before she could even begin to think about ordering up a full report, the power died. She rested her hand on the useless buttons, fighting a preposterous desire to pound vehemently on them. Centuries had not quite stilled the frustration of not being totally in control of the City she controlled.

She stared at the dulled scanner screen, musing over its last bit of information. She would not know more until morning.

Rising, she left the office and stepped along the quiet passageway to her suite. Inside, she entered a library where there were so many books to read, so many she'd forgotten, so many remembered, so *many* yet to be digested. Walking along the rows and rows of shelves, she sought some tangent of thought to divert her troubled mind.

Something caught her eye. She stopped

She plucked down an incredibly ancient volume, mouldering, brittle, but still readable. The gloomy poetry of a dying age. It had been one of her daughter's favorite books. She opened it and discovered that it had a tendency to break at a certain page. On it, there was a passage neatly underlined in marking more than a hundred years old.

*Thinks't thou existence doth depend on time?*
*It doth; but actions are our epochs; mine*
*Have made my days and nights imperishable,*
*Endless, and all alike, as sands on the shore,*
*Innumerable atoms; and one desert,*
*Barren and cold, on which the wild waves break,*
*But nothing rests, save carcasses and wrecks,*
*Rocks, and the salt-surf weeds of bitterness.*

She closed the book and closed her eyes. "Judith," she whispered, "Judith."

At dawn she rose, dressed in clean robes and hurried to her office. She liked mornings better. She sat, punched up the 274 key and watched the scanner light up. Quickly, she entered her instructions: 210—6427/4647. She had to know what made the Self-Gate call for such a colossal supercharge that the backup turned half the solar energy storage unit into fused slag.

The console hummed. Flickering, the screen informed her the analysis of the burnout would be in three stages:

I. 015/97—64/5491+++.

The first thing that happened was a sudden demand by the Self-Gate for an excessive amount of energy.

II. 015/97=**6447.˙.—04970~.

The synergizer responded by immediately weighing power priorities. The Self-Gate was at the top of the list, second only to the hospitals. An emergency decision was made: drain energy from all nonessential circuits.

III. 5417=7284+++!!!
?v?
248/0748=~771.46461.∴.09450: 248/0748.

The energy drain taxed systems not meant for such a heavy load. It quickly became certain to the synergizer that considerable danger and damage might occur on a widespread basis unless some deliberate sacrifice were made almost immediately. It calculated that the energy storage unit would not be totally destroyed, and even the part ruined might be rebuilt in time. Therefore, it ordered the burnout to take place there.

Clearing the screen, the woman began the second part of her probe: why the Self-Gate made such an unprecedented demand in the first place. The collation was already done, so she called for a report.

51v640? the synergizer asked.

She punched 640. The précis she received was one of the shortest and most puzzling ever produced by the synergizer: 231.

She frowned. The Self-Gate could cope with anyone foolish enough to attempt to enter the City. What did the synergizer mean by an *anomaly?*

Pressing the 51 key, she waited for a full report.

He left his horse with Korbin. The trader bid Arin good-by, and the young Shando started the last mile on foot. Several times he thought about turning back to wait for Garick in Lorl, but every step brought him that much closer to the zone.

He'd covered most of the distance when he rounded a curve and saw a stout beam positioned across the path.

The merk in front of the barrier was a tall, gaunt, far-north Wengen. He made no effort to stand up straight when he saw the big red-haired stranger.

"Turn around," the merk yawned with a bored, falling tone. "Go back."

"Since when," he asked, walking up to the wood beam, "does City need *two* gates?"

*"Dunesk,"* the soldier shrugged. "New orders."

"And you're here to turn people back before they get to the Self-Gate?"

The other nodded, still leaning casually against the log barrier.

Without further conversation, he turned around and walked off. When he was hidden by the curve of the path, he took out the cap and belt from the sack, threw the carry-bag into the bushes and donned the instruments. Helmet adjusted, he snapped on the force field and continued his journey uninterrupted.

And then he was there.

The drowsy afternoon softened toward dusk. Bees droned homeward. The grass swayed in a breeze tipped with the cooler breath of evening. Wildflowers bordered open fields that stretched to the distant horizon.

Not a gate anywhere. Not even a fence.

But it was impossible to overlook the huge sign in both Mrikan and Old Language:

SELF-GATE
City begins here. Go back.
DANGER!

He regarded it for a long time.

Then he plunged on past the warning marker.

It was rare that she did not know how to proceed, rarer still to request direct audio-visual communication with another member of City. But the Self-Gate had been running the same way so long, she'd lost touch with the intricacies of the original concept and rather than spend too much time with the synergizer, rooting out data bits and pieces at a time, she punched up 64021: 4271/0294.

The man who was once her cohabitor appeared on the screen. It had been years since they'd seen one another, but he was the same as she remembered. His sandy hair was no thinner above his forehead, no fuller, either. His pale gray eyes shone serenely, joylessly.

He was doubtless surprised at the contact but, in characteristic City fashion, did not expend precious seconds on an emotion that led nowhere. He raised his eyebrows, signaling *question.*

She reviewed the problem of the anomaly at the Self-Gate and explained that though she'd appointed a border guard to stand watch over the zone, she needed referents toward a more satisfactory and permanent solution.

He nodded, punched a call into the synergizer, cross-switched it to her scanner, then cut off the connection.

They did not say good-by.

She depressed the key signaling start and the report began.

015/97 . . . 51/074.

Her lips compressed briefly with the ghost of an old emotion. Typical of Randall's thoroughness, but she should have made it clear she did *not* want an encyclopedic reply, she could have done the same thing without his help.

Sighing, she skimmed the material. Early history. Definition. How the Self-Gate got its name. Differing attitudes: City magic vs. empirical tool. Theory of operation—

64821/7(8)4 . . . Yes! She slowed the input and read, for the first time in centuries, the structural premise of the Self-Gate, key to the anomaly that caused the overload.

I. 7(8)70=197407=93910.

Thoughts are reducible to intricate electrical reactions within the brain and are, in turn, expressible in terms of complex chemical codes.

II. $197407.93910/97=67420^x$.

$(\sim 197407.93910/67420^x)$?

There are a finite number of chemical-electrical brain patterns based on psychological definition of character. City scientists codified and dissected them, postulating that there must be, for each, a negative chemical-electrical field.

(90361 . . .

$$\frac{329/76405}{\text{V-XII}}///\sim\frac{329/76405}{\text{V-XII}}$$

. . . ?)

For example, the synergizer explained, what would happen if a particular subtype of manic-depressive brain wave was subjected to its own matching negative set?

The answer was simple.

~.

Totally.

That was how the Self-Gate worked.

She dimly remembered an occasion when Judith, in her infancy, argued with her parents about the Gate. She was so young they had to converse in the wearyingly slow Old Language; Judith had not yet mastered the City's verbal shorthand.

"The Self-Gate," Judith complained, "is just a tool to you for keeping people out. But *how* does it stop them?"

Randall calmly tried to explain the mechanics, but the girl impatiently tossed her head.

"Yes, yes, I know all that! But have any of you thought about what it must be like to have your brain shredded?"

The question took them into a difficult problem of ethics, but it all happened so long before that it was hard to recall exactly what was said. Didn't Judith finally—

She cut off the thought, disturbed at her growing tendency to muse about Judith as each day drew to a close. It was becoming a definite antiproductive pattern, one that might eventually require corrective processing. This time, she'd wasted nearly a minute.

She went back to the original problem, ordering a precise analysis of the brain pattern that the synergizer labeled "anomaly."

The answer was upsetting.

$$\longrightarrow \frac{6427}{\text{I-II}} \longleftrightarrow 6481/9362077.$$

$\frac{6427}{\text{I-II}}$ was a classic paranoid pattern, complicated in this instance by partial compensation. In other words, the person who ran the Gate and caused the burnout—the anomaly—was a paranoid who had learned how to deal with his fixation to some extent.

It was too near dusk to call up detailed power statistics, but she could easily see such a pattern would demand a great energy input to negate it. Difficult, yes, but foreseen.

It was the $\longrightarrow$ that astonished her. She rephrased the call, but got the identical reply. So this was the final, unbelievable piece of the enigma, she thought. The anomaly was a *new* pattern! It only roughly approximated $\frac{6427}{\text{I-II}}$! When it triggered the Self-Gate, the system only had two alternatives: improvise across circuits till it found the most comparable negative set, or commit electronic suicide by failing to carry out the function it was intended to perform.

In the end, it did a bit of both.

At least the lesson of the anomaly made her warier about trusting the Self-Gate entirely to a machine any more—even one as sophisticated as the synergizer. Its circuits were now imprinted with a directive to notify her immediately of any further unusual invasion of the zone.

But what if it *did* happen again? The anomaly had been turned back, probably was dead, but there might be another, evolved over the ages. Or worse, if the original survived, it was now bolstered by a new awareness which inevitably had to alter the original to something yet more remote.

As she was considering the ramifications of her line of thought, suddenly the emergency buzzer sounded. She started; it was the first time the silence of her chambers had been so disturbed since the burnout.

She watched the scanner begin to flash the same message again and again and again.

7284: 015/97!!! 7284: 015/97!!! 7284: 015/97!!!
7284: 015/97!!! 7284: 015/97!!! 7284: 015/97!!!
7284: 015/97!!! 7284: 015/97!!! 7284: 015/97!!!

Acknowledging receipt, she asked the nature of the danger at the Self-Gate. She got the precise answer she both expected and feared.

231. Anomaly.

And then the power died.

Garick's column moved slowly toward Lorl. They rode easy, for the sake of the wounded. There was no hurry now.

Garick rode half a mile behind the point with Edan and the remaining Shando masters. By tacit agreement, no one bothered the god more than necessary.

Close behind, Shalane rode with her father, the two of them flanked by Jay and Bowdeen. Moss and his daughter shared silently a private grief they would not lessen with words.

Daylight was gone. Only the muffled, grinding clatter of hoofs broke the silence.

Sharing with Shalane, suddenly Moss grew chill with the too familiar fear, the bleak sense of isolation. His nostrils flared with the phantom sense of remembered rain. Then he heard the hiss of intaken breath; next to him, Shalane went rigid in the saddle. Her mind snapped free of his like a broken branch. Her eyes unfocused, stared into infinity.

*"Get out! Get away!"*

"Lane?" Moss reached for her hand. Jay turned at the sound of her voice.

*"Let it go! Or be crushed by it!"*

"What is it?" Jay worried.

Moss grabbed her bridle and led the stallion out of the column to the roadside. The old Kriss distrust of magic flared briefly in Jay, died. He and Bowdeen followed Moss off the road.

They lifted her down from the horse, unprotesting but still rigid, helped her lay on the grass.

*"All of them."* Her voice came, harsh and strangled. *"For this? Liar! Thief! Give them back!"*

As they watched helplessly, Shalane curled up, face to the grass, whimpering. Some of the sounds she made were words, hard to piece out from the guttural agony. Moss began to sweat; the old, dull pain throbbed behind his eyes, the rain smell suffocating him. He knew instinctively what it was.

"She's with Arin."

"Maybe Garick should know," Bowdeen said, but Moss stopped him with a hand on his arm.

"Garick can't help this. It'll pass. She's close to Arin, been with him all along, has to feel this."

*"Irrelevant!"* Shalane snarled. *"Not there. Not again."*

"It's tearing her apart," Jay whispered.

Moss looked up at him, not without kindness. "Don't try to know it, Jay. She's with him. Good as you are, cowan can't ever know *with.*"

*And you don't know the Self-Gate,* Bowdeen thought. *Because that's where Arin is, the only place he could be, getting killed like all the others who try the zone.*

Abruptly as it began, the convulsion ended. Shalane lay quiet, staring up at nothing. Her lips moved in a whisper: *"I remember you, wolf."*

Jay shook his head, still bewildered by it all. "Arin? How can you be *sure?*"

The answer came from Shalane's lips.

*"I am Arin. And I am alone."*

There was no choice. She punched in new commands on her emergency circuit to return full power to the synergizer, twilight or not.

The scanner warned her of power shortages it would create. She acknowledged the danger, but still insisted. Information was vital, the need immediate.

The ready bulb lit. Pressing 274, she ordered a profile of the anomaly pattern in the Self-Gate zone. Meanwhile, her mind raced, trying to think of a safe way to cope with another approximate $\frac{6427}{\text{I-II}}$.

But just then, the scanner flickered.

$$231/6451: \longrightarrow \frac{9362077 \longleftrightarrow \frac{6427}{\text{I-II}} \cdot \frac{09707}{\text{IV-X}} \longleftrightarrow 9362077}{\sim}.$$

She stared at the answer for a full fifteen seconds, an unheard-of time for any City person to spend digesting a single piece of synergizer data.

*The thing is impossible!* Her mind rejected it. She ordered a check of the reply, but the identical answer came. Then she asked the synergizer to analyze and collate the pattern thoroughly.

The answer was $\sim$.

Irrationally, her mind sought a haven in thoughts of her daughter, but she could not allow it, no matter how desperately she wanted to escape the incredible thing. At least she knew one fact: the anomaly, unchecked, could cause a power crisis immensely more dangerous than the previous burnout.

The thing had to be stopped, but she could only see one way left to do it, an unthinkable way. Yet she entered her idea into the synergizer—and discovered, to her dismay, that it agreed with the plan.

In a clearing in front of the small barracks, old Poke sat on a stump, drowsing over the last scraps of his supper. He dabbled pudgy pink fingers in the bowl for one final blob of meat. He yawned.

Zone duty was never very interesting. Once in a long while, the buzzer sounded and they put on protective helmets and went in to cart out some fool who'd picked the Self-Gate as a way to die. Once they'd even found a young runt kicking and moaning, yet alive, but that was the only time. Otherwise nothing much happened to break up the monotony except a card game for buttons or payday stakes. At least border guards still *got* paid.

Poke belched, set down the bowl, wiped his plump hands on a

clump of grass. He would have liked a game now, but Ab was away at the new barrier and the only one inside was the boy, Rigg, a real cocky pain in the ass. Probably polishing his goddam sheddy for the fourth time that week—like he knew how to use it.

Poke sighed. They often sent him and Ab the rawest, sassiest, dumbest recruits, to beat some soldiering into their thick heads. Rigg was typical: hated to be ordered, surely itching for the day he'd have some authority himself. He was never insolent to Ab, who'd give him a bloody nose for his badmouth, but the boy showed little respect for Poke. Well, Poke didn't care. His time was almost up, soon he'd leave service, buy a little tavern in Lorl or Towzen. Poke wasn't all that thrifty, but there just wasn't much for a border guard to spend his salary on. Over the years, Ab probably supported one or two crib girls, but the only thing Poke really cared about any more was staying dry and full.

The barracks door banged open. Rigg rushed out, buckling on his sheddy.

"Haul it, Poke!' he yelled. "Got to ride in."

"Easy, boy," the other wheezed. "Anything's in the zone, it'll wait. Don't have to kill ourselves just to lug out another hunk of meat."

Rigg shook his head impatiently. "This is different. The alarm rang. I—"

"Not the alarm, asshole, you mean the buzzer. Alarm don't ring."

"It *rang*, Poke. The alarm rang! I picked up, got direct voice from City. Somebody's running the Gate—and beating it."

"Sure, boy, sure." Poke thumbnailed between his teeth to prize out a shred of meat. "They do that every other week." The scrap came free, he flicked it away, stooped with difficulty to pick up his bowl. He'd underestimated Rigg, didn't think the boy had enough imagination for such a joke. He was good at it, though, jiggling with excitement.

"Dammit, it's true! We all have to go in, get the bastard out."

"*All* of us, Rigg?" The boy knew better than to joke with Ab.

"I said all."

Poke waited for the telltale smirk that would prove it *was* a joke, but it didn't come. "All right," Poke said ominously, "we ride. But if you're fooling, Ab'll fix you. Be walking around with a bone where your butt used to be. Go get his horse."

Poke began lumbering toward the barracks to fetch the helmets.

When the signal flashed green, it meant City reduced power on the Self-Gate enough so they could ride partway in, protected by the headgear, till they found the—

"Don't need the helmets," Rigg called after him.

Poke did an about-face faster than the recruit thought possible. "Damn you!" he roared, "it's not funny any more!"

"Serious, Poke . . . City said don't bother."

"And I suppose," Poke replied with heavy sarcasm, "they're going to turn off their goddam Gate special for us?"

For the first time, Rigg looked really worried. He lowered his voice. "Poke, they already have."

Ab figured Rigg was having a game with them, but he mounted without a word. He never had much to say. When they reached the warning marker, he reined up and motioned Rigg to go ahead.

"Go on, you took the call," he ordered. "Me and Poke'll wait a bit."

"Why me?" Rigg wondered.

"Look at it like this," Poke drawled. "You just volunteered."

Exasperated, Rigg urged his horse past the marker. Ten feet, twenty, fifty. Then, swiveling in the saddle, he waved the others to catch up.

"Goddam," Ab murmured. "It *is* shut off."

Poke nodded. "And fuzz-face up there still thinks he's zone commander. Let's go."

They started off. When they topped the nearest rise, the boy saw the far-off houses for the first time. He hauled on the reins, stopped, sat there, mouth open. The day was a long one, and the graying shafts of light painted the City black and huge against the far horizon. His head turned, trying but unable to see to the end; it just went on and on and on. Rigg tried to say something, but whatever it was faltered to dumb silence.

"Yeah," said Ab. "We know."

They ranged out, searching closer to the edge of the City than Ab or Poke had ever ridden before, but they found no one. Finally it was too dark. Poke had to ride to the furthest talk-post and report their failure. He listened, said something as if he was arguing, then returned the device to its cradle and waddled back to Ab.

"Them sonsabitches," he panted. "They're giving us five minutes to get out before they turn on the Gate again. I begged for more time, but—"

"Tell us later!" Ab barked. "We're using our five. Come on!"

With great strain, Poke threw his leg over the horse, succeeding on the third try. Yanking the animal's nose around, Poke kicked its flanks into a lurching run. He dashed back after Ab along the route they came.

They got all the way to the final rise before they discovered Rigg wasn't following.

Poke peered back into the gloom. He tried to swear, but it just wouldn't come. "We should have figured."

Ab nodded. "City fever."

Poke agreed. First sight of City could do funny things to a new recruit's mind, it was hard enough to take even after seeing it time and again. They should have been watching Rigg, only they were both too scared of getting caught in the zone without helmets.

"The helmets," Poke whispered, exchanging a bleak glance with Ab. No matter what City told Rigg—if they'd only brought them, maybe they could still reach him in time before he got so far in even helmets wouldn't help.

"The helmets, yes," Ab grimly echoed. "Better get them. We're going to have one piece of meat to haul out, anyway." Lashing his horse, he started for safety, calling over his shoulder to Poke, "Come on! I don't want to *hear* him!"

They had to use lanterns to search for Rigg's body. While they cut into the dark with the powerful sun-batteried beams, helmets strapped securely to their heads, Poke asked Ab whether he'd seen anyone try to jump the barrier.

"Just one big, red-haired mofo. Deepwoods. Went home again."

Poke had his doubts. They were much increased when they found Rigg, body pierced through with the long Shando shaft.

He glanced uneasily about. "Where could he hide? *Where?*"

Lacking an answer, Ab just shrugged. He *did* know the Self-Gate and realized, at least, that the mysterious trespasser was merciful. Compared to the Gate, an arrow was not a cruel death.

At the far side of the Gate, he fell exhausted. He knew he'd made it, he was through. There was another marker indicating the end of the danger zone. He exulted: *I made it! Me!* But it was too dark to see the City, and he had no energy left. He flopped down under a bush and let sleep wash over him.

Bird songs wakened him just before light. The sky was gray and he could see faint shapes that were the City stretching out right and left, filling almost his entire angle of vision. It was like Lishin, but incredibly bigger, there was no end to it! Houses and houses and houses brightening in the coming dawn: stone, glass, red clay molded into brick. Walkways, flat, hard and gray, poured in blocks the way he'd heard about, and some of the squares glittered with flecks of shiny material that came alive in the early beams of sun. Spires higher than Lishin, and one of them bore on its side a great round thing with Old Language numbers and big arrows pointing in two places. As he watched, a deep, majestic sound came from it or someplace near it, a rolling music like the voice of a vast animal, king of silent forests.

The music ended, the stillness returned. The City stunned him, beckoned to come walk the empty streets and stare into the windows. *Come,* the City seemed to whisper in invitation. *See me, love the things I hold, the beautiful things that belong to nobody but me.*

His eyes drank in the vast distance as he walked. The Girdle was still switched on, but there was nobody to see him. The streets were as deserted and hushed as if the City had waited empty down all the centuries for this one pair of feet to tread its pavements, and he walked and caressed the glass of a large window, felt the texture of a metal doorknob, stared without name or knowledge at the paused profusion of things untouched for dusty years.

But it was not like Lishin, it was not dead. The silence was an unclosed bracket in time. The City *continued,* though he could not track its essence yet.

And still he walked down wide avenues, stepping over deep ruts in the sidewalk where the indomitable grass pushed up and broke the great blocks into puzzle-jogs. The great arc of the City swam before his eyes, no longer shading on an old map but five hundred endless miles of seeking. *Where do I start? Which way do I go?* At first he thought there would be people fanned out to find him, but then realized they would all be indoors, afraid to expose themselves to the threat of a contaminated outsider. *Then how do I find them? How do I learn who's in charge?*

His aimless, fascinated wandering took him north. The houses grew fewer, smaller and prettier, many made with white-stained wood arranged in overlapping slats, a method unknown to the covens.

Great age was a perceptible patina on all buildings. Weeds and trees. More grass sticking up between paving cracks, tumbling the great concrete blocks in a single bursting gesture sunward.

It was here he came upon the odd road.

It was neither eroded by time nor warped from beneath. It glinted peculiarly, but was not made of metal, polished wood or stone. The nearest thing it resembled was the pouch containing MacCauley's diary that Webb found in the swamp.

The road was wide, so wide that fifteen men might stand side by side with arms spread out and touching. As he approached, he saw the roadbed was not a single, unbroken surface but many adjacent strips laid next to one another.

He stepped on the nearest one. There was a grumbling, whirring sound. He glanced about, startled. The trees began to glide slowly past. The entire road had sprung to life, moving north, the strip he was on proceeding at a crawl, the one to its left running a bit faster, the next accelerating about a third more, and so on till the final ribbon speeding along at a dizzying clip.

He conquered his initial panic. The slow strip did not change speed. It was obviously designed for safe entry onto the road, and acceleration or deceleration could be accomplished simply by stepping from one strip to another.

Since he had no real idea of where to go, he decided he could do worse than stay on the road, reasoning that it would not be kept in operation if it did not lead someplace possibly vital.

Deliberately, he began crossing the highway to reach the fastest strip north.

349(8)20! 07/2740! . . .

She repeated the emergency notice of the night before, informing the entire City: EMERGENCY. STAY INDOORS. ANOMALY UNCHECKED. POSSIBLE CONTAMINATION.

. . . 07/2740! 231/2897! 6061/9273282!

The anomaly was *past* the Self-Gate, somewhere in the City since the previous evening: the first time anyone ever crossed the impregnable barrier! Her mind was too flexible to dash against the rocks of impossibility for very long: it happened and she had to accept the fact. Eventually she would analyze with the synergizer the exact way in which the age-old system broke down, but for now she was reduced to a policy of expediency: find the interloper, prevent the spread of some virulent bacteria to her long-insulated people.

Again she sent out the warning. SELF-GATE BREACHED! STAY INDOORS!

Calls had been lighting up for hours along the scanner banks, the first one very likely from Randall. But she was prepared, had set all incoming queries the same automatic answer REFER TO FILE 6427. Let them follow the same series of steps and deductions she pursued, she had no time to instruct them all personally.

As she waited for an update on the anomaly's position, she was haunted by an irrational thought: Judith has somehow invaded the City's solitude. Foolish to consider, she was dead by now, had to be. The Self-Gate read her decades earlier, detected the incipient biological breakdown and rejected her. Yet who but her daughter could be intelligent enough—and stubborn enough—to dare the Gate and *succeed?*

The buzzer sounded. More information. She watched the scanner. Every circuit was locked in, all data that could be channeled to her was on tap so the synergizer could inform her of the progress and intent of the anomaly.

231: 3529/47.

At last!

She punched in a demand for exact positional data and got an immediate answer.

3529/247(8)/7——

The anomaly was some forty miles below the old Pennsylvania line, heading north at a speed close to one hundred miles an hour.

She calculated, derived an estimate and knew what to do. If. She instructed the synergizer, then sat back and waited for the clock to catch up with her racing mind.

If only the seldom-used circuits still worked.

The City flowed and ebbed about him like a mighty river, now narrow and rapid between high banks, now broad and vast. Once he saw more lofty buildings, so far away the mist shrouded their tops, but if he reckoned the distance accurately they were even bigger than any he'd already seen. And then great rockfaces loomed up and cut them off from view and all he saw were straggling tiny dwellings enfolded by the thick tangle of centuries-old ivy. These latter houses were too small to be remarkable, except they looked so sturdy and they went on and *on,* and how could the City never end?

The early morning sun was bright and hot as he sat on the road surface, his stomach turning a little from the speed but more from hunger. There would be a time when he would eat; for now, he was content to watch the marvels of a land no covener ever saw before.

The road ran mostly arrow-straight, curving gently only now and then, weaving a slender thread through old hills and bare cliffs. Sometimes he spied a broad band of water east, and at times it was close, but mostly it stayed several bowshots distant. To his left, a creek broke out of the undergrowth and established itself, narrow, swift-running, clear. In the western distance where the road did not run, he saw a high bridge spanning the far reaches of the creek. It was not wide compared to the one in Lishin, but its height compensated. His neck muscles protested the painful angle at which he tilted his head to see the span.

Suddenly the road swept past the last cling of tangle-choked rockface, and there was the river, close below, broad and gentle-flowing in the same direction as the highway. The road traced its edges where small houses clustered at waterside. The broad sheet sparkled in the sunlight.

He rounded a curve, looked up. His mouth opened. On a great prominence not far away there was a building like none he had ever seen before. Immense and square, it was fronted and supported by huge white columns, fluted and scrolled; some were broken and lay chipped on their sides but most stood straight, supporting an enormous triangle that workers once shaped for a roof.

His mind reeled from the meaningless size. *Why?* What was that big they had to make the house so large to fit it inside?

Yet there were more such places to come, of varying shapes and patterns, but all colossal in scale: more great squares, oblongs with rounded edges, great, slant walls of gleaming glass, slim needles thrust straight and deep into the sky. Finally, he had to cover his eyes, surfeited with the scope of the City.

And when he looked once more, the buildings were gone, and there was grass and there were trees again, and the modest houses he'd grown used to.

Still the road rushed north.

After a time, he thought the roadstrip to his right was speeding up, but then, noticing it still in phase with the other bands, realized his own strip was slowing down. Jumping up, he leaped onto the faster ribbon before the difference grew too great to make the crossing. But as soon as he did, his new foothold also began to lose momentum.

He hurried to the next right-hand section. As soon as his feet touched, it, too, decelerated. His initial impression that he'd unwittingly done something to cause the slowdown gave way to the far more likely thought that someone in the City was deliberately manipulating him off the road.

He had no choice but to do as prompted. All segments on the left slowed and finally stopped, so he found himself at last on the first snail's-pace strip he'd originally stepped on. It crept around a brake of walnut and then, like the rest, ground to silence. In front of him stood a tall wooden pole, a crosspiece at its top something like the god sign of the Kriss. A strange device was affixed to the apex of the artificial tree: a gray molded horn big enough for a giant's fist; its sides coned outward to a lip which rolled gently back on itself. The horn crackled, and she spoke:

"If you've business in the City, follow the road till it stops again. Then I'll direct you further."

The sound was soft, yet held a faintly chiding edge that disturbed him.

The road started up once more.

He almost lost control during the final part of his journey.

The road slowed again very soon, stopped on a high ridge not far from a turbid river weaving along nearby. It was far different from the one that swept by the white-columned giant house; though it did not stink like the one at Lishin, it had its share of rotting flotsam.

When he got off, her voice sounded a second time, as she promised it would. She told him where to walk, and he obeyed, taking an ordinary footpath branching away from the moving road. He came to a place where the cliff above fell away and there he saw the heart of the City in one breathstopping instant.

The wonders he'd seen that morning, the gleaming silent streets, the dazzling windows opening on remnants of past wants and needs, the colonnaded façades and spires shouting upward in frozen defiance, all were only prologue to the ultimate spectacle, the glory and sorrow that was the supreme essence of the City.

The island lay on the far side of a majestic harbor. Thousands upon thousands of buildings cramped and shoved for what space there was, and even the least impressive stunned him while the biggest . . .

*No!* the worm that tried to tutor him clamored. *There's no reason to go on, it's too big. We're too small and insignificant.*

That was true; nevertheless, he set his feet resolutely upon the road that spiraled down and led past the shattered arches into the gaping dark tunnel which she told him to enter.

*Why trust her?*

Because there's no other way. The river's too fast, wide and deep and there are no boats. There's only the tunnel left. It goes straight across, beneath the river.

In the tunnel, his footsteps echoed and reverberated loudly. A few feet in, a stairway rose to a narrow path built into the tunnel wall. Clutching the grimy metal guide rail, he started forward.

*The dark. We remember the dark, Kon and I. We knew the rats and the wolves that laughed at the death of meaning. What if she lets the river run in?*

If she does, there's an end to everything. It's not important.

Step by step, he made his way in the dark, and there *were* creatures squealing and slithering below in the dirt; he shuddered, thinking of the closet in Lishin. Then his outstretched hand encountered a projection that cut off progress. He felt cautiously—it was a boxlike structure opening into the narrow path. He could not avoid going into it. The closet-smell choked his memory, but he forced himself through and was out of it in less than a second. He wondered what it was.

There were several more boxes along the way. In one, much further along, his hand brushed a small wall switch . . .

The sudden flood of light made him blink. The open box was just an empty rectangle of steel and glass, but a globe in its ceiling shone brighter and steadier than a dozen candles. The light did not spill far out into the tunnel, but he saw enough to be glad he was on the higher path, it was freer of filth. The light reflected red in the eyes of rats scurrying back into the gloom.

He let the light burn and walked on, though soon he found himself in darkness again. The air was close and pungent with the odor of animal droppings. Further along, he found another light, turned it on and continued walking. Another . . .

The huge letters on the far wall sprang out in the new glare. Faint, too faint to read completely, but impressive in their magnitude. Old Language.

The walk seemed interminable, but finally he perceived a distant round of sunlight and knew he was approaching the further opening of the tunnel. He hurried his pace. By the last hundred yards, he was running.

The afternoon glare blinded him. As he emerged from the tunnel, he wiped his eyes free of tears and looked up, grateful to return to the sweet, strong light of day.

And there was the City. Massive hulks of steel, brick, stone and glass staring down impassively at the insect who called himself a man. Roadways curving far above his head. Signs bigger than a whole room of Garick's house in new symbols and abbreviations he could not read.

*A bug,* the worm said sadly.

And then she spoke again.

"I can't see you, but know you're there. The sensors picked you up when you passed. Can you hear me?"

"Yes!" he spun around, confused at the sound of her voice coming from too many directions at once, like audible lep.

"Will you meet with me?"

"Yes." His own voice sounded pitifully thin to his ears.

"Follow this route," she said. He listened carefully, memorizing the turns he must take. It was no great distance, ten minutes walk south, perhaps fifteen minutes further to the east.

"You'll see a building. You won't mistake it."

It took longer than either anticipated, though he set out at once. The hush of empty avenues, the crumbling blocks that once were shops weighted him down. He knew the City was cut off from the world, but its own utter isolation he had not anticipated.

He proceeded south as she instructed, intensely curious, yet much depressed by what he saw. He reached the turning place. Entering the wide cross thoroughfare, he faced east—

—and stopped.

The building, she said, was unmistakable.

It was.

Before it, he sank down, knees crumpling, resting on the naked sidewalk in the attitude of a praying Kriss. Up and up and up he gaped at the tower whose top could not be seen, shrouded from his gaze by summer clouds.

*Shake your fist at it,* the worm mocked. *Bring it down.*

A long time passed. He stared at it and thought.

When his voice came back, it was not the worm's. He spoke with the bleak self-knowledge that carried him past Holder, past the Gate, past Lishin and Salvation and the vengeance that was Callan's.

"Bring it down?" he murmured. "If I have to . . . yes."

Alone.

He walked along the street and came to the massive door. He entered, footsteps tolling in the vaulting emptiness. He found the small room where she said to look. He hesitated only a moment before entering.

Neatly printed in Old Language, the message on the wall instructed him to press a certain three-digit button set in a long panel on the side of the room. He did so.

A portion of the wall slammed shut. *Trapped!* He dashed forward, pounded at the barrier, could not make it budge. He was sealed in the small closet. The floor shook and trembled. Before he could decide what to do about his predicament, the motion stopped and the door hissed open. He lost no time stepping out.

The room was narrow and the gray curtains on either side were drawn shut. The walls were gray, the ceiling was gray and all was illuminated by a gray light reminiscent of the tunnel's globe, but duller.

At the far end, he saw a door and a window next to it. She waited behind the glass.

He stared at her, forgetting to breathe. Once, just before the test of power he won over his brother, her face and form appeared to him, but that was only an image while this woman was vividly real.

He advanced, still shocked, but keeping himself firmly under control. His fingers sought the toggle of the Girdle, snapped it off. He plucked the helmet from his head. His sudden appearance must have surprised her, but her calm features retained their composure as she catalogued every detail of him in her memory, from his great height and reddish hair to the peculiar set of one poorly mended arm.

When she spoke, her voice harbored neither rancor nor challenge, merely a gentle curiosity. "Why did you run the Gate and enter the City?"

"I promised someone I would."

"Promised whom?"

"Someone who resembled you very much."

Though her eyes widened, the announcement did not much surprise her. "Who *are* you?"

Raising his head with grim pride, he said, "I am Singer, son of Judith Randall Singer, late of the Department of History, subsection on technology." He twisted Arin's lips in sardonic amusement. "Guess you'd better decontaminate me before we have a long, long talk . . ."

By the time Garick's force made camp on the outskirts of Lorl, the streets were empty. Even the crib girls locked up. The moneymen knew by virtue of Spitt and innate shrewdness that Garick meant no harm to anyone who didn't oppose him crossing the border, but the ordinary folk were terrified. They saw only that the northern merks were sitting unconcerned in Filsberg while the invincible southern force had been crushed out of existence.

Business was bad in Lorl. Everyone was staying home, afraid to get in Garick's way. Korbin's was empty. Philosophically, he opened a jug of his own sida (Shando, last autumn's hoarded best) and waited for the conqueror. Two glasses later, he heard the clop-clop of several horses break the silence beyond his fly-buzzing porch. The horses drew up; his half-open door swung wider. He saw the tall man in tabard and skins, one useless arm wrapped tight across his chest.

Korbin did not alter his posture, paunch resting against the bar. But he languidly raised one hand in the air. "I surrender. You want a drink?"

Garick moved to the counter. Korbin noted the old silent ease of movement, but also saw the gray in the Shando's beard, sensed the sorrow that helped put it there. He avoided staring at the arm, pouring a stiff one. They both drank.

"Jenna?" Korbin asked delicately.

A slight, weary shaking of the head. Garick emptied the glass and filled it again.

"Your crop coming in this year?"

The tall man rubbed wearily at his eyes; the deepening lines were filled with grit and dust. "It'll be in."

Circle folk didn't talk much about their dead; still, there was Garick in front of him, the richest man within a month's travel and still the saddest, sorriest, used-up thing Korbin had ever seen. "I'm sorry about the goddess. Saw her once. A *proud* woman."

"Yes. There's a lot of people outside Lorl. Need food and grain for the horses."

Korbin gestured to his denuded shelves. "Ain't much come in. You people were all off fighting."

"Can you get it?"

The trader spread his hands. "Gonna cost. What there is comes high."

Garick dropped three hundred krets on the counter. "Buy it, take your commission. If you need money, see me. I'll need Spitt, too."

Korbin counted the money tidily. "You got it."

"Where's Arin?"

"Been and gone. Left his horse in the stable, though."

"He's on foot? Which way'd he go?"

"Took the east road."

"Toward City?"

Korbin nodded; his double chins trembled.

Then Jenna was right, Garick reflected bitterly. Arin, too. All gone. While Singer did nothing, Arin hurled himself through the Self-Gate to prove his love for his father. And now there was no Girdle to put on Singer, and the old debt to Judith remained uncanceled and—

"That oldest boy of yours was in last summer. He ever find you?"

The arm still pained. Garick hoped it would die soon like a sick branch. When it was safe, he'd have it off and be done with it.

"I have only one son, Korbin. You got any pain-killer? Dump it in my glass."

—and they were all dead, all of them, Judith who he loved too soon, Jenna who he loved too late, Arin whom he'd hardly known, not loved enough while there was time—

*These are my folk, Jude, my world, and I can help them. But first I had to change it all and pay for it. But why me, who said it had to be me?*

And lastly, Singer. Singer, maybe most of all. Looking at him with her eyes, lacerating him with a life that poured out of *her*. Gone, too, gone like all the others, a dead limb to be cut away. For the love he'd once felt for Judith's son was dead like all the others.

They decontaminated him in an empty room on a lower floor of the same building. The doctor, wearing a translucent protective mask and suit, tested him and fed the data into the synergizer. When the readout came, he made doleful, clucking noises.

"We can only manage a temporary series of measures," he said, opening a black case and removing bottles and needles like the one Matthew had.

The doctor pierced his arm several times, not a particularly pleasant experience. He had to swallow a variety of powders, tablets, liquids. One of the latter was so vile he almost threw up.

The doctor was solicitous. "Something wrong?"

"Worse than Kriss cooking." The doctor didn't understand.

He was allowed to return to her chambers, riding back on the same elevator, the only car in operation. When he got out, an impulse made him twitch aside one of the curtains concealing the windows from his view. He saw nothing through the glass; a white vapor swirled before his eyes.

"They're clouds," she said.

He dropped the curtain and quickly stepped to the center of the room. It made her laugh.

"Don't be afraid, the place hasn't tumbled down yet. Come forward, let me see you."

She stood waiting at the far end of the corridor, framed in the doorway. When he drew near enough for her to study his face, she spoke again.

"You don't look much like Judith." Standing aside, she gestured for him to enter her office.

"You knew her, then."

"She was my daughter."

He looked at her intently, but her large brown eyes betrayed no deeper emotion than curiosity. Taking her usual chair by the scanner, she smoothed out her robes and motioned for him to sit where he would.

"Yes," she nodded, "we're related, you and me. However . . . I don't know how much Judith told you about the City . . ."

He inclined his head. "You don't touch."

"Rarely."

He held up one hand. "I'd better explain something right away—if I can, if you'll accept it. The reason I don't resemble my mother is because you aren't actually seeing Singer. This is my half brother, Arin. Right at this moment, *I'm* outside the Gate—my body—just riding into Lorl."

Her eyebrows rose. Silently, she evaluated what he claimed, provisionally decided that whatever he might be saying, it wasn't a lie. "You'd best explain."

"I can't give you a complete history, not everything that's happened outside since the City sealed itself off, but I'll start by telling you about lep. It was new to my mother at first."

She listened carefully, absorbing each word, pigeonholing it till it could be processed. Singer spoke of the power of masters, the reading and the sharing, how the cowans called it magic but what it really was—

"Telepathy!" she interrupted, recalling the ancient word. She swiveled in her chair and punched several input buttons. The scanner lit up.

7167(8)/75282: 7497/3271/932982.

Singer regarded the glowing green surface with amazement. "What the hell is that?"

"Part of the synergizer."

"And the numbers?"

"The definition of telepathy—direct mental communication, a matter of like frequencies. We don't study it."

"Why not?"

She entered his question. The synergizer explained.

7167(8): 1377/0=645710/74982.

She translated. "The usage and boundaries of telepathy are too limited to be of interest."

He cocked a doubtful eyebrow: "It's grown some."

"According to the synergizer, it's a profitless direction."

"Perhaps." He shrugged. "But I've carried it beyond the masters. They can't *steal,* but I can."

She asked the meaning of the word, strange in its context.

"When I was maybe seven, I discovered I could *steal* people, go inside their minds, take control, make them do what *I* wanted."

She nodded. The mind-boggling symbol she received when Singer entered the Self-Gate for the second time was coming clear. *He* was the compensated paranoid pattern, and the impossible link-up was his sharing of the same body with a compensated schizoid, his half brother, Arin. Aloud, she merely remarked, "What you call stealing would be a new extension of sympathetic fields. Theoretically possible, but quite unlikely."

"You want me to demonstrate?"

She held his eyes with her own level gaze. "You wouldn't."

"No, I guess not." He waved it away. "Anyway, it used to be I had to touch anyone I wanted to control, but the power's grown over the years. I didn't know it myself till I met Arin in the woods. I was hunting a deer, and all of a sudden I was Arin watching *me* through his eyes! I realized I could steal Arin without touching him. Later on, I learned I was even able to manage a certain amount of manipulation of others *through* Arin."

She looked at him disapprovingly. "Then you forced your brother to risk the Self-Gate against his will."

"There was no other choice. I tried it once, alone. It beat me. Thoroughly."

"And why were you so anxious to try again?"

He began to tell her, but stopped. It was not good enough to say he wanted to see the City because his mother woke a hunger in his heart, or that he dreamed of the place where he, Singer, might find a home and a people and not be lonely ever again. Maybe that was his basic motive, but now there was a lot more. It was important to pick out for her the parts she would consider valid.

So he told her of the war and how the Kriss spread a plague, still not effectively checked, that decimated the covens over the years; the subornation of the mercenaries under Callan, how the disguised, fanatic Kriss intercepted Garick's letter to the City; the consequent, desperate massing of the forest nation under his father's genius; the battle at Dannyline. How they waited now at the City's door.

And he told her about Uriah and how Judith might have been right if *he* had gained possession of the Girdle. "A weapon my mother must have been afraid would bring the destruction of the City if it was found and the wrong person used it. She originally thought it might block out some of the Self-Gate signals. My father may have thought that, too, though he never said. Anyway . . . it doesn't."

There was still more, he knew, but he could not yet find the words to express it; the idea was almost there but the more he tried to summon it, the more it eluded him.

She rose, tired from the long, cumbersome conversation in Old Language. "We'll talk more tonight. Now you'll come to my quarters and rest. Later there'll be food."

He nodded, realizing he, too, was tired. During the long journey, he'd given Arin little rest and forgotten to feed him. *I'm a hell of a tenant.*

She led the way out of the office and into the corridor. As they walked, he asked her name.

Her lips curved at an unexpected memory. "I'm Marian Singer, chief administrator of the City."

"You're smiling. Why?"

"Nothing. Something your mother used to call me."

"What?"

She shook her head. "I'm afraid it's rather fresh."

He echoed the word, puzzled.

Marian sighed. It was difficult enough to converse in anything but verbal shorthand; explaining an Old Language idiom was particularly tedious. But she tried. "Fresh is—a kind of flippant disrespect, light irony, sarcasm at worst. But in a society without religion, I'm afraid your mother was, well, rather fresh when she called me 'the priestess.'"

"Priestess?"

She nodded, surprised and pleased that the memory held something more than sorrow. "She'd get angry. When she did, her eyes went—"

"Black."

"Yes!" She almost pressed his hand. Instead, she opened the door to her private chambers, stark and gray as her office. "When Judith became annoyed, she'd refer to me as 'the priestess of solitude.'"

For the first time in his life, Bowdeen had found a man to follow, respect, even care about. That care took its toll. Right now, the Wengen was exasperated.

"But, Garick, dammit, listen to a little plain sense!"

"No," Garick repeated for the third time, "you're not coming with me. You watch and wait. The rest can do as they please until I get back."

"*If* you get back."

"Bow—shut up."

Bowdeen sighed and gave up. "You going now?"

"After we eat. Spitt's here, I want to talk to him."

"How 'bout if I just sort of follow behind, not too close—"

"Alone." Garick bit off the words. "Arin is *my* son."

Garick went back into Korbin's, leaving Bowdeen in the empty street with Shalane.

"Stubborn."

Shalane touched his arm. "He's going for Arin, isn't he?"

He looked down into her sad young face, lined with fatigue and something worse, then reached out and patted her shoulder. "Don't you go burying Arin yet. I've fought him, I've trailed him. They don't come no smarter."

He was more concerned about Garick. If Arin was dead, there was nothing they could do, but the god was a different matter. Garick was half out of his head with grief, exhaustion and pain, making foolish decisions now. No *way* should he go to the zone by himself, but that's what Garick was going to do.

City food was mostly synthetics designed for nutrition, certainly not savor. Singer didn't mind and if Arin objected, he said nothing about it.

For the past several hours, Marian—he could not bring himself to think of her as his grandmother—had been working. She returned at sundown.

"I've spoken with the doctor. You'll leave tomorrow."

"Why? Doesn't the decontamination last longer than that?"

"Yes, but we're disturbed about the plague. He'll give you medicines and instruct you in the treatment of the disease, how to control it and the carrier rats."

He shook his head. "It's not enough, Marian."

"What do you mean? Isn't that why you came?"

"For a start, but now Garick wants more. There's the memory of my mother driving him."

"I don't understand. Judith left the City to prevent that portable force field you've been wearing from falling into the wrong hands. Nothing more."

"No, there *was* more, Marian. Garick knew it, maybe not in words. Took me nearly twenty years to piece it together."

She waited for him to explain.

Singer rose, employing what he thought might be the psychological advantage of Arin's height. "When my mother was dying, I think she tried to tell me she wanted an alliance between City and the covens."

"That's impossible."

Her bland denial irritated him. "Why? Does it *have* to be?"

"Singer, the City deliberately shut itself away from those who didn't join it. Except for the schism, no one has entered or left since your mother. And you."

"What schism?"

She gestured impatiently. "Early City history. Not pertinent. There were those who couldn't accept the inevitable pattern that City life took. They left."

He tried to question her further on it, but Marian refused to spend time on anything other than the main topic of their talk.

"Unification," she said, "wouldn't serve any City purpose. Our population is frozen in number. We don't talk much, even our own compacted language is tedious to us. Work is our major activity, and we're alone when we do it."

He shook his head. "I see why my mother called you 'priestess of solitude.' "

Her lips twisted with a rueful memory. "City life chafed Judith, though she loved her work. But City people aren't forbidden to touch, Singer. The urge simply withers away."

Sitting down, he leaned forward till their heads were close, resisting the need to reach out, touch her hand. "Marian, my father says that something that doesn't grow eventually dies. If City can't change—"

"Not applicable. Argument doesn't reflect City rationale."

He ignored her. "During her life among the covens, my mother concluded there were things about coven ways important for the City to know. Doesn't that at least suggest limited contact? What can you lose?"

"Time."

*"Time?"* He gaped at her. "Why should time matter to people who practically live forever?"

"Practically: that's the operant word." She rose. "Singer, come with me." She conducted him back to her office, pointed at the lifeless scanner. "What do you see?"

"Nothing. It doesn't work."

"Precisely. For the time being, we can't use the synergizer at night."

"So?"

"It's a great hardship," she said, emphatically. "We have nothing but our work, and every second is vital."

"Even with your endless lives?"

"Singer, forget your coven notions of time, they aren't valid here. Yes, we live nine hundred, a thousand years, but it's still *not enough.* We each dread the statistically inevitable accident that will finally kill us, or the time when our brains refuse to store any further data, or the possible laboratory malfunction that destroys some vital organ that can't be recloned."

He remembered a City expression his mother once used. "Forever is in the future."

"Yes! We're still doing all we can to add life, preserve the knowledge of every City brain, shorten the educative process. When we plan a new baby here, it's perhaps eighty years before the child gains enough historical perspective to begin to be useful. Usually it's much longer before emotional maturity is also attained."

"And have you replaced my mother yet?"

She winced, but did not reply.

"So," he mused with a tinge of bitterness, "you live impossibly extended lives stuffing that electric sponge with everything that possibly can be known—or at least all that you and *it* consider important, and to hell with the world outside."

She started to answer, but the sheer weight of the effort it would take crushed the impulse. Marian shrugged. "Something like that, Singer."

He poked aside a curtain, tried to see the City far below, but it was too dark. Suddenly, he spun on her. "And what happens, Marian, if one day you finish feeding data into the synergizer and decide it's time to add it all up and—"

She interrupted. "And we press the button, and the answer comes back, 'no correlation.'"

Silence.

Her smile was gentle and ageless. "Was that your question?"

"Approximately," he murmured. "Thought you had no lep."

"Judith asked the same question once. So did I . . . when I was young."

"Is that a rebuke?"

"No, just a memory." She closed her eyes. "I can hear Judith now, brilliant as she was, breaking herself on that supposition. We trained her too soon."

Marian held his eyes earnestly. "Singer, we don't make a god out of the synergizer, we're beyond that need. In the early days of City, there *was* a church, but it became superfluous finally, and faded away."

He gestured impatiently. "What's that have to do—"

"With the synergizer? The only way to answer you is to tell a bit of early City history. It's difficult, I wish you could speak our language."

"You mean, those numbers you punch into that thing?"

"No, that's computer talk. Our oral communication is based on the same principle, but we employ digital adjuncts to speed it up. The whole purpose of our language is to *save time* . . . and it's still not as streamlined as we'd like."

"All right, tell me. I'll try to follow."

She pointed to the scanner. "It's all stored in there. If the power were only on, you could watch what they called newsreels."

Marian cleared her throat; the unaccustomed use of protracted speech was straining it. "Long ago, Singer, there were many religions. Their adherents wrangled about which was the true faith, basing their arguments and appeals principally on emotional persuasion, rather than logic. Logic examines, belief accepts. It was fashionable then to indulge in debates on the nature of god. Most creeds postulated a personal deity, some transmuted godhead into a vague force binding together all things. Even those who rejected religion regarded god as a vital issue; some claimed he/she/it had died, others merely contended that god's nature was beyond man's power to know.

"And then a new philosophy was formed. It was called the Church of the Irrelevation. Its members refused even to discuss the old issues of god and spirit and immortality. They said they were unprovable theories, wastes of energy and time when the world is sick and hungry."

"Irrelevation," he echoed, feeling a premonitory chill. "Meaning 'irrelevant'?"

"Yes, Singer. Gods, heavens and hells, incarnations and passages, universal forces—all *irrelevant* to making human life better. Things that can't be proven, disproved or even intelligently, empirically debated are childish to fight about."

Singer thought of the Kriss. "Yet the religious mind thinks its faith *can* be confirmed, by death at least."

"Yes, by death," Marian said gravely. "Dissolution, immolation, surrender. The religious mind doesn't think in these matters, Singer, the religious heart *feels*. Priests persuade, they know better than to try to convince. 'We *know* it's revealed word, trust us, we're right.' Irrelevationists protested: 'We don't want to take it on faith, we want proof. Your personal convictions satisfy *your* emotions, not *our* minds.' "

"And the priests, I imagine, countered with a withering mockery of mind. You should have known Uriah."

"More than just the priests," Marian said. "There was a whole generation of antirationalists. They sneered at pitting the fallible brain against thousands of years of tradition. Irrelevationists dismissed tradition as ancient error compounded by millennia of accreted ceremony."

"So," Singer asked, "the Irrelevationists tried to stamp out religion?"

"Only at first—before what's usually referred to as the Jing invasion, when established society was destroyed."

"What did they do then?"

"Irrelevationists grew subtle. Before the invasion, knowledge had advanced so far in the world that rituals had to be overhauled drastically, priests compromised with modern views to soothe their people's accelerating doubts. It was an age without spiritual moorings. The invasion brought anarchy, brutalism, the collapse of many faiths. Yet the frightened masses still craved security against the real and immediate dangers of personal insignificance and death.

"The Irrelevationists spoke up then. 'Never mind theology now,' they said, 'save your own skins, heal the country's wounds. Let *us* worry for you about god and immortality.' In other words, Singer, they developed a popular appeal for shunting aside religious issues until they could be examined on some other basis than unquestioning faith."

"And that was the beginning of the City?"

"Not as it is now. There was no Self-Gate at first. But we were—still are—a minority. There's only a few thousand of us in some fifteen thousand square miles. City leaders feared religion would grow again, try to fight us. So—"

"So you invented a way to shut us all out and place yourselves beyond time and emotion."

"Emotion." Marian echoed the word ironically. "That was a luxury once. Long ago."

"My mother learned to love."

"And died for it." Slowly, she shook her head. "Yearning for personal security—comfort, happiness—created religion, Singer, and religion, in turn, made death desirable, inevitable. That's a repugnant premise in the City."

"But, Marian, all you substitute is long life. Without joy, without emotion—why *deliberately* choose such a thing?"

"There's joy in our work. Or at least, satisfaction. The love and joy you allude to, Singer, are toys amplified beyond their importance by your ephemeral lifespans. Given a City life, the passions—even the most constant, companionate loves—grow stale. But meanwhile, intellectual activities become increasingly enticing. We follow them, and as we do, our lives flow toward serenity."

"And solitude." He felt very cold.

"Yes."

"It's not *enough,* Marian."

Wearily, she massaged her temples. "My head aches. I could've told you all this in a tenth of the time." Allowing a few of her precious seconds to elapse, the priestess smiled bleakly at him. "You should've been educated here, Singer. You've got your mother's intelligence. She also demanded a reason for the agony of a life without myth, for denying the distractions of naked flesh. Maybe you'll understand what I told her then, I'm not sure Judith ever did.

"Singer, perhaps it does take a certain amount of courage to choose to work solely for what someday *might* come about, but in our solitude we achieve one precious thing. Self-knowledge. It's a consolation itself like sorrow."

He could say nothing at first. Then, eyes closed, Singer spoke and each word was a distinct and separate pang. "Once my mother told me pain defines and exacts the price of its wisdom."

Marian looked up at him. "Judith said that?"

"Yes."

"I'm glad." It was a whisper.

He studied his brother's big hands, flexing the fingers, clenching them into fists. "I practically told Arin the same thing. Yet one part of me always thought, No, Singer, go to City! That's where there's—"

*Meaning?* his worm gently mocked.

She nodded, understanding. "The need to believe, Singer, is an almost inescapable trap of the ego."

*Now you know?*

Yes, worm, yes.

The reason why it wouldn't matter to the City whether or not the synergizer ever derived a final solution to the riddle of existence.

*Say it all.*

"Random. Irrelevant."

*Now,* said the worm, *meaning has meaning.*

Clean as the arc of Forever. *And shove it up your ego, big brother.*

Marian left Singer alone to think. Somewhere far off, a clock tolled the hour of nine.

Poke did not hear Garick coming.

It was dark. Crickets chirped, the breeze soughed in the maples. On the other side of the barrier, the warning marker was a pale, glowing ghost.

Ab wouldn't relieve him till daylight, a long way off. Poke yawned. Zone duty, always uneventful, was a goddam bore lately, what with City insisting on setting up the new patrol at—

The noise at his elbow startled him. Poke whirled, sheddy drawn before he finished turning: "Who's there?"

"Easy," said the tall man within arm's reach. "I'm Garick. I don't want trouble. Just information."

Shaken, Poke snatched up his battery lamp and played it over the visitor. He'd seen Garick now and then in Lorl; this was him all right. The man looked drawn and sick, but he'd eaten up the whole southern division and now he was clear up to their lousy barracks and there might be a hundred coveners behind him in the darkness.

Garick inclined his head toward the distant warning marker. "That the Gate?"

"All you'll ever see of it. What you want?"

"As I said, information." Garick hesitated. "There's talk someone went through yesterday."

Poke wasn't paid to talk, but you couldn't figure what a man like Garick might do. "Maybe."

Garick fought down the urge to walk away, leave it unsaid. It wouldn't be real if he didn't hear it. But he had to. "Heard you buried someone."

Poke sheathed the sword. "We did."

Garick slumped against the stout wooden beam, slid down till he was sitting on the ground. His head drooped and his shoulders heaved with the fatigue and dry misery he couldn't hold back any longer. He sobbed, deep, ugly, awkward sounds.

It was an hour for lonely philosophies. *The god of the Shando,* Poke thought, feeling cosmic, *and he's just a man like anyone else, and here I am in the middle of the night feeling sorry for him.* Then something connected in his mind: the Shando arrow.

"Hey, wait—you got it wrong, Garick." The other man said nothing. Poke squatted laboriously by him. "I mean, it was one of ours we buried."

Garick stared up at him blankly. The words took awhile to register in his exhausted mind. "One of yours?"

"Merk. Boy name Rigg."

". . . not Arin?"

Poke shook his head. "Somebody went through. Far as I know, he's still in there. Might've made it to City, we couldn't find 'im in the zone."

Garick felt hope stir. He knew if Arin had the Girdle on, he could be dead and nobody'd ever know it unless they actually stumbled over his body. But still—his son—his and Jenna's . . .

*Let him sit at my left hand in the hall when we go home.*

Poke remembered Ab's description of the man at the barrier. "This Arin, was he tall like you, red hair?"

"Yes . . . yes! You saw him?"

"Not me. Other zone guard. Ab."

"Where is he?"

"Ab? Asleep. Be here come morning."

". . . in the morning." Garick slumped back against the barrier trestle, shifting a little to ease the strain on his cradled arm. "I'll wait."

He took something from the pocket of his tabard. Poke recognized it as a packet of pain depressant, regular merk issue. In the spill of the lamp, he could see, under the tabard, the charred holes in Garick's buckskins.

"Merk, you got something to wash this down?"

Rummaging in his carry-bag, Poke extracted an earthenware bottle and a tin cup. He didn't use the cup all that often; he had to shake out two furiously copulating insects before handing it to Garick, pouring the drink like a polite host.

Garick dumped the powder into it, took a swallow and choked, wheezing: "What *is* this pig sweat? Not sida."

Poke laughed and drank himself. "That is Wengen gin, sir. Made from prime potatoes. Bet you never tasted it."

Garick forced himself to finish it. With the pain-killer, it worked quickly to numb him. He settled back against the trestle, willing his worn-out body to sleep.

"Potatoes," he mumbled.

Poke gently retrieved the cup from Garick's slackening grasp. Tipping the bottle again, he took another swallow from the refilled cup. The merk grumbled to himself, "Aww, shit, some company he is. Thought them Shando knew how to *drink* . . ."

Wandering through her suite, he found a room with many books inside. Plucking down a few at random—ones whose Old Language didn't seem too difficult—he dropped them on a plain metal table and took a chair, browsing for a while, noticing with a quickening pulse the occasional margin-penciled notations in his mother's unmistakable handwriting. Singer liked the book of poetry best. He'd grown up hearing the old song-stories, but these were different, more complex, cleverer, and some were funny and some were sad. One of the simpler stanzas clutched him like a cold hand on his heart.

*Bleaker than a winter wind blowing on a hill*
*Chiller than a freezing stream flowing through a mill*
*Is the victor and the victory*
*The willing and the will*

But what victory could he claim? His mother's desperate efforts to educate him to City ways in the last months of her life—all for nothing. The plague would be cured, but the covens were to be left in ignorance.

He had a frustrated feeling that he was almost on the brink of some discovery, a suggestion which might persuade Marian Singer to reconsider. But it wouldn't come, and in the morning, they'd send him away from the City and again he'd be alone, a single cowan in a sea of coven.

A sea of coven. Where did he hear that phrase before? Had to be the Kriss. Uriah. He thought about the honed intelligence, the crippled but questing mind, the keen relish for strategies for the sake of *inventing*. The game played out in Salvation. Uriah told Arin something that time . . . what?

*Nothing is free. There's always a price.*

But Singer told Arin then, if he gave something away, make a profit on it. What was the profit here? Would City gain, or coven, or both?

*There's always a price.*

That was why he couldn't force the birthing thought to come. The price was too high, he couldn't pay it.

*And yet we have a great deal in common, prince.* A knife-edge of thought: Uriah challenging Arin. *You have the makings of an exquisite bastard . . . not easy to carry a king's mission in this world . . .*

*Do I have to?* A long, slow, easy death for the covens. Not—

His mother's face. Fragments of a memory so dim he couldn't remember the words she spoke, he was too young to understand them, and he refused to remember, except nothing ever was lost, she told him and told him, *Hear what I say and don't worry if it doesn't make sense, it'll be there when you need it.*

And it was. The sound came back, her breath rasping against advancing death. "My baby, the City and the covens will break each other, as on a wheel. But the wheel won't turn till—"

Till. Till Singer went to Lishin, found the Girdle, put it on, went through the Gate, declared himself before City: Damn you, see me. *I exist!*

Yes. The block was gone. The thing he had to tell the priestess, the little fact to tip the balance, open up City, absorb the covens and swallow them and their dirty, ignorant and . . . *beautiful* way of life.

He arose, feeling cold, and Arin was cold and there might never be any more warmth, but every unwilling footstep brought him closer to where she was.

"The lep is more than just words, Marian. It includes a thing they call *sharing*."

"Meaning?"

"A wordless communication, transference of emotion and knowledge, pictures, complexities. It can pass between two, a dozen, even hundreds of people at once."

"So? Why are you telling me this?"

"City language," he said, wishing he could stop the words from coming. "You said it's *too slow*."

She waited for him to go on.

"Do you know that Garick, using lep, taught Arin Old Language in two months? *Two months!* With linked minds, it's like hooking up an output to a memory bank. What you've done with the synergizer, they have, in a way, done with their own minds. And the power doesn't switch off at sundown."

A brief silence. The ramifications clicked through her mind as fast as the synergizer might process them. She nodded. "Two directions. Eventual, deliberate breeding of the characteristic. More immediate: linkage with coven minds the way we connect with the synergizer."

"Yes," said Singer. "*How* would be up to you, but look at the tool you could make of lep, think of the tremendous leap in knowledge that could take place in ten, twenty years. Think of the *time* it could save you."

"What do the covens gain?"

"City education, technology."

She considered it, taking longer than necessary; the dead weight of tradition also operated in the City. But Singer, anticipating the force of inertia, had a suggestion to make.

"Marian—ask the synergizer."

It was near dawn, she knew she ought to wait a little longer, but the idea was too important and yet, as she punched the demand for power, she felt almost frivolous.

The feeling disappeared when she received the answer.

Marian sat for a time in silent thought. When she looked at him again it was with the stirrings of an emotion she couldn't even remember the name for.

"Singer, when you saw this building for the first time, what did you feel?"

"Shock."

"Slight or deep?"

"Profound, Marian. I literally fell on my knees."

"Yes," she said, and was silent again.

*When we've gone where we must—*

"And now, Singer . . . what will you do?"

*Done what we have to—*

"Singer?"

*How much of it will be left?*

All the distant voices: Judith intermingled with Kon-Magill, Elin, Sand-Teela, Webb, Hara, Clay and Holder—and the one cry stabbing at Garick over and over through the years, *his* cry that never stopped.

*"You can read it!"*

Listening to Ab, Garick knew it was Arin who went through the Gate.

"When someone tries to run it," he pressed, "how do you get him? Do they shut off the power?"

"Not completely, City never does that," said Ab, not mentioning the one time, when Rigg died. "We use helmets. We can get pretty far in with them. Not all the way, though."

"Get me one," Garick told him. Though quiet, it was unmistakably an order.

Ab shook his head. "Won't help. City has to cut back the power first."

Garick scarcely hesitated. "Then get me two."

"Two?" Poke spluttered. "Who's the other for? Not me!"

"When somebody runs the Gate and it hits them," Garick went on, "*then* they lower the power, right?"

"Sure," said Ab, "but—"

"Then I'll go in second."

The two merks gaped at him. Ab found his voice first. "You'd shove some poor bastard through that Gate full power?"

Garick's serenity was ice cold. "Cowan, I know a bastard just made for it. He's even done it. Now, get me those helmets."

Ab's hand rested on his sheddy hilt. "Forget it."

Garick sighed. "Now look, soldier. My son's in there and one way or another, I'm bringing him out. And if you plan to stop me," he pointed over the guard's shoulder, "*he's* going to be awful mad."

They followed his point. A tall figure emerged from the bush at roadside, grinning foolishly. Garick growled at him, "Bowdeen, a man your age should know enough to follow orders."

"Ain't you glad I don't?" Bowdeen waved casually to the two merks. "Poke and Ab! You sad-asses still on pay?"

Poke hooted in recognition. "Hey, Bow! Heard you retired."

"Sort of." The black man clapped them both on the shoulder. "Sidele back in town yet?"

"Sure," said Poke. "I seen her yesterday."

"Good." Bowdeen patted him. "Now you get them helmets like the man says—"

"Goddammit, Bow, we can't *do* that!"

"—so *he* don't have to shoot you." Where Bowdeen had emerged from the bush, Jay waited with an arrow ready.

"Bowdeen, *wait.*" Garick leaned over the barrier, straining eyes and ears into the eastern distance. "Listen!"

They all heard the sound then, a raucous, growling noise like none they'd ever known, coming nearer.

Motors.

At the top of the rise, beyond the Gate marker, three small wheeled carts rolled rapidly in their direction, each carrying two riders. Bowdeen squinted into the morning sun. "Master Garick, that's . . . ain't that—"

"Yes," Garick breathed. "It's Arin. It's *Arin,* Bow. And—"

Garick broke off, staring at the tiny, delicate black-haired woman. For a moment, he thought he might pass out, but his will held his body in check.

It *couldn't* be Judith.

The carts rolled to a stop. Arin alighted first, wearing the strange belt, the Girdle, over his robe. He approached his father and bowed with deep respect before him.

"I brought them, sir."

"Yes." Garick didn't try to stop the tears welling in his eyes. *All. You did it all. No one else.* He thought how proud Jenna would have been of Arin, let the boy share it wordlessly.

Arin said nothing. Singer wouldn't let him.

Garick felt lightheaded and weak, and through the blur of tears, his son's weather-burned face seemed bathed in a compassion and pity as vast as it was remote. Then Arin's arms were around him, and Arin's lips moved, murmuring at his ear.

"Before you meet her . . . whatever comes . . . I love you."

*Why does he say it like it's good-by?*

"Yes," Garick said softly. "That was needed."

"At least once," said his son.

"Garick," he introduced his father. "Marian Singer, mother of—of Judith."

Like the rest, she was encased from head to foot in a light translucent suit that protected her from contamination, but the face was clear enough.

"You," Garick swallowed, "you look so much like her."

"Yes," she acknowledged. "It appears we're related. And that we have a great deal to talk about." Marian looked at his arm and turned to one of the three City men who had accompanied her. "Doctor, please examine this."

Garick sat down, supported by Arin while the doctor studied the arm. "We could amputate later or restore limited use, it's hard to say without X-ray." He prepared a hypodermic and was about to administer it when he glanced up at the dark, streak-painted savage hovering protectively over Garick. "Tell your man, this is only to help you. It won't hurt."

"Tell him yourself," Garick said mildly. "He used to be Kriss. Speaks your language."

Tucked into the young man's belt that carried his black knife was a book bound in raw leather. The doctor was not unimpressed. "I see you read?"

"The Apocalypse." Jay tapped the book. "You know it?"

"Oh yes. On tape."

"Strange to feel like the Fifth Horseman." Jay pointed to the needle. "You be gentle with him."

Korbin's was agreed on for the initial conference. It was where Judith first stayed when she left City.

Before climbing into one of the carts, Garick offered several krets to Poke.

"What's that for?"

"The drink. And the kindness."

Poke stiffened. "Keep your money, Garick."

"Why?"

"Shouldn't have to say." The merk turned his back on Garick and waddled away toward the barracks.

"Damfool dumb sonvabitch," Ab remarked to Poke as the carts rolled away. "He's got money he ain't even seen yet. You shoulda took it."

"Ab," Poke glared at him, "I don't need no tight-ass Wengen advice. Last night I give Garick 'cause he was my guest. Poke's guest don't pay!"

The stout guard watched the carts moving off into the forest. Sighing, Poke scraped his hand thoughtfully against the stubble of his chin. Maybe Garick was important at home *but goddam, that old Shando sure could learn some* manners!

The first session was only between Garick, Arin and the City people. Neither Hoban, Tilda, nor the other masters felt any insult in being excluded. They had seen the small, fragile people in their queer clothes and their carts that went without horses: pretty enough and with powerful magic, they guessed, but they would leave it to Garick and not accept these new people or their ways just like that.

Shalane stood in front of Korbin's door, waiting for the conference to end. She'd ridden an errand for Tilda to the Karli outside Lorl and missed Arin. She'd heard about the shiny material City people wore and wondered how she'd look in it, instead of her own ragged skins. "Like a wet cat, I guess," she said ruefully.

*Will he come out soon?*

Moss kissed her hair. "Sure as frost, baby girl."

Arin emerged alone, before any of the others. He had a pained, drawn look that tightened the skin about his forehead and temples. Hand shielding his eyes, he looked like a man too quickly awakened from bad dreams. Blinking in the sun, withdrawn, he sat down on the edge of the wooden sidewalk, against a post, feet splayed in the dust of the street.

*Arin—*

Her lep caressed his mind before he saw her coming out of the group of Karli. He didn't get up, and the girl didn't run to him as she had a year or a hundred years ago. She came slowly with her woman's grace, her hand extended, and he drew her down beside him.

"You cut your hair."

"It'll grow," she said.

Leaning together, their foreheads touching, they still did not lep or share, their minds did not mingle yet, and it was bad to feel like this, bursting and empty all at the same time, and then Arin felt it well up in him. He buried her in his arms, face pressed into her throat. *Lane . . . Lane . . .*

*I know.* She cupped his face in her hands. *Don't share yet. We can't. Too much, Arin.*

*Yes.*

They held each other, and the joy was there, would always be there, but heavy with ghosts and no more like morning.

"But they're charming. Absolutely beautiful!" The City woman named Diane whispered to Randall Singer as they came out of the conference. "Garick is like a sculpture."

"A Rodin," Randall agreed, "in weathered granite. But see how they age." They'd agreed to use Old Language outside the Gate; even so, they whispered. One of these proud, clannish people might understand and think them condescending.

Diane glowed with a fever of discovery and purpose. "They'll be fascinating to study. I could spend fifty years on it and probably will. Look, Randall, there's the boy who came through the Gate." She began to putter with her camera.

"Don't embarrass them, Diane. They're not used to us."

"Nonsense, he won't mind. Marian says he's quite intelligent. And that *girl*. Look at her bone structure. She's a primitive Dürer!"

She planted herself in front of the boy and girl. Unmoving, absorbed in each other, they glanced incuriously at the oblong thing she held to her eye. It clicked at them. She pushed a minute lever and clicked again.

"Just babies," she whispered to Randall. "I do wish they'd smile."

In her view finder, Arin and the girl looked at her, seemed to look through her. But they would not smile.

Before the next scheduled conference began, Garick sent for Singer. He arrived several minutes later, hands still shrouded in skins and bound securely.

"I'm going to let you go," Garick told him.

"About time, daddy."

Garick came close and spoke in a low, dead voice. "Don't call me that. Arin did everything while you just sat there and watched your people die."

"Not *my* people."

"Then you're not my son." Garick lepped to Arin: *come, bring an extra horse.* To Singer he said: "You're leaving. Don't ever come near Charzen again."

Singer swallowed with difficulty, said nothing.

Arin arrived with a saddled horse in tow. "You found him in the woods," Garick ordered, "so leave him there. Far enough away so he won't cause anybody any trouble." He bent one last cold glance on the outcast. "I'm through paying for Jude."

Without another word, the god of Shando turned his back on Singer and crossed the street into Korbin's.

Arin had his mouth open to say something to his father, but couldn't make the words come. And suddenly, he found himself leading Singer to his horse.

When they were past the last houses, the brothers dismounted. Without Singer's prompting, Arin cut away the rope, stripped off the gloving skins and chucked them into the bushes. *Lot of good they did,* he lepped, ironical. Arin seemed to be struggling to express a complexity of thoughts.

*What, Arin?*

"You were there from the first, weren't you?"

Singer said nothing.

*The worm. The wolf.*

"Near the end, Arin, you made a pretty good worm yourself."

*Had a good teacher.*

Arin was oddly loath to end it, ride away. By unspoken assent, they sat down, side by side, backs to the bole of a large oak. It was just past high sun. They listened to the birds.

"Go on," Singer urged gently. "Ask it."

"You know. The Samman circle at Karli. Me and Lane."

"Yes, Arin, I was with you."

*Why?*

*Moment of weakness.* "For what it's worth, I'm sorry."

Arin said nothing.

*Does it still matter?*

Arin shook his head. "No. Not now."

Moments passed. A curious look came into Singer's eyes. "Look, Arin, now I think, you have nothing you should complain about. Leastways, *you* didn't have to sleep with Bowdeen."

It only took Arin a second to catch it. His eyes widened. "Sidele, *too?*"

"How else was I going to drag your big ass into that box? And did you ever try to tie yourself up?" Singer gave him a wry grin. *Dunesk.*

The picture was too much for Arin. For the first time since the long nightmare began he had a reason to laugh, and Singer joined him. They chuckled, then roared with the absurdity of it and though there were other things than mirth in their laughter, it took them a long time to stop wheezing and sputtering from it. Wiping the tears away, Arin finally caught his breath.

"Why, Singer? What was it all for?"

His brother shrugged. "Started out with one thing, changed along the way. Remember the day you came to test that shiny new power of yours? When you hit me with an image of my mother?"

"Yes. That was cruel."

"I got mad, that made me decide faster, but the thought had already come. There you were, Arin, so full of yourself and your mission. I decided then I might play god. Shape the world my way." *My mother's way.*

Arin understood more than Singer was saying, he knew his brother now. *Shape a world where Singer wouldn't still be a misfit.*

He hadn't meant his brother to read it, but Singer suddenly scrambled to his feet. "Must be about time for you to get on back, Arin." He held out his hand. "Let me have the Girdle. Misfits are practically invisible, anyhow."

Arin glanced down. "Almost forgot I was still wearing it. But you left the helmet back in City."

*The Girdle, Arin.*

"Garick'll ask about it eventually. Why do you want it?"

"Gods don't look too good up close." He waited, hand still outstretched. Arin did not move. "Do I have to steal you again?"

"First time, you *let* me win. Wonder how'd I do in a real test of power . . . ?"

*Little brother . . . shove it up your ego.*

Arin grinned sheepishly. Then reluctantly, he unbuckled the belt, gave it to Singer. "All right, you sad bastard, take it. You'll need it more than Garick." He watched his brother cinch it about his middle. "Where you going? City?"

"No."

"Then come on home!"

*Home? Where's that?*

"Singer, there's no reason for this. I'll tell Garick what you really did, and—"

"NO!"

"Why *not?* What are you trying to prove?"

Singer passed a hand over his eyes, shaded them, stood silent for a moment before looking up at his brother. "Arin," he said softly, "I've carried that hate nineteen years. It's time for me to stop hurting him."

*?*

*He can finally bury my mother. Unless he learns he owes me, instead of you.*

"But it must hurt you."

"I'm Singer." *Used to it.*

"No, dammit," Arin protested, "you *want* to hurt, it's how you know who you are! Me and Lane, we've been hurt bad, we'll never be clean, but we'll try. Come home, Singer!"

"I've spent too much time already alone in Charzen." He raised a hand in farewell. *Good-by, Arin.*

Singer started off into the forest on foot.

"Take the horse, anyway."

"No, Arin. Nothing of his."

"He won't ask."

"Where've I got to go so fast I need to ride?"

He walked in a southeasterly direction. He'd pass between Lorl and the zone, giving both plenty of berth. Arin watched him. Soon Singer was too far off to call, so he lepped.

*You left something out, big brother.*

*?*

Arin's lep slashed into Singer's mind. *Why don't you admit it? You're alone because you want it that way.*

*No other choice, Arin.*

*Because you define yourself as Singer, the misfit.*

*Not the only one who does.*

*You reshaped the world, but you can't do the same magic on yourself!*

*Arin—*

*No, you can't shut me up! I was through the Gate with you, remember? I know you. You and Garick, shaping worlds, shaping me, leaving me to understand too much or not enough and not believe in any of it. You think Garick fits? Is there room in his skull for all he's learned and going to learn? Will Lane fit when she prays to earth 'be full of life' and smells the death in it? Fool everybody but me, Singer. Marian taught me, too. I don't believe, I don't have to believe. If I stink of the world, I'll still live in it, because it's the only one I've got.*

No response from his brother.

*You don't fit because you won't fit because you can't fit because you won't let yourself fit because*

And then he couldn't see Singer any longer.

In spite of the dizzying sensation without the helmet, he had to shut Arin out, jumble his thoughts. But it didn't help. *You're not alone no matter what you think because you couldn't make it into your goddam City without me!*

It took a long time for Arin's lep to fade. Singer wanted to curse his brother, scream at him to shut up, but he couldn't.

*Once through myself. Once with Arin. Once looking up at her building. Once talking to the priestess. And now—*

Wouldn't he ever stop running the Self-Gate?

Marian was waiting for him, as arranged, just outside Lorl. She reached into the motorized cart, brought out the helmet and handed it to him.

"It's the first time I've actually seen you," she said.

"I know."

"There *is* a family resemblance."

"Won't Garick wonder where you are?"

"He's busy with a little man with a bald head. They have this old book and Randall—your grandfather—is helping them translate part of it." A faint smile twitched the corners of her mouth. "They'll be tied up quite some time, I can assure you."

Singer put the helmet on his head and reached again for the switch . . .

"Singer?"

He paused. "Yes, Marian?"

"You're welcome there now, you know. In the City."

"Thanks. But I can't. Not yet. It's too much."

"All right." She sounded doubtful. "But don't wait *too* long."

He shook his head. "City preoccupation with time."

"What about Garick? You *could* reconsider—"

"No, Marian, *no,* you promised. Arin did it all."

Without further discussion, he flicked the switch. Just as he did, she was seized by an irresistible impulse. It was absurd, she knew, yet Marian reached out her hand to touch Singer once, gently.

But he was already gone.

He hadn't intended to go by the tree. Not at first—but then he knew he must finish it. He went alone, cloaked in the Girdle, by a route he knew better than anyone else.

The pain was old and dull, the years had blunted the barbs, and yet—

*They are a beautiful dying flower.*

The deep-cut letters, stretched and distorted with the tree's growth . . . the labor of two days as he bruised and tore eight-year-old flesh to carve it deep enough.

*—the recurring bitter experience never turns them sour. Life is their religion, so all-pervading—*

Like the City that would bury them.

*Hardship, suffering and death, and yet they have a sense of joy and oneness too deep to speak.*

He struggled with his emotions, delving deep for the answer he knew he had now, the final thing that would close a bracket in time.

JUDITH SINGER BURYED HERE
WIFE OF GARIK
MASTER OF SHANDO
BORN IN THE CITE
DYED OF

The thing Singer had been too young to name or understand.

His knife bit again into the bark, surer, stronger, swifter, carving the last of it for himself and his father, burying her for good.

DYED OF
TOO MUCH LIFE

Yes. That said it all. And no. Everything and nothing. All that could be spelled.

And then it was time to go.

Stepping carefully, thinking only of the need to move with the deer's soundless tread, the misfit god, outcast of the covens, started off through the forest toward the distant, empty hills. About his waist he wore the Girdle of Solitude, at once a badge of honor and a stripe of shame, and he was neither Circle nor City, but he was Singer.

And he was alone.

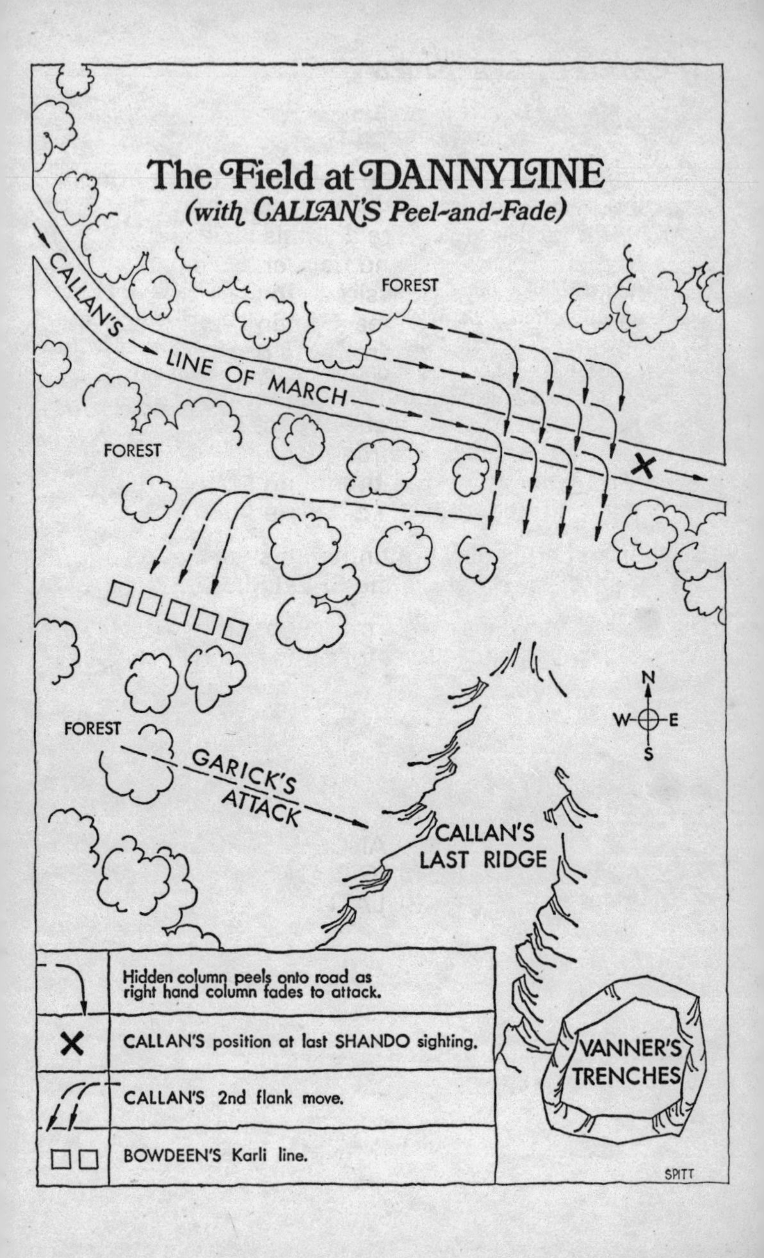
The Field at DANNYLINE
(with CALLAN'S Peel-and-Fade)
CALLAN'S LINE OF MARCH
FOREST
FOREST
FOREST
GARICK'S ATTACK
CALLAN'S LAST RIDGE
VANNER'S TRENCHES
N
W
E
S
Hidden column peels onto road as right hand column fades to attack.
CALLAN'S position at last SHANDO sighting.
CALLAN'S 2nd flank move.
BOWDEEN'S Karli line.
SPITT

## THE SPELLSINGER SERIES

**Alan Dean Foster**

Jonathan Meriweather is an indolent student and aspiring rock guitarist – until he's snatched from his own world to a world where animals walk and talk as men, armed with sword and dagger. He's been summoned there for a mission – to save the peace-loving (well, fairly peace-loving) animals from the evil forces emanating from the dreaded Greendowns.

And so Jonathan forms a strange fellowship which includes Clothahump, a sorcerous turtle, Mudge, a lecherous otter, and a fire-breathing Marxist dragon and sets out to combat the deadly enemy.

Soldier and crusader, fighting with sword and song, Jonathan Meriweather is the SPELLSINGER.

But even if he can lead his motley band to victory, what other perils lie in wait for him? And will he ever be able to return to earth?

THE SPELLSINGER SERIES

SPELLSINGER
THE HOUR OF THE GATE
THE DAY OF THE DISSONANCE
THE MOMENT OF THE MAGICIAN
PATHS OF THE PERAMBULATOR

**THE RIVER OF DANCING GODS**

**Jack L. Chalker**

BEYOND THE SEA OF DREAMS

Life had not been kind to Joe and Marge. Now, according to the stranger who met them on a road that wasn't there, they were due to die in nineteen minutes, eighteen seconds. But the ferryboat that waited to take them across the Sea of Dreams could bring them to a new and perhaps better life.

There lay a world where fairies still danced by moonlight and sorcery became real. Joe could become a mighty-thewed barbarian warrior. Marge could be more beautiful and find her magical self.

But there was much more than they realised to this strange land.

This was a world where Hell still strove to win its ancient war and demon princes sent men into battles of dark magic. It was a world where Joe and Marge must somehow help prevent the coming of Armageddon.

FUTURA PUBLICATIONS
FANTASY
AN ORBIT BOOK

ISBN 0–7088–8163–7

**THE ROAD TO CORLAY * A DREAM OF KINSHIP * A TAPESTRY OF TIME**
**The three books of the glowing, magical fantasy THE WHITE BIRD OF KINSHIP**

**Richard Cowper**

*The first coming was the Man;*
*The second was Fire to burn Him;*
*The third was Water to drown the Fire;*
*The fourth is the Bird of Dawning*

The Drowning, the great rising of the seas, had left Britain as seven island kingdoms; a millenium later, their people occupied a mediaeval world dominated by the Church Militant.

To the ancient city of York came Old Peter the Talespinner and the Boy, Tom, whose unearthly piping could bring men joy and sorrow beyond imagining. It was Tom's martyrdom on the walls of York that established a movement that would sweep the world, and a message of hope – the legend of the White Bird of Kinship.

The movement faces persecution, struggle and destruction, but from the ashes of strife new hope arises – another boy whose piping can charm nature itself, another Tom imbued with the spirit of the White Bird.

But new hopes breed new fears – the way is difficult and dark and Tom must face its dangers or despair.

'Moving, beautifully envisioned by the excellent Richard Cowper' *Daily Telegraph*

'Brilliant' *Tribune*

**HOSPITAL STATION**

**James White**

A vast hospital complex floating in space, built to cater for the medical emergencies of the galaxy. There are patients with eight legs – and none; stricken aliens that breathe methane or feed on radiation; an abandoned baby that weighs half a ton. And there are doctors and nurses to match, with a bewildering array of tentacles, and mental powers stretching all the way to telepathy.

Faced by the illnesses and accidents of the universe, fired by the challenge of galactic medicine, O'Mara, the hospital chief, and his crack team, including the altogether human Conway, with his insatiable curiosity, and Prilicla, the brilliant and fragile insect telepath, battle to preserve life in all its myriad forms.

HOSPITAL STATION – the astonishingly inventive saga of a vast hi-tech community, a cross between an emergency clinic and a zoo.

FUTURA PUBLICATIONS
AN ORBIT BOOK
SCIENCE FICTION

ISBN 0–7088–8181–5

## A NOOSE OF LIGHT

**A magical new fantasy of the Arabian nights**

**Seamus Cullen**

On a bare desert hillside overlooking a glittering city, an old man sits, keeping silent vigil. No man knows how long he has sat there, nor how old Anwar is . . .

But his tranquil life is soon to end, for there are those who would use him for their own ends: offering him to the people as the new prophet. And the Djmin Hawwaz wants Anwar's soul, while his brother Hutti plays dangerous games with mortal girls. When the beautiful Maryam comes to Anwar for advice in avoiding an unwelcome marriage, he sends her to Mecca. Baffled, she obeys his instruction to become a prostitute – and sets in motion a bizarre sequence of events, turning the worlds of human and demon alike upside-down.

A NOOSE OF LIGHT

Sensual, erotic, humorous and magical: an enchanting fantasy of an enchanted land.

FUTURA PUBLICATIONS
FANTASY/AN ORBIT BOOK

ISBN 0–7088–8178–5

**THE WILD SHORE**

**Kim Stanley Robinson**

'Simply one of our best writers' Gene Wolfe

'A powerful new talent' Damon Knight

2047: for 60 years America has been quarantined after a devastating nuclear attack. For the small community of San Onefre on the West Coast, life is a matter of survival: living simply on what the sea and land can provide, preserving that knowledge and skills they can in a society without mass communications. Until the men from San Diego arrive, riding the rails on flatbed trucks and bringing news of the new American Resistance. And Hank Fletcher and his friends are drawn into an adventure that marks the end of childhood . . .

A stunning debut by a powerful new talent.

'There's a fresh wind blowing in THE WILD SHORE . . . welcome, Kim Starley Robinson' Ursula K Le Guin

'Beautifully written . . . with a vivid depth rarely encountered in science fiction' *Washington Post Book World*

FUTURA PUBLICATIONS
SCIENCE FICTION

ISBN 0–7088–8147–5